JEANNE-MARIE LEPRINCE de BEAUMONT (1711–1780) first earned her living as a governess in England before publishing short stories and works for children, including *Le Magasin des Enfants* (1757), which contains her famous version of *Beauty and the Beast*. After returning to France in 1762, she retired to a country estate and continued to write, publishing more than seventy books in her lifetime.

CHARLES PERRAULT (1628–1703), born into a distinguished French family, began his career as a poet, but his transformation of the best-known French folk tales into provocative, beautifully written stories immortalized him as a writer. Among his famous works are *Sleeping Beauty, Little Red Riding Hood, Blue Beard, Cinderella,* and *Puss in Boots.*

MARIE-CATHERINE d'AULNOY (c. 1650–1705) lived a life of adventure and notoriety, filled with lovers, plots, and narrow escapes from death, as well as the establishment of the most interesting literary salon of the period. Her fairy tales include *The Island of Happiness, Beauty with the Golden Hair, The Blue Bird,* and *The Golden Branch*.

JACK ZIPES, translator, is a professor of German at the University of Minnesota. A specialist in folklore, fairy tales, and children's literature, he is the author of several books on fairy tales, including *Breaking the Magic Spell, Don't Bet on the Prince, Fairy Tales and the Art of S_____ The Complete Tales o_____ ed a number of vo_____ ics including *Comp_____ le, Arabian Nights, a_____

...roduction, and a translation of ...
... of the Brothers Grimm. He has edited
... volume of tales for Signet Clas...
... the Fairy Tales of Oscar Wild...
... and Aesop's Fables

BEAUTY AND THE BEAST

And Other
Classic French Fairy Tales

Translated and with an
Introduction by Jack Zipes

A SIGNET CLASSIC

SIGNET CLASSIC
Published by New American Library, a division of
Penguin Putnam Inc., 375 Hudson Street,
New York, New York 10014, U.S.A.
Penguin Books Ltd, 27 Wrights Lane,
London W8 5TZ, England
Penguin Books Australia Ltd, Ringwood,
Victoria, Australia
Penguin Books Canada Ltd, 10 Alcorn Avenue,
Toronto, Ontario, Canada M4V 3B2
Penguin Books (N.Z.) Ltd, 182–190 Wairau Road,
Auckland 10, New Zealand

Penguin Books Ltd, Registered Offices:
Harmondsworth, Middlesex, England

Published by Signet Classic, an imprint of New American Library,
a division of Penguin Putnam Inc.

First Signet Classic Printing, March 1997
10 9 8 7 6 5 4 3

 REGISTERED TRADEMARK—MARCA REGISTRADA

Library of Congress Catalog Card Number: 96-70085

Printed in the United States of America

BOOKS ARE AVAILABLE AT QUANTITY DISCOUNTS WHEN USED TO PROMOTE
PRODUCTS OR SERVICES. FOR INFORMATION PLEASE WRITE TO PREMIUM
MARKETING DIVISION, PENGUIN PUTNAM INC., 375 HUDSON STREET, NEW YORK,
NEW YORK 10014.

For my daughter Hanna
avec tendresse
encore et toujours

CONTENTS

INTRODUCTION
The Rise of the French Fairy Tale
and the Decline of France

> Your people, . . . whom you ought to love as
> your children, and who up to now have been
> passionately devoted to you, are dying of
> hunger. The culture of the soil is almost aban-
> doned; the towns and the country are being
> depopulated; every trade is languishing and no
> longer supports the workers. All commerce is
> destroyed. . . . The whole of France is nothing
> but a huge hospital, desolated and without
> resources.
> —Fénelon, *Letter to King Louis XIV,* 1694

UNTIL the 1690s the oral folk tale in France was not
deemed worthy of being transcribed and transformed into
literature, that is, written down and circulated among literate persons. In fact, with the exception of several significant collections of tales in Italy, *The Entertaining
Nights* (1550–53) by Giovan Francesco Straparola and
The Pentameron (1634–36) by Giambattista Basile, most
of the European aristocracy and intelligentsia considered
the folk tale part of the vulgar people's tradition, beneath
the dignity of cultivated people and associated with
pagan beliefs and superstitions that were no longer rele-
vant in Christian Europe. If the literate members of the
upper classes acknowledged the folk tale at all, it was as
crude entertainment, divertissement, anecdote, or homily
in its oral form transmitted through such intermediaries
as wet nurses, governesses, servants, peasants, merchants, and village priests.

From the late Middle Ages up through the Renais-
sance, folk tales were told by non-literate peasants
among themselves at the hearth, in spinning rooms, or

in the fields. They were told by priests in the vernacular as part of their sermons to reach out to the peasantry. Literate merchants and travelers transmitted them to people of all classes in inns and taverns. They were told to children of the upper class by nurses and governesses. They were remembered and passed on in different forms and versions by all members of society and told to suit particular occasions—*as talk.* Gradually, however, this talk became elevated, cultivated, made acceptable, and entered French salons by the middle of the seventeenth century. Only by 1690, in fact, was it regarded worthy of print, and by 1696 there had arisen a veritable vogue of printed fairy tales: the literary fairy tale had come into its own, and French aristocratic writers for the most part established the conventions and motifs for a genre that is perhaps the most popular in the western world—and not only among children.

How did all this come about? Why the change in attitude toward the lowly oral folk tale? What kinds of literary fairy tales were created?

Though it is impossible to fix a date for the rise of the literary fairy tale in France, its origins can be located in the conversation and games developed by highly educated aristocratic women in the salons that they formed in the 1630s in Paris and that continued to be popular up through the beginning of the eighteenth century. Deprived of access to schools and universities, French aristocratic women began organizing gatherings in their homes to which they invited other women and gradually men in order to discuss art, literature, and topics important to them such as love, marriage, and freedom. In particular, the women wanted to distinguish themselves as individuals who were above the rest of society and deserved special attention. Generally speaking, these women were called *précieuses* and tried to develop a *précieux* manner of thinking, speaking, and writing to reveal and celebrate their innate talents that distinguished them from the vulgar elements of society. Most important here was the emphasis placed on wit and invention in conversation. A *précieux* (and numerous men were included in this movement) was capable of transforming the most banal cliché into a brilliant and unique bon mot. Although they had a tendency to be effete and elitist, these women were by no means dilettantes. On the contrary, some of the most gifted writers of the time, such as Mlle. de Scudéry, Mlle. de Montpensier, Mme. de Sévigné, and Mme. de Lafayette, came out of this movement, and their goal was to gain more independence for women of their class and to be treated more seriously as intellectuals. In fact, one of the most important consequences of *préciosité* was its effect on women from the lower aristocracy and bourgeoisie, who were inspired to struggle for more rights and combat the arbitrary constraints placed on their lives in a patriarchal social system.

The women who frequented the salons were constantly seeking innovative ways to express their needs and to embellish the forms and style of speech and communication that they shared. Given the fact that they had all been exposed to folk tales as children and that they entertained themselves with conversational games that served as models for the occasional lyric and the serial novel, it is not by chance that they turned to the folk tale as a source of amusement. About the middle of the seventeenth century aristocratic women started to invent parlor games based on the plots of tales with the purpose of challenging one another in friendly fashion to see who could create the more compelling narrative. Such challenges led the women, in particular, to improve the quality of their dialogues, remarks, and ideas about morals, manners, and education, and at times to question male standards that governed their lives. The subject matter of the conversations consisted of literature, mores, taste, love, and etiquette, whereby the speakers all endeavored to portray ideal situations in the most effective oratory style, which would gradually be transmuted into literary forms and set the standards for the *conte de fée,* or what we now call the literary fairy tale.

By the 1670s we find various references in letters about the fairy tale as an acceptable jeu d'esprit in the salons. In this type of game, the women would refer to

folk tales and use certain motifs spontaneously in their
conversations. Eventually they began telling the tales
as a literary divertimento, intermezzo, or as a kind of
after-dinner dessert invented to amuse other listeners.
This social function of amusement was complemented
by another purpose, namely, that of self-portrayal and
representation of proper aristocratic manners. The
telling of fairy tales enabled women to picture themselves, social manners, and relations in a manner that
represented their interests and those of the aristocracy.
Thus, they placed great emphasis on certain rules of
oration such as naturalness and spontaneity and themes
such as freedom of choice in marriage, fidelity, and justice. The teller of the tale was to make it "seem" as
though the tale were made up on the spot, as though it
did not follow prescribed rules. Embellishment, impro-
visation, and experimentation with known folk or literary motifs were stressed. The procedure of telling a
tale as bagatelle worked as follows: the narrator was
requested to devise a tale based on a particular motif;
the adroitness of the narrator was measured by the
degree with which she was inventive and natural; the
audience responded politely with a compliment; then
another member of the audience was requested to tell a
tale, not in direct competition with the other teller, but
in order to continue the game and vary the possibilities
for invention and symbolic expression that often used
code words such as *galanterie, tendresse,* and *esprit* to
signal the qualities that distinguished their protagonists.

By the 1690s the "salon" fairy tale became so acceptable that women and men began writing down their
tales for publication. The "naturalness" of the tales
was, of course, feigned, since everyone prepared their
tales very carefully and rehearsed them before going to
a salon. Most of the notable writers of the fairy tale
learned to develop this literary genre by going to
the salons or homes of women who wanted to foster
intellectual conversation. And some writers, such as
Mme. d'Aulnoy, Mme. de Murat, and Mlle. L'Héritier,
even had their own salons. Moreover, for festivities at
Louis XIV's court and at aristocratic homes, especially
during the Carnival period, people attended dressed as

nymphs, satyrs, fauns, or other fairy-tale figures. There
were spectacular ballets and plays that incorporated
fairy-tale motifs, as in the production of Molière and
Corneille's *Psyché* (1671), which played a role in the
development of the beauty-and-the-beast motif in
the works of Mme. d'Aulnoy. In this regard, the attraction to the fairy tale had a great deal to do with the Sun
King's desire to make his court the most radiant in
Europe, for the French aristocracy and bourgeoisie
sought cultural means to translate and represent this
splendor in form and style to themselves and the outside world. Thus, the peasant contents and the settings
of the oral folk tales were transformed to appeal to
aristocratic and bourgeois audiences.

The transformation of the oral folk tale into a literary
fairy tale was not superficial or decorative. The aes-
thetics that the aristocratic women developed in their
conversational games and in their written tales had a
serious aspect to it: though they differed in style and
content, these tales were all anticlassical and were
written in implicit opposition to the leading critic of
the literary establishment, Nicolas Boileau, who championed Greek and Roman literature in the famous
"Quarrel of the Ancients and Moderns" (1687–96) as
the models for contemporary French writers to follow.
Instead, the early French fairy-tale writers used models
from French folklore and the medieval courtly tradition. In addition, since the majority of the writers and
tellers of fairy tales were women, these tales displayed
a certain resistance toward male rational precepts and
patriarchal realms by conceiving pagan worlds in which
the final say was determined by female fairies, extraordinarily majestic and powerful fairies, if you will. To
a certain extent, *all* the French writers of fairy tales,
men and women, "modernized" an oral genre by institu-
tionalizing it in literary form with utopian visions that
stemmed from their desire for better social conditions.

Despite the fact that their remarkable fairy tales set
the tone and standards for the development of most of
the memorable literary fairy tales in the West up to the
present, they and their utopian visions are all but forgotten, not only in English-speaking countries but also

in France itself. The major representative of this genre
known today is Charles Perrault, who published the
verse fairy tales *Donkey-Skin* and *The Foolish Wishes*
in 1694 and a slim volume of eight prose fairy tales,
Histoires ou contes du temps passé, in 1697. Though
finely wrought, these tales are not indicative of the
great vogue that took place, nor are they representative
of the utopian (and sometimes dystopian) verve of the
tales. To appreciate the value of Perrault's tales and
how different they are, they must be seen in their historical context.

There were approximately three waves of the French
fairy-tale vogue: (1) the experimental salon fairy tale,
1690–1703; (2) the Oriental tale, 1704–20; and (3) the
conventional and comical fairy tale, 1721–89. These
waves overlap somewhat, but if we understand the reasons for their origins and changes, we will grasp some
of the underlying meanings in the symbols of the tales
that are not readily apparent.

THE SALON FAIRY TALE

When Marie-Catherine d'Aulnoy included the fairy
tale *The Island of Happiness* in her novel *Histoire
d'Hippolyte, Comte de Douglas* in 1690, she was not
aware that she was about to set a trend in France.
Within five years the literary fairy tale became the talk
of the literary salons, or what had been the talk of these
salons now came to print: her tales were followed
by Mlle. L'Héritier's *Oeuvres Meslées* (1695); Mlle.
Bernard's *Inès de Cordoue* (1695), a novel that includes
a version of *Riquet à la houppe*; Mlle. de la Force's *Les
Contes des Contes* (1697); Perrault's *Histoires ou
contes du temps passé* (1697); Mme. d'Aulnoy's four-
volume *Les Contes des fées* (1697–98); the Chevalier
de Mailly's *Les Illustres Fées, contes galans* (1698);
Mme. de Murat's *Contes de fées* (1698); Nodot's *Histoire de Mélusine* (1698); Prechac's *Contes moins
contes que les autres* (1698); Mme. Durand's *Comtesse
de Mortane* (1699); Mme. de Murat's *Histoires sublimes et allégoriques* (1699); Eustache Le Noble's

Gage touché (1700); Mme. d'Auneuil's *Tiranie des fées détruite* (1702); and Mme. Durand's *Petits Soupers de l'année 1699* (1702).

The main reason for the publication of these tales—and perhaps the stress should be on making the tales *public,* or letting a greater public outside the salons know about the tales that were told in them—is that France had entered a major crisis about 1688, and conditions of living began to deteriorate at all levels of society. Indeed, even the aristocracy and haute bourgeoisie were not exempt. Due to the fact that Louis XIV continued to wage costly wars and sought to annex more land for France, the taxes for all classes became exorbitant, and at various times during the latter part of his reign there were years of bad crops due to terrible weather and devastation of human lives due to the wars. The steady increase of debt, taxation, and poor living conditions resulted in extreme misery for the peasantry and an austere life for the bourgeoisie and aristocracy. Moreover, this was the period when Louis XIV became more orthodox in his devotion to Catholicism under the influence of Madame de Maintenon, became more rigid in his cultural taste, and more arbitrary and willful as absolutist king. His reign, which had begun during an "Age of Reason," turned reason against itself to justify his desires, tastes, and ambition for glory, and this solipsism led to irrational policies that were destructive for the French people and soundly criticized by the highly respected Fénelon, the Archbishop of Cambrai, who in some way became the moral conscience of the ancien régime during its decline.

Given these dark times and the fact that writers were not allowed to directly criticize Louis XIV due to censorship, the fairy tale was regarded as a means to vent criticism and at the same time project hope for a better world. The very first fairy tale that Mme. d'Aulnoy wrote in 1690 is a good example of how writers saw the fairy tale as a narrative strategy to criticize Louis XIV and to elaborate a code of integrity, for many French writers were intent at that time to establish standards of manners, correct speech, justice, and

love. In d'Aulnoy's *The Happy Island,* Prince Adolph
fails to attain complete happiness because he sacrifices
love for glory in war. It is because he does not esteem
the tenderness of Princess Felicity enough to remain
faithful to her that he destroys himself. *The Happy
Island* is a utopian tale because it confronts male desire
as a destructive force and suggests that there is an ele-
ment missing in life that women can provide if utopia
is to be attained and maintained. The paradise associated with the Princess Felicity will remain beyond our
reach, and it is this longing for paradise, for a realm
that is just and allows for natural feelings to flow, that
was the basis for most of the literary fairy tales
produced during the 1690s in France. In this sense,
the utopian impulse was not much different from the
utopian impulse that led peasants to tell their folk tales.
But the wish fulfillment in the oral tales of the peasants
rose from completely different circumstances of
oppression and longing. The salon tales were marked
by the struggles within the upper classes for recogni-
tion, sensible policies, and power.

Interestingly, almost all of the major fairy-tale
writers of the 1690s were on the fringe of Louis XIV's
court and were often in trouble with him or with the
authorities. For instance, Mme. d'Aulnoy had been
banished from the court in 1670, returned to Paris in
1690, and became involved in a major scandal when
one of her friends killed her husband. Mme. de Murat
was banished from the court in 1694 when she published a political satire about Madame de Maintenon,
Scarron, and Louis XIV. Mlle. de La Force was sent to
a convent in 1697 for publishing impious verses.
Catherine Bernard was not accepted at court and
remained single to maintain her independence. The
Chevalier de Mailly was an illegitimate son of a
member of the Mailly family, and though accepted at
court, he caused difficulties by insisting that his bas-
tard status be recognized as equal to that of the legiti-
mate sons of the de Mailly family. Even Charles
Perrault, who had been a loyal civil servant as long as
his protector, Jean Baptiste Colbert, controller general
of finances, was alive, fell into disfavor in 1683 and

opposed the official cultural policy of Louis XIV until his death in 1701.

It would be an exaggeration to say that the first wave of salon fairy-tale writers were all malcontents opposed to Louis XIV's regime, for they all mixed in the best circles and were considered highly respectable and talented writers. Nevertheless, with the exception of Perrault, they were not part of the literary establishment and made names for themselves in a new genre that was looked upon with suspicion. Even the respectable Fénelon, who was a member of the court's inner circle and as the preceptor of the Duc de Bourgogne, Louis XIV's grandson, wrote fairy tales in the 1690s in an experiment to expand the Dauphin's mind through pleasurable reading, did not publish these tales until the 1730s. In other words, there was something inherently suspicious and perhaps subversive about the development of the literary fairy tale, and the French writers always felt compelled to apologize somewhat for choosing to write fairy tales. Though apologetic, they knew what they were doing.

Most of the early writers came to Paris from the provinces and were steeped in the folklore of their region. Before they published their tales, we must remember, they first practiced them orally and recited them in the salons. Whenever they wrote them down, they circulated them among their friends—they all knew one another and moved in the same circles—and made changes before the tales were printed. Some of them, like Perrault and Mlle. L'Héritier, were relatives and exchanged ideas. In addition, Perrault clearly had contact with Catherine Bernard, as their two versions of *Riquet with the Tuft* reveal. In particular, the women shared their ideas for their tales and discussed their dreams and hopes with one another in private and in their letters. When Madame de Murat was banished to the provinces, she used to stay up into the early hours of the morning, telling tales to her friends, among whom was Mlle. de La Force, who used to distribute her tales among her friends and discuss them before being placed in a convent.

All the writers revised their tales to develop a

précieux tone, a unique style, that was not only supposed to be gallant, natural, and witty, but inventive, astonishing, and modern. Their tales are highly provocative, extraordinary, bizarre, and implausible. They wrote in hyperbole to draw attention to themselves and their predicaments, and they were not afraid to include sadomasochistic elements and the macabre in their tales.

Many critics and educators have often complained that the Grimms' tales are too harsh and cruel to be read to children, and some have even gone so far as to maintain that German fairy-tale writers indulged themselves in violence. But in fact, the salon tales of the refined French ladies make the Grimms' tales look prudish. In particular, Mme. d'Aulnoy was a genius in conceiving ways to torture her heroines and heroes. She had them transformed into serpents, white cats, rams, monkeys, deer, and birds. Some of her heroines are whipped, incarcerated, and tantalized by grotesque fairies or sinister princes. Some of her heroes are treated brutally by ugly fairies who despise them because they want to marry an innocent, beautiful princess. A good many of her tales end tragically because the protagonists cannot protect themselves from those forces undermining their natural love.

The cruel events, torture, and grotesque transformations in d'Aulnoy's tales were not exceptional in the fairy tales written by women. In *The Discreet Princess* (1695) Mlle. L'Héritier has Finette brutalize the prince on three different occasions before she mercifully allows him to die. In *Riquet with the Tuft* (1696) Mlle. Bernard ends her tale by placing her heroine in a most cruel dilemma with two ugly gnomes. Mlle. de la Force depicts a brutal king as a murderer whose ferocity knows no bounds in *The Good Woman* (1697), while in *Fairer than a Fairy* (1697) she has a prince and princess demeaned and compelled to perform arduous tasks before they can marry and live in peace. Finally, Mme. de Murat has a sadistic sprite place two lovers in an unbearable situation at the end of *The Palace of Revenge* (1698), and she often has sets of lovers deceive and maltreat each other, as in *Anguillette* (1698) and *Perfect Love* (1698).

However, it was not only the women writers who wove violence and brutality into their tales. Perrault dealt with incest in *Donkey-Skin* (1694) and portrayed an ogre cutting the throats of his own daughters in *Little Thumbling* (1697). The Chevalier de Mailly had a penchant for transforming his protagonists into beasts, and in *The Queen of the Island of Flowers* (1698) he has a princess persecuted in a sadistic manner.

The brutality and sadomasochism in French fairy tales can be interpreted in two ways. On the one hand, it is apparent that the protagonist, whether male or female, has to suffer in order to demonstrate his or her nobility and *tendresse*. Therefore, a cruel trial or suffering became a conventional motif in the tales, part of the compositional technique to move the reader to have sympathy for the protagonist. On the other hand, much of the cruelty in the tales is connected to forced marriage or the separation of two lovers who come together out of tender feelings for each other and not because their relationship has been arranged. Since many of the female writers had been victims of forced marriages or refused to marry in order to guard their independence, there is an apparent comment on love, courtship, and marriage in these tales that, despite all the sentimentality, was taken seriously by the writers and their audiences.

In general, the fairy tales of the first phase of the vogue were very serious in tone and intent. Only here and there in the works of Mme. d'Aulnoy and Perrault do we find ironic and humorous touches. The fairy tales were meant to make readers realize how deceived they were if they compared their lives to the events in these tales. There was no splendid paradise in Louis XIV's court, no genuine love, no reconciliation, no tenderness of feeling. All this could be, however, found in fairy tales, and in this regard the symbolic portrayal of the impossible was a rational endeavor on the part of the writers to illuminate the irrational and destructive tendencies of their times.

THE ORIENTAL FAIRY TALE

The second phase of the fairy-tale vogue was only partially connected to the utopian critique of the first phase. The major change, the attraction to oriental fairy tales, stemmed from two factors: the salons had abandoned the fairy-tale games, and the major writers of fairy tales had either died or been banished from Paris by 1704. To fill the gap, so to speak, some writers began to turn toward oriental literature (it is interesting to note that the classical literature of Greece and Rome was ignored again). The most significant work of this period was Antoine Galland's translation *Les Mille et Une Nuits* (1704–17) of the Arabian collection of *The Thousand and One Nights.* Galland (1646–1715) had traveled and lived in the Middle East and had mastered Arabic, Hebrew, Persian, and Turkish. After he published the first four volumes of *The Thousand and One Nights,* they became extremely popular, and he continued translating the tales until his death. The final two volumes were published posthumously. Galland did more than translate. He actually adapted the tales to suit the tastes of his French readers, and he invented some of the plots and drew material together to form some of his own tales. His example was followed by Pétis de La Croix (1653–1713), who translated a Turkish work by Sheikh Zadah, the tutor of Amriath II, entitled *L'Histoire de la Sultane de Perse et des Visirs. Contes turcs* (*The Story of the Sultan of the Persians and the Visirs. Turkish Tales*) in 1710. Moreover, he also translated a Persian imitation of *The Thousand and One Days,* which borrowed material from Indian comedies. Finally, the Abbé Jean Paul Bignon's collection, *Les Aventures d'Abdalla, fils d'Anif* (1712–14), purported to be an authentic Arabic work in translation, but was actually Bignon's own creative adaptation of oriental tales mixed with French folklore.

Why all this interest in oriental fairy tales?

One explanation is that the diminishing grandeur of Louis XIV's court and the decline of France in general compelled writers to seek compensation in portrayals of exotic countries. Certainly for the readers of that time, the oriental tales had a unique appeal because so little was known about the Middle East, and whereas the French had developed extensive commercial relations with the Orient, this appeal became even greater. Of course, the men who stimulated the interest in the oriental fairy tales were scholars, and their reason for turning to Arabic, Persian, and Turkish folklore had more to do with their academic interests than with compensation for the decline of French glory. Whatever the reason for the second phase, it is important to point out that women stopped playing the dominant role and that the tales were no longer connected to the immediate interests of the aristocracy and haute bourgeoisie.

THE COMIC AND CONVENTIONAL FAIRY TALE

By 1720 the interest in the literary fairy tale had so diminished that writers began parodying the genre, developing it along conventional lines or utilizing it for children's literature. Claude Philippe de Caylus' tales in *Féerie novelles* (1741) and *Contes orientaux tirés des manuscrits de la bibliothèque du roi de France* (1743) are indicative of attempts to poke fun at the fairy-tale genre. De Caylus is not overly sarcastic, but he does reverse the traditional courtly types to reveal how ridiculous they and the court are. Most of his narratives are short, dry, and witty, and are connected to the style of caricature that he was developing at that time. Actually, his work had been preceded by Anthony Hamilton (1644–1719), who had earlier written much longer burlesques of the oriental trend in such tales as *Fleur d'Epine* and *Les Quatre Facardins* that were only published after his death in 1730.

In a more serious vein, Mlle. de Lubert and Mme. de Villeneuve carried on the salon tradition. For instance, Mlle. de Lubert, who rejected marriage in order to

devote herself to writing, composed a series of long,
intricate fairy tales from 1743 to 1755. Among them,
Princesse Camion (1743) is a remarkable example of a
sadomasochistic tale that is intriguing because of the
different tortures and transformations that she kept
inventing to dramatize the suffering of her protagonists. Mlle. de Villeneuve's major contribution to the
fairy tale had more to do with her ability to transcribe a
discourse on true love and class differences in marriage
into a classic fairy tale, *Beauty and the Beast* (1740),
than with writing a horror fairy tale like Mlle. de
Lubert. Mme. de Villeneuve's tale employs almost all
the traditional fairy-tale and folklore motifs in a conventional manner, but to her credit, she was the first
writer to develop the plot of *Beauty and the Beast* as
we generally know it today, and her addition of dream
sequences was an innovative touch that later writers of
fairy tales such as Novalis and E.T.A. Hoffman developed more fully.

The "conventionalization" of the salon tale meant that
the genre had become part of the French cultural heri-
tage and was open to parody, as we have seen, but also
open to more serious cultivation as in the works of Mlle.
de Lubert and Mme. de Villeneuve. More important, it
meant that the literary fairy tale could convey standard
notions of propriety and morality that reinforced the
socialization process in France. What might have been
somewhat subversive in the salon fairy tale was often
"conventionalized" to suit the taste and values of the
dominant classes and the regime by the middle of
the eighteenth century. This was the period when there
was a great debate about the meaning of *civilité*, and
literature was regarded as a means of socialization
through which norms, mores, and manners were to be
diffused. Therefore, it is not by chance that the literary
fairy tale for children was established during the eighteenth century by Mme. Leprince de Beaumont and not
by Mme. d'Aulnoy or Perrault. Both the debate about
civility and the acceptance of the fairy tale as a proper
literary genre had to reach a certain stage before the tale
could be conventionalized as children's literature.

It is extremely important to note that Mme. Leprince

de Beaumont's shorter version of Mme. de Villeneuve's *Beauty and the Beast* was published in an educational book entitled *Le Magasin des Enfants* in 1757. In fact, she published several fairy tales in this volume, all with the didactic purpose of demonstrating to little girls how they should behave in different situations. Therefore, her *Beauty and the Beast* preaches domesticity and self-sacrifice for women, and her *Prince Désir and Princess Mignone,* based on an old Breton folk tale, teaches a lesson about flattery and narcissism. One of the dangers in Mme. Leprince de Beaumont's conventionalizing the fairy tale for pedagogic purposes led to the undermining of the subversive and utopian quality of the earlier tales. However, conventionalization did not necessarily bring about a total watering down and depletion of the unusual ideas and motifs of the literary fairy tale and folk tale. It actually led to a more general acceptance and institutionalization of the literary fairy tale as genre for all ages and classes of readers. Such institutionalization set the framework within which other writers would create, play with those motifs, characters, and *topoi* that had been developed, and revise them in innovative ways to generate new forms, ideas, and motifs.

For instance, many of the literary fairy tales of the 1690s and early part of the eighteenth century found their way into cheap popular books published in a series called the *Bibliotheque Bleue* (known in England as chapbooks) and distributed by traveling book pedlars called *colporteurs.* The tales were rewritten (often drastically) and reduced to a more simple language so that the tales, when read in villages, were taken over by the peasants again and incorporated into the folklore. These tales were told and retold thousands of times and reentered the literary fairy tale genre through fairy-tale writers exposed to this amalgamated "folklore." The interaction between the oral and literary retellings of tales became one of the most important features in the development of the literary genre as it was institutionalized in the eighteenth century. The most obvious sign that the literary fairy tale had become an institution in France was the publication by Charles Mayer of the

Cabinet des fées (1785–89), a forty-one-volume set of
the best-known salon fairy, comical, and conventional
tales of the preceding century. From this point on, the
French literary fairy tales were diffused and made their
mark through translations in most of the western world.

In point of fact, then, though the original French
fairy tales are no longer read, they have never been
forgotten. They have come down to us today in various forms and have inspired writers like Wieland,
Goethe, the Brothers Grimm, Andersen, George Sand,
and numerous others. Thus, the literary fairy tale
keeps thriving and makes itself felt not only through
literature in remarkable works by such contemporary
authors as Angela Carter, A. S. Byatt, Margaret At-
wood, Michael Ende, and others, but through stage
adaptations and film productions. The best of the contemporary fairy tales also keep alive the utopian quest
and questioning spirit of the earlier salon tales. Written
because of dissatisfaction with their times, these fairy
tales still have a certain captivating charm that is not
confined to the particular historical period in which
they were conceived and written. They embrace the
future. They anticipate hopes and wishes that we ourselves have yet to fulfill. In that sense, they are still
modern, and—who knows?—may even open up alter-
natives to our postmodern dilemmas.

A NOTE ON THE TRANSLATION

I BEGAN this project with the intention of editing John Robinson Planché's translations of French fairy tales that were published in two nineteenth-century collections entitled *Four-and-twenty Fairy Tales selected from those of Perrault, etc.* (1858) and *Countess d'Aulnoy's Fairy Tales* (1885). Planché (1796–1880) was a distinguished British archaeologist and versatile writer who wrote over seventy works including numerous fairy-tale plays, a history of costumes, poems, songs, and essays. Initially I believed that his translations would enable me to accomplish two purposes at the same time: publish the major French fairy tales that led to a great vogue and brought about the establishment of the fairy tale as a serious literary genre in Europe; and reintroduce the gifted Planché to the English-speaking world. Historically, both the tales and Planché have suffered from neglect by critics and the general reading public.

The more I examined Planché's translations, however, the more I realized that they were somewhat too anachronistic and inaccurate. Once I had compared the original tales in the *Cabinet des Fées* (1785–89), a vast collection of forty-one volumes, with Planché's translations, I decided to create my own selection and to retranslate the tales using Planché's versions as the basis for my work since, to his credit, his renditions contained a certain style and idiomatic characteristics that I felt helped recapture the highly mannered style of the French authors. Moreover, as an expert in clothes, customs, and architecture, Planché provided accurate descriptions of the garments, buildings, and manners of French society during the ancien régime and even documented his translations with footnotes.

Since Planché did not include all the tales that I chose for my collection, I did completely new translations of Perrault's *Little Red Riding Hood, The Fairies, The Donkey Skin,* and *The Foolish Wishes,* d'Aulnoy's *The Island of Happiness,* Bignon's *Princess Zeineb and the King Leopard,* Leprince de Beaumont's *Beauty and the Beast,* L'Héritier's *The Discreet Princess,* and Bernard's *Riquet with the Tuft.* In the case of Perrault's *The Donkey Skin* and *The Foolish Wishes,* which were written in rhymed verse, I decided to render them into prose because I found it extremely difficult to recapture the seventeenth-century puns, historical references, and courtly style in English verse. To my knowledge, the only other translations of these two tales are also in prose and are inaccurate in many instances. I have endeavored to be as faithful to the text as one can be when translating a poem into prose, and in certain instances where the meaning was unclear, I have tried to make the prose version more cogent.

One of the major difficulties in doing these translations involved the transcribing of the verse morals that appear at the end of Perrault's, d'Aulnoy's, and de Murat's tales, and are also embedded in d'Aulnoy's tales. In most cases I sacrificed meter and style to meaning; in some cases, particularly in d'Aulnoy's tales, I endeavored to temper the bombastic and lavish tone and style. There are, of course, major stylistic differences among the authors, and I have tried to respect them as much as possible so that the reader can see how these French authors experimented with language and set standards of courtly and civil discourse. For instance, it will become obvious that the women writers were more inventive and imaginative in their discourse and in conceiving intrigues and plots in their tales, which were highly elaborate, while the male writers tended to be more succinct and make one major point in language that was highly economical. It was through language that all these writers tried to represent themselves as unique and gifted individuals, whose words about values, norms, politics, and civility were to be taken seriously.

The French fairy tales written from 1690 to 1789

formed part of a serious debate about the manners, politics, and values of that time. They were *not* intended for children at first, though some of the tales were later adapted for young people. The only writer in this collection who wrote expressly for children was Marie-Jeanne Leprince de Beaumont, whose version of *Beauty and the Beast* supplanted an earlier, more intricate version by Gabrielle-Suzanne de Villeneuve published in 1740. In general, all the tales in the present collection have had a remarkable influence on western culture and bear the impact of oral tales and folklore. In this sense, the French literary fairy tales were among the first in history to bring together the interests of the upper and lower classes in tales that are often stunning because of their extravagant ideas, incredible violence, and utopian longing.

I would like to express my gratitude to LuAnn Walther, who has been most supportive of my work, to Susan Rogers, who assumed control of the project at a crucial transitional period and to Rosemary Ahern, who has been the guiding spirit behind this edition. Catherine Vellay-Vallantin and Jacques Barchilon, whose work in the field is exemplary, both gave me invaluable advice about the social and historical background of the tales, while Carol Dines helped me revise many of the tales and gave me excellent suggestions for changes. Last but not least, I owe a great debt to John Paine, whose skillful and sensitive editing of the tales has helped keep their magic alive.

—Jack Zipes
Minneapolis, 1996

A NOTE ON THIS EDITION

THIS edition of *Beauty and the Beast and Other Classic French Fairy Tales* is based on my book, *Beauties, Beasts and Enchantment: Classic French Fairy Tales*, published by New American Library in 1989. Several tales by Charlotte-Rose Caumont de la Force, Jean Mailly, Gabrielle-Suzanne de Villeneuve, Philippe de Caylus, and Marie-Catherine d'Aulnoy have regrettably been omitted due to space constraints. Nevertheless, the present selection should provide readers with the most representative tales produced during the flowering of the literary fairy tale in France.

Corrections and slight changes have been made in the texts. Otherwise, the tales and introductions remain essentially as they were in the earlier edition.

—Jack Zipes
Minneapolis, 1996

Charles Perrault

Charles Perrault (1628–1703) was born in Paris into one of the more distinguished bourgeois families of the time. His father, Pierre Perrault, was a lawyer and member of the Paris Parlement, and his four brothers—he was the youngest—all went on to become renowned in such fields as architecture, theology, and law. In 1637 Perrault began studying at the Collège de Beauvais (near the Sorbonne), but at the age of fifteen he stopped attending school and largely taught himself all he needed to know so he could later take his law examinations.

It was about this time that Perrault took an interest in the popular movement against King Louis XIV, and his early poetry expressed a sympathy for bourgeois opposition to the crown because the king had deprived the bourgeoisie of certain privileges and offices. However, Perrault became somewhat fearful and gradually switched his position to support the king as the bourgeoisie made peace with Louis XIV in 1649. In 1651 he passed the law examinations at the University of Orléans, and after working for three years as a lawyer, he left the profession to become a secretary to his brother Pierre, who was the tax receiver of Paris.

Perrault, who had already written some minor poems, became more and more interested in literature. In 1659 he published two important poems, "Portrait d'Iris" and "Portrait de la voix d'Iris," and by 1660 his public career as a poet was in full swing when he composed several poems in honor of Louis XIV. In 1663 Perrault was appointed secretary to Jean Baptiste Colbert, controller general of finances, perhaps the most influential minister in Louis XIV's government. For

the next twenty years, until Colbert's death, Perrault
was able to accomplish a great deal in the arts and sciences due to Colbert's powerful support.

In 1671 he was elected to the French Academy and
was also placed in charge of the royal buildings. He
continued writing poetry and took an active interest in
cultural affairs of the court. In 1672 he married Marie
Guichon, with whom he had three sons. She died at
childbirth in 1678, and he never remarried, supervising
the education of his children by himself.

When Colbert died in 1683, Perrault was dismissed
from government service, but he had a pension and was
able to support his family until his death. Released
from administrative duties, Perrault concentrated more
on literary affairs, and in 1687 he helped inaugurate the
"Quarrel of the Ancients and the Moderns" (la
Querelle des Anciens et des Modernes) by reading a
poem entitled "Le Siècle de Louis le Grand." Perrault
took the side of modernism and believed that France
and Christianity—here he sided with the Jansenists,
who sought to purify Catholicism and make it more
mystical—could progress only if they incorporated
pagan beliefs and folklore and developed a culture of
enlightenment. On the other hand, Nicolas Boileau, the
literary critic, and Jean Racine, the dramatist, took the
opposite viewpoint and argued that France had to imitate the great empires of Greece and Rome and maintain stringent classical rules in respect to the arts. This
literary quarrel, which had great cultural implications,
lasted until 1697, at which time Louis XIV decided to
end it in favor of Boileau and Racine. This decision did
not stop Perrault, however, from incorporating his
ideas into his poetry and prose.

Perrault had always frequented the literary salons of
his niece Mlle. L'Héritier, Mme. d'Aulnoy, and other
women, and he had been annoyed by Boileau's satires
written against women. Thus, he wrote three verse
tales, *Griselidis* (1691), *Les Souhaits Ridicules* (The
Foolish Wishes, 1693) and *Peau d'Ane* (Donkey Skin,
1694) along with a long poem, *Apologie des femmes*
(1694), in defense of women, a defense which is, however, questionable. His poems use a highly mannered

style and folk motifs to stress the necessity of an enlightened attitude of fairness toward women, but fairness on male terms.

In 1696 Perrault embarked on a more ambitious project. He transformed several popular folk tales, including all their superstitious beliefs and magic, into moralistic tales that would appeal to children and adults and demonstrate a modern approach to literature. He had a prose version of *La Belle au Bois Dormant* (The Sleeping Beauty in the Woods) printed in the journal *Mercure Galant* in 1696, and in 1697 he published an entire collection of tales entitled *Histoires ou contes du temps passé,* which consisted of a new version of *Sleeping Beauty, Le Petit Chaperon Rouge* (Little Red Riding Hood), *Barbe Bleue* (Blue Beard), *Cendrillon* (Cinderella), *Le Petit Poucet* (Little Thumbling), *Riquet à la Houppe* (Riquet with the Tuft), *Le Chat botté* (Puss in Boots), and *Les Fées* (The Fairies).

Although *Histoires ou contes du temps passé* was published under the name of Pierre Perrault Darmancour, Perrault's son, and although some critics have asserted that the book was indeed written or at least cowritten by his son, recent evidence has shown clearly that this could not have been the case, especially since his son had not published anything up to that point. Perrault was simply using his son's name to mask his own identity so that he would not be blamed for reigniting the Quarrel of the Ancients and the Moderns.

Numerous critics have regarded Perrault's tales as written directly for children, but they overlook the fact that no children's literature per se existed at that time and that most writers of fairy tales were composing and reciting their tales for their peers in the literary salons. Certainly, if Perrault intended them to make a final point in the Quarrel of the Ancients and the Moderns, he obviously had an adult audience in mind that would understand his humor and the subtle manner in which he transformed folklore superstition to convey his position about the "modern" development of French civility.

There is no doubt but that, among the writers of fairy tales during the 1690s, Perrault was the greatest stylist,

which accounts for the fact that his tales have with-
stood the test of time. Furthermore, Perrault claimed
that literature must become modern, and his transformation of folk motifs and literary themes into refined
and provocative fairy tales still speaks to the modern
age, ironically in a way that may compel us to ponder
whether the Age of Reason has led to the progress and
happiness promised so charmingly in Perrault's tales.

THE MASTER CAT OR
PUSS IN BOOTS

A MILLER bequeathed to his three sons all his worldly goods, which consisted just of his mill, his ass, and his cat. The division was made quickly, and neither notary nor attorney were called, for they would have soon consumed all of the meager patrimony. The eldest received the mill; the second son, the ass; the youngest got nothing but the cat.

Of course, the youngest was upset at inheriting such a poor portion. "My brothers may now earn an honest living as partners," he said, "but as for me, I'm bound to die of hunger once I have eaten my cat and made a muff of his skin."

The cat, who had heard this speech but pretended not to have been listening, said to him with a sober and serious air, "Don't trouble yourself, master. Just give me a pouch and a pair of boots to go into the bushes, and you'll see that you were not left with as bad a share as you think."

Although the cat's master did not place much stock in this assertion, he had seen the cat play such cunning tricks in catching rats and mice—hanging himself upside down by the heels or lying in the flour as if he were dead—that he did not abandon all hope.

As soon as the cat had what he had asked for, he boldly pulled on his boots. Then he hung the pouch around his neck, took the strings in his forepaws, and went to a warren where a great number of rabbits lived. He put some bran and lettuce into his pouch and, stretching himself out as if he were dead, he waited for a young rabbit little versed in the wiles of the world to look for something to eat in the pouch. He had hardly lain down when he saw his plan work. A young scatterbrain of a rabbit entered the pouch, and master cat instantly pulled the strings, bagged it, and killed it without mercy. Proud of his catch, he went to the king's palace and demanded an audience. He was ushered up to the royal apartment, and upon entering, he made a low bow to the king. "Sire," he said, "here's a rabbit from the warren of my lord, the Marquis de Carabas (such was the name he fancied to call his master). He has instructed me to present it to you on his behalf."

"Tell your master," replied the king, "that I thank him and that he's given me great pleasure."

After some time had passed, the cat hid in a wheatfield, keeping the mouth of the pouch open as he always did. When two partridges entered it, he pulled the strings and caught them both. Then he went straight to the king and presented them to him just as he had done with the rabbit. The king was equally pleased by the two partridges and gave the cat a small token for his efforts.

During the next two or three months the cat continued every now and then to carry presents of game from his master to the king.

One day, when he knew the king was going to take a drive on the banks of a river with his daughter, the most beautiful princess in the world, he said to his master, "If you follow my advice, your fortune will be made. Just go and bathe in the river where I tell you, and leave the rest to me."

The "Marquis de Carabas" did as his cat advised, little expecting that any good would come of it. While he was bathing, the king passed by, and the cat began to shout with all his might, "Help! Help! My lord, the Marquis de Carabas is drowning!"

At this cry the king stuck his head out of the coach window. Recognizing the cat who had often brought game to him, he ordered his guards to rush to the aid of the Marquis de Carabas. While they were pulling the poor marquis out of the river, the cat approached the royal coach and told the king that some robbers had come and carried off his master's clothes while he was bathing, even though he had shouted "Thieves!" as loud as he could. But in truth the rascal had hidden his master's clothes himself under a large rock. The king immediately ordered the officers of his wardrobe to fetch one of his finest suits for the Marquis de Carabas. The king embraced the marquis a thousand times, and since the fine clothes brought out his good looks (for he was handsome and well built), the king's daughter found him much to her liking. No sooner did the Marquis de Carabas cast two or three respectful and rather tender glances at her than she fell in love with him. The king invited him to get into the coach and to accompany them on their drive.

Delighted to see that his scheme was succeeding, the cat ran on ahead and soon came upon some peasants mowing a field.

"Listen, my good people," he said, "you who are mowing, if you don't tell the king that this field belongs to my lord, the Marquis de Carabas, you'll all be cut into tiny pieces like minced meat!"

Indeed, the king did not fail to ask the mowers whose field they were mowing.

"It belongs to our lord, the Marquis de Carabas," they said all together, for the cat's threat had frightened them.

"You can see, sire," rejoined the marquis, "it's a field that yields an abundant crop every year."

Master cat, who kept ahead of the party, came upon some reapers and said to them, "Listen, my good people, you who are reaping, if you don't say that all this wheat belongs to my lord, the Marquis de Carabas, you'll all be cut into tiny pieces like minced meat!"

A moment later the king passed by and wished to know who owned all the wheatfields that he saw there.

"Our lord, the Marquis de Carabas," responded the reapers, and the king again expressed his joy to the marquis.

Running ahead of the coach, the cat uttered the same threat to all whom he encountered, and the king was astonished at the great wealth of the Marquis de Carabas. At last master cat arrived at a beautiful castle owned by an ogre, the richest ever known, for all the lands through which the king had driven belonged to the lord of this castle. The cat took care to inquire who the ogre was and what his powers were. Then he

requested to speak with him, saying that he could not
pass so near his castle without paying his respects. The
ogre received him as civilly as an ogre can and asked
him to sit down.

"I've been told," said the cat, "that you possess the
power of changing yourself into all sorts of animals.
For instance, it has been said that you can transform
yourself into a lion or an elephant."

"It's true," said the ogre brusquely. "And to prove it,
watch me become a lion."

The cat was so frightened at seeing a lion standing
before him that he immediately scampered up into the
roof gutters, and not without difficulty, for his boots
were not made to walk on tiles. Upon noticing that the
ogre resumed his previous form a short time afterward,
the cat descended and admitted that he had been terribly frightened.

"I've also been told," said the cat, "but I can't
believe it, that you've got the power to assume the
form of the smallest of animals. For instance, they say
that you can change yourself into a rat or mouse. I confess that it seems utterly impossible to me."

"Impossible?" replied the ogre. "Just watch!"

Immediately he changed himself into a mouse,
which began to run about the floor. No sooner did
the cat catch sight of it than he pounced on it and devoured it.

In the meantime the king saw the ogre's beautiful
castle from the road and desired to enter it. The cat
heard the noise of the coach rolling over the draw-
bridge and ran to meet it.

"Your Majesty," he said to the king, "welcome to the
castle of my lord, the Marquis de Carabas."

"What!" exclaimed the king. "Does this castle also
belong to you, Marquis? Nothing could be finer than
this courtyard and all these buildings surrounding it. If
you please, let us look inside."

The marquis gave his hand to the young princess,
and they followed the king, who led the way upstairs.
When they entered a grand hall, they found a magnificent repast that the ogre had ordered to be prepared for
some friends who were to have visited him that day.

(But they did not presume to enter when they found the king was there.) The king was just as much delighted by the accomplishments of the Marquis de Carabas as his daughter, who doted on him, and now, realizing how wealthy he was, he said to him, after having drunk five or six cups of wine, "The choice is entirely yours, Marquis, whether or not you want to become my son-in-law."

After making several low bows, the marquis accepted the honor the king had offered him, and on that very same day, he married the princess. In turn, the cat became a great lord and never again ran after mice, except for his amusement.

MORAL

Although the advantage may be great
When one inherits a grand estate
From father handed down to son,
Young men will find that industry
Combined with ingenuity,
Will lead more to prosperity.

ANOTHER MORAL

If the miller's son had quick success
    In winning such a fair princess,
By turning on the charm,
Then regard his manners, looks, and dress
    That inspired her deepest tenderness,
For they can't do one any harm.

CINDERELLA
OR THE GLASS SLIPPER

ONCE upon a time there was a gentleman who took the haughtiest and proudest woman in the world for his second wife. She had two daughters with the same temperament and the exact same appearance. On the other hand, the husband had a daughter whose gentleness and goodness were without parallel. She got this from her mother, who had been the best person in the world.

No sooner was the wedding over than the stepmother's ill-humor revealed itself. She could not abide the young girl, whose good qualities made her own daughters appear all the more detestable. So she ordered her to do all the most demeaning tasks in the house. It was she who cleaned the plates and the stairs, who scrubbed the rooms of the mistress and her daughters. She slept on a wretched straw mattress in a garret at the top of the house while her stepsisters occupied rooms with parquet floors and the most fashionable beds and mirrors in which they could regard themselves from head to toe. The poor girl endured everything with patience and did not dare complain to her father, who would have only scolded her since he was totally under the control of his wife. Whenever she finished her work, she would sit down near the chimney corner among the cinders. Consequently she was commonly called Cindertail. The second daughter, however, was not as malicious as her elder sister, and she dubbed her Cinderella. Nevertheless, Cinderella looked a thousand times more beautiful in her shabby clothes than her stepsisters, no matter how magnificent their clothes were.

Now, the king's son happened to give a ball and to invite all the people of quality. Our two young ladies were included in the invitation, for they cut a grand figure in this country. Of course, they were very pleased and began planning which would be the best gowns and headdresses to wear. This meant more misery for Cinderella because she was the one who ironed her sisters' linen and set their ruffles. Nothing was talked about but the style in which they were to be dressed.

"I'll wear my red velvet dress," said the elder sister, "and my English point-lace trimmings."

"I only have my usual petticoat to wear," said the younger, "but to make up for that I'll put on my gold-flowered mantua and my necklace of diamonds."

They sent for a good hairdresser to make up their double-frilled caps and brought their patches from the best shopkeeper. They summoned Cinderella and asked her opinion, for she had excellent taste. Cinderella gave them the best advice in the world and even offered to dress their hair for them, a favor they were eager to accept. While she went about it, they said to her, "Cinderella, wouldn't you like to go to the ball?"

"Alas! Ladies, you're playing with me. That would not befit me at all."

"You're right. People would have a great laugh to see a Cindertail at a ball!"

Any other person but Cinderella would have messed up their hairdos, but she was good-natured and dressed them to perfection. They could eat nothing for nearly two days because they were so excited. More than a dozen laces were broken in making their waists as small as possible, and they were constantly standing in front of their mirrors. At last the happy evening arrived. They set off, and Cinderella followed them with her eyes as long as she could. When they were out of sight, she began to cry. Her godmother, who came upon her all in tears, asked what was troubling her.

"I should so like—I should so like—" She sobbed so much that she could not finish the sentence.

"You'd like to go to the ball. Is that it?"

"Ah, yes!" said Cinderella, sighing.

"Well, if you'll be a good girl, I shall enable you to

go." She led her from her chamber into the yard and said, "Go to the garden and bring me a pumpkin."

Cinderella left immediately, gathered the finest pumpkin she could find, and brought it to her godmother, unable to guess how a pumpkin would enable her to go to the ball. Her godmother scooped it out, leaving nothing but the rind. Then she struck it with her wand, and the pumpkin was immediately transformed into a beautiful coach gilded all over. Next she looked into the mousetrap, where she found six live mice. She told Cinderella to lift the door of the trap a little, and as each mouse ran out, she gave it a tap with her wand. Each mouse sprouted into a fine horse, producing a fine team of six handsome, dappled, mouse-gray horses. Since her godmother had some difficulty in choosing something for a coachman, Cinderella said, "I'll go and see if there's a rat in the rattrap. We could make a coachman out of him."

"You're right," said her godmother. "Go and see."

Cinderella brought her the rattrap, which contained three large rats. The fairy selected one with the most ample beard, and after touching it, the rat was changed into a fat coachman, who had the finest moustaches that had ever been seen. Then she said, "Go into the garden, where you'll find six lizards behind the watering pot. I want you to bring them to me."

Cinderella had no sooner brought them than her godmother transformed them into six footmen, who immediately climbed up behind the coach in their braided liveries and perched there as though they had done nothing else all their lives. Then the fairy said to Cinderella, "Well, now you have something to take you to the ball. Are you satisfied?"

"Yes, but am I to go in these dirty clothes?"

Her godmother merely touched her with her wand, and her garments were instantly changed into garments of gold and silver dotted with jewels. She then gave her a pair of glass slippers, the prettiest in the world. When she was thus attired, she got into the coach, but her godmother warned her, "Above all, do not stay past midnight. If you remain at the ball one moment too long, your coach will again become a pumpkin; your horses, mice; your footmen, lizards; and your clothes will become cinder-covered rags." She promised her godmother she would not fail to leave the ball before midnight, and so she departed, overcome with joy.

Upon being informed that a grand princess had arrived whom nobody knew, the king's son went forth to greet her. He gave her his hand to help her out of the coach and led her into the hall where the company was assembled. All at once there was dead silence. The guests stopped dancing and the fiddlers ceased playing, so engrossed was everybody in regarding the beauty of the unknown lady. All that was heard was a low murmuring, "Oh, how lovely she is!" The king himself, old as he was, could not take his eyes off her and whispered to the queen that it was a long time since he had seen anyone so beautiful and so pleasant. All the ladies were busy examining her headdress and her clothes because they wanted to obtain some similar garments the very next day, if they could find the appropriate materials and tailors.

The king's son conducted her to the place of honor and then led her out to dance. She danced with so much grace that everyone's admiration increased. A very fine supper was served, but the prince could not eat anything because he was so wrapped up in watching her.

She sat beside her sisters and showed them a thousand civilities. She shared with them oranges and citrons that the prince had given her, and her sisters were quite surprised because they did not recognize her at all. While they were conversing, Cinderella heard the clock strike a quarter to twelve. She immediately made a low curtsy to the company and departed as quickly as she could.

As soon as she arrived home, she looked for her godmother, and after having thanked her, she said she wished very much to go to the ball again the next day because the king's son had invited her. While she was busy in telling her godmother all that had happened at the ball, the two sisters knocked at the door, and Cinderella opened it.

"How late you are!" she said to them, yawning, rubbing her eyes, and stretching as if she had only just awoke. However, she had not had the slightest inclination to sleep since she had left them.

"If you had been at the ball," said one of her sisters, "you would not have been bored. The most beautiful princess attended it—the most beautiful in the world. She paid us a thousand attentions, and also gave us oranges and citrons."

Cinderella was beside herself with delight. She asked them the name of the princess, but they replied that nobody knew her. Moreover, the king's son was stumped and would give anything in the world to know who she was. Cinderella smiled and said, "She was very beautiful, then? Heavens! How fortunate you are!—Couldn't I have a chance to see her? Alas! Jayotte, would you lend me the yellow gown you wear every day?"

"Indeed," said Jayotte, "I like that! Lend my gown to a dirty Cindertail like you! I'd have to be quite mad to do something like that!"

Cinderella fully expected this refusal and was delighted by it, for she would have been greatly embarrassed if her sister had lent her the gown.

The next evening the two sisters went to the ball, and so did Cinderella, dressed even more splendidly than before. The king's son never left her side and kept saying sweet things to her. The young lady enjoyed herself so much that she forgot her godmother's advice and was dumbfounded when the clock began to strike twelve, for she did not even think it was eleven. She rose and fled as lightly as a fawn. The prince followed her, but could not catch her. However, she dropped one of the glass slippers, which the prince carefully picked up. Without coach or footmen, Cinderella reached home out of breath and in shabby clothes. Nothing remained of her finery, except one of her little slippers, the companion to the one that she had dropped. The guards at the palace gate were asked if they had seen a princess depart. They answered that they had only seen a poorly dressed girl pass by, and she had more the appearance of a peasant than a lady.

When the two sisters returned from the ball, Cinderella asked them if they had enjoyed themselves as much as the first time and if the beautiful lady had been present. They said yes, but that she had fled as soon as the clock had struck twelve, and she had been in such haste that she had dropped one of her glass slippers, the prettiest in the world. The king's son had picked it up and had done nothing but gaze at it during the remainder of the evening. Undoubtedly, he was very much in love with the beautiful person who had worn the slipper.

They spoke the truth, for a few days later there was a flourish of trumpets. The king's son proclaimed that he would marry her whose foot would exactly fit the slipper. His men began by trying it on the princesses, then on the duchesses, and so on throughout the entire court. However, it was all in vain. Soon it was taken to the two sisters, who did their utmost to force one of their feet into the slipper, but they could not manage to do so.

Cinderella, who witnessed their efforts and recognized the slipper, said with a smile, "Let me see if it will fit me."

Her sisters began to laugh and ridicule her. The gentleman who had been entrusted to try the slipper looked attentively at Cinderella and found her to be very beautiful. So he said, "It is a proper request. I have been ordered to try the slipper on everyone without exception." He asked Cinderella to sit down, and upon placing the slipper under her little foot, he saw it go on easily and fit like wax.

The astonishment of the two sisters was great, but it was even greater when Cinderella took the other little slipper out of her pocket and put it on the other foot. At that moment the godmother arrived. With a tap of her wand Cinderella's clothes became even more magnificent than all the previous garments she had worn. The two sisters then recognized her as the beautiful person they had seen at the ball. They threw themselves at her feet, begging her pardon for the harsh treatment they had made her endure.

Cinderella raised and embraced them, saying that she forgave them with all her heart and begged them to love her well in the future. Adorned as she was, she

was conducted to the young prince. He found her more
beautiful than ever, and a few days later he married
her. Cinderella, who was as kind as she was beautiful,
gave her sisters apartments in the palace and had them
married the very same day to two great noblemen of
the court.

MORAL

A woman's beauty is quite a treasure
We never cease to admire.
Yet graciousness exceeds all measure.
There's nothing of virtue higher.
The fairy, according to our story,
Contributed it to Cinderella's glory
And taught her what becomes a queen,
(Left in a moral to be gleaned.)

Beautiful ladies, it's kindness more than dress
That wins a man's heart with greater success.
So, if you want a life filled with bliss,
The truest gift is graciousness.

ANOTHER MORAL

No doubt it is a benefit
To have strong courage and fine wit,
To be endowed with common sense
And other virtues to possess
That Heaven may dispense.
But these may prove quite useless—
As well as many others—
If you strive to gain success
And neglect godfathers or godmothers.

BLUE BEARD

ONCE upon a time there was a man who had fine town and country houses, gold and silver plates, embroidered furniture, and gilded coaches. Unfortunately, however, this man had a blue beard, which made him look so ugly and terrifying that there was not a woman or girl who did not run away from him.

Now, one of his neighbors was a lady of quality who had two exceedingly beautiful daughters. He proposed to marry one of them, leaving the choice up to the mother which of the two she would give him. Yet neither one would have him, and they kept sending him back and forth between them, not being able to make up their minds to marry a man who had a blue beard. What increased their distaste for him was that he had already had several wives, and nobody knew what had become of them.

In order to cultivate their acquaintance, Blue Beard took the sisters, their mother, three or four of their most intimate friends, and some young people who resided in the neighborhood, to one of his country estates, where they spent an entire week. Their days were filled with excursions, hunting and fishing, parties, balls, entertainments, and feasts. Nobody went to bed, for their nights were spent in merry games and gambols. In short, all went off so well that the younger daughter began to find that the beard of the master of the house was not as blue as it used to be and that he was a very worthy man.

The marriage took place immediately upon their return to town. At the end of a month Blue Beard told his wife that he was obliged to take a journey concerning a matter of great consequence, and it would occupy him at least six weeks. He asked her to amuse herself as best as she could during his absence and to take her closest friends into the country with her if she pleased, and to offer them fine meals.

"Here are the keys to my two great storerooms," he said to her. "These are the keys to the chests in which the gold and silver plates for special occasions are kept. These are the keys to the strongboxes in which I keep my money. These keys open the caskets that contain my jewels. And this is the passkey to all the apartments. As for this small key," he said, "it is for the little room at the end of the long corridor on the ground floor. Open everything and go everywhere except into that room, which I forbid you to enter. My orders are to be strictly obeyed, and if you dare open the door, my anger will exceed anything you have ever experienced."

She promised to carry out all his instructions exactly as he had ordered, and after he embraced her, he got into his coach and set out on his journey. The neighbors and friends of the young bride did not wait for her invitation, so eager were they to see all the treasures contained in the country mansion. They had not ventured to enter it while her husband was at home because they had been frightened of his blue beard. Now they began running through all the rooms, closets, and wardrobes. Each apartment outdid the other in beauty and richness. Then they ascended to the storerooms, where they could not admire enough the elegance of the many tapestries, beds, sofas, cabinets, stands, tables, and mirrors in which they could see themselves from head to foot. Some mirrors had frames of glass, and some of gold gilt, more beautiful and magnificent than they had ever seen. They could not stop extolling and envying the good fortune of the new bride.

In the meantime, she was not in the least entertained by all these treasures because she was so impatient to open the little room on the ground floor. Her curiosity increased to such a degree that, without reflecting how rude it was to leave her company, she ran down a back staircase so hastily that she nearly tripped and broke her neck on two or three occasions. Once at the door she paused for a moment, recalling her husband's prohibition. What misfortune might befall her if she disobeyed? But the temptation was so strong that she could not withstand it. She took the small key, and with a trembling hand she opened the door of the little room.

At first she could make out nothing, since the windows were shuttered. After a short time, though, she began to perceive that the floor was covered with clotted blood of the dead bodies of several women suspended from the walls. These were all the former wives of Blue Beard, who had cut their throats one after the other. She thought she would die from fright, and the key to the room fell from her hand. After recovering her senses a little, she picked up the key, locked the door again, and went up to her chamber to compose herself. Yet she could not relax because she was too upset. Then she noticed that the key to the room was stained with blood. She wiped it two or three times, but the blood would not come off. In vain she washed it, and even scrubbed it with sand and grit. But the blood remained, for the key was enchanted, and there was no way of cleaning it completely. When the blood was washed off one side, it came back on the other.

That very evening Blue Beard returned from his journey and announced that he had received letters on the road informing him that the business on which he had set forth had been settled to his advantage. His wife did all she could to persuade him that she was delighted by his speedy return. The next morning he asked her to return his keys. She gave them to him, but her hand trembled so much that he did not have any difficulty in guessing what had occurred.

"Why is it," he said, "that the key to the little room is not with the others?"

"I must have left it upstairs on my table," she replied.

"Bring it to me right now," said Blue Beard.

After several excuses she was compelled to produce the key. Once Blue Beard examined it, he said to her, "Why is there blood on this key?"

"I don't know," answered the poor woman, paler than death.

"You don't know?" Blue Beard responded. "I know well enough. You wanted to enter the room! Well, madam, you will enter it and take your place among the ladies you saw there."

She flung herself at her husband's feet, weeping and begging his pardon. One glance at her showed that she truly repented of disobeying him. Her beauty and affliction might have melted a rock.

"You must die, madam," he said, "and immediately."

"If I must die," she replied, looking at him with eyes bathed in tears, "give me a little time to say my prayers."

"I shall give you a quarter of an hour," Blue Beard answered, "but not a minute more."

As soon as he had left her, she called for her sister and said, "Sister Anne"—for that was her name—"go up, I beg you, to the top of the tower and see if my brothers are coming. They promised me that they would come to see me today. If you see them, give them a signal to make haste."

Sister Anne mounted to the top of the tower, and the poor distressed creature called to her every now and then, "Anne! Sister Anne! Do you see anyone coming?"

And sister Anne answered her, "I see nothing but the sun making dust, and the grass growing green."

In the meantime Blue Beard held a cutlass in his hand and bellowed to his wife with all his might, "Come down quickly, or I'll come up there."

"Please, one minute more," replied his wife. Immediately she repeated in a low voice, "Anne! Sister Anne! Do you see anyone coming?"

And sister Anne replied, "I see nothing but the sun making dust, and the grass growing green."

"Come down quickly," roared Blue Beard, "or I shall come up there!"

"I'm coming," answered his wife, and then she called, "Anne! Sister Anne! Do you see anyone coming?"

"I see," said sister Anne, "a great cloud of dust moving this way."

"Is it my brothers?"

"Alas! No, sister, I see a flock of sheep."

"Do you refuse to come down?" shouted Blue Beard.

"One minute more," his wife replied, and then she cried, "Anne! Sister Anne! Do you see anything coming?"

"I see two horsemen coming this way," she responded, "but they're still at a great distance." A moment afterward she exclaimed, "Heaven be praised! They're my brothers! I'm signaling to them as best I can to hurry up."

Blue Beard began to roar so loudly that the whole house shook. So his poor wife descended to him and threw herself at his feet, all disheveled and in tears.

"It's no use," said Blue Beard. "You must die!"

He seized her by the hair with one hand and raised his cutlass with the other. He was about to cut off her head when the poor woman looked up at him. Fixing her dying gaze upon him, she implored him to allow her one short moment to collect herself.

"No, no," he said, lifting his arm, "commend yourself as best you can to Heaven."

At that moment there was such a loud knocking at the gate that Blue Beard stopped short. The gate was opened, and two horsemen burst through. With drawn swords they ran straight at Blue Beard, who recognized them as the brothers of his wife—one a dragoon, the other a musqueteer. Immediately he fled, hoping to escape, but they pursued so quickly that they overtook him before he could reach the step of his door and passed their swords through his body, leaving him dead on the spot. The poor woman, who was nearly as dead as her husband, did not have the strength even to rise and embrace her brothers.

Since Blue Beard had no heirs, his widow inherited all his wealth. She employed part of it to arrange a marriage between her sister Anne and a young gentleman who had loved her a long time. Another part paid for commissions for her two brothers so they could become captains. The rest she used for her marriage to a worthy man who made her forget the miserable time she had spent with Blue Beard.

MORAL

Curiosity, in spite of its charm,
Too often causes a great deal of harm.
A thousand new cases arise each day.
With due respect, ladies, the thrill is slight,
For as soon as you're satisfied, it goes away,
And the price one pays is never right.

ANOTHER MORAL

Provided one has common sense
And learns to study complex texts,
It's easy to trace the evidence
Of long ago in this tale's events.

No longer are husbands so terrible,
Or insist on having the impossible.
Though he may be jealous and dissatisfied,
He tries to do as he's obliged.
And whatever color his beard may be,
It's difficult to know who the master be.

LITTLE THUMBLING

ONCE upon a time there was a woodcutter and his wife who had seven children, all boys. The eldest was but ten years old and the youngest only seven. People were astonished that the woodcutter had had so many children in such a short time, but the fact is that his wife did not mince matters and seldom gave birth to less than two at a time. They were very poor, and having seven children was a great burden to them, since not one was able to earn his own living.

What distressed them even more was that the youngest son was very delicate and rarely spoke, which they considered a mark of stupidity instead of good sense. Moreover, he was very little. Indeed, at birth he was scarcely bigger than one's thumb, and this led everyone to call him Little Thumbling. This poor child became the family scapegoat and was blamed for everything that happened. Nevertheless, he was the shrewdest and most sensible of all the brothers, and if he spoke but little, he listened a great deal.

One year there was a disastrous harvest, and the famine was so severe that these poor people decided to get rid of their children. One evening, when they were all in bed and the woodcutter was sitting by the fire with his wife, he said with a heavy heart, "It's plain that we can no longer feed our children. I can't let them die of hunger before my eyes, and I've made up my mind to lose them tomorrow in the forest. We can do this without any trouble when they are making bundles of firewood. We only have to disappear without their seeing us."

"Ah!" the woodcutter's wife exclaimed. "Do you really have the heart to abandon your own children?"

Her husband tried in vain to convince her how their terrible poverty necessitated such a plan, but she would not consent to the deed. However poor, she was their mother. After reflecting on how miserable she would be to see them die of hunger, though, she finally agreed and went to bed weeping.

Little Thumbling had heard everything they said, for while he had been lying in his bed, he had realized that they were discussing their affairs. He had got up quietly, slipped under his father's stool, and listened without being seen. Going back to bed, he did not sleep a wink the rest of the night because he was thinking over what he should do. He rose early the next morning and went to the banks of a brook, where he filled his pockets with small white pebbles and then returned home. Little Thumbling revealed nothing of what he had heard to his brothers.

Later they set out all together. They entered a dense forest, where they were unable to see one another once they were ten paces apart. The woodcutter began to chop wood, and his children, to pick up sticks and make bundles. Seeing them occupied with their work, the father and mother gradually stole away and then fled in an instant by a small, winding path. When the children found themselves all alone, they began to cry with all their might. Little Thumbling let them scream since he was fully confident that he could get home again. He had dropped the white pebbles in his pockets all along the path.

"Don't be afraid, brothers," he said. "Our father and mother have abandoned us here, but I'll lead you safely home. Just follow me."

They followed him, and he led them back to the house by the same path that they had taken into the forest. At first they were afraid to enter the house. Instead, they placed themselves next to the door to listen to the conversation of their parents.

Now, after the woodcutter and his wife had arrived home, they found ten crowns that the lord of the manor had sent them. He had owed them this money for a long time, and they had given up all hope of ever receiving it. This put new life into these poor, starving people. The woodcutter sent his wife to the butcher's right away, for it had been many a day since they had eaten anything. She bought three times as much as was necessary for two persons, and when they sat down at the table again, she said, "Alas! Where are our poor children now? They would make a good meal out of our leftovers. But it was you, Guillaume, who wanted to lose them. I told you we'd repent it. What are they doing now in the forest? Alas! Heaven help me! The wolves have probably eaten them already! What a monster you must be to get rid of your children this way!"

When she repeated more than forty times that they would repent it and that she had told him so, the woodcutter lost his temper. He threatened to beat her if she did not hold her tongue. It was not that the woodcutter was not perhaps even more sorry than his wife, but that she browbeat him. He was like many other people who are disposed to women who can talk well but become irritated by women who are always right.

"Alas!" His wife was in tears. "Where are my children now, my poor children!"

She uttered these words so loudly that the children began to cry at the door, "Here we are! Here we are!"

She rushed to open the door, and embracing them, she exclaimed, "How happy I am to see you again, my dear children! You're very tired and hungry. And how dirty you are, Pierrot! Come here and let me wash you."

Pierrot was her eldest son, and she loved him most of all because he was somewhat redheaded, which was the color of her hair too. They sat down to supper and ate with an appetite that pleased their father and mother. They all talked at once and related how frightened they had been in the forest. The good souls were delighted to see their children around them once more, but their joy lasted just as long as the ten crowns. When the money was spent, they relapsed into their former misery and decided to lose the children again. And to do so they were determined to lead them much farther from home than they had the first time.

They discussed this in secret, but were overheard by

Little Thumbling, who counted on getting out of the predicament the way he had before. Yet when he got up early to collect some pebbles, he found the house door double-locked. He could not think of what to do until the woodcutter's wife gave them each a piece of bread for their breakfast. Then it occurred to him that he might use the bread in place of the pebbles by throwing crumbs along the path as they went. So he stuck his piece in his pocket.

The father and mother led them into the thickest, darkest part of the forest, and as soon as they had done so, they took a sidepath and left them there. Little Thumbling was not at all worried, for he thought he would easily find his way back by following the crumbs he had scattered along the path. But he was greatly surprised when he could not find a single crumb: the birds had eaten them all up. Now the poor children were in great trouble. The farther they wandered, the deeper they plunged into the forest. Night arrived, and a great wind arose, filling them with fear. They imagined that they heard wolves howling on every side of them. "They're coming to devour us!" They scarcely dared to turn their heads. Then it began raining so heavily that they were soon drenched to the skin. With each step they took, they slipped and tumbled into the mud. They got up all covered with mud and did not know what to do with their hands. Little Thumbling climbed up a tree to try to see something from the top. After looking all around, he saw a little light, like that of a candle, faraway on the other side of the forest. When he climbed down from the tree and reached the ground, he could no longer see the light. This was a great disappointment to him, but after having walked on with his brothers for some time in the direction of the light, he saw it again as they emerged from the forest. Then again when they descended into the ravines, they kept losing sight of the beaming light and became frightened. Eventually, however, they reached the house where the light was burning and knocked at the door. A good woman came to open it and asked them what they wanted. Little Thumbling told her that they were poor children who had lost their way in the forest and begged her for a night's lodging out of charity. Seeing how lovely the children were, she began to weep and said, "Alas! My poor boys, don't you know where you've landed? This is the dwelling of an ogre who eats little children!"

"Oh, madam!" replied Little Thumbling, who trembled from head to toe just as all his brothers did. "What shall we do? It's certain that the wolves of the forest will devour us tonight if you refuse to take us under your roof. That being the case, we'd rather be eaten by your husband. If you're kind enough to plead for us, perhaps he'll take pity on us."

The ogre's wife, who believed she could manage to hide them from her husband till the next morning, allowed them to come in and led them to a spot where they could warm themselves by a good fire, for there was a whole sheep on the spit roasting for the ogre's supper. Just as they were beginning to get warm, they heard two or three loud knocks at the door. The ogre had come home. His wife immediately made the children hide under the bed and went to open the door. The ogre first asked if his supper were ready and if she had drawn the wine. With that he sat down to his meal. The mutton was almost raw, but he liked it all the better for that. He sniffed right and left, saying that he smelt fresh meat.

"It must be the calf that you smell. I've just skinned it," said his wife.

"I smell fresh meat, I tell you," replied the ogre, looking suspiciously at his wife. "There's something here I don't understand." Upon saying these words, he rose from the table and went straight to the bed. "Ah!" he exclaimed. "This is the way you deceive me, cursed woman! I don't know what's holding me back from eating you as well! It's a lucky thing that you're an old beast!"

He dragged the boys from under the bed one after the other. "Here's some game that comes just in time for me to entertain three ogre friends of mine who are coming to see me tomorrow." The poor children fell on their knees, begging for mercy, but they were facing the most cruel of all the ogres. Far from feeling pity for

them, he was already devouring them with his eyes. He
said to his wife, "They will be perfect as dainty bits
once you make a good sauce for them." He fetched a
large knife, and as he approached the poor children, he
whetted it on a long stone that he held in his left hand.
He had already grabbed one of the boys when his wife
said to him, "Why do you want to do it at this hour of
the night? Won't you have time enough tomorrow?"

"Hold your tongue," the ogre replied. "They'll be all
the more tender."

"But you already have so much meat," his wife
responded. "Here's a calf, two sheep, and half a pig."

"You're right," the ogre said. "Give them a good
supper to fatten them up, and then put them to bed."

Overjoyed, the good woman brought them plenty for
supper, but they could not eat because they were so
paralyzed with fright. As for the ogre, he seated himself to drink again, delighted to think he had such a
treat in store for his friends. So he emptied a dozen
goblets, which was more than usual and affected his
head somewhat, and he was obliged to go to bed.

Now, the ogre had seven daughters who were still
quite young. These little ogresses had the most beautiful complexions due to eating raw flesh like their
father. But they had very small, round gray eyes,
hooked noses, and large mouths with long teeth,
extremely sharp and wide apart. They were not very
vicious as yet, but they showed great promise, for they
had already begun to bite little children to suck their
blood. They had been sent to bed early, and all seven
were in a large bed, each having a golden crown on her
head. In the same room there was another bed of the
same size. It was in this bed that the ogre's wife put the
seven little boys to sleep, after which she went to sleep
with her husband.

Little Thumbling noticed that the ogre's daughters
had golden crowns on their heads. Fearing that the ogre
might regret not having killed him and his brothers that
evening, he got up in the middle of the night. He took
off his nightcap and those of his brothers, crept over
very softly, and swapped them for the crowns of the
ogre's seven daughters. These he put on his brothers

and himself so that the ogre might mistake them for his daughters, and his daughters for the boys whose throats he longed to cut.

Everything turned out exactly as he had anticipated. The ogre awoke at midnight and regretted that he had postponed what he might have done that evening until the next morning. Therefore, he jumped out of bed and seized his large knife. "Let's go and see how our little rascals are doing. We won't make the same mistake twice." So he stole up to his daughters' bedroom on tiptoe and approached the bed in which the little boys were lying. They were all asleep except Thumbling, who was dreadfully frightened when the ogre placed his hand on his head to feel as he had in turn felt those of his brothers.

After feeling the golden crowns, the ogre said, "Upon my word, I almost made a mess of a job! It's clear I must have drunk too much last night." He then went to the bed where his daughters slept, and after feeling the nightcaps that belonged to the boys, he cried, "Aha! Here are our sly little dogs. Let's get to work!" With these words he cut the throats of his seven daughters without hesitating. Well satisfied with his work, he returned and stretched himself out in bed beside his wife. As soon as Little Thumbling heard the ogre snoring, he woke his brothers and told them to dress themselves quickly and follow him. They went down quietly into the garden and jumped over the wall. As they ran throughout the night, they could not stop trembling, for they did not know where they were going.

When the ogre awoke the next morning, he said to his wife, "Go upstairs and dress the little rascals you took in last night."

The ogress was astonished by her husband's kindness, never suspecting the sort of dressing he meant her to give them. Thus she merely imagined that he was ordering her to go and put on their clothes. When she went upstairs, she was greatly surprised to find her daughters murdered and swimming in their blood. All at once she fainted (for this is the first thing that most women do in similar circumstances). Fearing that his wife was taking too long in carrying out her task, the ogre went upstairs to help. He was no less surprised than his wife when he came upon the frightful spectacle.

"Ah! What have I done?" he exclaimed. "The wretches shall pay for it, and right now!" He threw a jugful of water in his wife's face, and after reviving her, he said, "Quick! Fetch my seven-league boots so I can go and catch them."

After setting out, he ran far and wide and at last came upon the track of the poor children, who were not more than a hundred yards from their father's house. They saw the ogre striding from hill to hill and stepping over rivers as easily as if they were the smallest brooks. Little Thumbling noticed a hollow cave nearby and hid his brothers in it, and while watching the movements of the ogre, he crept in after them. Now the ogre, feeling tired because his long journey had been to no avail, needed to rest, especially since seven-league boots make the wearer quite exhausted. By chance he sat down on the very rock in which the little boys had concealed themselves. Since the ogre was worn out, he soon fell asleep and began to snore so terribly that the poor children were just as frightened as they had been when he had grabbed the large knife to cut their throats.

Little Thumbling was not so much alarmed and told his brothers to run straight into the house while the ogre was sound asleep and not to worry about him. They took his advice and quickly ran home. Little Thumbling now approached the ogre and carefully pulled off his boots, which he immediately put on himself. The boots were very large and very long, but since they were fairy boots, they possessed the quality of increasing or diminishing in size according to the leg of the person who wore them. Thus they fit him just as if they had been made for him. He went straight to the ogre's house, where he found the wife weeping over her murdered daughters.

"Your husband is in great danger. He's been captured by a band of robbers, who have sworn to kill him if he doesn't give them all his gold and silver," Thumbling said to her. "He saw me just at the moment they had their daggers at his throat, and he begged me to

come and ask you to give me all his valuables without
holding anything back. Otherwise, they'll kill him
without mercy. Since time was of the essence, he
insisted I take his seven-league boots so that I might go
faster and also so that you'd be sure I wasn't an
imposter."

The good woman was very much alarmed by this
news and immediately gave Thumbling all the money
she could find, for the ogre was not a bad husband to
her, even though he ate little children. So, loaded down
with the ogre's entire wealth, Little Thumbling rushed
back to his father's house, where he was received with
great joy.

Many people differ in their account of this part of
the story. They assert that Little Thumbling never committed the theft, and that he only considered himself
justified in taking the ogre's seven-league boots
because the ogre had used them expressly to run after
little children. These people argue that they got their
story from good authority and had even eaten and
drunk in the woodcutter's house.

They maintain that after Little Thumbling had put on
the ogre's boots, he went to the court. There, he knew,
they were anxious to learn about the army and the outcome of a battle that was being fought two hundred
leagues away. He went to the king and told him, "If
you so desire, I will bring back news of the army
before dusk." The king promised him a large sum of
money if he did so, and Little Thumbling brought news
that very evening.

Since this first journey gave him a certain reputation,
he earned whatever he chose to ask. Not only did the
king pay liberally for taking his orders to the army, but
numerous ladies gave him any price he named for news
of their lovers, and this became the best source of his
income. Occasionally he met some wives who
entrusted him with letters for their husbands, but they
paid him so poorly that he did not even bother to put
down what he got among his receipts.

After he had been a courier for some time and saved
a great deal of money, he returned to his father. You
cannot imagine how joyful his family was at seeing

him again. He made them all comfortable by buying
newly created positions for his father and brothers. In
this way he made sure they were all established, and at
the same time he made certain that he did perfectly
well at the court himself.

MORAL

No longer may children be such a hardship,
If possessed of charm, good looks, and wit.
But if one's weak and falters in the fray,
He'll soon be mocked until he runs away.
Yet there are times when the child, the least expected,
May return with a fortune, his honor resurrected.

Children
are the
wealth of
the family

THE SLEEPING BEAUTY
IN THE WOODS

ONCE upon a time there was a king and a queen who were quite disturbed at not having any children. Indeed, they were so disturbed that no words can express their feelings. They visited all the baths in the world. They took vows, pilgrimages—everything was tried, and nothing succeeded. At last, however, the queen became pregnant and gave birth to a daughter. At the christening all the fairies who could be found in the realm (seven altogether) were asked to be godmothers so that each would give the child a gift. According to the custom of the fairies in those days, the gifts would endow the princess with all the perfections that could be imagined.

After the baptismal ceremonies the entire company returned to the king's palace, where a great banquet was held for the fairies. Places were laid for each, consisting of a magnificent plate with a massive gold case containing a spoon, fork, and knife of fine gold, studded with diamonds and rubies. But as they were all about to sit down at the table, an old fairy entered the palace. She had not been invited because she had not left the tower in which she resided for more than fifty years, and it was supposed that she had either died or had become enchanted.

The king ordered a place to be set for her, but he could not give her a massive gold case as he had with the others because the seven had been made expressly for the seven fairies. The old fairy thought that she was being slighted and muttered some threats between her teeth. One of the young fairies who chanced to be nearby overheard her, and thinking that she might wish the little princess bad luck, hid herself behind the tapestry as soon as they rose from the table. "That way

I'll have the last word and repair any evil the old woman might do."

Meanwhile, the fairies began to bestow their gifts upon the princess. The youngest fairy decreed, "She will be the most beautiful person in the world." The next fairy declared, "She will have the temperament of an angel." The third, "She will evince the most admirable grace in all she does." The fourth: "She will dance to perfection." The sixth: "She will play every instrument in the most exquisite manner possible."

Finally the turn of the old fairy arrived. Her head shook more with malice than with age as she declared, "The princess will pierce her hand with a spindle and die of the wound."

This terrible gift made the entire company tremble, and no one present could refrain from tears. At this moment the young fairy stepped from behind the tapestry and uttered in a loud voice, "Comfort yourselves, King and Queen, your daughter will not die. It's true that I don't have sufficient power to undo entirely what my elder has done. The princess will pierce her hand with a spindle. But instead of dying, she'll only fall into a deep sleep that will last one hundred years. At the end of that time, a king's son will come to wake her."

In the hope of avoiding the misfortune predicted by the old fairy, the king immediately issued a public edict forbidding all his subjects to spin with a spindle or to have spindles in their house under pain of death.

After fifteen or sixteen years had passed, the royal couple and their court traveled to one of their country residences, and one day the princess happened to be exploring it. She went from one chamber to another, and after arriving at the top of a tower, she entered a little garret, where an honest old woman was sitting by herself with her distaff and spindle. This good woman had never heard of the king's prohibition of spinning with a spindle.

"What are you doing there, my fair lady?" asked the princess.

"I'm spinning, my lovely child," answered the old woman, who did not know her.

"Oh, how pretty it is!" the princess responded. "How do you do it? Let me try and see if I can do it as well."

No sooner had she grasped the spindle than she pricked her hand with the point and fainted, for she had been hasty, a little thoughtless, and moreover, the sentence of the fairies had ordained it to be that way. Greatly embarrassed, the good old woman called for help. People came from all quarters. They threw water on the princess's face. They unlaced her stays. They slapped her hands. They rubbed her temples with Queen of Hungary's water. Nothing could revive her. Then the king, who had run upstairs at the noise, remembered the prediction of the fairies and wisely concluded that this must have happened as the fairies said it would. Therefore, he had the princess carried to the finest apartment in the palace and placed on a bed of gold and silver embroidery. One would have said she was an angel, so lovely did she appear, for her swoon had not deprived her of her rich complexion: her cheeks preserved their crimson color, and her lips were like coral. Her eyes were closed, but her gentle breathing could be heard, and that indicated she was not dead. The king commanded that she be left to sleep in peace until the hour arrived for her waking.

The good fairy who had saved her life by decreeing that she should sleep for one hundred years was in the Kingdom of Mataquin, twelve thousand leagues away. When the princess met with her accident, she was informed of it instantly by a little dwarf who had a pair of seven-league boots (that is, boots that enable the wearer to cover seven leagues at a single stride). The fairy set out immediately, and an hour afterward she was seen arriving in a chariot of fire drawn by dragons. The king advanced and offered his hand to help her out of the chariot. She approved of all that he had done. Yet since she had great foresight, she thought to herself that when the princess awoke, she would feel considerably embarrassed at finding herself all alone in that old castle. So this is what the fairy did:

With the exception of the king and queen, she touched everyone in the castle with her wand—governesses, maids of honor, ladies-in-waiting, gentlemen, officers, stewards, cooks, scullions, boys, guards, porters, pages, footmen. She also touched all the horses in the stables, their grooms, the great mastiffs in the courtyard, and little Pootsie, the princess's tiny dog lying on the bed beside her. As soon as she touched them, they all fell asleep, and they were not to wake again until the time arrived for their mistress to do so. Thus they would all be ready to wait upon her if she should want them. Even the spits that had been put down to the fire, laden with partridges and pheasants, went to sleep, and the fire as well.

All this was done in a moment, for the fairies never lose much time when they work. Then the king and queen kissed their dear daughter without waking her and left the castle. They issued a proclamation forbidding anyone to approach it. These orders were unnecessary, for within a quarter of an hour the park was surrounded by such a great quantity of trees, large and small, interlaced by brambles and thorns, that neither man nor beast could penetrate them. Nothing more could be seen than the tops of the castle turrets, and these only at a considerable distance. Nobody doubted but that was also some of the fairy's handiwork so that the princess might have nothing to fear from the curiosity of strangers during her slumber.

At the end of the hundred years, a different family from that of the sleeping princess had succeeded to the throne. One day the son of the king went hunting in that neighborhood and inquired about the towers that he saw above the trees of a large and dense wood. Every person responded to the prince according to the story he had heard. Some said that it was an old castle haunted by ghosts. Others, that all the witches of the region held their Sabbath there. The most prevalent opinion was that it was the abode of an ogre who carried away all the children he could catch and ate them there at his leisure, since he alone had the power of making a passage through the wood. While the prince tried to make up his mind what to believe, an old peasant spoke in his turn and said to him, "Prince, it is more than fifty years since I heard my father say that the most beautiful princess ever seen is in that castle.

He told me that she was to sleep for a hundred years and was destined to be awakened by a chosen king's son."

Upon hearing these words, the young prince felt all on fire. There was no doubt in his mind that he was destined to accomplish this wonderful adventure, and impelled by love and glory, he decided on the spot to see what would come of it. No sooner had he approached the wood than all those great trees and all those brambles and thorns opened on their own accord and allowed him to pass through. Then he began walking toward the castle, which he saw at the end of the long avenue that he had entered. To his surprise, the trees closed up as soon as he passed, and none of his attendants could follow him. Nevertheless, he continued to advance, for a young and amorous prince is always courageous. When he entered a large forecourt, everything he saw froze his blood with terror. A frightful silence reigned. Death seemed to be everywhere. Nothing could be seen but the bodies of men and animals stretched out and apparently lifeless. He soon discovered, however, by the shining noses and red faces of the porters that they were only asleep; their goblets, which still contained a few drops of wine, sufficiently proved that they had dosed off while drinking. Passing through a large courtyard paved with marble, he ascended a staircase. As he entered the guardroom, he saw the guards drawn up in a line, their carbines shouldered, and snoring their loudest. He traversed several apartments filled with ladies and gentlemen all asleep; some standing, others seated. Finally he entered a chamber completely covered with gold and saw the most lovely sight he had ever looked upon—on a bed with curtains open on each side was a princess who seemed to be about fifteen or sixteen. Her radiant charms gave her such a luminous, supernatural appearance that he approached, trembling and admiring, and knelt down beside her. At that moment the enchantment ended. The princess awoke and bestowed on him a look more tender than a first glance might seem to warrant.

"Is it you, my prince?" she said. "You have been long awaited."

Charmed by these words, and still more by the tone in which they were uttered, the prince hardly knew how to express his joy and gratitude to her. He assured her he loved her better than he loved himself. His words were not very coherent, but they pleased her all the more because of that. The less eloquence, the more love, so they say. He was much more embarrassed than she was, and one ought not to be astonished at that, for the princess had had time enough to consider what she should say to him. There is reason to believe (though history makes no mention of it) that the good fairy had procured her the pleasure of very charming dreams during her long slumber. In short, they talked for four hours without expressing half of what they had to say to each other.

In the meantime the entire palace had been roused at the same time as the princess. They all remembered what their tasks were, and since they were not all in love, they were dying with hunger. The lady-in-waiting, as hungry as any of them, became impatient and announced loudly to the princess that dinner was ready. The prince assisted the princess to rise. She was fully dressed, and her gown was magnificent, but he took care not to tell her that she was attired like his grandmother, who also wore stand-up collars. Still, she looked no less lovely in it.

They passed into a salon of mirrors, in which stewards of the princess served them supper. The violins and oboes played antiquated but excellent pieces of music. And after supper, to lose no time, the chaplain married them in the castle chapel, and the maid of honor pulled the curtains of their bed closed.

They did not sleep a great deal, however. The princess did not have much need of sleep, and the prince left her at sunrise to return to the city, where his father had been greatly worried about him. The prince told him that he had lost his way in the forest while hunting, and that he had slept in the hut of a charcoal-burner, who had given him some black bread and cheese for his supper. His father, who was a trusting soul, believed him, but his mother was not so easily persuaded. Observing that he went hunting nearly every day and always had some story ready as an excuse when he had slept two or three nights away from home, she was convinced that he had some mistress. Indeed, he lived with the princess for more than two years and had two children by her. The first was a girl named Aurora, and the second, a son, called Day because he seemed even more beautiful than his sister.

In order to draw a confession from him, the queen often said to her son that he ought to settle down. However, he never dared to trust her with his secret. Although he loved her, he also feared her, for she was of the race of ogres, and the king had married her only because of her great wealth. It was even whispered about the court that she had the inclinations of an ogress: whenever she saw little children passing, she had the greatest difficulty restraining herself from pouncing on them. Hence, the prince refused to say anything about his adventure.

Two years later, however, the king died, and the prince became his successor. Thereupon, he made a public declaration of his marriage and went in great state to fetch his queen to the palace. With her two children on either side of her, she made a magnificent entry into the capital.

Some time afterward the king went to war with his neighbor, the Emperor Cantalabutte. He left the regency of the kingdom to his mother, the queen, and placed his wife and children in her care. Since he was likely to spend the entire summer in battle, the queen mother sent her daughter-in-law and the children to a country house in the forest, as soon as he was gone, so that she might gratify her horrible longing more easily. A few days later, she followed them there, and one evening she said to her steward, "I want to eat little Aurora for dinner tomorrow."

"Ah, madam!" exclaimed the steward.

"That is my will," said the queen (and she said it in the tone of an ogress longing to eat fresh meat), "and I want her served up with *sauce Robert*."

The poor man plainly saw that it was useless to trifle

with an ogress. So he took his knife and went up to little Aurora's room. She was then about four years old, and when she skipped over to him, threw her arms around his neck with a laugh, and asked him for some sweets, he burst into tears. The knife fell from his hands. Soon he went down into the kitchen court, killed a little lamb, and served it with such a delicious sauce that his mistress assured him she had never eaten anything so good. In the meantime he carried off little Aurora and gave her to his wife to conceal in the lodging she occupied at the far end of the kitchen court.

A week later, the wicked queen said to her steward, "I want to eat little Day for supper."

Determined to deceive her as before he did not reply. He went in search of little Day and found him with a tiny foil in his hand, fencing with a large monkey, though he was only three years old. He carried him to his wife, who hid him where she had concealed his sister. Then he cooked a tender little goat in place of little Day, and the ogress thought it most delicious.

Thus far all was going well, but one evening the wicked queen said to the steward, "I want to eat the queen with the same sauce that I had with the children."

This time the poor steward despaired of being able to deceive her again. The young queen was now twenty years old, not counting the hundred years she had slept. Her skin was a little tough, though it was white and beautiful. Thus, where in the menagerie was he to find an animal that was just as tough as she was?

To save his own life he resolved he would cut the queen's throat and went up to her apartment intending to carry out this plan. He worked himself up into a fit and entered the young queen's chamber, dagger in hand. However, he did not want to take her by surprise and thus repeated respectfully the order he had received from the queen mother.

"Do your duty!" said she, stretching out her neck to him. "Carry out the order given to you. Then I shall behold my children, my poor children, that I loved so much."

She had thought they were dead ever since they had been carried off without explanation.

"No, no, madam!" replied the poor steward, touched to the quick. "You shall not die, and you shall see your children again, but it will be in my house, where I have hidden them. And I shall again deceive the queen mother by serving her a young hind in your stead."

He led her straight to his own quarters, and after leaving her to embrace her children and weep with them, he cooked a hind that the queen ate at supper with as much appetite as if it had been the young queen. She felt content with her cruelty and intended to tell the king on his return that some ferocious wolves had devoured his wife and two children.

One evening when she was prowling as usual around the courts and poultry yards of the castle to inhale the smell of fresh meat, she overheard little Day crying in a lower room because his mother wanted to slap him for having been naughty. She also heard little Aurora begging forgiveness for her brother. The ogress recognized the voices of the queen and her children and, furious at having been duped, she gave orders in a tone that made everyone tremble, "Bring a large copper vat into the middle of the court early tomorrow morning."

When it was done the next day, she had the vat filled with toads, vipers, adders, and serpents, intending to fling the queen, her children, the steward, his wife, and his maidservant into it.

"Bring them forth with their hands tied behind them," she commanded.

When they stood before her, the executioners began preparing to fling them into the copper vat when the king, who was not expected back so soon, entered the courtyard on horseback. He had ridden posthaste, and greatly astonished, he demanded to know the meaning of the horrible spectacle, but nobody dared to tell him. Then the ogress, enraged at the sight of the king's return, flung herself headfirst into the vat and was devoured by the horrible reptiles that she had commanded to be placed there. The king could not help but feel sorry, for she was his mother, but he speedily

consoled himself in the company of his beautiful wife
and children.

MORAL

To wait so long,
To want a man refined and strong,
Is not at all uncommon.
But: rare it is a hundred years to wait.
Indeed there is no woman
Today so patient for a mate.

Our tale was meant to show
That when marriage is deferred,
It is no less blissful than those of which you've heard.
Nothing's lost after a century or so.
And yet, for lovers whose ardor
Cannot be controlled and marry out of passion,
I don't have the heart their act to deplore
Or to preach a moral lesson.

RIQUET WITH THE TUFT

ONCE upon a time there was a queen who gave birth to a son so ugly and misshapen that for a long time everyone doubted if he was in fact human. A fairy who was present at his birth assured everyone, however, that he could not fail to be pleasant because he would have a great deal of intelligence. She added that he would also have the ability to impart the same amount of intelligence to that person he came to love by virtue of this gift she was giving him. All this somewhat consoled the poor queen, who was very much distressed at having brought such a hideous little monkey into the world. Sure enough, as soon as the child was able to talk, he said a thousand pretty things. Furthermore, there was an indescribable air of thoughtfulness in all his actions that charmed everyone. I have forgotten to say that he was born with a little tuft of hair on his head, and this was the reason why he was called Riquet with the Tuft (Riquet being the family name).

At the end of seven or eight years, the queen of a neighboring kingdom gave birth to two daughters. The first of them was more beautiful than daylight, and the queen was so delighted that people feared her great joy might cause her some harm. The same fairy who had attended the birth of little Riquet with the Tuft was also present on this occasion, and to moderate the queen's joy, she declared that this little princess would be as stupid as she was beautiful. The queen was deeply mortified by this, but a few minutes later her chagrin became even greater still, for she gave birth to a second child who turned out to be extremely ugly.

"Don't be too upset, madam," the fairy said to her. "Your daughter will be compensated in another way. She'll have so much intelligence that her lack of beauty will hardly be noticed."

"May heaven grant it," replied the queen. "But isn't there some way to give a little intelligence to my older daughter who is so beautiful?"

"I can't do anything for her, madam, in the way of wit," said the fairy, "but I can do a great deal in matters of beauty. Since there's nothing I would not do to please you, I shall endow her with the ability to render any person who pleases her with a beautiful or handsome appearance."

As these two princesses grew up, their qualities increased in the same proportion. Throughout the realm everyone talked about the beauty of the older daughter and the intelligence of the younger. It is also true that their defects greatly increased as they grew older. The young daughter became uglier, and the older more stupid every day. She either gave no answer when addressed, or she said something foolish. At the same time she was so awkward that she could not place four pieces of china on a mantel without breaking one of them, nor drink a glass of water without spilling half of it on her clothes. Despite the great advantage of beauty in a young person, the younger sister always outshone the elder whenever they were in society. At first everyone gathered around the more beautiful girl to admire her, but soon left her for the more intelligent sister to listen to the thousand pleasant things she said. In less than a quarter of an hour, not a soul would be standing near the elder sister while everyone would be surrounding the younger. Though very stupid, the elder sister noticed this and would have willingly given up all her beauty for half the intelligence of her sister.

The queen, discreet though she was, could not help reproaching the elder daughter whenever she did stupid things, and that made the poor princess ready to die of grief. One day, when she had withdrawn into the woods to bemoan her misfortune, she saw a little man coming toward her. He was extremely ugly and unpleasant, but was dressed in magnificent attire. It was young Riquet with the Tuft. He had fallen in love with her from seeing her portraits, which had been sent all around the world, and he had left his father's kingdom to have the pleasure of seeing and speaking to her. Delighted to meet her thus alone, he approached her with all the respect and politeness imaginable. After paying the usual compliments, he remarked that she was very melancholy.

"I cannot comprehend, madam," he said, "how a person so beautiful as you are can be so sad as you appear. Though I may boast of having seen an infinite number of lovely women, I can assure you that I've never beheld one whose beauty could begin to compare with yours."

"It's very kind of you to say so, sir," replied the princess, and there she stopped.

"Beauty is such a great advantage," continued Riquet, "that it ought to surpass all other things. If one possesses it, I don't see anything that could cause one much distress."

"I'd rather be as ugly as you and have intelligence," said the princess, "than be as beautiful and stupid as I am."

"There's no greater proof of intelligence, madam, than the belief that we do not have any. It's the nature of the gift that the more we have, the more we believe we are deficient in it."

"I don't know whether that's the case," the princess said, "but I know full well that I am very stupid, and that's the cause of the grief which is killing me."

"If that's all that's troubling you, madam, I can easily put an end to your distress."

"And how do you intend to manage that?" the princess asked.

"I have the power, madam, to give as much intelligence as anyone can possess to the person I love," Riquet with the Tuft replied. "And as you are that person, madam, it will depend entirely on whether or not you want to have so much intelligence, for you may have it, provided that you consent to marry me."

The princess was thunderstruck and did not say a word.

"I see that this proposal torments you, and I'm not surprised," said Riquet with the Tuft. "But I'll give you a full year to make up your mind."

The princess had so little intelligence, and at the same time had such a strong desire to possess a great deal, that she imagined the year would never come to an end. So she immediately accepted his offer. No sooner did she promise that she would marry Riquet with the Tuft twelve months from that day than she felt a complete change come over her. She found she possessed an incredible facility to say anything she wished and to say it in a polished yet easy and natural manner. She commenced right away, maintaining an elegant conversation with the prince. Indeed, she was so brilliant that he believed that he had given her more wit than he had kept for himself.

When she returned to the palace, the whole court was at a loss to account for such a sudden and extraordinary change. Whereas she had formerly said any number of foolish things, she now made sensible and exceedingly clever observations. The entire court rejoiced beyond belief. Only the younger sister was not quite pleased, for she no longer held the advantage of intelligence over her elder sister. Now she merely appeared as an ugly woman by her side, and the king let himself be guided by the elder daughter's advice. Sometimes he even held the meetings of his council in her apartment.

The news of this change spread abroad, and all the young princes of the neighboring kingdoms exerted themselves to the utmost to gain her affection. Nearly all of them asked her hand in marriage, but since she found none of them sufficiently intelligent, she listened to all of them without promising herself to anyone in particular. At last a prince arrived who was so witty and handsome that she could not help feeling attracted to him. Her father noticed this and told her that she was at perfect liberty to choose a husband for herself and that she only had to make her decision known. Now, the more intelligence one possesses, the greater the difficulty one has in making up one's mind about such a weighty matter. So she thanked her father and requested some time to think it over.

By chance she took a walk in the same woods where she had met Riquet with the Tuft to ponder with greater freedom what she should do. While she was walking, deep in thought, she heard a dull rumble beneath her feet, as though many people were running busily back and forth. Listening more attentively, she heard voices say, "Bring me that cooking pot." "Give me that kettle." "Put some wood on the fire." At that same moment the ground opened, and she saw below what appeared to be a large kitchen full of cooks, scullions, and all sorts of servants necessary for the preparation of a magnificent banquet. A group of approximately twenty to thirty cooks came forth, and they took places at a very long table set in a path of the woods. Each had a larding pin in hand and a cap on his head, and they set to work, keeping time to a melodious song. Astonished at this sight, the princess inquired who had hired them.

"Riquet with the Tuft, madam," the leader of the group replied. "His marriage is to take place tomorrow."

The princess was even more surprised than she was before, and suddenly she recalled that it was exactly a year ago that she had promised to marry Prince Riquet with the Tuft. How she was taken aback! The reason why she had not remembered her promise was that when she had made it, she had still been a fool, and after receiving her new mind, she had forgotten all her follies. Now, no sooner had she advanced another thirty steps on her walk than she encountered Riquet with the Tuft, who appeared gallant and magnificent, like a prince about to be married.

"As you can see, madam," he said, "I've kept my word to the minute, and I have no doubt but that you've come here to keep yours. By giving me your hand, you'll make me the happiest of men."

"I'll be frank with you," the princess replied. "I've

yet to make up my mind on that matter, and I
don't believe I'll ever be able to do so to your
satisfaction."

"You astonish me, madam."

"I can believe it," the princess responded, "and
assuredly, if I had to deal with a stupid person—a man
without intelligence—I'd feel greatly embarrassed. 'A
princess is bound by her word,' he'd say to me, 'and
you must marry me as you promised to do so.' But
since the man with whom I'm speaking is the most
intelligent man in the world, I'm certain he'll listen to
reason. As you know, when I was no better than a fool,
I could not decide whether I should marry you. Now
that I have the intelligence that you've given me and
that renders me much more difficult to please than
before, how can you expect me to make a decision
today that I couldn't make then? If you seriously
thought of marrying me, you made a big mistake in
taking away my stupidity and enabling me to see
clearer."

"If a man without intelligence would be justified
in reproaching you for your breach of promise,"
Riquet with the Tuft replied, "why do you expect,
madam, that I should not be allowed to do the
same? This matter affects the entire happiness of my
life. Is it reasonable that intelligent people should be
placed at a greater disadvantage than those who have
none? Can you presume this, you who have so much
intelligence and have so earnestly desired to possess
it? But let us come to the point, if you please. With
the exception of my ugliness, is there anything about
me that displeases you? Are you dissatisfied with
my birth, my intelligence, my temperament, or my
manners?"

"Not in the least," replied the princess. "I admire
you for everything you've just mentioned."

"If so," Riquet with the Tuft responded, "I'll gain
my happiness, for you have the power to make me the
most pleasing of men."

"How can that be done?"

"It can if you love me sufficiently to wish that it
should be. And to remove your doubts, you should

know that the same fairy who endowed me at birth with the power to give intelligence to the person I chose also gave you the power to render handsome any man who pleases you."

"If that's so," the princess said, "I wish with all my heart that you may become the most charming and handsome prince in the world."

No sooner had the princess pronounced these words than Riquet with the Tuft appeared to her eyes as the most handsome, strapping, and charming man she had ever seen. There are some who assert that it was not the fairy's spell but love alone that caused this transformation. They say that the princess, having reflected on her lover's perseverance, prudence, and all the good qualities of his heart and mind, no longer saw the deformity of his body nor the ugliness of his features. His hunch appeared to her as nothing more than the effect of a man shrugging his shoulders. Likewise, his horrible limp appeared to be nothing more than a slight sway that charmed her. They also say that his eyes, which squinted, seemed to her only more brilliant for the proof they gave of the intensity of his love. Finally, his great red nose had something martial and heroic about it. However this may be, the princess promised to marry him on the spot, provided that he obtained the consent of the king, her father.

On learning of his daughter's high regard for Riquet with the Tuft, whom he also knew to be a very intelligent and wise prince, the king accepted him with pleasure as a son-in-law. The wedding took place the next morning, just as Riquet with the Tuft had planned it.

MORAL

That which you see written down here
Is not so fantastic because it's quite true:
We find what we love is wondrously fair,
In what we love we find intelligence, too.

ANOTHER MORAL

Nature very often places
Beauty in an object that amazes,

Such that art can ne'er achieve.
Yet even beauty can't move the heart
As much as that charm hard to chart,
A charm which only love can perceive.

LITTLE RED RIDING HOOD

ONCE upon a time there was a little village girl, the prettiest in the world. Her mother doted on her, and her grandmother even more. This good woman made her a little red hood which suited her so well that wherever she went, she was called Little Red Riding Hood.

One day, after her mother had baked some biscuits, she said to Little Red Riding Hood, "Go see how your grandmother's feeling. I've heard that she's ill. You can take her some biscuits and this small pot of butter."

Little Red Riding Hood departed at once to visit her grandmother, who lived in another village. In passing through the forest she met old neighbor wolf, who had a great desire to eat her. But he did not dare because of some woodcutters who were in the forest. Instead he asked her where she was going. The poor child, who did not know that it is dangerous to stop and listen to a wolf, said to him, "I'm going to see my grandmother, and I'm bringing her some biscuits with a small pot of butter that my mother's sending her."

"Does she live far from here?" the wolf asked.

"Oh, yes!" Little Red Riding Hood said. "You've got to go by the mill, which you can see right over there, and hers is the first house in the village."

"Well, then," said the wolf, "I'll go and see her, too. You take that path there, and I'll take this path here, and we'll see who'll get there first."

The wolf began to run as fast as he could on the shorter path, and the little girl took the longer path. What's more, she enjoyed herself by gathering nuts, running after butterflies, and making bouquets of small flowers that she found along the way. It did not take the wolf long to arrive at the grandmother's house, and he knocked:

"Tick, tock."

"Who's there?"

"It's your granddaughter, Little Red Riding Hood," the wolf said, disguising his voice. "I've brought you some biscuits and a little pot of butter that my mother's sent for you."

The good grandmother, who was in her bed because she was not feeling well, cried out to him, "Pull the bobbin, and the latch will fall."

The wolf pulled the bobbin, and the door opened. He pounced on the good woman and devoured her quicker than a wink, for it had been more than three days since he had eaten last. After that he closed the door and lay down in the grandmother's bed to wait for Little Red Riding Hood, who after a while came knocking at the door.

"Tick, tock."

"Who's there?"

When she heard the gruff voice of the wolf, Little Red Riding Hood was scared at first, but she thought her grandmother had a cold and responded, "It's your granddaughter, Little Red Riding Hood. I've brought you some biscuits and a little pot of butter that my mother's sent for you."

The wolf softened his voice and cried out to her, "Pull the bobbin, and the latch will fall."

Little Red Riding Hood pulled the bobbin, and the door opened.

Upon seeing her enter, the wolf hid himself under the bedcovers and said to her, "Put the biscuits and the pot of butter on the bin and come lie down beside me."

Little Red Riding Hood undressed and got into the bed, where she was quite astonished to see how her grandmother appeared in her nightgown.

"What big arms you have, grandmother!" she said to her.

"The better to hug you with, my child."

"What big legs you have, grandmother!"

"The better to run with, my child."

"What big ears you have, grandmother!"

"The better to hear you with, my child."
"What big eyes you have, grandmother!"
"The better to see you with, my child."
"What big teeth you have, grandmother!"
"The better to eat you with!"

And upon saying these words, the wicked wolf pounced on Little Red Riding Hood and ate her up.

MORAL

One sees here that young children,
Especially pretty girls,
Who're bred as pure as pearls,
Should question words addressed by men.
Or they may serve one day as feast
For a wolf or other beast.
I say a wolf since not all are wild
Or are indeed the same in kind.
For some are winning and have sharp minds.
Some are loud, smooth, or mild.
Others appear plain kind or unriled.
They follow young ladies wherever they go,
Right into the halls of their very own homes.
Alas for those girls who've refused the truth:
The sweetest tongue has the sharpest tooth.

THE FAIRIES

ONCE upon a time there was a widow who had two daughters. The older one was often mistaken for her mother because she was so much like her in looks and character. Indeed, both mother and daughter were so disagreeable and haughty that it was impossible to live with them. The younger daughter, who looked exactly like her father and took after him in her kindness and politeness, was one of the most beautiful girls ever seen.

Since we naturally tend to be fond of those who resemble us, the mother doted on her elder daughter while she hated the younger. She made her eat in the kitchen and work from morning till night. Among the many things that this poor child was forced to do, she had to walk a mile twice a day to fetch water from a spring and tote it back in a large jug. One day, when she was at the spring, a poor woman came up to her and asked her for a drink.

"Why, of course, my good woman," she said, and the pretty maiden at once stooped and rinsed out the jug. Then she filled it with water from the clearest part of the spring and offered it to the woman, helping to keep the jug raised so that she might drink more easily.

After the woman had finished drinking, she said, "You are so beautiful, so good and kind, that I can't resist bestowing a gift on you"—for she was a fairy who had assumed the form of a poor peasant in order to discover just how kind this young girl was. "I shall give you a gift," continued the fairy, "that will cause every word you utter to become either a flower or precious stone."

When this beautiful girl arrived home, her mother scolded her for returning so late.

"I'm sorry for having taken so long," the poor girl said, and on saying these words, two roses, two pearls, and two large diamonds fell from her mouth.

"What do I see here!" said her mother, completely astonished. "I believe I saw pearls and diamonds dropping from your mouth. Where do they come from, my daughter?" (This was the first time she had ever called her "my daughter.")

As countless diamonds fell from her mouth, the poor child naively told her all that had happened.

"Upon my word," said the mother, "I must send my daughter. Come here, Fanchon! Do you see what's falling from your sister's mouth when she speaks? Wouldn't you like to have the same gift? You only have to fetch some water from the spring, and if a poor woman asks you for a drink, you're to give it to her nicely and politely."

"You'll never get me to walk to the spring!" the rude girl responded.

"I'm insisting," her mother replied, "and you'd better go this instant!"

She left, sulking as she went. With her she took the most beautiful silver bottle in the house. No sooner did she arrive at the spring than a magnificently dressed lady emerged from the forest and asked her for a drink. This was the same fairy who had appeared to her sister, but she now put on the airs and the garments of a princess to see just how rude this girl could be.

"Do you think I came here just to fetch you a drink?" the rude and arrogant girl said. "Do you think that I carried this silver bottle just to offer a drink to a fine lady? Get your own drink if you want one!"

"You're not at all polite," the fairy replied without anger. "Well, then, since you're not very obliging, I'll bestow a gift on you. Every word uttered from your mouth will become either a snake or a toad."

As soon as her mother caught sight of her, she cried out, "Well then, daughter!"

"Well then, my mother," her rude daughter responded, spitting two vipers and two toads from her mouth.

"Oh heavens!" her mother exclaimed. "What do I see? Your sister's to blame, and she'll pay for it!"

She dashed off to beat her, but the poor child fled and took refuge in a nearby forest. The king's son, who was returning from a hunt, encountered her there, and observing how beautiful she was, he asked her what she was doing there weeping all alone.

"Alas, sir! My mother has driven me from home."

Seeing five or six pearls and as many diamonds fall from her mouth, the king's son asked her to tell him where they came from. She told him the entire story, and the king's son fell in love with her. When he considered that such a gift was worth more than a dowry anyone else could bring, he took her to the palace of the king, his father, where he married her.

As for the sister, she made herself so hated that her own mother drove her out of the house. This wretched girl searched about in vain for someone who would offer her shelter, and finally she went off to a corner of the forest, where she died.

MORAL

Diamonds and gold
Can do wonders for one's soul.
Yet kind words, I am told,
Are worth more on the whole.

ANOTHER MORAL

Virtue demands a great deal of effort,
For one must indeed be very good-natured.
Sooner or later it reaps its reward,
Which comes indeed when it's least sought.

THE FOOLISH WISHES

ONCE upon a time there was a poor woodcutter whose life was so hard that he longed to rest in the infernal regions of the world beyond. This tormented soul maintained that in all his days on earth, heaven had never granted him a single wish.

One day he was grumbling to himself in the forest when Jupiter appeared with thunderbolt in hand. It is impossible to describe the fear of the good man, who threw himself on the ground and cried, "I don't want a thing. No wishes. No thunder. My lord, let me live in peace!"

"Have no fear," said Jupiter. "I've come because I've been moved by your complaints, and I want to show you how unfair you've been to me. So listen: I, who reign supreme over the entire world, promise to grant you the first three wishes you make, no matter what they are. Just see that they make you happy. And since your happiness depends on your wishes, think carefully before you make them." With these words Jupiter returned to the heavens.

The woodcutter, now cheerful, picked up his bundle of sticks and carried them home on his back. Never had his burden seemed so light. As he was running along, he said to himself, "I mustn't be hasty in this matter. It's important, and I must ask my wife's advice."

Upon entering his cottage, he called, "Hey, Fanchon! Let's make a large fire, my dear. We're going to be rich for the rest of our lives. All we have to do is to make some wishes."

He told her what had happened, and on hearing the story his wife promptly began forming a thousand vast schemes in her mind. Nevertheless, she realized the importance of doing everything prudently.

"Blaise, my dear," she said to her husband, "let's not spoil anything by our impatience. Let's both mull over in our minds what's best for us. I suggest that we sleep on it and put off our first wish until tomorrow."

"I agree with you," said the good man Blaise. "But now, get some of the good wine behind the stack of sticks."

On her return, he leisurely drank the wine by a large fire and enjoyed the sweetness of relaxation. Leaning back in his chair, he said, "Since we have such a good blaze, I wish we had some sausage. That would go well with it."

He had hardly finished speaking when his wife was astonished to see a very long sausage approaching her from the chimney corner like a serpent. First she screamed, but then realized that this incident had been caused by her husband's foolish wish. Overcome by vexation, she began to scold and berate the poor man.

"You can have an empire of gold, pearls, rubies, diamonds, or fine clothes," she said, "but all you seem to want is a sausage!"

"Ah well, I was wrong," he replied. "I made a bad choice. In fact, I made an enormously bad choice. I'll do better next time."

"Sure, you will," she snapped. "I'll be long gone before that happens. You've got to be an ass to make a wish like that!"

Her husband became enraged and thought how nice it would be to be a widower, and—between you and me—this was not a bad idea.

"Men," he said, "are born to suffer! A curse on this sausage and all other sausages. I wish to God that the sausage was hanging from your nose, you vile creature!"

The wish was heard in heaven, and moments after he had uttered those words, the sausage attached itself to the nose of the agitated woman. This unforeseen miracle made her immensely angry. Fanchon was pretty and had a great deal of grace. And, to tell the truth, this ornament did not improve her looks. Even though it merely hung down over her face, it prevented her from speaking easily. Her husband now had such a wonderful advantage that he thought his wish was not all that bad.

"Despite this terrible disaster, I could still make myself king," he said to himself. "In truth, there's nothing that can compare to the grandeur of sovereignty. But I must take the queen's feelings into account, for she'd suffer immensely if she had to take her place on the throne with a nose more than a yard long. I must see whether she wants to be a grand princess with that horrible nose or whether she wants to keep living as a woodcutter's wife with a nose like everyone else's."

Fanchon knew that she who wielded a scepter had a lot of power and that people swear you have a well-formed nose if you wear a crown. Yet after thinking about the matter carefully, she realized that nothing could surpass the desire to be pleasant-looking. Thus she decided to keep her own nose rather than to become an ugly queen.

So the woodcutter did not change his lot. He did not become a potentate, nor did his purse become filled with gold coins. Happily he employed his last wish to have his wife restored to her former state.

Moral

No doubt, men who are quite miserable,
Or blind, dumb, worried, and fickle
Aren't fit to make those wishes they should.
In fact, there are few among them who're able
To use such heaven's gifts for their own good.

DONKEY-SKIN

ONCE upon a time lived the most powerful king in the world. Gentle in peace, terrifying in war, he was incomparable in all ways. His neighbors feared him while his subjects were content. Throughout his realm the fine arts and civility flourished under his protection. His better half, his constant companion, was charming and beautiful. Such was her sweet and good nature that he was less happy as king and more happy as her husband. Out of their tender, pure wedlock a daughter was born, and she had so many virtues that she consoled them for their inability to have more children.

Everything was magnificent in their huge palace. They had an ample group of courtiers and servants all around them. In his stables the king had large and small horses of every kind, which were adorned with beautiful trappings, gold braids, and embroidery. But what surprised everyone on entering the stables was a master donkey in the place of honor. This discrepancy may be surprising, but if you knew the superb virtues of this donkey, you would probably agree that there was no honor too great for him. Nature had formed him in such a way that he never emitted an odor. Instead he generated heaps of beautiful gold coins that were gathered from the stable litter every morning at sunrise.

Now, heaven, which always mixes the good with the bad, just like rain may come in good weather, permitted a nasty illness to suddenly attack the queen. Help was sought everywhere, but neither the learned physicians nor the charlatans who appeared were able to arrest the fever, which increased day by day. When her last hour arrived, the queen said to her husband,

"Before I die, you must promise me one thing, and that is, if you should desire to remarry when I am gone—"

"Ah!" said the king, "your concern is superfluous. I'd never think of doing such a thing. You can rest assured about that."

"I believe you," replied the queen, "if your ardent love is any proof. But to make me more certain, I want you to swear that you'll give your pledge to another woman only if she is more beautiful, more accomplished, and wiser than I."

Her confidence in her qualities and her cleverness were such that she knew he would regard his promise as an oath never to remarry. With his eyes bathed in tears, he swore to do everything the queen desired. Then she died in his arms.

Never did a king make such a commotion. Day and night he could be heard sobbing, and many believed that he could not keep mourning so bitterly for long. Indeed, some said he wept about his deceased wife like a man who wanted to end the matter in haste.

In truth, this was the case. At the end of several months he wanted to move on with his life and choose a new queen. But this was not easy to do. He had to keep his word, and his new wife had to have more charms and grace than his dead one, who had become immortalized. Neither the court, with its great quantity of beautiful women, nor the city, the country, or foreign kingdoms, where the rounds were made, could provide the king with such a woman.

The only one more beautiful was his daughter. In truth, she even possessed certain attractive qualities that her deceased mother had not had. The king himself noticed this, and he fell so ardently in love with her that he became mad. He convinced himself that this love was reason enough for him to marry her. He even found a casuist who argued logically that a case could be made for such a marriage. But the young princess was greatly troubled to hear him talk of such love and grieved night and day.

Thus the princess sought out her godmother, who lived at some distance from the castle in a grotto of

coral and pearls. She was a remarkable fairy, far superior to any of her kind. There is no need to tell you
what a fairy was like in those most happy of times, for
I am certain that your mother has told you about them
when you were very young.

Upon seeing the princess, the fairy said, "I know
why you've come. I know your heart is filled with sadness. But there's no need to worry, for I am with you.
If you follow my advice, there's nothing that can harm
you. It's true that your father wants to marry you, and
if you were to listen to his insane request, it would be a
grave mistake. However, there's a way to refuse him
without contradicting him. Tell him that before you'd
be willing to abandon your heart to him, he must grant
your wishes and give you a dress the color of the sky.
In spite of all his power and wealth and the favorable
signs of the stars, he'll never be able to fulfill your
request."

So the princess departed right away, and trembling,
went to her amorous father. He immediately summoned his tailors and ordered them to make a dress the
color of the sky without delay. "Or else, be assured I
will hang you all."

The sun was just dawning the next day when they
brought the desired dress, the most beautiful blue of
the firmament. There was not a color more like the sky,
and it was encircled by large clouds of gold. Though
the princess desired it, she was caught between joy and
pain. She did not know how to respond or get out of
her promise. Then her godmother said to her in a low
voice, "Princess, ask for a more radiant dress. Ask for
one the color of the moon. He'll never be able to give
that to you."

No sooner did the princess make the request than the
king said to his embroiderer, "I want a dress that will
glisten greater than the star of night, and I want it
without fail in four days."

The splendid dress was ready by the deadline set by
the king. Up in the night sky the luster of the moon's
illumination makes the stars appear pale, mere scullions in her court. Despite this, the glistening moon
was less radiant than this dress of silver.

Admiring this marvelous dress, the princess was almost ready to give her consent to her father, but urged on by her godmother, she said to the amorous king, "I can't be content until I have an even more radiant dress. I want one the color of the sun."

Since the king loved her with an ardor that could not be matched anywhere, he immediately summoned a rich jeweler and ordered him to make a superb garment of gold and diamonds. "And if you fail to satisfy us, you will be tortured to death."

Yet it was not necessary for the king to punish the jeweler, for the industrious man brought him the precious dress by the end of the week. It was so beautiful and radiant that the blond lover of Clytemnestra, when he drove his chariot of gold on the arch of heaven, would have been dazzled by its brilliant rays.

The princess was so confused by these gifts that she did not know what to say. At that moment her godmother took her by the hand and whispered in her ear, "There's no need to pursue this path anymore. There's a greater marvel than all the gifts you have received. I mean that donkey who constantly fills your father's purse with gold coins. Ask him for the donkey skin. Since this rare donkey is the major source of his money, he won't give it to you, unless I'm badly mistaken."

Now this fairy was very clever, and yet she did not realize that passionate love counts more than money or gold, provided that the prospects for its fulfillment are good. So the forfeit was gallantly granted the moment the princess requested it.

When the skin was brought to her, she was terribly frightened. As she began to complain bitterly about her fate, her godmother arrived. She explained, "If you do your best, there's no need to fear." The princess had to let the king think that she was ready to place herself at his disposal and marry him while preparing at the same time to disguise herself and flee alone to some distant country in order to avoid the impending, evil marriage.

"Here's a large chest," the fairy continued. "You can put your clothes, mirror, toilet articles, diamonds, and

rubies in it. I'm going to give you my magic wand.
Whenever you hold it in your hand, the chest will
always follow your path beneath the ground. And
whenever you want to open it, you merely have to
touch the ground with my wand, and the chest will
appear before you. We'll use the donkey's skin to
make you unrecognizable. It's such a perfect disguise
and so horrible that once you conceal yourself inside,
nobody will ever believe that it adorns anyone so beautiful as you."

Thus disguised, the princess departed from the
abode of the wise fairy the next morning as the dew
began to drop. When the king started preparations
for the marriage celebration, he learned to his horror that his bride-to-be had taken flight. All the
houses, roads, and avenues were promptly searched,
but in vain. No one could conceive of what had happened to her. Sadness and sorrow spread throughout
the realm. There would be no marriage, no feast, no
tarts, no sugar-almonds. The ladies at the court were
quite disappointed not to be able to dine, but the
priest was most saddened, for he had been expecting a
heavy donation at the end of the ceremony as well as a
hearty meal.

Meanwhile the princess continued her flight,
dirtying her face with mud. When she extended her
hands to people she met, begging for a place to work,
they noticed how much she smelled and how disagreeable she looked, and did not want to have anything to
do with such a dirty creature, even though they themselves were hardly less vulgar and mean. Farther and
farther she traveled and farther still until she finally
arrived at a farm where they needed a scullion to wash
the dishclothes and clean out the pig troughs. She was
put in a corner of the kitchen, where the servants, insolent and nasty creatures all, ridiculed, contradicted, and
mocked her. They kept playing mean tricks on her and
harassed her at every chance they had. Indeed, she was
the butt of all their jokes.

On Sundays she had a little time to rest. After finishing her morning chores, she went into her room,
closed the door, and washed herself. Then she opened

the chest and carefully arranged her toilet articles in their little jars in front of her large mirror. Satisfied and happy, she tried on her moon dress, then the one that shone like the sun, and finally the beautiful blue dress that even the sky could not match in brilliance. Her only regret was that she did not have enough room to spread out the trains of the dresses on the floor. Still, she loved to see herself young, fresh as a rose, and a thousand times more elegant than she had ever been. Such sweet pleasure kept her going from one Sunday to the next.

I forgot to mention that there was a large aviary on this farm that belonged to a powerful and magnificent king. All sorts of strange fowls were kept there: chickens from Barbary, rails, guinea fowls, cormorants, musical birds, quacking ducks, and a thousand other kinds, which were the match of ten other courts put together. The king's son often stopped at this charming spot on his return from the hunt to rest and enjoy a cool drink. He was more handsome than Cephalus and had a regal and martial appearance that made the proudest batallions tremble. From a distance Donkey-Skin admired him with a tender look. Thanks to her courage, she realized that she still had the heart of a princess beneath her dirt and rags.

"What a grand manner he has!" she said, even though he paid no attention to her. "How gracious he is, and how happy must be the woman who has captured his heart! If he were to honor me with the plainest dress imaginable, I'd feel more decorated than in any of those I have."

One Sunday the young prince was wandering adventurously from courtyard to courtyard, and he passed through an obscure hallway, where Donkey-Skin had her humble room. He chanced to peek through the keyhole, and since it was a holiday, she had dressed herself up as richly as possible in her dress of gold and diamonds that shone like the sun. Succumbing to fascination, the prince kept peeking at her, scarcely breathing because he was filled with such pleasure. Her magnificent dress, her beautiful face, her lovely manner, her fine traits, and her young freshness moved

him a thousand times over. But most of all, he was captivated by the air of grandeur mingled with modest
reserve that bore witness to the beauty of her soul.

Three times he was on the verge of entering her
room because of the ardor that overwhelmed him, but
three times he refrained out of respect for the seemingly divine creature he was beholding.

Returning to the palace, he became pensive. Day and
night he sighed, refusing to attend any of the balls even
though it was Carnival. He began to hate hunting and
attending the theater. He lost his appetite, and everything saddened his heart. At the root of his malady was
a deadly melancholy.

He inquired about the remarkable nymph who lived
in one of the lower courtyards at the end of the dingy
alley where it remained dark even in broad daylight.

"You mean Donkey-Skin," he was told. "But there's
nothing nymphlike or beautiful about her. She's called
Donkey-Skin because of the skin that she wears on her
back. She's the ideal remedy for anyone in love. That
beast is almost uglier than a wolf."

All this was said in vain, for he did not believe it.
Love had left its mark and could not be effaced. However, his mother, whose only child he was, pleaded
with him to tell her what was wrong, yet she pressured
him in vain. He moaned, wept, and sighed. He said
nothing, except that he wanted Donkey-Skin to make
him a cake with her own hands. And so, his mother
could only repeat what her son desired.

"Oh, heavens, madam!" the servants said to her.
"This Donkey-Skin is a black drab, uglier and dirtier
than the most wretched scullion."

"It doesn't matter," the queen said. "Fulfilling his
request is the only thing that concerns us." His mother
loved him so much that she would have served him
anything on a golden platter.

Meanwhile, Donkey-Skin took some ground flour,
salt, butter, and fresh eggs in order to make the dough
especially fine. Then she locked herself alone in her
room to make the cake. She washed her hands, arms,
and face and put on a silver smock in honor of the task
that she was about to undertake. It is said that in

working a bit too hastily, a precious ring happened to fall from Donkey-Skin's finger into the batter. But some claim that she dropped the ring on purpose. As for me, quite frankly, I can believe it because when the prince had stopped at the door and looked through the keyhole, she must have seen him. Women are so alert that nothing escapes their notice. Indeed, I pledge my word on it that she was convinced her young lover would gratefully receive her ring.

There was never a cake kneaded so daintily as this one, and the prince found it so good that he immediately began ravishing it and almost swallowed the ring. However, when he saw the remarkable emerald and the narrow band of gold, his heart was ignited by an inexpressible joy. At once he put the ring under his pillow. Yet that did not cure his malady. Upon seeing him grow worse day by day, the doctors, wise with experience, used their great science to come to the conclusion that he was sick with love.

Whatever else one may say about marriage, it is a perfect remedy for love sickness. So it was decided that the prince should marry. After he deliberated for some time, he finally said, "I'll be glad to get married provided that I marry only the person whose finger fits this ring."

This strange demand surprised the king and queen very much, but he was so sick that they did not dare to say anything that might upset him. Now a search began for the person whose finger might fit the ring, no matter what class or lineage. The only requirement was that the woman be ready to come and show her finger to claim her due.

A rumor was spread throughout the realm that to claim the prince, one had to have a very slender finger. Consequently, every charlatan, eager to make a name for himself, pretended that he possessed the secret of making a finger slender. Following such capricious advice, one woman scraped her finger like a turnip. Another cut a little piece off. Still another used some liquid to remove the skin from her finger and reduce its size. All sorts of plans imaginable were concocted by women to make their fingers fit the ring.

The selection was begun with the young princesses, marquesses, and duchesses, but no matter how delicate their fingers were, they were too large for the ring. Then the countesses, baronesses, and all the rest of the nobility took their turns and presented their hands in vain. Next came well-proportioned working girls who had pretty and slender fingers. Finally, it was necessary to turn to the servants, kitchen help, minor servants, and poultry keepers, in short, to all the trash who with their reddened or blackened hands hoped for a happy fate just as much as those with delicate hands. Many girls presented themselves with large and thick fingers, but trying the prince's ring on their fingers was like trying to thread the eye of a needle with a rope.

Everyone thought that they had reached the end because the only one remaining was Donkey-Skin in the corner of the kitchen. And who could ever believe that the heavens had ordained that she might become queen?

"Why not?" said the prince. "Let her try."

Everyone began laughing and exclaimed aloud, "Do you mean to say that you want that dirty wretch to enter here?"

But when she drew a little hand as white as ivory and of royal blood from under the dirty skin, the destined ring fit perfectly around her finger. The members of the court were astonished. So delirious were they that they wanted to march her to the king right away, but she requested that she be given some time to change her clothes before she appeared before her lord and master. In truth, the people could hardly keep from laughing because of the clothes she was wearing.

Finally, she arrived at the palace and passed through all the halls in her blue dress whose radiance could not be matched. Her blonde hair glistened with diamonds. Her blue eyes, so large and sweet, whose gaze always pleased and never hurt, were filled with a proud majesty. Her waist was so slender that two hands could have encircled it. All the charms and ornaments of the ladies of the court dwindled in comparison. Despite the rejoicing and commotion of the gathering, the good king did not fail to notice the many charms of his future daughter-in-law, and the queen was also terribly delighted. The prince, her dear lover, could hardly bear the excitement of his rapture.

Preparations for the wedding were begun at once. The monarch invited all the kings of the surrounding countries, who left their lands to attend the grand event, all radiant in their different attire. Those from the East were mounted on huge elephants. The Moors arriving from distant shores were so black and ugly that they frightened the little children. People embarked from all the corners of the world and descended on the court in great numbers. But neither prince nor king seemed as splendid as the bride's father, who had purified the criminal and odious fires that had ignited his spirit in the past. The flame that was left in his soul had been transformed into devoted paternal love. When he saw her, he said, "May heaven be blessed for allowing me to see you again, my dear child."

Weeping with joy, he embraced her tenderly. Everyone wanted to share in his happiness, and the future husband was delighted to learn that he was to become the son-in-law of such a powerful king. At that moment the godmother arrived and told the entire story of how everything had happened and culminated in Donkey-Skin's glory.

Evidently, the moral of this tale implies it is better for a child to expose oneself to hardships than to neglect one's duty.

Indeed, virtue may sometimes seem ill-fated, but it is always crowned with success. Of course, strongest reason is a weak dike against mad love and ardent ecstasy, especially if a lover is not afraid to squander rich treasures.

Finally, we must take into account that clear water and brown bread are sufficient nourishment for all young women provided that they have good habits, and that there is not a damsel under the skies who does not imagine herself beautiful and somehow carrying off

the honors in the famous beauty contest between Hera,
Aphrodite, and Athena.

The tale of Donkey-Skin is hard to believe,
But as long as there are children on this earth,
With mothers and grandmothers who continue to give birth,
This tale will always be told and surely well received.

Marie-Jeanne L'Héritier

Marie-Jeanne L'Héritier de Villandon (1664–1734) was a niece of Charles Perrault and the daughter of Nicolas L'Héritier, seigneur de Nouvelon et de Villandon, a noted historian and writer. Her mother was reported to be quite erudite; her brother led a distinguished career as mathematician and man of letters; her sister, Mlle. de Nouvelon, was a poet. Given such a literary and scholarly family, it was not by chance that Mlle. L'Héritier decided to dedicate herself to writing. Unlike many other women writers of her time, however, she did not become involved in any scandals nor suffered banishment to a convent. She never married or had any lovers. She was known for being studious, clever, honorable, and on close terms with the most influential women of her time. She was invited to attend the gatherings at the more illustrious of the salons in Paris and eventually maintained her own literary salon, in which she often recited her tales, poetry, and other works before she published them.

Mlle. L'Héritier's first major work was *Oeuvres meslées* (1695–98), which contained *L'Innocente tromperie, L'Avare puni, Les Enchantements de l'éloquence ou Les Effets de la Douceur,* and *L'Adroite Princesse ou Les Aventures de Finette,* which was dedicated to Henriette Julie de Murat. It was followed immediately by *Bigarrures ingénieuses* (1696), which reprinted *Les Enchantements* and *L'Adroite Princesse* and included a new fairy tale entitled *Ricdin-Ricdon.* These early collections were influenced by Perrault, Mme. d'Aulnoy, and Mme. de Murat, who were all close friends of hers, and contained her major contributions to the fairy-tale mode.

As her reputation grew, she won various literary prizes and was elected member of the Académie des Ricovrati de Padova in 1697. Mlle. L'Héritier was supported in her work by her patron, the Duchess of Nemours, Marie d'Orléans de Longueville, whose memoirs she edited in 1709. After her patron's death, she received a modest pension from Chauvelin that enabled her to live in a proper way until her death. In addition, she inherited Mlle. de Scudéry's salon, for whom she wrote the eulogy *L'Apothéose de Mlle Scudéry* (1702).

All Mlle. L'Héritier's works tended to be moralistic and conformed to the general literary taste of the day. For example, two of her works, *La Pompe Dauphine* (1711) and *Le Tombeau du Dauphin* (1711), were dedicated to the king and the royal family and are filled with short, didactic pieces that celebrated virtuous courtly manners. Mlle. L'Héritier also liked to display her extensive knowledge in works such as *L'Erudition Enjouée* (1703) and *Les Caprices du Destin* (1718), which included short literary essays, histories, poems, and tales.

Even though Mlle. L'Héritier published few fairy tales after her three major works in 1695, she is historically important because her first three prose tales signaled the beginning of the mode of fairy-tale writing that was to become so popular in France for the next hundred years. *L'Adroite Princesse* (The Discreet Princess) is undoubtedly her most significant tale and reveals Mlle. L'Héritier's attitudes about the standards of proper comportment for young ladies. As in most of her tales, magical elements and imagination are not celebrated so much as reason and sobriety. In fact, *The Discreet Princess* was written in such a dry, succinct manner that it was considered to be one of Perrault's tales for over one hundred fifty years. However, Perrault would never have allowed a young woman to triumph over a man, no matter how villainous he was. To Mlle. L'Héritier's credit, she demonstrated the qualities women needed to survive in courtly society, and her skillful transformation of folk motifs and themes rendered *The Discreet Princess* one of the more amusing narratives of that period.

THE DISCREET PRINCESS OR
THE ADVENTURES OF FINETTE

DURING the time of the First Crusade, a king of a country in Europe decided to go to war against the infidels of Palestine. Before undertaking such a long journey, he put the affairs of his kingdom into such good order and placed the regency in the hands of such an able minister that he was entirely at ease. What worried this king most, though, was the care of his family. He had recently lost his wife, who had failed to give birth to a son before her death. On the other hand, he was the father of three princesses, all of marriageable age. My chronicle has not indicated what their true names were. I only know that people were quite simple during these happy times, and customarily gave eminent people surnames according to their good or bad characteristics. Thus they called the eldest princess "Nonchalante," the second "Babbler," and the third "Finette." All of these names suited the characters of the three sisters.

Never was anyone more indolent than Nonchalante. The earliest she ever woke up was one in the afternoon, and she was dragged to church in the same condition as when she got out of bed. Her clothes were all in disarray, her dress loose, sans belt, and often she wore mismatched slippers. They used to correct this mistake during the day, but could never prevail upon this princess to wear anything but slippers, for she found it extremely exhausting to put on shoes. Whenever Nonchalante finished eating, she would camp at her dressing table until evening. She employed the rest of her time until midnight by playing and snacking. Since undressing her took almost as long as getting her dressed, she never succeeded in going to bed until dawn.

Babbler led a different kind of life. Extremely active, this princess spent little time caring about her looks, but she had such a strong propensity for talking that from the moment she woke to the time she fell asleep again, her mouth was never shut. She knew everything about the bad households, the love liaisons, and the intrigues not only at the court, but also among the most petty of the bourgeoisie. She kept a record of all those wives who stole from their families at home in order to make a more dazzling impression when they went out into society. She was informed precisely about what a particular countess's lady-in-waiting and a particular marquis's steward earned. In order to be on top of all these insignificant affairs, she listened to her nurse and seamstress with greater pleasure than she would to an ambassador. Finally, she shocked everyone, from the king down to his footmen, with her pretty stories. She did not care whom she had for a listener provided she could prattle. Such a longing to talk had another bad effect on this princess. Despite her high rank, her familiarity emboldened young men around the court to talk sweetly to her. She listened to their flowery speeches merely so that she could have the pleasure of responding to them. No matter what the consequences of her actions might be, she had to hear others talk or gossip herself from morning till night.

Neither Babbler nor Nonchalante ever bothered to occupy herself by thinking, reflecting, or reading. They never troubled themselves about household chores or entertained themselves by sewing or weaving. In short, these two sisters lived in eternal idleness and ignorance.

The youngest of the three sisters had a very different character. Her mind and hands were continually active, and she had a surprising vivacity that was put to good use. She knew how to sing and dance and play musical instruments to perfection. She was remarkably nimble and successful in all those little manual chores with which her sex generally amused themselves. Moreover, she put the king's household into perfect order and prevented the pilferings of the petty officers through her care and vigilance, for even in those days princes were cheated by those who surrounded them.

Finette's talents did not stop there. She had great judgment and such a wonderful presence of mind that she could immediately find ways to get out of any kind of predicament. By using her insights, this young princess had discovered a dangerous trap that a perfidious ambassador of the neighboring kingdom had set for her father in a treaty that he was about to sign. To punish the treachery of this ambassador and his master, the king changed the articles of the treaty, and by wording it in the terms that his daughter dictated to him, he in turn deceived the deceiver. Another time the princess discovered some cheating by a minister against the king, and through the advice she gave her father, he managed to foil this disloyal man. In fact, she gave so many signs of her intelligence that this is why the people called her Finette.

The king loved her far more than his other daughters and depended so much on her good sense that if he had not had any other child but her, he would have departed for the Crusade without feeling uneasy. However, his faith in Finette's good behavior was offset by his distrust of his other daughters. Therefore, to make sure that his family would be safeguarded in the way he believed he had done for his subjects, he adopted the following measures that I am now going to relate.

The king was on intimate terms with a fairy, and went to see her in order to express the uneasiness he felt concerning his daughters.

"It's not that the two eldest have ever done the least thing contrary to their duty," he said. "But they have so little sense, are so imprudent, and live so indolently that I fear that they will get caught up in some foolish intrigue during my absence or do something foolish merely to amuse themselves. As for Finette, I'm sure of her virtue. However, I'll treat her as I do her sisters to make everything equal. This is why, wise fairy, I'd like you to make my daughters three distaffs out of glass. And I'd like you to make each one so artfully that it will break as soon as its owner does anything against her honor."

Since this fairy was extremely skillful, she presented the king with three enchanted distaffs within seconds, taking great care to make them according to his conditions. But he was not content with this precaution. He put the princesses into a high tower in a secluded spot. The king told his daughters that he was ordering them to live in that tower during his absence and prohibited them from admitting any people whatsoever. He took all their officers and servants of both sexes from them, and after giving them the enchanted distaffs, whose qualities he explained to them, he kissed the princesses, locked the doors of the tower, took away the keys, and departed.

You may perhaps believe that these princesses were now in danger of dying from hunger. Not at all. A pulley had been attached to one of the windows of the tower, and a rope ran through it, to which the princesses tied a basket that they let down to the ground. Provisions were placed into this basket on a daily basis, and after they pulled up the basket, they carefully coiled the rope in the room.

Nonchalante and Babbler led a life of despair in this desolate place. They became bored beyond expression, but they were forced to have patience because they had been given such a terrible picture of their distaffs that they feared that their least slip might cause them to break.

As for Finette, she was not bored in the least. Her needlework, spinning, and music furnished her with abundant amusement. Besides this, the minister who was governing the state had the king's permission to place letters into the basket, which kept the princesses informed about what was happening in the kingdom or outside it. Finette read all the news with great attention and pleasure, but her two sisters did not deign to participate in the least. They said they were too sorrowful to have the strength to amuse themselves with such weighty matters. They needed cards to entertain themselves during their father's absence.

Thus they spent their time by grumbling continually about their destiny, and I believe they even said, "It is much better to be born happy than to be born the

daughter of a king." They often went to the windows of
the tower to see at least what was happening in the
countryside, and one day, when Finette was absorbed
in some pretty work in her room, her sisters saw a poor
woman clothed in rags and tatters at the foot of the
tower. She pathetically cried out to them about her
misery and begged them with clasped hands to let her
come into the castle. "I'm an unfortunate stranger who
knows how to do a thousand things, and I shall serve
you with the utmost fidelity."

At first the princesses recalled their father's orders
not to permit anyone to enter the tower, but Nonchalante was so weary of attending herself, and Babbler
was so bored at having nobody to talk to but her sisters,
that the desire of the one to be groomed and the other to
gossip made them decide to admit this poor stranger.

"Do you think," Babbler said to her sister, "that the
king's order was meant to include this unfortunate
wretch? I believe we can admit her without anything
happening."

"Sister, you may do whatever you please," Nonchalante responded.

Babbler had only waited for her sister to consent,
and she immediately let down the basket. The poor
woman got into it, and the princesses pulled her up
with the help of the pulley.

When this woman drew nigh, her horrid dirty clothes
almost turned their stomachs. They would have given
her others, but she told them she would change her
clothes the next day. At present, she could think of
nothing but her work. As she said these words, Finette
entered the room. She was stunned to see this unknown
person with her sisters. They told her the reasons that
had induced them to pull her up, and Finette, who saw
that she could do nothing about it, concealed her disappointment at their imprudence.

In the meantime the princesses' new servant explored the tower a hundred times under the pretext of
doing her work, but in reality to see what was located
where in it. In truth, this ragged creature was none
other than the elder son of a powerful king, a neighbor
of the princesses' father. One of the most cunning men

of his time, this young prince completely controlled his father. Actually, this did not require much ability, because the king had such a sweet and easy disposition that he had been named "The Gentle." As for this young prince, who always acted with artifice and guile, the people called him Rich-in-Craft, a name commonly shortened to Rich-Craft.

His younger brother had as many good qualities as Rich-Craft had bad ones. Despite their different characters, however, such a tight bond existed between these two princes that everyone was surprised by it. Besides the younger prince's good qualities, his handsome face and graceful figure were so remarkable that he was generally called Bel-a-voir.

It was Rich-Craft who had instigated the deceitful act of his father's ambassador who had tried to change the treaty, an act that had been foiled by Finette's quick mind. Ever since she had turned the tables on them, Rich-Craft, who had not shown a particularly great love for the princess's father before this, now developed an even stronger aversion for him. Thus, after he had learned about the precautions that the king had taken in regard to his daughters, he decided to have some pernicious fun by undermining the prudence of such a distrustful father. Accordingly, Rich-Craft obtained permission from his father to take a journey, and he found a way to enter the tower, as you have already seen.

In examining the castle, Rich-Craft observed that the princesses could easily make themselves heard by people passing by, and he concluded that he'd best stay in his ragged disguise for the rest of the day because if they realized who he was, they could easily call out and have him punished for his rash undertaking. That night, however, after the princesses had dined, he pulled off his rags and revealed himself as a cavalier in rich attire dotted with gold and jewels. The poor princesses were so frightened by this disclosure that they all ran from him as fast as they could. Finette and Babbler, who were very nimble, quickly reached their rooms, but Nonchalante, who was not accustomed to moving fast, was soon overtaken.

Rich-Craft threw himself at her feet. He declared
who he was and told her that the reputation of her
beauty and the sight of her portraits had induced him to
leave his delightful court in order to pledge his eternal
devotion and propose to her. Nonchalante was at such a
loss for words that she could not answer the prince,
who remained kneeling. Meanwhile he kept saying a
thousand sweet things and made a thousand protestations, and he ardently implored her, "Take me this very
moment for your husband." Due to her weak backbone,
she did not have the strength to gainsay him and told
him without thinking that she believed him to be sincere and accepted his proposal. No greater formalities
than these concluded the marriage.

At that moment, however, her distaff broke into a
thousand pieces.

Babbler and Finette were extraordinarily anxious.
They had made it back to their separate rooms and
locked themselves in. These rooms were at some distance from each other, and since neither princess knew
anything about the other's fate, they did not sleep a
wink all night long.

The next morning the wicked prince led Nonchalante
into a ground apartment at the end of the garden, where
she told him how greatly she was disturbed about her
sisters. She dared not show herself to them, for fear
they would find fault with her marriage. The prince
told her he would make sure that they would approve
and, after talking some more, he locked Nonchalante in
her room. Then he searched carefully all over the castle
to locate the other princesses. It took some time before
he could discover in what rooms they had locked themselves, but eventually Babbler's longing to talk all the
time caused her to grumble to herself.

Rich-Craft went to the door, looked through the keyhole, and spoke to her. He told her everything that he
had previously told her sister. "I swear I entered the
tower only to offer my hand and heart to you." This
seducer was the consummate actor and played his role
perfectly, for he had had a lot of practice. He praised
her wit and beauty in exaggerated terms, and Babbler,
who was convinced that she had great qualities, was

foolish enough to believe everything he told her. She answered with a flood of words that showed how receptive she was. Certainly this princess had an extraordinary capacity for chatter to have acquitted herself as she did, for she was extremely faint after not having eaten a morsel all day. In fact, she had nothing fit to eat in her room because she was extremely lazy and had not thought of anything but endless talking. Whenever she needed anything, she usually depended on Finette, who was always prudent and kept an abundance of fine biscuits, pies, macaroons, and jams of her own making in her room. Weakened by her severe hunger pangs, Babbler was moved by the protestations that the prince made through the door. At last she opened it and was at the mercy of the artful seducer.

Given her hunger, they decided to adjourn to the pantry, where he found all sorts of refreshments, since the daily basket furnished the princesses with more than enough. Babbler was still at a loss to know what had happened to her sisters, but she got it into her head—and I am not sure what her reasons were—that they were both locked up in Finette's room and had all they needed. Rich-Craft used all the arguments he could to substantiate this belief and told her that they would go and find the princesses toward evening. Not entirely in agreement with him on this matter, she said they would go and find them as soon as they had finished eating.

In short, the prince and princess began eating with big appetites. When they were finished, Rich-Craft asked to see the most beautiful apartment in the castle. He gave his hand to the princess as she led him there, and when they entered, he began to exaggerate his love and the advantages she would have in marrying him. He told her, just as he had done with her sister Nonchalante, that she should accept his proposal immediately because if she were to see her sisters beforehand, they would certainly oppose it. "Since I'm one of the most powerful of the neighboring princes, they'll probably think I'm better suited for your elder sister, and she'll never consent to a match she might desire herself." After many words that signified nothing,

Babbler acted just as extravagantly as her sister had done; she agreed to become Rich-Craft's wife.

She never thought about her glass distaff until it shattered into a hundred pieces.

Toward evening Babbler returned to her room with the prince, and the first thing she saw was the shards of her glass distaff littering the floor. She was very troubled by this sight, and the prince asked why she was so concerned. Since her passion for talking made her incapable of holding her tongue about any subject, she foolishly told Rich-Craft the secret of the distaff. The prince laughed evilly to himself because the princesses' father would now be wholly convinced of his daughters' bad conduct.

Meanwhile, Babbler no longer wished to search for her sisters, for she had reason to fear that they would not approve of her conduct. The prince himself proposed that he undertake this task and told her, "I know how to win their approval, never fear." After this assurance the princess, who had not slept at all that night, grew very drowsy, and when she fell asleep, Rich-Craft locked her in her room as he had previously done with Nonchalante.

Once this devious prince had locked up Babbler, he went into all the rooms of the castle, one after another. When he found them all open except one that was locked from the inside, he concluded that was where Finette had gone. Since he had created a routine of compliments, he used the same ones at Finette's door that he had used with her sisters. But this princess was not so easy to dupe, and listened to him for a good while without responding. At last realizing that he knew she was in that room, she told him if it were true that he had such a strong and sincere affection for her, he should go down into the garden and shut the door after him. Then she would talk to him as much as he wanted from the window of her room that overlooked the garden.

Rich-Craft would not agree to this, and since the princess persisted in refusing to open the door, this wicked prince lost his patience. Fetching a large wooden log, he broke the door in. However, he found

Finette armed with a large hammer, which had been accidentally left in a wardrobe in her room. Her face was red with emotion, and her eyes sparkled with rage, making her appear even more enchanting and beautiful to Rich-Craft. He would have cast himself at her feet, but as she retreated, she said boldly, "Prince, if you approach me, I'll split your skull with this hammer."

"What's this I hear, beautiful princess!" Rich-Craft exclaimed in his hypocritical tone. "Does the love I have for you inspire you with such hatred?"

He then began to speak to her across the room, describing the passionate ardor that the reputation of her beauty and wonderful wit had aroused in him. "The only reason I put on such a disguise was to offer my hand and heart." He told her she ought to pardon the violent love that caused him to break open her door. Finally he tried to persuade her, as he had with her sisters, that it was in her interest to take him for a husband as soon as possible, and he assured her he did not know where her sisters had gone. This was because his thoughts had been wholly fixed on her, and he had not gone to the trouble of looking for them.

The discreet princess pretended to be appeased and told him, "I simply must find my sisters, and after that we will do what has to be done together." But Rich-Craft answered that he could not agree to search for her sisters until she had consented to marry him, for her sisters would certainly oppose their match due to their seniority. Finette, who had good reason to distrust this treacherous prince, became even more suspicious at this answer. She trembled to think of what disaster had befallen her sisters and was determined to revenge them. So this young princess told Rich-Craft that she would gladly consent to marry him, but since she was of the opinion that marriages made at night always turned out to be unhappy, she requested that he postpone the ceremony until the next morning. She added that she would certainly not mention a word of this to her sisters and asked him to give her only a little time to say her prayers. Afterward she would take him to a room where there was a very good bed, and then she would return to her own room until the morning.

Rich-Craft was not very courageous, and as he watched the large hammer, which she played with like a fan, he consented and retired to give her some time to pray. No sooner was he gone than Finette rushed to one of the rooms of the tower, and made a bed over the hole of a sink. This room was as clean as any other, but all the garbage and dirty water were thrown down the hole which was very large. Finette put two weak sticks across it and then made a clean bed on top of them. After that she quickly returned to her room. A few minutes later Rich-Craft made his appearance, and the princess led him into the room where she had made his bed and then retired.

Without undressing, the prince hastily threw himself onto the bed. His weight immediately broke the small sticks, and he began falling to the bottom of the drain, unable to stop himself. Along the way he received twenty blows on his head and was bruised all over. The prince's fall made a great noise in the pipe, and since it was not far from Finette's room, she knew that her trick had worked. It is impossible to describe the pleasant feeling and joy she had as she heard him muttering in the drain. He certainly deserved his punishment, and the princess had every reason to feel satisfied.

But her joy was not so consuming that she forgot her sisters, and her first concern was to go and look for them. It was quite easy to find Babbler. Rich-Craft had double-locked that princess in her room and had left the key in the door. So Finette entered eagerly, and the noise she made startled her sister, throwing her into a great state of confusion. Finette told how she had defeated the wicked prince who had come to insult them, and on hearing that news, Babbler was thunderstruck, for despite all her talk about how smart she was, she had been foolish enough to have ridiculously believed every word Rich-Craft had told her. The world is still full of such dopes like her. However, she managed to cover up the extent of her sorrow and left the room with Finette to look for Nonchalante.

They searched all the rooms of the castle, but in vain. At last Finette thought to herself that they should look in the garden apartment, where, indeed, they found Nonchalante half dead with despair and fatigue, for she had not had anything to eat all day. Her sisters gave her all the assistance she needed. Then they recounted their adventures to one another, and Nonchalante and Babbler were overcome with remorse. Afterward, all three went to bed.

In the meantime Rich-Craft spent a very uncomfortable night, and when day came, he was not much better. The prince found himself in an underground sewer, though he could not see how horrible it was because no light could penetrate there. Nevertheless, after he had struggled painfully for some time, he found the end of the drain, which ran into a river at a considerable distance from the tower. Once there, he was able to make himself heard by some fishermen, who dragged him out in such a state that he aroused their compassion.

Rich-Craft ordered the men to carry him to his father's kingdom to recover from his wounds in seclusion. The disgrace that he had experienced caused him to develop such an inveterate hatred for Finette that he thought less about getting well than he did about getting revenge.

Meanwhile, Finette was very sad. Honor was a thousand times dearer to her than life, and the shameful weakness of her sisters had thrown her into such despair that she had great difficulty overcoming it. At the same time, the constitution of her sisters took a turn for the worse as a result of their worthless marriages, and Finette's patience was put to the test.

Rich-Craft, long a cunning villain, had continued to hatch ideas since this incident so that he could perpetrate even greater villainy. Neither the drain nor the bruises disturbed him as much as the fact that he had encountered someone more clever than he was. He knew the effects that his two marriages had had, and to tempt the princesses, he had great boxes filled with the finest fruit placed beneath the windows of the castle. Nonchalante and Babbler, who often sat at the windows, could not help but see the fruit, and they immediately felt a passionate desire to eat some. They

insisted that Finette go down in the basket to get some
of the fruit for them. So great was the kindness of that
princess and so willing was she to oblige her sisters
that she did as they requested and brought back some
fruit, which they devoured with great avidity.

The next day fruits of another kind appeared, and
again the princesses wanted to have some. And again
Finette complied with kindness. But Rich-Craft's officers, who were hiding and who had missed their target
the first time, did not fail the second. They seized
Finette and carried her off in plain view of her sisters,
who tore out their hair in despair. Rich-Craft's guards
were efficient and took Finette to a house in the
country, where the prince was residing in order to
regain his health. Since he was so infuriated with the
princess, he said a hundred brutal things to her, which
she answered with courage and greatness of soul
worthy of the heroine she was. At last, after having
kept her prisoner for some days, Rich-Craft had her
brought to the top of an extremely high mountain,
where he immediately followed. There he announced
to her they were going to put her to death in such a
manner that would sufficiently avenge all the injuries
she had caused him. Then the wicked prince demonstrated his barbaric nature by showing her a barrel
lined with knives, razors, and hooked nails all around
the inside. "In order to punish you the way you
deserve," he said, "we're going to put you into that
barrel and roll you from the top of this mountain down
into the valley."

Though Finette was no Roman, she was no more
afraid of this punishment than Regulus was at the sight
of a similar destiny. Instead of admiring her heroic
character, however, Rich-Craft became more enraged
than ever. Determined to put a quick end to her life, he
stooped to look into the barrel, the instrument of his
vengeance, to see whether it was properly furnished
with all its murderous weapons.

Finette, who saw her persecutor absorbed in examining the barrel, swiftly pushed him into it and kicked
the barrel down the mountain. As she ran away, the
prince's officers, who had been appalled at how cruelly

their master had planned to treat this charming princess, did not make the slightest attempt to stop her. Besides, they were so frightened by what had happened to Rich-Craft that they could think of nothing but how to stop the barrel, which was rolling pell-mell down the mountain. However, their efforts were for naught. He rolled down to the bottom, where they drew him out wounded in a thousand places.

Rich-Craft's accident made the gentle king and Prince Bel-a-voir extremely sad. As for the people of their country, they were not at all moved, since Rich-Craft was universally hated. They were astonished that the young prince, who had such noble and generous sentiments, could love his unworthy elder brother. But that was due to the loyalty and good nature of this prince, and Rich-Craft was always astute enough to exploit his compassionate feelings and make his brother beholden to him. Therefore, Bel-a-voir did not leave a thing undone to cure him as soon as possible. Yet despite all the care everyone took of Rich-Craft, nothing did him any good. On the contrary, his wounds grew worse every day, and it appeared that he would be suffering from them for a long time.

After escaping from this terrible danger, Finette returned safely to the castle, where she had left her sisters, but it was not long before she was faced with new troubles. Both of her sisters gave birth to sons, and Finette was mortified by such a predicament. However, her courage did not abate, and her desire to conceal her sisters' shame made her determined to expose herself to danger once more.

To accomplish her plan, she first took the precaution to disguise herself as a man. The children of her sisters she put into boxes in which she made little holes so they could breathe. Then she took these boxes and several others and rode on horseback to the capital of the gentle king.

When Finette entered the city, she learned of the generous manner in which Bel-a-voir was paying for any medicine that might help his brother. Indeed, such generosity had attracted all the charlatans in Europe. At that time there were a great many adventurers

without jobs or talent who pretended to be remarkable
men that had been endowed by heaven to cure all sorts
of maladies. These men, whose entire science consisted of bold deceit, found great credence among the
people because of the impression they created by their
outward appearance and by the bizarre names they
assumed. Such quacks never remain in the place where
they were born, and the exoticism of coming from a
distant place is often considered a proof of quality by
the common people.

The ingenious princess, who knew all this, gave herself a very strange name for that kingdom. Then she let
it be known that the Cavalier Sanatio had arrived with
marvelous secrets that cured all sorts of wounds, no
matter how dangerous and infected. Bel-a-voir immediately sent for this supposed cavalier, and Finette
swept in with all the airs of one of the best physicians
in the world and said five or six words in a cavalier
way. That is, she was the perfect doctor.

The princess was surprised by the good looks and
pleasant manner of Bel-a-voir, and after conversing
with him some time with regard to Rich-Craft's
wounds, she told him she would fetch a bottle with an
extraordinary elixir. "In the meantime I'll leave two
boxes I've brought that contain some excellent oint-
ments appropriate for the wounded prince." After the
supposed physician left and did not return, everyone
began to feel anxious. When at last they were going to
send for him, they heard the bawling of young infants
in Rich-Craft's room. This surprised everybody, for no
one had seen any infants there. After listening attentively, however, they found that the cries came from
the doctor's boxes. The noise was caused by Finette's
little nephews. The princess had given them a great
deal to eat before she came to the palace, but since they
had now been there a long time, they were hungry and
expressed their needs by singing a most doleful tune.
Someone opened the boxes, and the people were
greatly surprised to find two pretty babes in them.
Rich-Craft realized immediately that Finette had
played a new trick on him and threw himself into a
rage. His wounds grew worse and worse because of

this, and everyone realized that his death could not be prevented.

Seeing Bel-a-voir overcome with sorrow, Rich-Craft, treacherous to his last breath, thought to exploit his brother's affection. "You've always loved me, Prince," he said, "and you're now lamenting my imminent loss. I can have no greater proof of your love for me. It's true I'm dying, but if you've really ever cared for me, I hope you'll grant me what I'm going to ask of you."

Bel-a-voir, who was incapable of refusing anything to a brother in such a condition, gave him his most solemn oath to grant him whatever he desired.

As soon as he heard this, Rich-Craft embraced his brother and said to him, "Now I shall die contented because I'll be revenged. The favor I want you to do is to ask Finette to marry you after I die. You'll undoubtedly obtain this wicked princess for your wife, and the moment she's in your power, I want you to plunge your dagger into her heart."

Bel-a-voir trembled with horror at these words and repented the imprudence of his oath. But now was not the time to retract it. He did not want his despair to be noticed by his brother, who died soon after. The gentle king was tremendously affected by his death. His subjects, however, far from mourning Rich-Craft, were extremely glad that his death guaranteed the succession for Bel-a-voir, whom everyone considered worthy of the crown.

Once again Finette had returned safely to her sisters, and soon thereafter she heard of Rich-Craft's death. Some time later, news reached the three princesses that the king, their father, had returned home. He rushed to the tower, and his first wish was to see the distaffs. Nonchalante went and brought the distaff that belonged to Finette and showed it to the king. After making a very low curtsy, she returned it to the place whence she had taken it. Babbler did the same. In her turn, Finette brought out the same distaff, but the king now grew suspicious and demanded to see them all together. No one could show hers except Finette. The king was so enraged by his two elder daughters that he

immediately sent them away to the fairy who had given
him the distaffs, asking her to keep his daughters with
her as long as they lived and to punish them the way
they deserved.

To begin the punishment of these princesses, the
fairy led them into a gallery of her enchanted castle
where she had ordered the history of a vast number of
illustrious women who had made themselves famous
by leading busy, virtuous lives to be depicted in paintings. Due to the wonderful effects of fairy art, all these
figures were in motion from morning until night. Tro-
phies and emblems honoring these virtuous ladies were
everywhere, and it was tremendously mortifying for
the two sisters to compare the triumphs of these heroines with the despicable situation to which their imprudence had reduced them. To complete their grief, the
fairy told them gravely that if they had occupied themselves like those they saw in the pictures, they would
not have gone astray. She told them, "Idleness is the
mother of all vice and the source of all your misery."
Finally the fairy added that to prevent them from ever
falling into the same bad habits again and to make up
for the time they had lost, she was going to employ
them in the most coarse and mean work. Without any
regard for their lily-white complexions, she sent them
to gather peas in the garden and to pull out the weeds.
Nonchalante could not help but despair of leading such
a disciplined life, and she soon died from sorrow and
exhaustion. Babbler, who some time afterward found a
way to escape from the fairy's castle by night, broke
her skull against a tree and died in the arms of some
peasants.

Finette's good nature caused her to grieve a great
deal over the fate of her sisters, but in the midst of her
sorrow, she was informed that Prince Bel-a-voir had
requested her hand in marriage. What's more, her
father had already consented without notifying her, for
in those days the inclination of the partners was the last
thing one considered in arranging marriages. Finette
trembled at the news. She had good reason to fear that
Rich-Craft's hatred might have infected the heart of
a dear brother, and she was worried that this young

prince only sought to victimize her for his brother's sake. So concerned was she about this that she went to consult the wise fairy, who appreciated her fine qualities in the same way she had despised Nonchalante's and Babbler's bad ones.

The fairy would reveal nothing to Finette and only remarked, "Princess, you're wise and prudent. Up to now you've taken the proper precautions with regard to your conduct, and that has enabled you to bear in mind that *distrust is the mother of security.* Remember the importance of this maxim, and you'll eventually be happy without needing the help of my art."

Since she was not able to learn anything more from the fairy, Finette returned to the palace extremely upset. Some days later she was married by an ambassador in the name of Prince Bel-a-voir and conducted to her spouse in a splendid equipage. After she crossed the border, she was escorted in the same magnificent manner upon entering the first two cities of King Gentle's realm, and in the third city she met Bel-a-voir, who had been ordered by his father to go and welcome her. Everybody had been surprised by the prince's sadness at the approach of a marriage that he had so zealously pursued. Indeed, the king had to reprimand him and send him to meet the princess against his inclinations.

When Bel-a-voir saw how charming she was, he complimented her in such a confused manner that the courtiers, who knew how witty and gallant he was, believed him so strongly moved by love that he had lost his presence of mind. The entire city shouted for joy, and there were concerts and fireworks everywhere. After a magnificent supper, preparations were made for conducting the royal couple to their apartment.

Finette, who kept thinking about the fairy's maxim, had a plan. She won over one of the women, who had the key of the closet of the apartment designated for her. She gave orders to the woman to carry into that closet some straw, a bladder, some sheep's blood, and the entrails of some of the animals that had been prepared for supper. Then the princess used a pretext to go in. Making a figure from the straw, she put into it the

entrails and bladder full of blood. Then she dressed it
up in a woman's night-clothes. After she had finished
making this pretty dummy, she rejoined her company,
and some time later, she and her husband were conducted to their apartment. When they had allowed as
much time at the dressing table as was necessary, the
ladies of honor took away the torches and retired.
Finette immediately placed the straw dummy in the bed
and hid herself in a corner of the room.

After heaving two or three deep sighs, the prince
drew his sword and ran it through the body of the supposed Finette. All at once he saw the blood trickle out,
and the straw body did not move.

"What have I done?" Bel-a-voir exclaimed. "What!
After so many cruel struggles with myself—after
having weighed everything carefully whether I should
keep my word at the expense of a dreadful crime, I've
taken the life of a charming princess, whom I was born
to love! Her charms captivated me the moment I saw
her, and yet I didn't have the strength to free myself
from an oath that a brother possessed by fury had
exacted from me. Ah, heavens! How could anyone
think of punishing a woman for having too much
virtue? Well, Rich-Craft, I've satisfied your unjust
vengeance, but now I'll revenge Finette by my own
death. Yes, beautiful princess, this same sword will—"

As he was saying these words, Finette heard the
prince looking for his sword, which he had dropped in
his great agitation. Since she did not want him to
commit such a foolish act, she cried, "My prince, I'm
not dead! Your good heart made me anticipate your
repentance, and I saved you from committing a crime
by playing a trick that was not meant to harm you."

She then told Bel-a-voir about the foresight she had
had in regard to the straw figure. The prince was
ecstatic to find Finette alive, and expressed his gratitude to her for her prudence and preventing him from
committing a crime which he could not think about
without horror. He could not understand how he could
have been so weak and why he had not discovered the
futility of that wicked oath sooner that had been
exacted from him by his deceitful brother.

However, if Finette had not always been convinced that distrust is the mother of security, she would have been killed, and her death would have caused that of Bel-a-voir. Then afterward, people would have discussed the prince's strange emotions at their leisure.

Long live prudence and presence of mind! They saved this couple from the most dreadful of misfortunes and provided them with the most lovely destiny in the world. The prince and princess retained the greatest tenderness for each other and spent a long succession of beautiful days in such honor and happiness that would be difficult to describe.

Catherine Bernard

Catherine Bernard (1662–1712) was born in Rouen and moved to Paris during her youth. Since she was related to Corneille and Fontenelle, she was soon introduced to the literary circles of Paris and established herself in 1687 as a talented author with a series of novels under the general title *Les Malheurs de L'amour* (The Misfortunes of Love): *Eléonor d'Yvrée* (1688), *Le Comte d'Amboise* (1689), and *Inès de Cordoue* (1696). It was as a writer of tragedies, however, that she became famous. In 1689 her first play, *Léodamie*, was performed twenty times, and was followed by *Brutus* (1690), which had even greater success than the play by Voltaire, who had been influenced by her work.

Like many women writers of her time, who were not independently wealthy and remained single, Mlle. Bernard led an austere and modest life. In addition to her novels and tragedies, she wrote a number of poems that were published in different anthologies of the seventeenth century. Since she could not support herself from her writing alone, she accepted the patronage of the Chancelière de Pontchartrain, one of the more influential ladies at King Louis XIV's court.

Mlle. Bernard's *Riquet à la Houppe* (Riquet with the Tuft) appeared in her novel *Inès de Cordoue* in 1696 along with one other tale, *Le Prince Roiser*. There is some question as to whether she wrote her tale before Charles Perrault wrote his or vice versa. It is more than likely, since they moved in the same literary circles, that there was a mutual influence, and that both may have been acquainted with an oral folk tale that served as the basis of *Riquet*. The differences between the two versions are very interesting. Perrault's tale is more imaginative and optimistic from a male viewpoint. To bring about the happy end, he has his princess comply with a male code of reasoning. Bernard's version is more realistic and corresponds to the general theme of her novel *The Misfortunes of Love*. Unlike Perrault, she took a more critical view of forced marriages and depicted the quandary many women felt when they were obliged to enter into contractual marriages. To this extent, Bernard's tale, which helped inaugurate the fairy-tale mode in France, is a significant social document that can be considered part of the debate about the role of women and women's education that was prevalent during the ancien régime.

RIQUET WITH
THE TUFT

A GRAND nobleman of Grenada, whose wealth was equal to his high birth, experienced a domestic calamity that poisoned all the treasures of his fortune. His only daughter was so stupid that her naturally beautiful features only served to make her appearance distasteful. Her movements were anything but graceful. Her figure, though slender, made an awkward impression since it lacked sprightliness.

Mama—that was the name of this girl—did not possess enough intelligence to know that she was not intelligent, but she did have enough to realize she was looked upon with disdain, even though she could not figure out why. One day, when she was out walking by herself, as was her habit, she saw a man hideous enough to be a monster emerge from the ground. As soon as she caught sight of him, she wanted to flee, but he called her back.

"Stop," he said to her. "I have something unpleasant to tell you, but I also have something nice to promise you. Even with your beauty you have something—and I don't know what's caused it—that makes people regard you with disfavor. It has to do with your incapacity to think, and without my making a value judgment, this fault makes you as inferior as I am, for my body is like your mind. That's the cruel thing I have to say to you. But from the stunned manner in which you're looking at me, I think I've given your mind too little credit, for I fear I've insulted you. This is what makes me despair as I broach the subject of my proposition. However, I'm going to risk making it to you. Do you want intelligence?"

"Yes." Mama responded in a manner that might have indicated no.

"Very good," he said. "Here's the way. You must love Riquet with the Tuft. That's my name, and you must marry me at the end of the year. That's the condition I'll impose on you. Think it over. If you can't, repeat the words that I'm going to say to you as often as possible. They'll eventually teach you how to think. Farewell for a year. Here are the words that will dissipate your indolence and at the same time cure your imbecility:

> Love can surely inspire me
> To help me shed stupidity.
> And teach me to care with sincerity
> If I have the right quality."

As Mama began to utter these words properly, her poise improved immensely—she became more vivacious, and her movements more free. She kept repeating the verse and soon departed for her father's house, where she told him something coherent, then a little later, something intelligent, and finally, something witty. Such a great and rapid transformation did not go unnoticed. Lovers came in droves. Mama was no longer alone at the balls or during promenades. Soon she made men unfaithful and jealous. People talked only about her and for her.

Among the men who found her charming, it was easy for her to find someone more handsome than Riquet with the Tuft. The mind that her benefactor had given her started to work against him. The words that she conscientiously repeated filled her with love, but the effect was contrary to Riquet's intentions: the love was not for him.

She favored the most handsome of those men who sighed for her, although he was not the best match with regard to his wealth. Thus her father and mother, who saw that they had wished this misfortune on their daughter by desiring she should have a mind, and who realized that they could not deprive her of it, thought at least they should give her lessons against love. But

prohibiting a young and pretty person from loving is
like preventing a tree from bearing leaves in May. She
only loved Arada more—that was the name of her
lover.

She made sure not to tell anyone about how she happened to obtain her mind. Her vanity caused her to
keep this a secret. She had enough intelligence to
understand the importance of hiding the mystery of
how she had managed to become so.

The year that Riquet with the Tuft had given her to
make a decision drew to an end. With great anguish she
awaited the deadline. Her mind, now her bane, did not
let one single torturous consequence escape her. To
lose her lover forever, to be under the power of
someone about whom the only thing she knew was his
deformity, which was perhaps his least fault, and
finally to marry someone and to accept his gifts that
she did not want to return—these thoughts kept passing
through her mind.

One day, when she was contemplating her cruel destiny and wandering off alone, she heard a loud hubbub
and subterranean voices singing the words Riquet with
the Tuft had taught her. She shuddered when she heard
them, for it was the signal of disaster. Soon the ground
opened. She descended gradually and saw Riquet with
the Tuft surrounded by creatures who were just as
deformed as he was. What a spectacle for a person who
had been pursued by the most charming men in her
country! Her torment was even greater than her surprise. Unable to speak, she let loose a flood of tears.
This was the only human quality she possessed that
was beyond the control of the mind that Riquet with
the Tuft had given her. In turn, he regarded her sadly.

"Madam," he said, "it's not difficult to see that I'm
more distasteful to you than when I first appeared
before you. I myself am bewildered by what has happened in giving you a mind. But in the last analysis,
you're free to make a choice: marry me or return to
your former condition. I'll send you back to your
father's house the way I found you, or I'll make you
mistress of this kingdom. I am king of the gnomes, and
you would be queen. If you can excuse my shape and

overlook my repulsive deformities, you could enjoy a great many pleasures here. I am master of all the treasures locked up in the earth, and you would be mistress of them. With gold and intelligence, who could want more from life?" Seeing she was unconvinced, he continued, "I'm afraid that you've developed some kind of false squeamishness. I must seem inadequate in the midst of all my riches. But if I and my treasures don't please you, just speak up. I'll take you away from here and bring you home because I don't want anything to trouble my happiness here. You have two days to become acquainted with this place and to decide my fate and yours."

After leading her into a magnificent apartment, Riquet with the Tuft left her. She was attended by gnomes of her sex, whose ugliness did not repel her as much as that of the men. They entertained her with a meal and good company. After dinner she saw a play in which the deformities of the actors prevented her from developing any interest in the subject of the drama. That evening a ball was held in her honor, but she attended it without desiring to please anyone. Indeed, she felt an innate disgust that made it impossible for her to show Riquet her appreciation for all the pleasures he provided.

In order to save herself from this odious husband, she would have returned to her stupidity without feeling grief if she had not had a lover, but it would have meant losing a lover in a most cruel manner. It is also true that she would lose her lover by marrying the gnome—she would never be able to see Arada, speak with him, or send him news about herself, for Riquet would suspect her of infidelity. In sum, by getting rid of the man she loved, she was going to marry a husband who would always be odious even when he was pleasant. Moreover, he was a monster.

The decision was a wrenching one to make. When the two days had passed, her mind was not any more made up than before. She told the gnome that it had not been possible for her to reach a decision.

"That's a decision against me," he told her. "So now

I'll return you to your former condition that you didn't dare to choose."

She trembled. The idea of losing her lover through the disdain he would show her provided such a powerful spur that she felt compelled to renounce him.

"Well, then!" the gnome said to her. "You've decided. It must be up to you."

Riquet with the Tuft did not make it difficult. He married her, and Mama's intelligence increased even more through this marriage. Her unhappiness, though, increased in proportion to the growth of her mind. She was horrified to have given herself to a monster, and she couldn't comprehend how she spent one moment with him.

The gnome realized very well how much his wife hated him, and he was hurt by it, even though he prided himself on the force of his intelligence. This aversion was a constant reproach to his deformity and made him detest women, marriage, and curiosity so much so that he became distraught. He often left Mama alone, and since she was reduced to just thinking, she became convinced that she had to make Arada see with his own eyes that she was not unfaithful. She knew he could get to this place because she had so easily managed to get there herself. At the least she had to send him news about herself and explain her absence because of the gnome who had abducted her. Once Arada saw him, he would know she was faithful.

There is nothing that an intelligent woman in love cannot do. She won over a gnome attendant, who carried news about her to Arada. Fortunately, this was still during the time that lovers were faithful to each other. He had become despondent over Mama's absence without becoming bitter about it. He was not even plagued by suspicion. He maintained that if he died, he would not have the least negative thought about his mistress and did not want to seek a cure for his love. It is not difficult to believe that with such feelings, he was willing to risk his life to find Mama as soon as he knew where she was. Nor did she forbid him from coming there.

Mama's cheerfulness returned gradually, and her

beauty made her even more perfect, but the amorous gnome caused her to worry. He had too much intelligence and knew Mama's repugnance for him too well to believe that she had become accustomed to being there and had become sweeter so suddenly. Mama was imprudent enough to get dressed up, and he was smart enough to realize that he was not worthy of this. Long did he search until he discovered a handsome man hiding in his palace. As a result, he thought up an extremely fine way both to revenge himself and take care of the lover. First, Riquet ordered Mama to appear before him.

"It doesn't amuse me to make complaints and reproaches," he said. "I let human beings have their share of them. When I gave you a mind, I presumed I would enjoy it. However, you've used it against me. Still, I won't deprive you of it completely. You've submitted to the law that was imposed on you. But even if you did not break our agreement, you didn't observe it to the letter. Let us compromise. You shall have a mind during the night. I don't want a stupid wife, but you shall be stupid during the day for whomever you please."

All at once Mama felt a dullness of mind that she did not understand anymore. During the night her ideas were aroused again, and she wept over her misfortune. She was not able to console herself or find the ways through her wisdom to help herself.

The following night she noticed that her husband was sleeping soundly. She placed an herb on his nose that increased his oblivion and made it last as long as she wished. She got up and crept away from the object of her wrath. Led by her dreams, she went to the place where Arada was dwelling. She thought that he might be looking for her and found him in a lane where they had often met. He asked her all kinds of questions. Mama told him about her misfortunes, which abated because of the pleasure she derived in relating them to him.

The next night they met at the same place without being followed, and their meetings continued for such a long time that their misfortune now enabled them to taste a new kind of happiness. Mama's mind and love provided her with a thousand ways to be charming and to make Arada forget that she lacked intelligence half the time.

Whenever the lovers felt the dawn of day approaching, Mama went to wake the gnome. She took care to remove the herb that made him drowsy as soon as she was beside him. Although she now became an imbecile again, she used the time to sleep.

Such bittersweet happiness could not last forever. The leaf that made Riquet sleep also made him snore, and, thinking his master was grumbling, a half-asleep servant ran to him, saw the herb that had been placed on his nose, and removed it because he thought that was disturbing him—a cure that made three people unhappy all at the same time. Riquet saw that he was alone and searched for his wife in a rage. Either chance or his bad luck led him to the place where the two lovers had abandoned themselves to each other. As he approached, he heard them swear eternal love to each other. He did not say a word. He touched the lover with a wand that transformed his shape into one exactly like his own. And after looking back and forth and back and forth, Mama could no longer distinguish who her husband was. Thus she lived with two husbands instead of one, never knowing whom she should address her lamentations for fear of mistaking the object of her hatred for the object of her love.

But perhaps she hardly lost anything there. In the long run lovers become husbands anyway.

Henriette Julie de Murat

Henriette Julie de Castelnau, Comtess de Murat (1670–1716) was born in Brest, Brittany, and was strongly influenced by the traditions and folklore of that region. Both her parents came from old noble families, and at the time she was born, her father was governor of Brest. When Henriette Julie turned sixteen she was sent to Louis XIV's court in Paris to marry Comte de Murat. Soon after her arrival and marriage, she caused a sensation and impressed Queen Marie-Thérèse by wearing the traditional peasant costumes of Brittany.

Madame de Murat was known for her great beauty, wit, and independence. However, since she was courted by numerous famous people, she let this flattery go to her head. In addition, her nonconformism and flair for attention made important members of the court extremely envious. Given the enemies she made and her zest for adventure, she was often in trouble with the king. Finally, in 1694 when she published a pamphlet entitled *Histoire de la courtisane Rhodope,* a political satire about Scarron, Louis XIV, and Madame de Maintenon, she was banished. It appears that her husband, who had played a minor role in her life, had died before this banishment. At any rate, Madame de Murat was sent alone to Loches, a small city in the provinces of France, where she remained until 1715.

It was in Loches from 1694 to 1715 that Madame de Murat wrote and published her most significant works: *Histoire galante des habitants de Loches* (1696), *Les Mémoires de la Comtesse de Murat ou la defense des dames* (1697), *Contes de fées* (1698), *Les nouveaux contes de fées* (1698), and *Histoires sublimes et allégoriques* (1699). As in Paris, Madame de Murat, who missed the cultural life of the court, caused somewhat of a commotion in the provincial city of Loches. Given her vivacious temperament, she organized all kinds of gatherings at her house, which were reported to be scandalous. In fact, however, Mme. de Murat simply endeavored to recreate an atmosphere similar to Paris, and she loved to converse, dance, and stay up until late in the morning telling fairy tales with some of her best friends like Charlotte-Rose de la Force, who also published tales during this period. In addition to these soirees and numerous mysterious journeys, Madame de Murat astonished the people of Loches by wearing a red cloak to church every Sunday.

Though Madame de Murat constantly sought to obtain a pardon from Louis XIV, she was never successful. She returned to Paris briefly in 1715, after Louis XIV's death. But even then the duration of her residence there was very short because she was already suffering from chronic nephritis and kidney stones that caused her extreme pain. Therefore, she retired to her chateau, La Buzadière, where she died in 1716.

Madame de Murat composed her fairy tales during her exile in Loches to relieve herself of boredom. A born storyteller, she recalled the tales and legends that she had heard during her childhood in Brittany, and she amused herself by retelling them in her own versions to her friends. Then she would either record these oral versions in a journal that she kept or prepare them for publication. Most of her tales concern the issue of *tendresse,* marriage, and power struggles among the aristocracy. Madame de Murat's basic philosophy—live for the moment, and live according to your feelings—is the dominant theme in her tales. But she does not preach or predict a happy end when one subscribes to such a philosophy. In fact, nothing is predictable in her tales because even the power of fairies was never sufficient in her mind to guarantee a happy end. This becomes evident in one of her best tales, *Le Palais de la vengeance* (The Palace of Revenge), which was first published in *Les nouveaux contes de fées* in 1698. Moreover, *The Palace of Revenge* is interesting because it conveys her sentiments about banishment and boredom. What appears to be an idyllic dream for a couple living at a bustling court turns out to be a nightmare in disguise.

THE PALACE OF REVENGE

THERE was once a king and queen of Iceland, who had a daughter after twenty years of married life. Her birth gave them the greatest pleasure, since they had given up hope of having a successor to the throne. The young princess was named Imis, and from the very beginning her budding charms promised that she would be marvelously beautiful and radiant when she grew older.

No one in the universe would have ever been worthy of her if Cupid had not thought it a point of honor to bring such a wonderful person under his sway. Therefore, he arranged to have a prince born in the same court who was just as charming as the lovely princess. He was called Philax and was the son of a brother of the King of Iceland. He was two years older than the princess, and they were brought up together with all the freedom natural to childhood and close relatives. The first sensations of their hearts were mutual admiration and affection, and both found nothing more beautiful in their eyes as the other. Consequently, they could not find a single attraction in the world that interfered with the feeling each had for the other, even though they had yet to discover its name.

The king and queen were pleased to see the children's mutual affection grow. They loved young Philax, for he was a prince of their blood, and no child had ever wakened fairer hopes. Everything seemed to favor Cupid's plans to make Prince Philax the happiest of men.

The princess was about twelve years old when the queen, who was extremely fond of her, wanted to have her daughter's fortune told by a fairy whose extraordinary powers had created a sensation at that time. The queen set out in search of this fairy and took along Imis, who was despondent because she had to separate from Philax. Moreover, she wondered time and again why people troubled themselves about the future when the present was so pleasant. Philax remained with the king, and there was nothing at the court that could compensate for the absence of the princess.

Arriving at the fairy's castle, the queen was magnificently received, but the fairy was not at home. Her usual residence was on the summit of a mountain some distance away, where she absorbed herself in the profound study that had made her famous throughout the world. As soon as she heard about the queen's arrival, she returned to the castle. The queen presented the princess to her, told her her name and the hour of her birth, which the fairy already knew quite well even though she had not been there. The fairy of the mountain knew everything. She promised the queen an answer in two days and then returned to the summit of the mountain. On the morning of the third day she came back to the castle, requested that the queen descend into the garden, and gave her some tablets of palm leaves closely shut, which she was ordered not to open except in the presence of the king. To satisfy her curiosity to some degree, the queen asked her several questions in regard to the fate of her daughter.

"Great queen," the fairy of the mountain replied, "I can't tell you precisely what sort of catastrophe threatens the princess. I see only that love will have a large share in the events of her life, and that no beauty will ever arouse such passionate emotions as that of Imis will do."

One didn't have to be a fairy to foresee that the princess would have admirers. Her eyes already seemed to demand love from everyone's heart that the fairy assured the queen most people would feel for her. In the meantime, Imis, much less uneasy about her destiny than about her separation from Philax, amused herself by gathering flowers. Because she was only thinking about his love and was impatient to depart, however, she forgot the bouquet she had begun to make and unthinkingly threw them away. Then she hastened to rejoin the queen, who was taking her leave of the fairy of the mountain. The fairy also embraced Imis and gazed at her with the admiration she deserved.

"Since it's impossible for me, beautiful princess, to change the decree of destiny in your favor, I'll at least try to let you escape the disasters that it's preparing for you." Upon saying this, she gathered a bunch of lilies of the valley and addressed the youthful Imis again. "Always wear these flowers that I'm giving you," she said. "They'll never fade, and as long as you wear them, they'll protect you from all the evils with which fate threatens you."

Then she fastened the bouquet on the headdress of Imis. The flowers, obedient to the fairy's wishes, were no sooner placed in the princess's hair than they adjusted themselves and formed a sort of aigrette, whose whiteness seemed to prove only that nothing could eclipse Imis's fair complexion.

After thanking the fairy a thousand times, the queen bade her farewell and went back to Iceland, where the entire court impatiently awaited the princess's return. The eyes of Imis and her lover sparkled radiantly and beautifully with a joy that has never been seen before. The mystery of the lilies of the valley was revealed to the king alone. It had such a pleasing effect in the princess's beautiful brown hair that everyone assumed that it was simply an ornament that she herself had culled in the fairy's gardens.

The princess told Philax much more about the grief she felt at her separation from him than about the misfortunes that the fates had in store for her. Although Philax was worried by them, he was happy just to be with her in the present; the evils of the future were as yet uncertain. In fact, they forgot them and abandoned themselves to the delight of seeing each other again.

In the meantime, the queen recounted the events of the journey to the king and gave him the fairy's tablets.

The king opened them and found the following words written in letters of gold: ·

> Fate for Imis hides despair
> Under hopes that seem most fair.
> She'll be miserable as can be
> Because of too much felicity.

The king and queen were very disturbed by this oracle and vainly tried to interpret it. They said nothing about it to the princess in order to spare her unnecessary sorrow.

One day, while Philax was hunting, a pleasure he indulged in frequently, Imis went walking by herself in a labyrinth of myrtles. She was melancholy because Philax had been gone so long, and she reproached herself for succumbing to an impatience that he evidently did not share. She was absorbed in her thoughts when she heard a voice:

"Why do you torment yourself, beautiful princess? If Philax does not appreciate the happiness of being loved by you, I've come to offer you a heart a thousand times more grateful—a heart deeply smitten by your charms—and a fortune remarkable enough to be the object of desire of everyone in the world except yourself."

The princess was astonished when she heard this voice. She had imagined herself alone in the labyrinth, and since she had not uttered a word, she was even more surprised that this voice had responded to her thoughts. She looked around and saw a little man appear in the air, seated upon a cockchafer.

"Fear not, fair Imis," he said to her. "You have no lover more submissive than I, and although this is the first time I've appeared to you, I've loved you for a long time and have gazed upon you every day."

"You astonish me!" the princess replied. "What's that you said? You've watched me and know my thoughts? If so, you must be aware that it's useless to love me. Philax, to whom I've given my heart, will continue to rule over it because of his charm, and although I'm unhappy with him, I've never loved him so much as I do at this moment. But tell me who you are, and where you first saw me."

"I'm Pagan the Enchanter," he replied, "and I have power over everyone but you. I saw you first in the gardens of the fairy of the mountain. I was hidden in one of the tulips you had gathered, and I took it as a good sign that you were induced to choose the flower I was concealed in. I had hoped you would carry me away with you, but you were too pleasantly occupied by thinking about Philax. You threw away the flowers as soon as you had gathered them and left me in the garden the most enamored of creatures. From that moment on, I've felt that nothing could make me happy except the hope of being loved by you. Think favorably of me, fair Imis, if this be possible, and permit me occasionally to remind you of my affection."

With these words he disappeared. The princess returned to the palace, where the sight of Philax dissipated the alarm she felt. She was so eager to hear him apologize for the length of time he had spent hunting that she nearly forgot to tell him what had occurred. But at last, she told him what she had seen in the labyrinth of myrtles. Despite his courage the young prince was alarmed at the idea of a winged rival because he could not fight for the hand of the princess with him on equal terms. Still, the plume of the lilies of the valley protected her against enchantments, and the affection Imis had for him gave him no cause to fear any change in her heart.

The day after this incident in the labyrinth, the princess woke and saw twelve tiny nymphs seated on honey bees fly into her room. They carried minuscule golden baskets in their hands and approached Imis's bed, where they greeted her, and then placed their baskets on a table of white marble that was standing in the center of the room. As soon as the baskets were placed on it, they grew to an ordinary size. The nymphs left them there and greeted Imis again. One approached the bed nearer than the rest, let something fall on it, and then flew away.

Although she was astonished by such a strange sight,

she picked up the object that the nymph had dropped beside her. It was a marvelously beautiful emerald, and the moment the princess touched it, the emerald opened and revealed a rose leaf on which she read these verses:

> Let the world learn to its surprise
> The wondrous power of your eyes.
> Such is the love I bear, you'll see,
> It makes even torture dear to me.

The princess had difficulty recovering from her surprise, and at last she called her attendants, who were just as surprised at the sight of the baskets. The king, queen, and Philax rushed to her chamber on hearing the news of this extraordinary event. When the princess revealed to them what had happened, she told them about everything except the letter of her lover. She thought she was not bound to say anything about it except to Philax. The baskets were carefully examined and found to be filled with extraordinarily beautiful jewels of such great value that everyone's astonishment increased.

The princess would not touch anything, and when she found a moment when nobody was listening, she drew close to Philax and gave him the emerald and the rose leaf. He read his rival's letter with much disquietude, and Imis consoled him by tearing the rose leaf to pieces before his eyes. Alas, how dearly were they to pay for that act!

Some days elapsed without the princess hearing anything from Pagan. She thought that her contempt for him would put an end to his passion, and Philax expected the same thing. So he returned to his hunting as usual. When he stopped beside a fountain to refresh himself, he had the emerald with him that the princess had given him. Recalling with pleasure how little value she had placed on it, he drew it from his pocket to look at it. But no sooner was it in his hand than it slipped through his fingers, and no sooner did it touch the ground than it changed into a chariot. Two winged monsters emerged from the fountain and harnessed themselves to it. Philax gazed at them without alarm, for he was incapable of fear. Nevertheless, he could not avoid feeling some distress when he found himself being transported into the chariot by an irresistible power, and at the same moment raised into the air by the winged monsters, who pulled the chariot along with alarming speed.

Night fell, and the huntsmen, after searching for Philax in vain throughout the wood, went back to the palace, where they imagined he had returned alone. But he was not to be found there, nor had anyone seen him since he had set out with them for the chase.

The king commanded them to renew their search. The entire court shared his majesty's anxiety. They returned to the wood and ran all over looking for him. It was daybreak before they retraced their steps to the palace; however, they had been unable to obtain any news about the prince's whereabouts. Imis had spent the night despairing of her lover's absence, which she could not comprehend. She had ascended to the battlements of the palace to watch for the return of the search party, hoping she would see him arrive in their company. No words can express her grief when Philax did not appear, and when she was informed that it had been impossible to discover what had happened to him, she fainted. Carrying her into the palace, one of her women undressed her and put her to bed. In her haste, however, she took the plume of the lilies of the valley out of the princess's hair that guarded her against the power of enchantment. The instant it was removed, a dark cloud filled the apartment, into which Imis vanished. The king and queen fell into deep despair when they learned about her disappearance, and there was nothing that could console them.

On recovering from her swoon, the princess found herself in a chamber of multicolored coral with a floor made of pearls. She was surrounded by nymphs, who waited on her with the most profound respect. They were very beautiful and dressed in a magnificent and tasteful manner. Imis first asked them where she was.

"You're in a place where you're adored," one of the nymphs said to her. "Fear nothing, fair princess, you'll find everything you can desire here."

"Then Philax is here!" the princess exclaimed, her eyes sparkling with joy. "My only desire is to be fortunate enough to see him again."

"You cherish the memory of an ungrateful lover too long," Pagan said, making himself visible to the princess. "Since that prince has deserted you, he's no longer worthy of your affection. Let resentment and respect for your own pride combine with the feelings I have for you. Reign forever in these regions, lovely princess. You'll find immense treasures in them, and every kind of conceivable delight will accompany your steps."

Imis replied to Pagan's words with tears alone, and since he was afraid to embitter these tears, he left her. The nymphs remained with her and used everything within their power to console her. They served her a magnificent meal, but she refused to eat. By the following morning, though, her desire to see Philax once more made her determined to live. She took some food, and the nymphs conducted her through various parts of the palace to take her mind off her sorrow. It was built entirely of shiny shells mixed with precious stones of different colors that produced the finest effect in the world. All the furniture was made of gold, and it was clear from such wonderful craftsmanship that only fairies could have made it.

After they had shown Imis the palace, the nymphs led her into the gardens, which were indescribably beautiful. She found a splendid chariot drawn by six stags and led by a dwarf, who requested that she get in. Imis complied, and the nymphs seated themselves at her feet. They were driven to the seaside, where a nymph informed the princess that Pagan, who reigned on this island, had used the power of his art to make it the most beautiful in the universe. The sound of instruments interrupted the nymph's talk. The sea appeared to be entirely covered with little boats built of scarlet

coral and filled with everything necessary to create a
splendid aquatic entertainment. In the middle of
the small craft was a much larger barque on which
Imis's initials, formed by pearls, could be seen everywhere. Drawn by two dolphins, the barque approached
the shore. The princess got in, accompanied by her
nymphs. As soon as she was on board, a superb meal
appeared before her, and her ears were entertained
at the same time by exquisite music that emanated
from the boats around her. Songs lauding her were
sung, but Imis did not pay any attention. She remounted her chariot and returned to the palace overcome with sadness.

In the evening Pagan appeared again, and he found
her more inappreciative of his love than ever before,
but he was not discouraged and was confident that his
constancy would have an effect. He had yet to learn
that the most faithful are not always the most happy
when it comes to love.

Every day he offered the princess entertainments
worthy of arousing the admiration of the entire world,
but they were lost upon the person for whom they were
invented. Imis thought of nothing but her missing
lover.

In the meantime, that unfortunate prince had been
transported by the winged monsters to a forest belonging to Pagan, called the Dismal Forest. As soon as
Philax arrived there, the emerald chariot and monsters
disappeared. Surprised by this miracle, the prince summoned all his courage to help himself. It was the only
aid on which he could count in that place. He first
explored several of the roads through the forest. They
were dreadful, and the sun could not illuminate a way
out of the gloomy forest. There was not a soul to be
found, not even an animal of any kind. It seemed as
though the beasts themselves were horrified of this
dreary abode.

Philax lived on wild fruit and spent his days in the
deepest sorrow. His separation from the princess
caused him great despair, and sometimes he occupied
himself by using his sword to carve the name of Imis
on the tree trunks. Although these rank growths were

hardly befitting for such a tender purpose, when we are truly in love, we frequently make the least suitable things express our feelings.

Continuing to advance through the forest every day, the prince had been journeying nearly a year when one night he heard some plaintive voices. Try as he might, he could not distinguish any words. Alarming as these wailing sounds were at such a dark hour—in a place where the prince had not encountered a soul—he desperately sought some kind of company. "If I could at least find someone as wretched as I," he said to himself, "he could console me for the misfortunes I have experienced." Thus he waited impatiently for morning, when he could search for the people whose voices he had heard. He walked toward that part of the forest where he thought the sounds had come from, but he searched all day in vain. At last, however, toward evening he discovered a spot barren of trees. There sprawled the ruins of a castle that appeared to have been enormous at one time. He entered a courtyard that had walls made of green marble and still seemed somewhat splendid. Yet he found nothing but huge trees standing irregularly in various spots of the enclosure. Noticing something elevated on a pedestal of black marble, he found on closer inspection a jumbled pile of armor and weapons, heaped one on top of the other. Ancient helmets, shields, and swords formed a sort of motley trophy. He had been looking for some inscription that might tell him who had been the former owners, and he found one engraved on the pedestal. Time had nearly effaced the characters, and he had great difficulty in deciphering these words:

TO THE IMMORTAL MEMORY OF THE GLORY OF THE FAIRY
CÉORÉ
IT WAS HERE
THAT ON THE SAME DAY
SHE TRIUMPHED OVER CUPID
AND PUNISHED HER UNFAITHFUL LOVERS

This inscription did not provide Philax with nearly enough information to solve the mystery. Therefore, he

was about to continue his search through the forest
when night overtook him. He sat down at the foot of a
cypress, and no sooner did he begin to relax than he
heard the same voices that had attracted his attention
the previous evening. He was not so much surprised by
this as when he noticed that it was the trees themselves
that uttered these complaints just as if they had been
human beings. The prince rose, drew his sword, and
struck the cypress nearest him. He was about to repeat
the blow when the tree exclaimed, "Stop! Stop! Don't
insult an unfortunate prince who's no longer in a position to defend himself!"

Philax stopped, and as he adjusted to the extraordinary nature of this happenstance, he asked the
cypress what miracle had transformed it into a man and
a tree at the same time.

"I'll gladly tell you," the cypress replied, "especially
since this is the first opportunity in two thousand years
that fate has afforded me the chance of relating my
misfortunes and I don't want to lose it. All the trees
you see in this courtyard were princes, renowned in
their time for their rank and valor. The fairy Céoré
reigned in this country. Beautiful though she was, her
powers made her more famous than her beauty. These
other charms she used to bring us under her spell. She
had become enamored of the young Orizée, a prince
whose remarkable qualities made him worthy of a
better fate—I should tell you," the cypress added, "he's
the oak you see beside me."

Philax looked at the oak and heard it breathe a heavy
sigh as it recalled its misfortune.

"To attract this prince to her court," the cypress continued, "the fairy had a tournament proclaimed. We
were all quick to seize this opportunity to acquire
glory, and Orizée was one of the princes who con-
tended. The prize consisted of a fairy armor that made
the wearer invulnerable. Unfortunately, I was the
winner. Céoré was annoyed that fate had not favored
her inclinations and, deciding to avenge herself on us,
she enchanted all the mirrors that lined a gallery in her
castle. Those who saw her reflection in these fatal mirrors just once could not resist having the most pas-

sionate feelings for her. It was in this gallery that she received us the day after the tournament. We all saw her in these mirrors, and she appeared so beautiful that those among us who had been indifferent to love up until then stopped being so from that point on, and those who were in love with others became unfaithful all at once. We no longer thought of leaving the fairy's palace. Our only concern was to please her. The affairs of our realms no longer mattered to us. Nothing seemed of consequence except the hope of being loved by Céoré. Orizée was the only one she favored, and the passion of the other princes merely gave the fairy opportunities of sacrificing them to this lover who was so dear to her, and causing the fame of her beauty to spread throughout the world. Love appeared for some time to soften Céoré's cruel nature, but at the end of four or five years she displayed her former ferocity. Abusing the power of her enchantment over us, she used us to avenge herself on neighboring kings for the slightest offence by the most horrible murders. Orizée tried in vain to prevent her cruel acts. She loved him but would not obey him. Having returned one day from subduing a giant whom I had challenged on her orders, I had the vanquished giant's arms brought before her. She was alone in the gallery of mirrors. I laid the giant's spoils at her feet and declared my feelings for her with indescribable ardor, augmented no doubt by the power of the enchantment that surrounded me. But far from showing the least gratitude for my triumph or for the love I felt for her, Céoré treated me with utmost contempt. Into a boudoir she withdrew and left me alone in the gallery in a state of utter despair and rage. I remained there for some time, not knowing what to do because the fairy's enchantments did not permit us to fight with Orizée. Since she was concerned about the life of her lover, the cruel Céoré had deprived us of the natural desire to avenge ourselves on a fortunate rival when she aroused our jealousy. Finally, after pacing the gallery for some time, I remembered that it was in this place that I had first fallen in love with the fairy and exclaimed, 'It's here that I first felt that fatal passion which now fills me with despair. You wretched

mirrors that have pictured the unjust Céoré to me so
often with a beauty that enslaved my heart and reason,
I'm going to punish you for the crime of making her
too appealing to me.' Upon saying this, I snatched the
giant's club that I had brought to give the fairy as a
present, and I dashed the mirrors to pieces. No sooner
were they broken than I felt an even greater hatred for
Céoré than my former love. At the same time, the other
princes who had been my rivals felt their spells broken,
and Orizée himself became ashamed of the love the
fairy had for him. Céoré vainly tried to retain her lover
by her tears, but he did not respond to her grief.
Despite her cries, we set out all together, determined to
flee from the terrible place. Yet as we passed through
the courtyard, the sky appeared to be on fire. A
frightful clap of thunder was heard, and we found we
could not move. The fairy appeared in the air, riding on
a large serpent, and she addressed us in a tone that
revealed her rage. 'Faithless princes,' she said, 'I'm
about to punish you by a torture that will never end
because of the crime you've committed in breaking my
chains, which were too great an honor for you to bear.
As for you, ungrateful Orizée, I'll triumph after all in
the love you've felt for me. I'm going to plague you
with the same misfortune that your rivals will experience. Now, I command in memory of this incident that
when mirrors become commonly used throughout the
world, it will always be a definite sign of infidelity
whenever a lover breaks one.' The fairy vanished after
having uttered these words. We were changed into
trees, but cruel Céoré left us our reason, undoubtedly
with the intention to increase our suffering. Time has
destroyed the superb castle that was the avenue of our
misfortune, and you're the only man we've seen during
the two thousand years that we've been in this frightful
forest."

   Philax was about to reply to the cypress tree's
story when he was suddenly transported into a beautiful garden. There he found a lovely nymph who
approached him with a gracious air and said, "If
you wish, Philax, I'll allow you to see Princess Imis in
three days."

The prince was ecstatic when he heard such an unexpected offer and threw himself at her feet to express his gratitude. At that same moment Pagan was aloft, concealed in a cloud with the Princess Imis. He had told her a thousand times that Philax was unfaithful, but she had always refused to believe a word of this jealous lover. He now conducted her to this spot, he said, to convince her of the fickleness of the prince. The princess saw Philax throw himself at the nymph's feet with an air of extreme delight, and she became despondent. No longer did she deceive herself of something that she was afraid to believe more than anything in the world. Pagan had placed her at a distance from the earth that prevented her from hearing what Philax and the nymph had said—it was by his orders that the nymph had appeared before Philax.

Pagan led Imis back to his island, where, after having convinced her of Philax's infidelity, he found that he had only increased the beautiful princess's grief without making her any more positive toward him. To his despair he found that his plan of alleged infidelity had failed despite the fact that it had seemed so promising. Therefore, he was now determined to avenge himself for the constancy of these lovers. He was not cruel like the fairy Céoré, his ancestress, so he conceived a different kind of punishment from the one she had used to torment her unfortunate lovers. He did not wish to destroy either the princess, whom he had loved so tenderly, or even Philax, whom he had already made suffer so much. Consequently he limited his revenge to the destruction of a feeling that had opposed his own.

Erecting a crystal palace on his island, he took great care to put everything in it that would make life pleasant. However, there would be no way to leave this castle. He enclosed nymphs and dwarfs to wait on Imis and her lover, and when everything was ready for their reception, he transported the two of them there. At first they thought themselves at the height of happiness and blessed Pagan a thousand times for softening his anger. As for Pagan, although he at first could not bear to see them together, he hoped that this spectacle would one

day prove less painful. In the meantime, he left the
crystal palace after engraving this inscription on it with
a stroke of his wand:

> Absence, danger, pleasure, pain,
> Were all employed, and all in vain.
> Imis and Philax could not be severed.
> Pagan, whose power they dared defy,
> Condemned them for their constant tie
> To dwell in this place together forever.

They say that at the end of some years, Pagan was as
much avenged as he had hoped and that the beautiful
Imis and Philax fulfilled the prediction of the fairy of
the mountain. Indeed, they fervently kept seeking to
recover the aigrette of the lilies to destroy their
enchanted palace in the exact same way that they had
previously used the lilies to protect themselves against
the evil that had been predicted for them.

> Until that moment a fond pair had been blessed
> And cherished in their hearts love's constant fire.
> But Pagan taught them by that fatal test
> That even of bliss human hearts could tire.

Jean-Paul Bignon

Jean-Paul Bignon (1662–1743), the son of Jérome II and Suzanne Phélypeaux de Pontchartrain, chose to enter the ecclesiastical orders at an early age in order to pursue his scholarly interests. In 1684 he was accepted into the Novitiate de l'Oratoire, and in 1685 he went to a retreat at St.-Paul-aux-Bois, the diocese of Soissons, for five years in order to devote himself to a systematic study of the classics. At the beginning of 1691 he was ordained a priest and became director of all the academies in the kingdom, one of the most important educational positions in the ancient régime. In 1693 he was made abbot of St.-Quentin-en-Isle, but continued to function as the director of academies. Bignon endeavored to keep out of the quarrels between the Jansenists and Jesuits, and he gradually became one of the most influential figures in the domain of the arts and sciences during his lifetime. As a member of the Académie Française and president of the Academy of Sciences for forty years, he constantly supported the work of the most promising intellectuals in France.

In 1700 he was appointed director of the libraries and the bureau of censorship. In 1702 Bignon took over the directorship of the *Journal des scavans* (Journal of Scholars and Scientists) and reorganized it so that more intellectuals could contribute to the publication and enhance the quality of the articles. Bignon constantly sought ways to improve the conditions of scholarship in France, and after he became royal librarian in 1718 he brought about major changes in the library system, increasing the holdings and providing wide public access to the libraries. Toward the end of his life he had an expensive chateau built for himself near Melun, and he gave his retreat the name *Isle-Belle,* or Beautiful Island.

Bignon was more than a strong administrator. He was a noted public speaker, poet, and scholar. He published numerous essays and wrote an important biography entitled *Vie de François Lévesque, prêtre de l'Oratoire* (1684). Since he was most active in intellectual circles during the height of the fairy-tale vogue, he evidently decided to make a contribution to it by writing a collection of tales entitled *Les Aventures d'Abdalla, fils d'Anif* (1712–14). Bignon combined oriental motifs with French folklore to depict the exotic adventures of Abdalla, who encounters Zeineb during his travels. Each episode of the book is a tale unto itself, and Zeineb's first-person narrative is extremely important because of the role it plays in the Beauty and the Beast tradition. It is more than likely that Madame de Villeneuve knew this version, and it may have served as the basis for her tale that later influenced Madame Leprince de Beaumont.

PRINCESS ZEINEB
AND KING LEOPARD

I AM the daughter of King Batoche, who rules over the easternmost part of the Island of Gilolo. My name is Zeineb, and I have five older sisters. One day my father went hunting in the mountains, and after he had gone a long way, he eventually reached a desolate spot and was extremely surprised to find a beautiful palace that he had never seen before. Anxious to find out more about this unknown mansion, he started to approach it. Yet he froze as a terrifying voice called him by name and threatened him with immediate death unless he sent one of his daughters within three days. King Batoche raised his eyes and saw a leopard at a window. The fire emanating from the eyes of this beast terrified him. In fact, so great was my father's fright that he fled the spot with his men without daring to reply.

My sisters and I were all upset by the sadness that overcame our father, especially since it was quite visible on his face. We hugged him and urged him to tell us what was troubling his heart. After we had persisted for a long time, he finally told us.

"It's a matter of my life or yours," he said. "Ah, I'd much rather die than lose the children I so dearly love."

Tears were in his eyes as he began telling us what he had seen and how he had been threatened in such a terrible way.

"If that's the only dreadful thing that's been disturbing you, my dear father," our eldest sister said, "console yourself. I'll depart tomorrow. Perhaps this leopard won't be as merciless as you think."

The king vainly tried to oppose her plan, for she let herself be guided to the secluded palace. But when the doors opened and the leopard showed himself, my sister found him so horrible that she forgot all her good resolutions, turned around, and fled. When my four other sisters saw her return, they scolded her harshly for having so little courage, and the next day they all tried their luck together. But their courage failed them in the same way that it had failed our eldest sister. As a result, the king's life depended solely on me.

When I took my turn, I was more fearless than they. Not only did I withstand the dreadful gaze of the leopard at the window when I arrived, but I also had the courage to enter the marvelous palace with my mind firmly made up not to leave until I had completely brought everything to light. As soon as I was in the courtyard, the doors closed. A group of nymphs who were quite comely but, due to some miracle, could not talk, appeared before me and began serving me. I was led into a magnificent apartment and spent the entire day regarding the beautiful features of the palace and its gardens. My evening repast was delicious, and I went to sleep in a bed that was better than any in King Batoche's palace. But a thousand troubling things were soon to follow.

Shortly after I was in bed, I heard his steps, and it would not have taken much to have frightened me to death. He rushed into my room and made a terrible noise, brandishing teeth, claws, and tail. Then he stretched his whole body alongside me. I had left him plenty of space because, believe me, I did not occupy much myself. The beast behaved himself in an astonishingly discreet way: he did not touch me at all and left before daybreak. I would have liked to have taken advantage of this time to have slept, but my fear was much too overwhelming. The same nymphs who had served me the day before came to wake me and get me dressed. They did not neglect a thing to make me comfortable. I had a royal lunch and heard a musical concert during the afternoon. My pleasure was made complete when I observed that the leopard did not appear during the entire day. Indeed, this day set the tone for all the days that followed, but, to tell the truth, I spent many nights without daring to sleep. Finally, the discretion demonstrated by the leopard enabled me to regain my tranquillity.

Ten months went by like this, and at the end of this time, I succumbed to a curious desire that had possessed me from the start and one I had continually resisted: I wanted to know whether the leopard by day was also a leopard by night.

I rose from the bed while he slept, avoiding any contact with him. Then I tiptoed all around the room, searching for something to light it. I suspected that the beast's skin was lying on the ground. In fact, I found it and was then overcome by a mad whim—for what else could I call my behavior? I boldly tore the skin to pieces without considering what might happen. After this rash act I lay down again on my edge of the bed as if nothing had happened.

My companion got up at his usual time, and when he discovered that his skin was gone, he began to wail. I responded by coughing to make him aware that I was awake.

"It's superfluous now to continue taking precautions," the groaning man said to me sadly. "I'm a powerful king who was placed under a magic spell by a magician serving my enemies. My enchantment would have been over now, and I had decided to share my throne and my bed with you. But alas, your curiosity has set me back, and it is now as if I had never suffered anything! Why did you act against your better judgment? Common sense should have told you that you can't act recklessly in a place where you don't know the laws."

I frankly confessed my mistake and begged him to consider that girls are naturally curious. I told him he should be grateful to me for not having looked sooner for the answer to his mysterious appearance. This excuse spoiled everything, and he heaped upon me a new flood of reproaches. Finally, the enchanted king calmed down and momentarily revealed his splendid face, which radiated a sudden light. But as he felt dark forces about to act on him again, he bade farewell and taught me some words that I was to pronounce against anyone I wanted to restrain from doing something until I pronounced some other words that would free that person to continue his actions. No sooner did I learn

them than the palace disappeared along with all its
pleasant things, and I found myself alone and completely naked lying on a rock.

Tears poured from my eyes as I cursed my curiosity
and imprudence. Daylight came, and I was obliged out
of shame to look around for something to cover me. I
noticed some clothes near the spot where I was lying
and went over to pick them up. They were my own
clothes, which had been almost worn out over those ten
months by all the abuses of exposure. I put on those
sad rags as best I could and, fearing that my mistake
had caused my father's death, I thought it wiser to
leave my country and to go begging rather than to
appear before my sisters in my sorry condition. Smear-
ing my face with dirt, I summoned up my courage to
begin my wandering.

After a long and fatiguing journey I arrived at a sea-
port where an old Moslem who was heading to Borneo
to do some trading took pity on me and took me on
board his ship. We had a safe voyage and let down the
anchor in a bay of that large island, even though I was
not sure why. After descending with many other people
weary of the sea, I left their company without anyone
noticing, since I had no desire to go with their leader,
who was on his way to the coastal cities where business called him. Instead, I went into the interior of the
island, which was very populous, and in three months I
reached the pretty city of Soucad, which got its name
from the large river that crosses it.

I noticed from the very first that the embroidery
decorating the clothes of the women was extremely
coarse, and I was convinced that I was more skillful in
doing this simple work than the women of Borneo, and
that I had found a source that would provide me with
work. Once my skill became known, I soon had success beyond my greatest expectations. I rented a small
cottage and in a short time established an honest business for myself. I did not have any difficulty learning
the language because people use approximately the
same language in Soucad as they do in Gilolo. For six
or seven months I was able to work in peace and gradually regained the beauty that people had flattered me

with having—good looks that had almost entirely disappeared due to the exhaustion and misery I had suffered. I drew the attention of many people. Among
them were three of the most distinguished young men
of the city, who conspired together to discover whether
I was a cruel beauty. They agreed among themselves
that one of them, who was considered an artful
seducer, would make the first attempt. He came to my
house that very evening and began the conversation by
asking me to make an embroidered belt for him. Then
he talked about his feelings for me: no beauty intended
for easy conquest has ever heard so many professions
of friendship and favors all at once. When dinnertime
arrived, he wanted to entertain me, and though he saw I
was repulsed by the idea, he insisted, and I consented.
The meal was exquisite, and he did not forget little
sweet songs to accompany it. In fact, my lover made it
quite clear from several brazen looks that he expected
me to be most obliging to him.

Since an open window in my room made him feel
uncomfortable, he went over to shut it. While he was
closing it, however, I pronounced those powerful
words King Leopard had taught me. I put him into a
trance so that he had to keep closing and reclosing the
window. As for me, I went to bed as I ordinarily did
without any difficulties. The poor spellbound man
spent the entire night closing that window. The next
morning I released him and let him go with a good
warning to behave better in the future.

His comrades, who had been waiting impatiently for
him in a street since daybreak, ran toward him as soon
as he appeared. He cleverly led them to believe that he
had been perfectly well received and described his
good fortune to them in glowing colors that set them
afire. They drew lots to see which one would enjoy the
expected happiness next, and the day seemed long to
the one who won. However, the night was much more
tedious for him because he was obliged to wind a reel
of silk for the exact same time that the other had spent
closing the window. The third young man was tricked
just like his friends, and he had to comb my hair the
entire night because of my orders.

These young men did not have the strength to conceal their misadventures for long. All three were outraged, and their tenderness changed into obsessive hate. Therefore, they agreed to denounce me to the judges as the most despicable sorceress in the world. As a result, I was taken from my house and imprisoned. My powerful and motivated adversaries worked ferverishly at getting ready for my trial. Since I did not deny a single fact they accused me of, the affair would not have lasted four days if I had not distributed some money among several of the judges through the help of a good friend who was kind enough to do this. The decision was postponed for three whole months due in part to the money and in part to the fact that two of the other judges were appreciative of my charms. They did everything they could to save me, convinced that I would not be ungrateful after such a great service. Nevertheless, in the end my persecutors won, and I was condemned to be burned alive.

After this cruel sentence had been pronounced, I was led to the stake set up in the most beautiful square in Soucad. When I arrived there, they told me what to expect when one is to be executed in a public ceremony, and they bound me to the stake with a large chain. The people hurled insults at me: "She's a sorceress!" "She's an enemy of the human race!" They accused me of all the bad things that had happened naturally or accidentally to all those people who had bought my work. They were delighted to see the executioner advance toward the stake with a flaming torch in his hand, but this unsuspecting crowd was greatly surprised a moment later to see this same executioner become immobile and entranced. The only thing he could do was to hold his burning torch. This effect had been induced by the words that I had secretly pronounced against him. Everyone was in suspense due to this strange incident. Then their mood changed all at once, and they could not stop themselves from laughing as they watched how ridiculous a figure the executioner cut.

The three young men were present and had a large number of partisans in the crowd. They became extra-

ordinarily furious at seeing an event that reminded
them of what had happened to them. They cried out
that this was public proof of my guilt and that they
should quickly reduce to ashes a woman who even at
the point of death had abominable ties with evil spirits.
The mob was moved by these words and ran to the
nearby houses to fetch firebrands. I prepared again to
stop this riot when an uproar mixed with acclamations
caught their attention in the main street that emptied
into the square.

The King of Soucad himself had caused this pleasant
commotion. After a long absence he had wanted to surprise his people by making a sudden appearance. Since
he was greatly beloved, everyone's attention was
drawn to him and away from the stake, executioner,
victim, and judges.

The king had gotten out of his carriage and was
riding slowly on horseback in order to be better
seen. He advanced right into the middle of the square
and saw a spectacle that he found rather strange,
since it did not fit the public joy that had been aroused
by his happy return. When he turned toward the
stake, he granted me the reprieve that only he could
give and had me untied. Immediately I ran to embrace the knees of my liberator, who looked at me
very attentively. He dismounted and embraced me
with a joy that equaled the amazement of all the
spectators. I did not dare to raise my eyes, but finally,
once I glimpsed the person from whom I had received
such a surprising reprieve, I recognized King Leopard, whose image had remained deeply engraved in
my mind.

It is impossible to express the feelings of my heart,
my thoughts, and what I wanted to say. I could not
form a single coherent sentence. My gratitude and joy
took away all the words that came to my mind. The
king had me climb into his carriage without getting in
himself and conducted me to his palace in triumph.
Some days later, he married me in a solemn ceremony
and empowered me to reign in his dominions. The
first merciful act I asked him to perform was to pardon my accusers. Then I gave the judges who had let

themselves be bribed by my money the punishment
they deserved. On the other hand, those judges who
had been moved by my beauty were punished in a more
lenient way.

Jeanne-Marie
Leprince de Beaumont

Jeanne-Marie Leprince de Beaumont (1711–80) was born in Rouen and was given an excellent education. She married M. de Beaumont, a dissolute libertine, in 1743, but the marriage was annulled after only two years. In 1746 she departed for England, where she earned her living as a governess, and she often returned to France for visits. She also remarried, this time to a certain M. Pichon, and raised several children in England. At the same time she began publishing novels and stories with a strong didactic bent. Her first work was a novel entitled *Le Triomphe de la Vérité* (1748), which was published in France. It was in London, however, that she made a name for herself by publishing short stories in magazines and producing collections of anecdotes, stories, fairy tales, commentaries, and essays directed at specific social and age groups. For instance, she published a series of pedagogical works with the following titles: *Le Magasin des Enfants* (1757), *Le Magasin des Adolescents* (1760), *Le Magasin des Pauvres* (1768), *Le Mentor moderne* (1770), *Manuel de la jeunesse* (1773), and *Magasin des dévotes* (1779).

In 1762 she returned to France, where she continued her voluminous production, and retired to a country estate in Haute-Savoie in 1768. Among her major works of this period were: *Mémoires de la Baronne de Batteville* (1776), *Contes moraux* (1774), *Oeuvres mêlées* (1775). By the time of her death, she had written over seventy books.

Mme. Leprince de Beaumont's major fairy tales were all published in *Le Magasin des Enfants*, and they include: *La Belle et la Bête, Le Prince Chéri, Le Prince Désir, Fatal et Fortuné, Le Prince Charmant, La*

Veuve et les deux filles, Aurore et Aimée, Le Pêcheur et le Voyageur, Joliette, and *Bellotte et Laidronette.* Her version of *Beauty and the Beast,* which was based on Mme. de Villeneuve's longer narrative, is perhaps the most famous in the world. Her emphasis was on the proper upbringing of young girls like Beauty, and she continually stressed industriousness, self-sacrifice, modesty, and diligence in all her tales as the qualities young ladies must possess to attain happiness. She was one of the first French writers to write fairy tales explicitly for children, and one can see from the tale presented here that she keeps her language and plot simple to convey her moral messages. Though her style is limited by the lesson she wants to teach, she is careful not to destroy the magic in her tales, which triumphs despite her preaching.

BEAUTY AND
THE BEAST

ONCE upon a time there was an extremely rich merchant who had six children, three boys and three girls. Since he was a sensible man, the merchant spared no expense in educating them, hiring all kinds of tutors for their benefit.

His daughters were very pretty, but everyone admired the youngest one in particular. When she was a small child, they called her simply "Little Beauty." The name stuck and as a result it led to a great deal of envy on the part of her sisters. Not only was the youngest girl prettier, she was also better natured. The two elder girls were very arrogant because their family was rich. They pretended to be ladies and refused to receive visits of daughters who belonged to merchant families. They chose only people of quality for their companions. Every day they went to the balls, the theater, and the park, and they made fun of their younger sister, who spent most of her time reading books.

Since these girls were known to be rich, many important merchants sought their hand in marriage. But the two elder sisters maintained that they would never marry unless they found a duke, or at the very least, a count. But Beauty—as I have mentioned, this was the name of the youngest daughter—thanked all those who proposed marriage to her and said that she was too young and that she wanted to keep her father company for some years to come.

Suddenly the merchant lost his fortune, and the only property he had left was a small country house quite far from the city. With tears in his eyes he told his children that they would have to go and live in this house and work like farmers to support themselves. His two elder daughters replied that they did not want to leave the city and that they had many admirers who would be only too happy to marry them even though they no longer had a fortune. But these fine young ladies were mistaken. Their admirers no longer paid them any attention now that they were poor. Moreover, since they were so arrogant, everyone disliked them and said, "They don't deserve to be pitied. It's quite nice to see pride take a fall. Now let's see them pretend to be ladies while minding sheep in the country."

Yet at the same time people said, "As for Beauty, we're distressed by her misfortune. She's such a good girl. She has always been kind to poor people. She's so sweet and forthright!"

Several gentlemen still wanted to marry her, despite the fact that she told them that she could not abandon her poor father in his distress. She was going to follow him to the country to console him and help him in his work. Poor Beauty had been greatly upset by the loss of her fortune, but she said to herself, "My tears will not bring back my fortune. So I must try to be happy without it."

When they arrived at the country house, the merchant and his three sons began farming the land. Beauty rose at four o'clock every morning and occupied herself by cleaning the house and preparing breakfast for the family. At first she had a great deal of difficulty because she was not accustomed to working like a servant. But after two months she became stronger, and the hard work improved her health. After finishing her chores, she generally read, played the harpsichord, or sung while spinning. On the other hand, her two sisters were bored to death. They rose at ten, took walks the entire day, and entertained themselves by bemoaning the loss of their beautiful clothes and the fine company they used to have.

"Look at our little sister," they would say to each other. "She's so thick and stupid that she's quite content in this miserable situation."

The good merchant did not agree with them. He knew that Beauty was more suited to stand out in company than they were. He admired the virtues of this young girl—especially her patience, for her sisters were not content merely to let her do all the work in the house, but also insulted her every chance they had.

After living a year in this secluded spot, the merchant received a letter informing him that a ship containing his merchandise had just arrived safely. This news turned the heads of the two elder girls, for they thought that they might put an end to their boredom and would finally be able to leave the countryside. When they saw their father getting ready to depart for the city, they begged him to bring them back dresses, furs, caps, and all sorts of finery. Beauty asked for nothing because she thought that all the profit from the merchandise would not be sufficient to buy what her sisters had requested.

"Don't you want me to buy you something?" her father asked her.

"Since you are so kind to think of me," she replied, "please bring me a rose, for there are none here."

Beauty was not really anxious to have a rose, but she did not want to set an example that would disparage her sisters, who would have said that she had requested nothing to show how much better she was.

The good man set out for the city, but when he arrived, he found there was a lawsuit concerning his merchandise, and after a great deal of trouble, he began his return journey poorer than before.

He had only thirty miles to go before he would reach his house and was already looking forward to seeing his children again, but in passing through a large forest to get to his house, he got lost in a raging snowstorm. The wind was so strong that he was twice knocked from his horse. When night fell, he was convinced that he would die of hunger and cold, or else be eaten by the wolves that were howling all around him. Suddenly he saw a light at the end of a long avenue of trees. It appeared to be quite some distance away, and he began walking in that direction. Soon he realized that the light was coming from a huge palace that was totally illuminated. Thanking God for sending this help, the merchant hurried toward the castle. Imagine his surprise, though, when he found nobody in the court-yards! His horse, which had followed him, saw a large, open stable and walked inside. Upon finding hay and oats, the poor animal, who was dying of hunger, began eating with a rapacious appetite. The merchant tied the horse up in the stable and walked toward the palace without encountering a soul. When he entered a large hall, however, he discovered a good fire and a table set with food for one. Since the sleet and snow had soaked him from head to foot, he approached the fire to dry himself. "The master of this house will forgive the liberty I'm taking," he said to himself, "and I'm sure that he'll be here soon."

He waited a considerable time, but when the clock struck eleven and he still did not see anyone, he could not resist his pangs of hunger anymore. Trembling all over, he took a chicken and devoured it in two mouthfuls. As he became more hardy, he left the hall and wandered through several large, magnificently furnished apartments. Finally he found a room with a good bed, and since it was past midnight and he was tired, he decided to shut the door and go to bed. It was ten o'clock when he woke the next day, and he was greatly surprised to find clean clothes in place of his own, which had been completely muddied.

"Surely," he said to himself, "this palace belongs to some good fairy who has taken pity on my predicament."

He looked out the window and no longer saw snow but an enchanting vista of arbors of flowers. He returned to the large hall where he had dined the night before and saw a small table with a cup of chocolate on it.

"I want to thank you, madam fairy," he said aloud, "for being so kind to think of breakfast for me."

After drinking his chocolate, the good man went to look for his horse. As he passed under an arbor of roses, he remembered Beauty's request, and he plucked a rose from a branch heavy with those flowers. All of a sudden he heard a loud noise and saw a beast coming toward him. It looked so horrible that he almost fainted.

"You're very ungrateful," the beast said in a ferocious voice. "I saved your life by receiving you in my castle, and then you steal my roses, which I love more than anything else in the world. You will have to die for this mistake. I'll give you a quarter of an hour to ask for God's forgiveness."

The merchant threw himself on his knees and pleaded with clasped hands: "Pardon me, my lord. I didn't think that I'd offend you by plucking a rose. One of my daughters had asked me to bring her one."

"I'm not called 'lord' but Beast. I prefer that people speak their minds, so don't think that you can move me by flattery," replied the monster. "But are you telling me that you have daughters ...? I'll pardon you on one condition, that one of your daughters comes here voluntarily to die in your place. Don't try to reason with me. Just go. And if your daughters refuse to die for you, swear to me that you'll return within three months."

The good man did not intend to sacrifice one of his daughters to this hideous monster, but he thought, "At least I'll have the pleasure of embracing them one more time."

So he swore he would return, and the Beast told him he could leave whenever he liked. "But," he added, "I don't want you to part empty-handed. Go back to the room where you slept. There you'll find a large, empty chest. You may fill it with whatever you like, and I shall have it carried home for you."

The Beast withdrew, and the good man said to himself, "If I must die, I shall still have the consolation of leaving my children with something to sustain themselves."

He returned to the room where he had slept, and upon finding a large quantity of gold pieces, he filled the chest that the Beast had mentioned. After closing it, he went to his horse in the stable, and left the palace with a sadness that matched the joy that he had experienced upon entering it. His horse took one of the forest roads on its own, and within a few hours the good man arrived at his small house, where his children gathered around him. But instead of returning their caresses, the merchant burst into tears at the sight of them. He held the branch of roses that he had brought for Beauty, and he gave it to her, saying, "Beauty, take these roses. They will cost your poor father dearly."

Immediately thereafter he told his family about the tempestuous adventure that he had experienced. On hearing the tale, the two elder daughters uttered loud cries and berated Beauty, since she did not weep.

"See what this measly creature's arrogance has caused!" they said. "Why didn't she settle for the same gifts as ours? But no, our lady had to be different. Now she's going to be the cause of our father's death, and she doesn't even cry."

"That would be quite senseless," replied Beauty. "Why should I lament my father's death when he is not going to perish? Since the monster is willing to accept one of his daughters, I intend to offer myself to placate his fury, and I feel very fortunate to be in a position to save my father and prove my affection for him."

"No, sister," said her three brothers, "you won't die. We shall go and find this monster, and we'll die under his blows if we can't kill him."

"Don't harbor any such hopes, my children," said the merchant. "The Beast's power is so great that I don't have the slightest hope of killing him. And I'm delighted by the goodness of Beauty's heart, but I won't expose her to death. I'm old, and I don't have much longer to live. Therefore, I'll lose only a few years of my life that I won't regret losing on account of you, my dear children."

"Rest assured, Father," said Beauty, "you won't go to this palace without me. You can't prevent me from following you. Even though I'm young, I'm not so strongly tied to life, and I'd rather be devoured by this monster than to die of the grief that your loss would cause me."

Arguments were in vain: Beauty was determined to depart for this beautiful palace. And her sisters were delighted because the virtues of their younger sister had filled them with a good deal of envy. The merchant was so concerned by the torment of losing his daughter that he forgot all about the chest that he had filled with gold. But as soon as he retired to his room to sleep, he was quite astonished to find it by the side of his bed. He decided not to tell his children that he had become rich, for his daughters would want to return to the city and he was resolved to die in the country. But he confided his secret to Beauty, who informed him that several gentlemen had come during his absence and that two of them loved her sisters. She pleaded with her father to let her sisters get married, for she was of such a kind nature that she loved them and forgave with all her heart the evil they had done her.

When Beauty departed with her father, the two nasty sisters rubbed their eyes with onions to weep. But her brothers wept in truth, as did the merchant. The only one who did not cry was Beauty, because she did not want to increase their distress.

The horse took the road to the palace, and by nightfall they spotted it all alight as before. The horse was installed in the stable, and the good man entered the large hall with his daughter. There they found a table magnificently set for two people. However, the merchant did not have the heart to eat. On the other hand, Beauty forced herself to appear calm, and she sat down at the table and served him. Then she said to herself, "It's clear that the Beast is providing such a lovely feast to fatten me up before eating me."

After they had finished supper, they heard a loud roar, and the merchant tearfully said good-bye to his daughter, for he knew it was the Beast. Beauty could not help trembling at the sight of this horrible figure, but she summoned her courage. The monster asked if she had come of her own accord and, continuing to shake, she responded yes.

"You are, indeed, quite good," said the Beast, "and I am very much obliged to you. As for you, my good man, you are to depart tomorrow, and never think of returning here. Good-bye, Beauty."

"Good-bye, Beast," she responded.

Suddenly the Beast disappeared.

"Oh, my daughter!" said the merchant, embracing

Beauty. "I'm half dead with fear. Believe me, it's best if I stay."

"No, my father," Beauty said firmly. "You're to depart tomorrow morning, and you'll leave me to the mercy of Heaven. Perhaps Heaven will take pity on me."

When they went to bed, they thought they would not be able to sleep the entire night. But they were hardly in their beds before their eyes closed shut. During her sleep Beauty envisioned a lady who said to her, "Your kind heart pleases me, Beauty. The good deed you're performing to save your father's life will not go unrewarded."

When Beauty woke the next morning, she told her father about the dream, and though this consoled him somewhat, it did not prevent him from sobbing loudly when he had to tear himself away from his dear child. After he departed, Beauty sat down in the great hall and began to weep as well. Yet since she had a great deal of courage, she asked God to protect her and resolved not to grieve anymore during the short time she had to live. Convinced that the Beast was going to eat her that night, she decided to take a walk in the meantime and explore the splendid castle. She could not help but admire its beauty, and was quite surprised when she found a door on which was written: "BEAUTY'S ROOM." She opened the door quickly and was dazzled by the magnificence that radiated throughout the room. But what struck her most of all was a glass-walled bookcase, a harpsichord, and numerous books of music. "He doesn't want me to get bored," she whispered to herself. "If I'm only supposed to spend one day here, he wouldn't have made all these preparations."

This thought renewed her courage. She opened the library, chose a book, and read these words on it: "Your wish is our command. You are queen and mistress here."

"Alas!" she said with a sigh. "My only wish is to see my poor father again and to know what he's doing at this very moment."

She had said this to herself, so you can imagine her surprise when she glanced at a large mirror and saw her house, where her father was arriving with an extremely sorrowful face. Her sisters went out to meet him, and despite the grimaces they made in pretending to be distressed, the joy on their faces at the absence of their sister was visible. A moment later, everything in the mirror disappeared, and Beauty could not but think that the Beast had been most compliant and that she had nothing to fear from him.

At noon she found the table set, and during her meal she heard an excellent concert, even though she did not see a soul. That evening as she was about to sit down at the table, she heard the noise made by the Beast. She could not keep herself from trembling.

"Beauty," the monster said to her, "would you mind if I watch you dine?"

"You're the master," replied Beauty, trembling.

"No," responded the Beast. "You are the mistress here, and you only have to tell me to go if I bother you. Then I'll leave immediately. Tell me, do you find me very ugly?"

"Yes, I do," said Beauty. "I don't know how to lie. But I believe that you're very good."

"You're right," said the monster. "But besides being ugly, I'm not intelligent at all. I know quite well that I'm just a beast."

"A stupid person doesn't realize that he lacks intelligence," Beauty replied. "Fools never know what they're lacking."

"Enjoy your meal, Beauty," the monster said to her, "and try to amuse yourself in your house, for everything here is yours. I'd feel upset if you were not happy."

"You're quite kind," Beauty said. "I assure you that I am most pleased with your kind heart. When I think of that, you no longer seem ugly to me."

"Oh, yes," the Beast answered, "I have a kind heart, but I'm still a monster."

"There are many men who are more monstrous than you," Beauty said, "and I prefer you with your looks rather than those who have pleasing faces but conceal false, ungrateful, and corrupt hearts."

"If I had the intelligence," the Beast responded, "I'd make a fine compliment to thank you. But I'm so stupid that I can only say that I'm greatly obliged to you."

Beauty ate with a good appetite, for she was no longer afraid of the Beast. She nearly died of fright, though, when he asked, "Beauty, will you be my wife?"

She did not answer right away, for she feared enraging the monster by refusing him. At last, however, she said with a quaver, "No, Beast."

The poor monster meant merely to sigh, but he made such a frightful whistle that it echoed through the entire palace. Beauty soon regained her composure, for the Beast said to her in a sad voice, "Farewell, then, Beauty."

He left the room, turning from time to time to look at her as he went. When Beauty was alone, she felt a great deal of compassion for the Beast. "It's quite a shame," she said, "that he's so ugly, for he's so good."

Three months Beauty spent in great tranquillity. Every evening at supper the Beast paid her a visit and entertained her in conversation with plain good sense, but not what the world calls wit. Every day Beauty discovered new qualities in the monster. She became so accustomed to seeing him that she adjusted to his ugliness, and far from dreading the moment of his visit, she often looked at her watch to see if it was nine o'clock yet, for the Beast never failed to appear at that hour.

Only one thing troubled Beauty. Before she went to bed every night, the Beast would ask her if she would be his wife, and he seemed deeply wounded when she refused.

"You're making me uncomfortable, Beast," she said one day. "I'd like to say I'll marry you, but I'm too frank to allow you to believe that this could ever happen. I'll always be your friend. Try to be content with that."

"I'll have to," responded the Beast. "I am honest with myself, and I know I'm quite horrid-looking. But I love you very much. However, I'm happy enough with the knowledge that you want to stay here. Promise me that you'll never leave me."

Beauty blushed at these words, for she had seen in

her mirror that her father was sick with remorse for
having lost her, and she wished to see him again.

"I could easily promise never to leave you," she
said. "But I have such a desire to see my father again
that I would die of grief if you were to refuse me this
request."

"I'd rather die myself than to distress you," the monster said. "I'll send you to your father's home. You will
stay with him, and your poor beast will die of grief."

"No," Beauty said. "I love you too much to want to
cause your death. I promise to return in a week's time.
You've shown me that my sisters are married and my
brothers have left home to join the army. Just let me
stay a week with my father since he's all alone."

"You will be there tomorrow morning," the Beast
said. "But remember your promise. You only have to
place your ring on the table before going to bed if you
want to return. Farewell, Beauty."

As was his custom, the Beast sighed when he said
these words, and Beauty went to bed very sad at having
troubled him. When she awoke the next morning, she
found herself in her father's house, and when she rang
a bell at her bedside, it was answered by a servant who
uttered a great cry upon seeing her. Her good father
came running when he heard the noise and almost died
of joy at seeing his dear daughter again. They kept
hugging each other for more than a quarter of an hour.
After their excitement subsided, Beauty recalled that
she did not have any clothes to wear. But the servant
told her that he had just found a chest in the next room,
and it was full of dresses trimmed with gold and diamonds. Beauty thanked the good Beast for looking
after her. She took the least sumptuous of the dresses
and told the servant to lock up the others, for she
wanted to send them as gifts to her sisters. But no
sooner had she spoken those words than the chest disappeared. Her father remarked, "The Beast probably
wants you to keep them for yourself." Within seconds
the dresses and the chests came back again.

As Beauty proceeded to get dressed, a message
was sent to inform her sisters of her arrival, and they
came running with their husbands. Both sisters were

what society extols is naturally more monstrous

exceedingly unhappy. The oldest had married a young gentleman who was remarkably handsome, but was so enamored of his own looks that he occupied himself with nothing but his appearance from morning until night and despised his wife's beauty. The second sister had married a man who was very intelligent, but he used his wit only to enrage everyone, first and foremost his wife. The sisters almost died of grief when they saw Beauty dressed like a princess and more beautiful than daylight. It was in vain that she hugged them, for nothing could stifle their envy, which increased when she told them how happy she was.

The two envious sisters descended into the garden to vent their feelings in tears. "Why is this little prig happier than we are?" they asked each other. "Aren't we just as pleasing as she?"

"Sister," said the oldest, "I've just had an idea. Let's try to keep her here more than a week. That stupid beast will become enraged when he finds out that she's broken her word, and perhaps he'll devour her."

"Right you are, sister," responded the other. "But we must show her a great deal of affection to succeed."

Having made this decision, they returned to the house and showed Beauty so much attention that she wept with joy. Once the week had passed, the two sisters tore their hair and seemed so distressed by her departure that she promised to remain another week. Even so, Beauty reproached herself for the grief she was causing her poor Beast, whom she loved with all her heart. In addition, she missed not being able to see him any longer. On the tenth night she spent in her father's house, she dreamt that she was in the palace garden and saw the Beast lying on the grass nearly dead and reprimanding her for her ingratitude. Beauty woke with a start and burst into tears.

"Aren't I very wicked for causing grief to a beast who's gone out of his way to please me?" she said. "Is it his fault that he's so ugly and has so little intelligence? He's so kind, and that's worth more than anything else. Why haven't I wanted to marry him? I'm more happy with him than my sisters are with their

[handwritten: love is not passionate is based on high regard marriage of excellent character]

husbands. It is neither handsome looks nor intelligence that makes a woman happy. It is good character, virtue, and kindness, and the Beast has all these good qualities. It's clear that I don't love him, but I have respect, friendship, and gratitude for him. So there's no reason to make him miserable, and if I'm ungrateful, I'll reproach myself for the rest of my life."

With these words Beauty placed her ring on the table and lay down again. No sooner did her head hit the pillow than she fell asleep, and when she woke the next morning, she saw with joy that she was in the Beast's palace. She put on her most magnificent dress to please him and spent a boring day waiting for the evening to arrive. But the clock struck nine, and Beast did not appear.

Now Beauty feared that she had caused his death. She ran throughout the palace, sobbing loudly. After searching everywhere, she recalled her dream and ran into the garden toward the canal, where she had seen him in her sleep. There she found the poor Beast stretched out unconscious. She thought he was dead. Without concern for his horrifying looks, she threw herself on his body and felt his heart still beating. So she fetched some water from the canal and threw it on his face.

Beast opened his eyes and said, "You forgot your promise, Beauty. The grief I felt upon having lost you made me decide to fast to death. But I shall die content since I have the pleasure of seeing you one more time."

"No, my dear Beast, you shall not die," said Beauty. "You will live to become my husband. I give you my hand and swear that I belong only to you from this moment on. Alas! I thought that I only felt friendship for you, but the torment I am feeling makes me realize that I cannot live without you."

Beauty had scarcely uttered these words when the castle radiated with light. Fireworks and music announced a feast. These attractions did not hold her attention, though. She returned her gaze to her dear Beast, whose dangerous condition made her tremble. How great was her surprise when she discovered that the Beast had disappeared, and at her feet was a prince more handsome than Eros himself, who thanked her for having put an end to his enchantment. Although she should have been only concerned about the prince, she could not refrain from asking what had happened to the Beast.

"You're looking at him right at your feet," the prince said. "A wicked fairy condemned me to remain in this form until a beautiful girl consented to marry me, and she prohibited me from revealing my intelligence. You were the only person in the world kind enough to allow the goodness of my character to touch you. In offering you my crown, I'm only discharging the debt I owe you."

Beauty was most pleasantly surprised and assisted the handsome prince in rising by offering her hand. Together they went to the castle, where Beauty was overwhelmed by joy in finding her father and entire family in the hall, for the beautiful lady who had appeared to her in her dream had transported them to the castle.

"Beauty," said this lady, who was a grand fairy, "come and receive the reward for your good choice. You've preferred virtue over beauty and wit, and you deserve to find these qualities combined in one and the same person. You're going to become a great queen, and I hope that a throne will not destroy your virtuous qualities. As for you, my young ladies," the fairy said to Beauty's two sisters, "I know your hearts and all the malace they contain. You shall become statues while retaining your ability to think beneath the stone that encompasses you. You will stand at the portal of your sister's palace, and I can think of no better punishment to impose on you than to witness her happiness. I'll allow you to return to your original shape only when you recognize your faults, but I fear that you'll remain statues forever. Pride, anger, gluttony, and laziness can all be corrected, but some sort of miracle is needed to convert a wicked and envious heart."

The fairy waved her wand and all at once transported everyone in the hall to the prince's realm, where his subjects rejoiced upon seeing him again. Then he married Beauty, who lived with him a long time in perfect happiness because their relationship was founded on virtue.

inner qualities are impt
  not beauty
each giving to other
development of one
   affects/ influences
(development of other
↳ Cupid + Psyche
   Singing Springing Lark
   B & B
actions of one influences
   ↳ actions of other

Mlle. de Lubert

Mademoiselle de Lubert (c.1710–c.1779) was the daughter of the president of Parlement in Paris. Not much is known about her life except that she rejected marriage in order to dedicate herself to her writing. She was able to do this because she was independently wealthy. As her career advanced, she developed good relations with Fontenelle, Voltaire, and La Condamine, who praised her works.

Mlle. de Lubert wrote poetry and prose and had a special talent for combining motifs from ancient romances with traditional folk tales to produce long fairy tales that are extraordinarily imaginative and complex. Her major works include: *Les Princes des Autruches* (1743), *Le Prince Glacé et la Princesse Etincelante* (1743), *La Princesse Camion* (1743), *La Princesse Couleur de Rose et le Prince Céladon* (1743), *La Veillée galante* (1747), *Histoire de la princesse Foirette, et d'autres contes* (1750), *Blancherose* (1751), *Mourat et Turquia* (1752), and *Léonille* (1755).

Writing in the tradition of Mme. d'Aulnoy, Mlle. de Lubert had a penchant for the grotesque and bizarre mixed with sadism. Monsters and tortures abound in her works, and there is an obvious influence of the theater, ballet, and opera on them. Mlle. de Lubert sought to transform the scenes in her works into theatrical spectacles. In turn, these unusual scenes created an atmosphere that allowed her to treat such serious themes as forced marriages, fidelity, and authority with a great deal of freedom. In *Princess Camion* are characters and incidents that prefigure the grotesque in Kafka, and although they are also somewhat ludicrous,

Mlle. Lubert's fairy tales may be interpreted as ironical commentaries about courtly manners that seemed absurd to her. In this respect, we must consider her perspective as that of a single woman opposed to marriage and traditional social norms, who saw her tales as a subversive means to make her critical private views extraordinarily public.

THE PRINCESS CAMION

ONCE upon a time there was a king and queen who placed all their hopes for a successor in their only son, for the queen did not bear any other children. By the time Prince Zirphil was fourteen, he was marvelously handsome and learned everything taught him with ease. The king and queen were tremendously fond of him, and their subjects adored him, for whereas he was friendly to everyone, he knew how to make distinctions among those who approached him. Since he was an only son, the king and queen decided he should marry as soon as possible in order to secure the succession to the crown.

Therefore, they had their men travel by foot and on horseback to look for a princess worthy of the heir apparent, but they failed to find anyone suitable. At last, after the long, careful search, the queen was informed that a veiled lady requested a private audience regarding an important affair. The queen immediately ascended her throne in the audience chamber and ordered the lady to be admitted. The lady approached without removing her white crepe veil, which hung all the way to the ground. Arriving at the foot of the throne, she said, "Queen, I'm astonished that you thought of marrying your son without consulting me. I'm the fairy Marmotte, and my name is sufficiently well-known to have reached your ears."

"Ah, madam," the queen said, quickly descending her throne and embracing the fairy, "I'm sure you'll pardon my fault when I tell you that people related stories to me about your wonders as though they were nursery tales. But now that you've graced this palace by coming here, I no longer doubt your power. I beg you, do me the honor of giving me your advice."

"That's not a sufficient answer for a fairy," Marmotte replied. "Such an excuse might perhaps satisfy a common person, but I'm mortally offended, and to begin your punishment, I command you to have Zirphil marry the person I've brought with me."

Upon saying these words, she felt around in her pocket and took out a toothpick case. When she opened it, out came a little ivory doll, so pretty and well made that the queen could not help admiring it despite her unease.

"This is my goddaughter," the fairy said, "and I had always destined her for Zirphil."

The queen soaked herself in her tears. She implored Marmotte in the most touching terms not to expose her to the ridicule of her people, who would laugh at her if she announced such a marriage.

"Laugh, will they, madam?" the fairy exclaimed. "Indeed, we shall see if they have reason to laugh! We shall see if they laugh at my goddaughter, and if your son doesn't adore her. I can tell you that she deserves to be adored. It's true that she's tiny, but she has more sense than your entire kingdom put together. When you hear her speak, you'll be surprised yourself—for she can talk, I promise you. Now, then, little Princess Camion," she said to the doll, "speak a little to your mother-in-law, and show her what you can do."

Then the pretty Camion jumped on the queen's fur tippet and paid her a little compliment so tender and sensitive that her majesty stopped crying and gave the Princess Camion a hearty kiss.

"Here, Queen, is my toothpick case," the fairy said. "Put your daughter-in-law in it. I want your son to become acquainted with her before marrying her. I don't think it will take long. Your obedience may soften my anger, but if you act contrary to my orders, you, your husband, your son, and your kingdom will all feel the effect of my wrath. Above all, take care to put her back into her case early in the evening because it's important that she doesn't stay out late."

As she finished saying this, the fairy raised her veil, and the queen fainted from fright when she saw an actual marmot—black, sleek, and as large as a human

being. Her attendants rushed to her assistance, and
when she recovered, she saw nothing but the case that
Marmotte had left behind her.

Putting her to bed, they went to inform the king
about the accident. He arrived very anxious, and the
queen sent everyone away. In a flood of tears she told
the king about what had just happened. At first the king
did not believe it, not until he saw the doll that the
queen drew from the case.

"Heavens!" he cried, and after reflecting a moment,
he asked, "Why is it that kings are exposed to such
great misfortunes? Ah, we're placed above other men
only to feel the cares and sorrows that are part of our
existence more acutely."

"And in order to set greater examples of fortitude,
sire," added the doll in a small, sweet distinct voice.

"My dear Camion," the queen said, "you speak like
an oracle."

After the three of them had conversed for an hour,
they decided not to reveal the impending marriage until
Zirphil, who had gone hunting for three days, returned
and agreed to obey the fairy's command. In the interim
the queen and the king withdrew to the privacy of their
rooms in order to talk to little Camion. Since she had a
highly cultivated intellect, she spoke well and with an
unusual turn of thought that was very pleasing.
Although she was vivacious, her eyes had a fixed
expression that was not very pleasant. Moreover, it disturbed the queen because she had begun to love
Camion and feared the prince might take a dislike
toward her.

More than a month passed since Marmotte had
appeared, but the queen still had not dared to show Zirphil his intended. One day he entered the room while
she was in bed. "Madam," he said, "the most unusual
thing happened to me some days ago while I was
hunting. I had wanted to keep it from you, but it's
come to seem so extraordinary that I must tell you
about it no matter what.

"I had followed a wild boar and chased it into the
middle of the forest without observing that I was alone.
When I saw him jump into a great hole that opened up

in the ground, my horse plunged in after it, and I continued falling for half an hour. At last I found myself at the bottom of this hole without having hurt myself. Instead of encountering the boar, which, I confess, I was afraid of facing, I saw a very ugly woman who asked me to dismount and follow her. I didn't hesitate giving her my hand, and she opened a small door that had previously been hidden from view. I entered with her into a salon of green marble, where there was a golden bathtub covered with a curtain of very rich material. The curtain rose, and I saw a person of such marvelous beauty in the tub that I thought I would faint. 'Prince Zirphil,' said the bathing lady, 'the fairy Marmotte has enchanted me, and it's only through your aid that I can be released.'

" 'Speak, madam,' I said to her. 'What must I do to help you?'

" 'You must either marry me this instant or skin me alive.'

"I was just as surprised by the first alternative as I was alarmed by the second. She read the embarrassment in my eyes and said, 'Don't think I'm jesting, or that I'm proposing something you may regret. No, Zirphil, dismiss your fears. I'm an unfortunate princess who's detested by a fairy. She's made me half woman, half whale because I wouldn't marry her nephew, the King of the Whiting—he's frightful and even more wicked than he is hideous. She's condemned me to remain in my present state until a prince named Zirphil fulfills one of the two conditions that I've just proposed. To expedite this matter, I had my maid of honor take the form of a wild boar, and it was she who led you to this spot, where you'll remain until you fulfill my desire in one way or the other. I'm not mistress here, and Citronette, who you see with me, will tell you that this is the only way it can be.'

"Imagine, madam," the prince said to the queen, who was listening attentively, "what a state I was in when I heard these words! Although the whale-princess's face was exceedingly pleasing and her charms and misfortunes made her extremely intriguing, the fact that she was half fish horrified me, and the idea of skinning her

alive threw me into utter despair. 'But, madam,' I said
to her at length (for my silence was as stupid as it was
insulting), 'isn't there a third way?' No sooner had I
uttered those unfortunate words than the whale-
princess and her attendant uttered shrieks and lamentations that were enough to pierce the vaulted roof of the
salon. 'Ungrateful wretch! Cruel tiger, and everything
that is most ferocious and inhuman!' the whale-
princess exclaimed. 'Do you want to condemn me to
the torture of seeing you perish as well? If you don't
grant my request, the fairy has assured me you'll die,
and I'll remain a whale my entire life.'

"Her reproaches pierced my heart. She raised her
beautiful arms out of the water and joined her
charming hands together to implore me to decide
quickly. Citronette fell at my feet and embraced my
knees, screaming loud enough to deafen me. 'But how
can I marry you?' I asked. 'What sort of ceremony
could be performed?' 'Skin me' she said tenderly, 'and
don't marry me. I prefer that.'

" 'Skin her!' screamed the other. 'You have nothing
to fear.'

"I was in an indescribable state of confusion, and
while I was trying to make up my mind, their shrieks
and tears increased until I had no idea what would
become of me. After a thousand and one struggles, I
cast my eyes once more on the beautiful whale. I confess, I found an inexpressible charm in her features.
Throwing myself on my knees close to the tub, I took
her hand. 'No, divine princess,' I said to her. 'I won't
skin you. I'd prefer to marry you!'

"As I said these words, joy lit the princess's countenance, but a modest joy, for she blushed and lowered
her beautiful eyes. 'I'll never forget the favor you're
doing for me,' she said. 'I'm so overwhelmed with
gratitude that you can demand anything from me after
this generous act.'

" 'Don't waste time,' the insufferable Citronette
said. 'Tell him quickly what he must do.'

" 'It's sufficient,' said the whale princess blushing
again, 'that you give me your ring, and that you take

mine. Here's my hand. Receive it as a pledge of my faith.'

"No sooner did I perform this tender exchange and kiss the beautiful hand she held out to me than I found myself on my horse again in the middle of the forest. After calling my attendants, they came to me, and I returned home unable to say a word because I was so completely astounded. Since then I've been transported every night, without knowing how, into the beautiful green salon, where I spend the night near an invisible person. She speaks to me and tells me that the time hasn't come yet for me to know who she is."

"Ah, my son," the queen interrupted, "is it really true that you're married to her?"

"I am, madam," the prince replied. "Yet even though I love my wife enormously, I would have given her up if I could have escaped the salon without resorting to the marriage."

Upon saying these words, a little voice that came from the queen's purse said, "Prince Zirphil, you should have flayed her. Your pity may perhaps be fatal to you."

Surprised by this voice, the prince was speechless. The queen vainly tried to conceal the cause of his astonishment from him, but he quickly searched the purse hanging on the armchair near the bed and drew out the toothpick case, which the queen took from his hand and opened. Princess Camion immediately emerged, and the dumbfounded prince threw himself onto his knees by the queen's bedside to inspect her more closely.

"I swear, madam," he cried, "this is my dear whale in miniature! Is this some jest? Did you only want to frighten me by allowing me to believe so long that you wouldn't approve of my marriage?"

"No, my son," the queen replied. "My grief is real, and you've exposed us to the most cruel misfortunes by marrying that whale. In fact, you were promised to the Princess Camion, whom you see in my hands."

Then she related to him what had happened between her and the fairy Marmotte. The prince did not interrupt because he was so astonished that she and his

father had agreed to a proposal that was so patently
ridiculous.

"Heaven forbid, madam," he said when the queen
had finished, "that I should ever oppose your majesty's
plans, or that I should act contrary to the wishes of my
father, even when he commands me to do something
impossible as this appears to be. But if I had consented,
could I really have fallen in love with this pretty
princess? Would your subjects ever have—"

"Time is a great teacher, Prince Zirphil," Camion
interrupted. "But what is done is done. You can't
marry me now, and my godmother is a person who
won't easily tolerate anyone breaking his word to her.
Tiny as I am, I feel the unpleasantness of this predicament as acutely as the largest woman would. But since
you're not so much to blame, except for having been a
mite too hasty, I may be able to persuade the fairy to
mitigate the punishment."

After saying these words, Camion fell silent,
exhausted from having said so much.

"My darling," the queen said, "I implore you to get
some rest. I fear you might become ill, and then you'll
be in no condition to speak to the fairy when she comes
to torment us. You're our only hope, and no matter
how she may punish us, I won't feel it so deeply if
Marmotte doesn't take you from us."

Princess Camion felt her little heart beat at these
words. Since she was quite exhausted, however, she
could only kiss her hand and let some tiny tears drop
on it. Moved by this incident, Zirphil begged Camion
to permit him to kiss her hand in turn. She gave it to
him with much grace and dignity and then reentered
her case. After this tender scene the queen rose in order
to tell the king what had happened and to take every
sensible precaution against the fairy's anger.

In spite of a double guard in front of Zirphil's apartment, he was carried off at midnight and found himself
as usual in the company of his invisible wife. But
instead of hearing the sweet, touching things she usually said to him, she wept and refused to speak at all.

"What have I done?" he asked after he tired of
asking her to confide in him. "You weep, dear princess,

when you ought to console me for all the danger I've incurred due to my tender feelings for you."

"I know everything," the princess said, her voice racked by sobs. "I know all the misery that may happen to me. But you, ungrateful man, you're the one I have most to complain about!"

"Oh, heavens!" Zirphil cried. "With what do you reproach me?"

"The love Camion has for you and the tenderness with which you kissed her hand."

"The tenderness!" the prince replied quickly. "You know too little about it if you can accuse me so lightly. Besides, even if Camion could love me—which is impossible, since she only saw me for a moment—how can you worry when you've had proofs of my commitment to you? I should accuse you of injustice. If I looked at her with any attention, it was because her features reminded me of yours, and being deprived of the pleasure of beholding you, anyone who resembles you gives me the greatest satisfaction. Show yourself to me again, my dear princess, and I'll never look at another woman."

The invisible lady appeared to be consoled by these words, and she approached the prince. "Pardon my spate of jealousy," she said. "I have too much reason to fear they'll take me from you not to feel troubled by an incident that seemed to announce the beginning of that separation."

"But," the prince said, "can't I know why you're no longer permitted to show yourself? If I've rescued you from Marmotte's tyranny, how can it be that you can be subjected to it again?"

"Alas!" the invisible princess said. "If you had decided to flay me, we would have been very happy. But you were so horrified by that proposal that I didn't dare push you further."

"Pray, how did Camion chance to learn about this adventure?" the prince interrupted. "She told me nearly the exact same thing."

No sooner did he finish saying these words than the princess uttered a frightful shriek. Surprised, the prince rose hastily. His alarm was enormous when he saw the

hideous Marmotte in the middle of the room. She held
the beautiful princess, who was now neither half whale
nor invisible, by the hair. He was about to grab his
sword when the princess tearfully begged him to
temper his anger because it would be to no avail
against the fairy's power. The horrible Marmotte was
grinding her teeth and spewed a blue flame that
scorched his beard.

"Prince Zirphil," she said to him, "a fairy protects
you and prevents me from exterminating you, your
father, your mother, and your kin. But since you've
married without consulting me, you'll at least suffer in
regard to everything that's dear to you. Neither your
torment nor that of your princess will ever end until
you've obeyed my commands."

When she finished speaking, the fairy, princess,
salon, and palace all disappeared together, and he
found himself in his own apartment in his nightdress
and with his sword in his hand. So astonished and infuriated was he that he did not feel the severity of the
cold, though it was the middle of winter. The cries he
made caused his guards to enter the room, and they
begged him to go to bed or to allow them to dress him.
Deciding to get dressed, he went to the queen's
chamber, who, for her part, had spent the night in the
cruelest state of anxiety. She had been unable to sleep,
and in order to induce slumber she had wanted to talk
over her despair with tiny Camion. When she had
looked for her toothpick case, though, Camion had disappeared. Afraid she might have lost her in the garden,
the queen got up, and after ordering torches to be lit,
she searched for her without success. Camion had vanished. Therefore, the queen retired to bed again in an
alarming state of sorrow. She was giving fresh vent to
her grief as her son entered, but he was so distressed
himself that he did not notice her tears. Yet she saw
how disturbed he was and exclaimed, "Ah! No doubt
you've come to bring some dreadful tidings to me!"

"Yes, madam," the prince replied. "I've come to tell
you that I'll die if I don't find my princess."

"What?" the queen cried out. "Do you already love
that unfortunate princess, my dear son?"

"Do you mean your Camion?" the prince asked. "Madam, how can you suspect me of such a thing? I'm speaking of my dear whale-princess. She's been torn away from me. It's for her alone that I live, and the cruel Marmotte has carried her away!"

"Ah, my son," the queen said, "I'm far more unhappy than you. They may have taken away your princess, but they've also robbed me of my Camion! She's been missing from her case since last night!"

Then they told each other their respective adventures and wept together over their common misfortunes. The king was informed about the sorrow of the queen and the grief of his son. He entered the apartment in which this tragic scene was taking place, and since he was an extremely clever man, it occurred to him immediately to post a large reward for finding Camion. Everybody agreed that this was a capital idea, and even the queen, in spite of her great grief, confessed that only an extraordinary mind could have thought of such a novel expedient. The handbills were printed and distributed, and the queen became rather calm in the hope of soon hearing some tidings of her little princess. As for Zirphil, Camion's disappearance interested him no more than her presence had. He decided to seek out a fairy about whom he had heard, and after receiving the permission of the king and queen, he departed with a single equerry to accompany him.

A great distance separated his country and that inhabited by the fairy, but neither time nor obstacles checked the ardor of young Zirphil. Through countless countries and kingdoms he passed. Nothing in particular happened to him because he was not looking for any adventures. Since he was as handsome as Cupid and brave as his sword, he could have had plenty of adventures if he had sought them.

After traveling for a year, he arrived at the beginning of the desert in which the fairy had her abode. He dismounted from his horse and left his equerry in a cottage with orders to wait for him there. Into the desert, which was frightful due to its desolation, he entered. Only screech owls inhabited it, but their cries did not alarm the valiant spirit of our prince.

One evening he saw a light at a distance, and this made him think, I must be approaching the famous grotto. Indeed, who but a fairy could live in such a horrible desert? He walked all night long, and finally at daybreak he discovered the grotto, but a lake of fire separated him from it, and all his valor could not protect him from the flames that spread left and right. He searched around for a long time to see what he could do, and his courage nearly failed him when he found not even a bridge.

Despair proved his best friend, for in a frenzy of love and anguish he decided, "I'll end my days in the lake if I cannot cross it." No sooner did he make this strange resolution than he threw himself bodily into the flames. From the first he felt a gentle warmth that hardly inconvenienced him, and he swam to the other side without the least trouble. As soon as he got there, a young and beautiful salamander emerged from the lake and said, "Prince Zirphil, if your love is as great as your courage, you may hope for everything from the fairy Lumineuse. She favors you, but she wants to test you."

Zirphil made a profound bow to the salamander in acknowledgment, for she plunged again into the flames before he had time to speak. He continued on his way, and after a while he arrived at the foot of an enormous rock that glowed so radiantly that it appeared to be on fire. It was such a large carbuncle that the fairy was lodged inside in a very comfortable manner. As soon as the prince approached, Lumineuse emerged from the rock, and he prostrated himself before her. Then she raised him and asked him to enter.

"Prince Zirphil," she said, "a power equal to mine has neutralized the benefits I bestowed on you at birth, but since I am very concerned for your future, I'll do the best I can for you. Indeed, you'll need as much patience as courage to foil the wickedness of Marmotte. I can tell you nothing more."

"At least, madam," the prince replied, "do me the favor of informing me if my beautiful princess is unhappy, and if I may hope to see her again soon."

"She's not unhappy," the fairy responded. "But you

won't be able to see her until you've pounded her in the mortar of the King of Whiting."

"Oh, heavens!" the prince cried. "Is she in his power? Now I'll not only have to dread the consequences of his fury, but also the even greater horror of pounding her with my own hands!"

"Summon your courage," the fairy replied. "Don't hesitate to obey. Your entire happiness, and your wife's as well, depend on it."

"But she'll die if I pound her," the prince said, "and I'd rather die myself."

"Be off," the fairy said, "and don't argue! Each moment you lose adds to Marmotte's fury. Go and look for the King of the Whiting. Tell him you're the page I promised to send him, and rely on my protection."

Then she took a map and pointed on the road that he had to take to reach the dominions of the King of Whiting. Before she took leave of him, she informed him that the ring that the princess had given him would show him what he should do whenever the king commanded him to perform a difficult task. He departed, and after traveling some days, he arrived in a meadow that stretched down to the seashore, where a small sailing vessel made of mother-of-pearl and gold was moored. Looking at his ruby, he saw himself in it going on board the vessel. Therefore, he embarked and cast off, whereupon the wind took the boat out to sea. He had been sailing for several hours when the vessel finally docked at the foot of a crystal castle built upon wooden piles. He jumped ashore and entered a courtyard that led to a magnificent vestibule and countless apartments whose walls were remarkably cut from rock crystal, producing the most beautiful effect in the world. The castle appeared to be inhabited only by people with heads of all sorts of fish. Convinced this was the dwelling of the King of Whiting, he shuddered with rage. However, he restrained himself so he could ask a turbot, who had the manner of a captain of the guard, how he could manage to see the King of Whiting. The man-turbot made a grave signal for him to advance, and he entered the guard chamber, where

he saw a thousand armed men with pike heads formed
in rows through which he was to pass.

Making his way through this infinite crowd of fish-
men, he came to the throne room. There was not much
noise, for the courtiers could not speak since the
greater number of them had whiting's heads. He saw
several who appeared to be of a higher rank than the
rest due to the air they assumed with the crowd surrounding them. Once he arrived at the king's room, he
saw the council, composed of twelve men who had
shark heads, emerge. After a while the king himself
appeared. He had a whiting's head like many of the
others, but he could speak. He had fins on his shoulders, and from his waist down he was a veritable
whiting. He wore only an extremely radiant scarf made
of the skin of goldfish and a helmet in the form of a
crown, from which rose a codfish's tail as a plume.
Four whiting carried him in a bowl of Japanese porcelain as large as a bathful of sea water. His greatest
pride consisted in having it filled twice a day by the
dukes and peers of his kingdom, and this position was
extremely sought after.

Very large, the King of Whiting had more the air of
a monster than of anything else. After he had spoken to
several petitioners, he noticed the prince. "Who are
you, my friend?" he asked. "By what chance do I see a
man here?"

"My lord," Zirphil said, "I'm the page the fairy
Lumineuse promised you."

"I know what she's up to," the king laughed,
showing teeth like those of a saw. "Lead him into my
seraglio, and let him teach my crayfish to talk."

Immediately a squad of whiting surrounded him and
led him away. As he passed through the apartments
again, all the fish, even those in highest favor, professed a great deal of friendship for him by various
signs. The whiting led him through a delightful garden
at the end of which was a charming pavilion built
entirely of mother-of-pearl and ornamented with great
branches of coral. The favorite whiting brought him
into a similarly decorated apartment that had windows
overlooking a magnificent stretch of water. They indi-

cated that this was to be his residence, and after showing him a little room at one corner of the salon, which he understood was to be his bedroom, they retired, and he remained alone, astonished to find himself something like a prisoner in the palace of his rival.

He was contemplating his situation when the doors of his room opened. Ten or twelve thousand crayfish, who were conducted by one larger than the rest, entered and placed themselves in straight lines that nearly filled the apartment. The one marching at their head mounted a table near him and said, "Prince, I know you, and you owe much to my care, but since it is rare to find gratitude in men, I won't tell you what I've done for you, for fear you'd destroy the sentiments you've aroused in me. Therefore, let me merely inform you that these are the crayfish of the King of Whiting. They alone speak in this empire, and you've been chosen to teach them the language of refinement, the customs of the world, and the means of pleasing their sovereign. You'll find them intelligent, but you must choose ten every morning to pound in the king's mortar to make his broth."

Once this crayfish stopped speaking, the prince replied, "I had no idea, madam, that you had taken an interest in my affairs. The gratitude I already feel toward you should induce you to abandon the bad opinion you've developed toward men in general, for on the bare assurance you've given me of your friendship, I feel deeply obligated to you. But what I am anxious to learn is how I should go about reasoning with the beings whose education I am in charge of. If I could be sure that they had as much intelligence as you, I'd be honored to do this work. But if I find them difficult to teach, I'll have less courage to punish them for faults for which they are not responsible. And if I live with them, how can I have the heart to have them tortured?"

"You are obstinate and a great talker," the crayfish interrupted. "But we know exactly how to take care of you." Upon saying this, she rose from the table, and after jumping to the ground, she took her real form of Marmotte (for she was that wicked fairy).

"Oh heavens!" the prince cried. "So this is the person who boasts that she's interested in my affairs—she who's done nothing but make me miserable! Ah, Lumineuse, you've abandoned me!"

No sooner had he finished uttering those words than the marmot jumped through the window into the reservoir and disappeared, leaving him alone with twelve thousand crayfish. After reflecting somewhat on how he should proceed to educate them, during which time they waited in complete silence, it occurred to him that he might find his beautiful and unfortunate princess among them. "Hideous Marmotte has ordered me to pound ten of them every morning. And why should I be chosen to pound ten of them every morning if not to drive me mad? Never mind, let's look for her. Let's at least try to recognize her even if I die of grief before her eyes." Then he asked the crayfish if they would kindly permit him to search for one of his acquaintances among them.

"We know nothing about it, my lord," offered one of them. "But you can make whatever inquiry you please up to the time we must return to the reservoir, for we spend every night there."

Zirphil began his inspection, and the more he looked, the less he discovered, but he surmised from the few words that he drew from those he interrogated that they were all princesses transformed by Marmotte's wickedness. This caused him inconsolable grief because he had to choose ten for the king's broth.

When evening came, the crayfish repeated that they had to retire to the reservoir. Not without pain did he relinquish his search for the sweet princess. He had been able to interrogate only a hundred and fifty crayfish during the entire day, but since he was certain that at least she was not among them, he decided to take ten from that number. No sooner did he choose them than he proceeded to carry them to the king's offices. Suddenly he heard peals of laughter from the victims he was about to crush and stopped dead, so surprised that he could not speak. As he continued walking, he interrupted them to inquire what they found so amusing under their present circumstances. They renewed their

loud laughter so heartily that he could not help partici-
pating in their mirth in spite of himself. They wanted to
speak, but could not do so because they were laughing
so hard. They could only utter, "Oh, I can't say any
more!" "Oh, I'll die from it!" "No, there's nothing in
the world so amusing!" And then they roared again.

At last he reached the palace with them all laughing
together, and after he showed them to a pike-headed
man who seemed to be the head cook, a mortar of
green porphyry ornamented with gold was placed
before him. Into this he put his ten crayfish, and prepared to pound them. Just then the bottom of the
mortar opened and emitted a radiant flame that dazzled
the prince. Then it closed again and appeared perfectly
empty: the crayfish had vanished. This simultaneously
astonished and gratified him because he had been loath
to pound such merry creatures. On the other hand, the
man-pike seemed sadly distressed by this incident and
wept bitterly. The prince was just as much surprised by
this as he was by the laughter of the crayfish. However,
he could not determine the reason for this, since the
pike-head could not talk.

He returned to his pretty rooms and was disturbed to
find the crayfish had already gone back to the reservoir. The next morning they reentered without Marmotte, and he looked for his princess. Since he was still
not able to discover her, he again chose ten of the
youngest crayfish for pounding. Then the same thing
occurred—they laughed, and the man-pike wept when
they disappeared in the flame. For three months this
extraordinary scene was repeated every day. He heard
nothing from the King of Whiting, and he was uneasy
only because he had not discovered his beautiful
princess.

One evening, after returning from the kitchen to his
apartment, he crossed the king's gardens and passed
near a palisade surrounding a charming grove. In the
middle of it was a little sparkling fountain, where he
heard someone chatting. Since he believed that all
the inhabitants of that kingdom were incapable of
speaking, this surprised him. He advanced quietly and

heard a voice that said, "But, Princess, if you don't reveal yourself, your husband will never find you."

"What can I do?" said the other voice, which he recognized as the one he had so often heard. "Marmotte's cruelty compels me to remain silent, and I can't reveal myself without risking his life as well as my own. The wise Lumineuse, who's helping him, is hiding my features from him in order to protect both of us. It's absolutely necessary that he pound me. It's an irrevocable sentence."

"But why must he pound you?" the other inquired. "You've never told me your history. Your confidante, Citronette, would have told me if she hadn't been chosen for the king's broth last week."

"Alas!" the princess replied. "That unfortunate lady has already undergone the torture that still awaits me. If only I were in her place! I'm sure she's in her grotto by this time."

"But," the other voice replied, "since it's such a beautiful night, tell me now why you've been subjected to Marmotte's vengeance. I've already told you who I am, and I'm burning with impatience to know more about you."

"Although it will revive my grief," the princess remarked, "I can't refuse to satisfy you, especially since I must talk about Zirphil. I take pleasure in everything that pertains to him."

You can easily judge how delighted the prince felt at this fortunate moment. He glided quietly into the grove, but since it was very dark, he did not see anything. However, he listened with all his might, and this is what he heard word for word.

My father was king of a country near Mount Caucasus. He reigned to the best of his ability over a people of incredible wickedness. They were perpetually revolting, and often the windows of his palace were broken by stones they hurled. The queen, my mother, who was a very accomplished woman, composed speeches for him to make to the disaffected, but if he succeeded in appeasing them one day, the next produced new troubles. The judges became tired of condemning people to death, and the executioners of hanging them. At last things reached such a state that my father saw that all our provinces were united against us, and he decided to withdraw from the capital so that he would no longer have to witness so many unpleasant scenes. He took the queen with him and left the government of the kingdom to one of his ministers, who was very wise and less timid than my father. My mother was expecting to give birth to me and traveled with some difficulty to the foot of Mount Caucasus, which my father had chosen for his abode. Our wicked subjects joyfully fired guns at their departure and strangled our minister the next day, saying that he had wanted to carry matters with too high a hand and that they preferred their former sovereign. My father was not at all flattered by their preference and remained hiding in his little retreat, where I soon saw the light of day.

They named me Camion because I was so tiny. Moreover, since the king and queen were tired of the honors that had cost them so dearly, they concealed my high birth from me. I was brought up as a shepherdess. At the end of ten years (which appeared to them like ten minutes because they were so happy in their retreat), the fairies of the Caucasus, who had become infuriated by the wickedness of the people of our kingdom, decided to restore order there. One day, as I was tending my sheep in the meadow next to our garden, two old shepherdesses approached and begged me to give them shelter for the night. They had such a dejected air that my soul was moved with compassion. "Follow me," I said. "My father, who's a farmer, will gladly welcome you." I ran to the cottage to announce their arrival to him. He came to greet them and received them with a good deal of kindness, as did my mother. Then I brought in my sheep and set milk before our guests. Meanwhile, my father prepared them a nice little supper and the queen—who, as I told you before, was a clever woman—entertained them in a wonderful manner.

I had a little lamb of which I was extremely fond, and my father called me to bring it to him so he might

kill and roast it. I was not accustomed to oppose his
will and therefore took it to him. But I was so distressed that I sat down to weep beside my mother, who
was so occupied in talking to these good women that
she did not pay any attention to me. "What's the matter
with the little Camion?" one of them said, who saw me
in tears.

"Alas, madam!" I said to her. "My father's roasting
my pet lamb for your supper."

"What!" said the one who had not yet spoken. "Is it
on our account that pretty Camion is thus distressed?"
Standing up, she struck the ground with her stick, and a
magnificently set table rose from it. The two old
women became two beautiful ladies dressed in dazzling precious stones. I was so transfixed that I did not
even pay attention when my little lamb bounded into
the room and made a thousand capers that amused the
entire company. After kissing the hands of the beautiful ladies, I ran to pet him. Imagine my shock when I
found his wool made all of silver purl and covered with
knots of rose-colored ribbons.

My father and mother fell at the feet of the fairies,
for, I need not tell you, this is what they were. The
more majestic of them raised them, saying, "King and
queen, we've known you for a long time, and your
misfortunes have aroused our pity. Don't imagine
that greatness exempts anyone from the evils of
humankind. You must know through experience that
the more elevated the rank, the more keenly these evils
are felt. Your patience and virtue have raised you
above your misfortunes, and it's time to give you your
reward. I'm the fairy Lumineuse, and I've come to
inquire what your majesties would find most pleasant.
Come, speak! Don't worry about putting our power to
the test. Consult each other, and your wishes will be
fulfilled. But say nothing with regard to Camion: her
destiny is separate from yours. The fairy Marmotte has
been envious of the splendid fate promised her and has
obscured it for a time. But we do know Camion will
learn the value of her happiness only by experiencing
the evils of life. We can protect her only by softening
them. That's all we're permitted to tell you. Now,

speak. We can do anything you want with that one exception."

After this speech the fairies fell silent. The queen turned to the king so that he might reply, for she was crying because I was doomed to be unhappy. But my father was in no better condition to speak than she was. He uttered pitiful cries, and on seeing them in tears, I left my lamb to come weep with them. The fairies waited patiently and in perfect silence until our tears dried. At last my mother nudged the king gently: they were waiting for his reply. He took his handkerchief from his eyes and said that since it was fated that I should be miserable, they could offer him nothing that would please him. "I refuse the happiness you promise me because I'll always feel embittered by thinking about what dear Camion has to dread." Seeing that the poor man could say no more, the queen begged the fairies to take their lives on the day my sad destiny was to be fulfilled because her only wish was not to be compelled to witness my misery. The good fairies were touched by the extreme grief that reigned in the royal family and talked together in a whisper. At last Lumineuse said to the queen, "Be consoled, madam. The misfortunes threatening Camion are not so great and they'll end happily. Indeed, from the moment that the husband destined for her obeys the commands of fate, our sister's malevolence will have no more power over her. Believe me, she'll be happy with him, for the prince we've chosen is worthy of her.

"All we can tell you is that you must never forget to lower your daughter every morning into your well. She must bathe in it for half an hour, every morning. If you observe this rule strictly, she may escape the evil with which she is threatened. At the age of twelve, the critical period of her fate will commence. If she reaches the age of thirteen safely, there'll be nothing more to fear. This is all that concerns her. Now, make a wish for yourselves, and we'll satisfy your desires."

The king and queen looked at each other, and after a short silence the king asked to become a statue until I had completed my thirteenth year. The queen made a modest request, that the temperature of the well in which I was to be dipped always correspond to the season. The fairies were charmed by this excess of parental tenderness and added that the water would be orange-flowered water, and that the king could resume his natural form whenever the queen threw this water on him. "You can, of course, become a statue again whenever you please." After lauding the king and queen for their moderation, they eventually took their leave of us with the promise: "We'll aid you whenever you need help if you just burn a bit of the silver purl with which Camion's lamb is covered."

When they vanished, I felt anguish for the first time in my life as I watched my father become a great black marble statue. The queen burst into tears, and I did, too, but since everything must have an end, I stopped crying and occupied myself by consoling my mother because I felt a sudden increase of both sense and sensitivity.

The queen spent her days at the feet of the statue, and I milked my ewes after bathing each day as they had ordered. We lived off the food produced by the milk because the queen would not take anything else, and only out of love for me could she be prevailed upon to go on with a life so filled with bitterness. "Alas, my daughter!" she sometimes said. "Our grandeur and high birth have been of no use to us! (By this time she had revealed my rank to me.) It would have been better to have been born into the lower classes. A crown has brought such disaster to us! Only virtue and an affection for you, my dear Camion, enable me to withstand these catastrophes. There are moments when my soul seems eager to leave me, and I confess, I feel pleasure in thinking that I shall soon die. It's not for me you should weep, but for your father, whose grief is even greater than mine. It has brought him to the extremity of desiring a fate worse than death. Never forget, my dear, the gratitude you owe him."

"Alas, madam!" I said. "I'm incapable of ever forgetting it, and still less can I forget that you're keeping yourself alive only in order to help me."

I was bathed regularly every day, and every day my

mother sadly viewed the king as an inanimate statue. However, she did not dare recall him to life for fear of inflicting him with the pain of witnessing my threatened misfortune. Since the fairies had not specified what we were to fear, we lived in mortal dread. My mother in particular imagined no need of frightful things because her imagination had an unlimited scope to cover. As for me, I did not trouble myself much about it, for youth is the only time that we enjoy the present.

My mother told me repeatedly that she felt a great desire to bring my father back to life again, an inclination I shared as well. At last, after six months had passed and she found that the fairies' bath had greatly enriched both my body and mind, she decided to satisfy this longing, if only to give the king the pleasure of seeing my progress. Therefore, she asked me to bring her some water from the well. Accordingly, after my bath I drew up a vase of this marvelous water, and no sooner did we sprinkle the statue than my father became a man again. The queen threw herself at his feet to ask pardon for having troubled his repose. He raised her and after embracing her tenderly, he readily forgave her, and she introduced me to him.

"I'm ashamed to tell you that he was both delighted and surprised. For how can you believe me, beautiful princess, when I am the most hideous of crayfish?" the voice said hesitatingly.

"Alas! I don't have any trouble believing you," replied the one to whom she spoke. "I too might boast of having been beautiful, but how is it possible to appear so in these frightful shells? Please continue, for I'm eager to hear the rest of your story."

"Very well, then," said the other voice.

The king was enchanted with me and gave me numerous caresses. Then he asked the queen if she had any news to tell him. "Alas!" she said. "Who in this desolate spot could come and tell me any? Besides, since I've been solely occupied in lamenting your transformation, I've taken little interest in the world, which means nothing to me without you."

"Well," the king said, "I'll tell *you* some news then, for don't think that I've always been asleep. The fairies who are protecting us have disclosed to me the punishment of my subjects. They've made an immense lake out of my kingdom, and all the inhabitants are menfish. A nephew of the fairy Marmotte whom they have set up as their king persecutes them with unparalleled cruelty; he devours them for the least fault. At the end of a certain time a prince will arrive who'll dethrone him and reign in his stead. It's in this kingdom that Camion will attain perfect happiness. This is all I know, and it wasn't a bad way of spending my time, given the fact that I was able to discover these things," he said laughing. "The fairies came every night to inform me of what was going on, and I would have perhaps learned much more if you had let me remain a statue a little longer. However, I'm so delighted to see you once more that I don't think I'll want to become a statue again very soon."

We spent some time in the happiest manner possible. Nevertheless the king and queen were rather anxious as I approached the age of thirteen. Whenever the queen bathed me, she took great care to ensure the prediction would not be fulfilled. But who can boast of escaping her destiny? One morning, when my mother had risen early and was gathering some flowers to decorate our cottage—my father was fond of them—she saw an ugly animal, a marmot, come out from beneath a tuberose. This beast threw itself on her and bit her nose. She fainted from the pain of the bite, and when my father did not see her return at the end of an hour, he went looking for her. You can imagine how upset he was at finding her covered with blood and nearly dead! He uttered fearful cries and I ran to his aid. Together we carried the queen into the house and put her to bed, where it took more than two hours for her to revive. At last she began to give some signs of life, and we had the pleasure of seeing her recover from all but the pain of the bite, which caused her a good deal of suffering.

Right away she asked, "Did Camion go bathing?"

We had quite forgotten it, though, in our anxiety about her. She was very alarmed at hearing this. However, on seeing that nothing had happened to me as yet, she became reassured.

The day passed without any other trouble. The king had taken out his gun and went searching all over for the horrid beast without being able to find it. The next day at sunrise the queen awoke and came to fetch me to make up for the fault of the preceding morning. She lowered me into the well as usual, but alas, it was our unlucky day! Although the heavens were quite serene, all at once a dreadful clap of thunder pierced the air. Suddenly the sky was on fire, and a flaming dart soared from a burning cloud and flew into the well. In her fright my mother let go of the cord holding me, and I sank to the bottom. Although I was not hurt, you can imagine how horrified I was at discovering that I had been partially transformed into an enormous whale. I bobbed to the surface again and called the queen with all my might. She did not reply, and I wept bitterly as much for her loss as for my transformation. Then I felt an invisible power forcing me to descend to the bottom of the well. Upon reaching it I entered a crystal grotto where I found a kind of nymph. She was quite ugly, resembling an immensely fat frog. However, she smiled at my approach and said to me, "Camion, I'm the Nymph of the Bottomless Well. I have orders to welcome you and to make you undergo the penance to which you've been sentenced for having failed to bathe. Follow me, and don't try to object."

"Alas, what could I do? I was so distressed and so faint at finding myself on dry ground that I didn't have the strength to speak. She dragged me, not painlessly, into a salon of green marble adjoining the grotto. There she put me into an immense golden tub filled with water, and I began to recover my senses. The good nymph appeared delighted at this. "I'm called Citronette," she said. "I've been appointed to wait on you, so you can order me to do anything you want. I know the past and the present perfectly, but I cannot determine the future. Command me, and at least I can make the time of your penance less annoying to you."

I embraced the good Citronette after she said these words and told her about my past. Then I inquired about the fate of the king and queen. She was about to reply when a hideous marmot as large as a human being entered the salon. I was petrified with horror. She walked on her hind legs and leaned on a gold wand, giving her a dignified air. She approached the tub—in which I would gladly have drowned myself because I was so frightened—and she raised her wand to touch me. "Camion," she said, "you're in my power, and nothing can release you except your obedience and that of the husband whom my sisters have destined for you. Listen to me, and set aside your fear. It doesn't befit a person of your rank.

"Ever since your childhood I have wanted to care for you and marry you to my nephew, the King of Whiting. Lumineuse and two or three of my other sisters combined to deprive me of this right. I was provoked, and not being able to revenge myself on them, I decided to punish you for their audacity. Therefore, I condemned you to become a whale for at least half the term of your existence. My sisters protested so strongly against what they called my injustice that I reduced my term by over three-quarters, but I reserved the right of marrying you to my nephew in return for my compliance. Lumineuse, who's imperious and unfortunately my superior, would not listen to this arrangement. She had predestined you to a prince whom she protected. I was then compelled to consent to her plan in spite of my resentment. All that I could obtain was that the first person to rescue you from my claws would become your husband. Here are their portraits," she continued, showing me two gold miniature cases, "which will enable you to recognize them. But if one of them comes to rescue you, he must become your fiancé when you're in the tub, and he must tear off the whale skin before you can leave it. If he doesn't, you'll remain a fish forever. My nephew wouldn't hesitate a moment to carry out this order, but Lumineuse's favorite will consider it a horrible task because he has the air of a delicate gentleman. So you'd better put your mind to work and think up a way to make him skin you. After that you'll no longer be unhappy, if you can call it unhappiness to be a beautiful, fat, and well-fed whale up to your neck in water."

I did not reply, dejected as much by my present state as the thought of the flaying to which I had to submit myself. Marmotte disappeared and left me with the two miniature cases. I was weeping over my misfortunes without dreaming of looking at the portraits when sympathetic Citronette said, "Come, we mustn't lament over catastrophes that can't be remedied. Let's see if I can't help console you. But first, try not to weep so much, for I have a tender heart and can't see your tears without feeling inclined to mix mine with them. Let's chase them away by looking at these portraits."

Upon saying this, she opened the first case and showed it to me. We both shrieked like Melusine at seeing a hideous whiting's head. True, it was painted to give all the advantages that could be given, yet in spite of that, nothing so ugly has ever been seen in the memory of humankind. "Take it away," I cried. "I can't bear the sight of it any longer. I'd rather be a whale all my life than marry that horrible whiting!"

She didn't give me time to finish heaping abuse on this monster, but exclaimed, "Look at this darling young man! Oh, as far as he's concerned, if he were to skin you, I'd be delighted."

I looked quickly to see if what she said was true, and I was soon quite convinced. A noble, charming expression, with fine eyes full of tenderness, adorned a face both mild and majestic. An air of intelligence permeated this fascinating and delightful portrait. A profusion of black hair with natural curls gave him a look that Citronette mistook for indifference, but which I interpreted, and I think rightly so, as conveying precisely the opposite sentiment.

I gazed at this handsome face without being aware of how much pleasure I was having. Citronette noticed it first. "Without a doubt," she cried, "that's the one we'll choose."

This banter roused me from my reverie, and blushing at my ecstasy, I said, "Why should I trouble myself? Ah, my dear Citronette, this appears to me very much

like another one of cruel Marmotte's tricks. She's
made full use of her art to compel me to long for some
similar living being who's impossible to find.

"What?" Citronette commented. "You're already
having such tender thoughts about this portrait? Ah,
truly, I didn't expect that so soon." I blushed again at
this jest and became quite embarrassed at finding that I
had too innocently betrayed the effect this beautiful
painting had produced on my heart. Citronette again
read my thoughts. "No, no," she said, embracing me.
"Don't repent of your feelings. Your frankness charms
me, and to console you, I'll tell you that Marmotte is
not deceiving you. There really is a prince who's the
original of the portrait."

This assurance filled me with joy momentarily, but
the next instant that feeling departed when I remembered that this prince would never see me. I was in the
depths of the earth, and Marmotte would prefer to
allow her monster of a nephew to penetrate my abode
than give the least assistance to a prince she hated.
Hadn't her sisters destined him for me without her
consent? I no longer concealed what I thought from
Citronette. Indeed, the attempt would have been useless because she read my deepest secrets with surprising ease. Therefore, I decided it would be better
to be candid. Moreover, she deserved my trust since
she was so so attached to me. Naturally, I found it a
great consolation because I've felt from that time
on, one can have a lot of happiness in being able to
talk to someone when one's heart is consumed by
one object. In fact, this is when I began to fall in
love, and Citronette helped clear up the confusion that
the beginning of passion produces in the mind. Clever
and clear-sighted, she soothed my grief by allowing
me to talk about it, and when I had exhausted words,
she gently changed the subject to something that
almost always, however, touched on my troubles or my
affection.

She informed me that the king, my father, had been
transported to the abode of the King of Whiting and
that the queen had become a crayfish the very moment

she lost me. I could not understand this and maintained, "One cannot just become a crayfish."

"Well," she responded, "can you explain how you've become a whale any better?"

She was right, of course. We are often surprised by things that happen to others, even though we don't notice when we go through even more astonishing things ourselves. I simply lacked experience to grasp this. Citronette laughed frequently at my innocence and was surprised to find me so eloquent in my affection, for truly I was spellbinding on that subject. And I found that love makes the mind more active. I could not sleep and woke the good-natured Citronette a hundred times during the night to talk to her about my prince. She had told me his name, that he hunted almost every day in the forest, and it was beneath this forest that I was interred. She proposed that we try to attract him to our dwelling, but I would not consent, although I was dying to do so. I was afraid he would die for want of air. It was difficult for us since we were accustomed to it. I was also afraid that I would be taking too great a liberty. Besides, I was upset that I would have to appear to him in the form of a whale, and I judged that his aversion for me would equal that which the King of Whiting's portrait had aroused within me. Citronette reassured me, saying that despite the whale's body, my face was charming. I believed it sometimes, but more often I was uneasy, and after having looked at myself, I could not imagine I was sufficiently beautiful to inspire love in a man who had made me so well acquainted with it. My self-love came to the aid of my prudence. Alas, how rarely are our virtues traced to purer inspirations!

I spent my time by devising ways that I could catch sight of him and make him see me. Each one that occurred to me I rejected, one after the other. Citronette was a great help to me at this time, for she had plenty of sense and even more gentleness and amiability. One day, when I was even sadder than usual— for love has the peculiar property of infecting gentle souls with melancholy—I saw the frightful Marmotte

enter with two persons whom I did not recognize at
first. I imagined she had brought her wretched nephew
with her, and I uttered frightful shrieks as they
approached. "Why, she couldn't cry louder if they
were skinning her!" the horrid Marmotte exclaimed.
"Look what terrible harm's been done to her!"

"Good gracious, sister," said one of the persons
accompanying her and whom I then remembered with
joy as having seen previously in our village. "Let's set
a truce to your stories of skinning, and let's tell
Camion what we've come to tell her."

"Gladly," Marmotte said, "but on the conditions
agreed upon."

"Camion," the good fairy said, without replying to
Marmotte, "we've become too upset by your plight not
to think of a remedy, particularly since you've not
deserved your fate. My sisters and I have decided
to ameliorate it as much as we can. Therefore, this is
what we've decided to do. You're about to be presented at the court of the prince to whom I've destined you from birth. But, my dear child, you won't
appear there as you are. You're to return three nights a
week and to plunge back into your tub. Until you're
married—"

"And skinned!" interrupted the odious Marmotte,
laughing violently.

The good fairy merely turned toward her, shrugged
her shoulders, and continued, "Until you're married,
you'll be a whale in this place. We can tell you no
more. You'll be informed of the rest by degrees, but
above all keep your secret. If a word of this is revealed,
neither I nor my sisters can do anything for you, and
you'll be at the mercy of my sister Marmotte."

"That's what I hope," the wicked fairy said, "and I
daresay I already see her in my power. A secret kept by
a girl would be a miracle."

"That's her own affair," Lumineuse said, for it
was she who had already spoken. "To proceed, my
daughter," she said, "you'll become a little doll made
of ivory, but you'll be capable of thinking and
speaking, and we'll preserve all your features. I'll give
you a week to consider whether my proposal suits you.

Then we'll return, and you can tell me if you agree to it, or if you'd prefer one of the two husbands chosen for you."

I had no time to reply. The fairies departed after these words, leaving me astounded by what I had just seen and heard. I remained with Citronette, who believed that it was a great treat for me to become an ivory doll. I sighed when I thought that my prince would never take a fancy to such a bauble, but at last the desire to become acquainted with him overcame my anxiety to please him, and I decided to accept. In fact, I was quite eager because Zirphil (they had mentioned his name) might possibly be forestalled by the King of Whiting, and this idea made me nearly die of grief.

Citronette told me that Prince Zirphil hunted daily in the forest above, and I made her take the form of a stag, hound, or wild boar every day so that she might bring me some news of him who occupied my heart. She described him to me as a hundred times more handsome than his picture, and my imagination embellished him to such a degree that I decided to see him or die.

One day before the expected arrival of the fairies, Citronette was roaming the forest in the form of a wild boar to find food for my curiosity when suddenly I saw her return, followed by the too charming Zirphil. I can't describe my joy and astonishment. What enchanted me most, though, was that this charming prince appeared equally delighted with me. Perhaps I desired this too much not to help deceiving myself. However, I thought I saw a look in his eyes that he knew the impression he had made. Citronette was more worried about my happiness than about our ecstasy. She aroused us by begging him either to skin or to marry me. Then I came to my senses and felt the danger of my situation. I joined in her entreaties and, thanks to our tears and pleas, we induced him to pledge himself to me. No sooner did I accept him than he vanished. I don't know how, but I found myself in my ordinary form, lying on a good bed. I was no longer a whale, but I was still in the depths of the earth in the green salon, and Citronette had lost the power of leaving it and of transforming herself.

I expected the fairies to be infuriated. My love had increased since I had become personally acquainted with the object of my desire, and I feared that my charming husband might be included in the vengeance of the fairies for not having waited until they could witness my marriage. Citronette had all she could do to reassure me, for I could not overcome my apprehension. At dawn Marmotte appeared, but I saw neither Lumineuse nor her companion. Not seeming more irritable than usual, Marmotte touched me with her wand without a word, and I became a charming little doll, which she put in her toothpick case. Then she went to the queen-mother of my husband and gave me to her with orders to wed me to her son or to expect all the evil she could inflict. Moreover, she told her that I was her goddaughter and was called Princess Camion. In truth, I took a great fancy to my mother-in-law. I considered her charming since she was the mother of my adorable Zirphil, and my caresses were returned. Every night I was transported into the green salon and enjoyed the pleasure of meeting my husband, for the same power controlled him and transported him likewise into the subterraneous dwelling. I did not know why they forbade me to tell him my secret since I was married, but I kept it in spite of my great desire to tell him.

"You'll see," the speaker continued with a sigh, "how impossible it is to avoid one's fate. But it's beginning to get light, and I'm quite weary from being out of the water so long. Let's return to the reservoir, and tomorrow, if we're not selected for the soup of that worthless king, we'll resume the thread of our conversation at the same hour. —Come, let's go."

Zirphil did not hear any more and returned to his apartment, quite concerned at not having given some indication to his princess that he was so near. Yet the fear of increasing her misfortunes by such an indiscretion consoled him. The misery of knowing she was likely to perish by his hand made him determined to continue his diligent search among the crayfish.

He went to bed but not to sleep, for he did not close his eyes all night. To have found his princess in the form of a crayfish, ready to be made into soup for the King of Whiting, seemed a torture more frightful than even death itself. He believed that this had been her fate and was becoming terribly upset when he heard a great noise in the garden. At first he heard a jumbled sound, but after listening attentively, he distinguished flutes and conch shells. He rose and went to the window, from which he saw the King of Whiting, accompanied by the dozen sharks who composed his council, advancing toward the pavilion. He rushed to open the door, and after the retinue entered, the king had his tub filled with sea water by the peers of the realm who had been carrying it. After a short repose he made the council take their places and addressed the young prince. "Whoever you may be," he said, "you've apparently decided to make me die of hunger because you've been sending me a broth everyday that I can't swallow. However, I must tell you, young man, that if you are in league with evil powers to poison me, you're on the wrong side. As nephew of the fairy Marmotte, nothing can harm me."

The prince was astonished at being suspected of such a base act and was about to make a proud reply. As he raised his hand, however, he happened to gaze at his ring and saw Lumineuse, who placed her finger to her lips to warm him to be silent. (He had not thought of consulting his ring before this because he had been so overwhelmed by his grief). Accordingly, he held his tongue, but he betrayed his indignation by his expression, which the sharks noticed because they made signs that appeared to say that they agreed with him.

"Ho, ho!" the king said. "Since this myrmidon appears so angry, we must make him work in front of us. Let them go to my kitchen. Let them bring the mortar for the crayfish. I'll give my council a treat."

A pike-head began carrying out the king's commands at once. At the same time the twelve sharks took

a large net, threw it from the window into the reservoir,
and drew in three or four thousand crayfish. While the
council fished and the pike-head fetched the king's
mortar, Zirphil contemplated the situation. "The most
crucial moment of my life is approaching. My happiness or misery will depend on what I do right now." He
armed himself with resolve for whatever might happen,
placing all his hopes in the fairy Lumineuse. He
implored her, "Take my side," and at the same time he
looked at his ring and saw the beautiful fairy, who
made a sign to him to pound courageously. This signal
revitalized him and relieved him of some of the pain he
felt in consenting to such a cruel act.

At last the horrid mortar was produced. Zirphil
approached it boldly, prepared to obey the king. The
council ceremoniously put in the crayfish, and the
prince tried to pound them. Yet the same thing that had
happened to the ones in the kitchen happened to them
as well—the bottom of the mortar opened and flames
devoured them. The king and his odious sharks amused
themselves for a long time with this spectacle, never
tiring of refilling the mortar. Finally, a single crayfish
was left of the four thousand, one surprisingly large
and fine. The king commanded it to be shelled so he
could see if he would like to eat it raw. They gave it to
Zirphil to shell, and he trembled all over at having to
inflict this new torture. His trembling became even
worse when this poor fish joined her two claws and
said with eyes filled with tears, "Alas, Zirphil, what
have I done to you to make you want to harm me so
much?"

The prince was moved by these words, and his heart,
pierced with grief. He looked at her sadly and at length
took it upon himself to beg the king to allow her to be
pounded. Ever covetous of his authority, the king was
firm in his resolution. Indeed, he was enraged by this
humble request and threatened to pound Zirphil himself if he did not shell it. The poor prince quivered as
he touched the crayfish with a knife they supplied him.
Again he looked at his ring and saw Lumineuse
laughing and talking to a veiled person she held by the
hand. He was baffled by this, and the king gave him no

time to reflect. He cried out to him loudly to finish. The prince stuck the knife with such force under the shell of the crayfish that it cried piteously. He turned his eyes away from hers, unable to help shedding tears. Finally he resumed his task, but to his great astonishment, as he was about to finish the shelling, he found the wicked Marmotte in his hands. She jumped to the ground and uttered shrieks of mocking laughter. They were so loud and unpleasant that they prevented him from fainting; otherwise he would have slumped to the floor.

The king cried in surprise, "Why, it's my aunt!"

"Yes, it's no one but me," this annoying beast said. "But, my dear Whiting, I've come to tell you a terrible piece of news." Whiting grew pale at these words, and the council assumed an air of satisfaction that increased the bad mood of the king and his terrible aunt. "The fact is, my darling," Marmotte continued, "you must return to your watery dominions because this rash young man before you has chosen to display a constancy that nothing can shake. He's triumphed despite all the traps I set to prevent him from carrying off the princess I had destined for you."

Upon hearing these words, the King of Whiting fell into such a rage that he could not contain himself. He flailed about and showed his violent temper. Despite Marmotte's attempts to calm him, he broke his bowl into a thousand pieces, and since he was on dry ground, he fainted. Mad with rage, Marmotte turned to Zirphil, who had remained a silent spectator during this tragic scene. "You've triumphed, Zirphil," she said, "thanks to the power of a fairy whom I must obey. But your troubles haven't ended yet. You won't be happy until you give me the case that contained the cursed Camion. Even Lumineuse has agreed to this, and I've obtained her consent to make you suffer until that time." After saying this she took the King of Whiting on her shoulders and threw him into the reservoir along with the sharks, the palace, and all its inhabitants.

Zirphil found himself alone at the foot of a great mountain, in a country as arid as a desert. There was

nothing to be seen—not a single house or even the
large reservoir. Everything had vanished all at once.
The prince was more upset than astonished by such an
extraordinary event: he was accustomed to wonders but
the continued persecution of the fairy Marmotte caused
him to grieve.

"I'm sure that I've pounded my princess," he said.
"Yes, I must have pounded her. Yet I'm none the
happier for it. Ah, barbarous Marmotte! And you,
Lumineuse, you've left me helpless even after I obeyed
you at the expense of all that a heart as sensitive as
mine could suffer!"

Grief and his scant rest of the night before threw him
into such a state of weakness that he would have collapsed altogether if he had not summoned the courage
to survive. "If I could only find some nourishment," he
said. "However, I'm sure I can't find a single fruit in
this horrible desert that can refresh me." No sooner had
he uttered these words than his ring opened, and a tiny
table covered with excellent viands emerged from it.
Within seconds it grew large enough to accommodate
him, and on it he found everything that could tempt his
eyes and his appetite, for the repast was so beautifully
arranged and the wine so delicious that nothing was
lacking. He gave thanks to Lumineuse, for who else
could have helped him so opportunely? He ate, drank,
and felt his strength return.

After he had finished, the table shrank back into the
ring. Since it was late, he did not make much progress
in climbing the mountain, but stretched himself out
under a wretched tree that had hardly enough leaves to
protect him from the dew. "Alas!" he said as he lay
down. "Such is the nature of man. He forgets the good
that is past and concerns himself only with the evil in
the present. Right now I'd gladly exchange that table
for a couch a little less hard than this."

A moment later he felt himself lying in a comfortable bed, though he could see nothing because the
darkness had seemingly increased. He ascertained that
this was caused by large curtains surrounding his bed
and protecting him from the cold and dew. After
thanking the attentive Lumineuse again, he dropped off

to sleep. At daybreak he awoke and found himself in a bed walled by curtains of yellow taffeta and silver. This bed had been placed in the middle of a satin tent of the same color, embroidered all over with bright silver letters forming Zirphil's name, and all of these supported by whales outlined by rubies. Everything that one could possibly need was to be found in this beautiful tent. If the prince had been in a more tranquil state of mind, he would have admired this elegant habitation, but he only glanced at the whales, dressed himself, and went out of the tent, which folded itself up and returned to the ring from which it had emerged.

He began to climb the mountain, no longer going to the trouble of looking for food or lodging because he was certain to have both as soon as he wished for them. His only worry was how to find Lumineuse, for his ring was mute on that subject, and he found himself in a country so unfamiliar and deserted that he was compelled to trust to chance.

After having spent several days in climbing without discovering anything, he arrived at the brink of a well that was cut into the rock. Seating himself beside it to rest, he began to exclaim as usual: "Lumineuse, why can't I find you?"

When he finished uttering these words, he heard a voice coming from the well. "Is it Zirphil who's speaking to me?"

His joy at hearing the voice was increased when he recognized whose it was. He rushed to the brink of the well and said, "Yes, it's Zirphil. And aren't you Citronette?"

"Yes," Citronette replied, emerging from the well and embracing the prince.

It is impossible to relate what pleasure Zirphil felt in seeing Citronette again. He overwhelmed the nymph with questions about the princess and herself. Finally, after the excitement of their initial encounter had subsided, they spoke more soberly with each other.

"I'm going to tell you everything you don't know," she said. "Ever since you pounded us, we've been enjoying a happiness lessened only by your absence.

I've been awaiting your arrival here in behalf of
the fairy Lumineuse to tell you what you still have
to do in order to possess a princess who loves you
as much as you love her. But since some time must
elapse before you can attain this happiness, I'll tell
you the rest of the marvelous story about your charming bride."

Zirphil kissed Citronette's hand a thousand times
and followed her into her grotto, where he thought he
would die of intermixed pleasure and woe, for in this
spot had he seen his divine princess for the first time.
After sharing a meal that sprang from the ring, he
begged the good Citronette kindly to resume the narrative from the point that the princess had left off in the
palace garden.

Since this is the spot where Lumineuse is to meet
you, you'll learn all you want while waiting for her—
you realize it's useless for you to run after her. She's
entrusted you to my care, and a lover is less impatient
when one talks to him about the lady he loves.

The fairy Marmotte knew about your marriage, and
she had transformed our friend into an ivory doll,
believing that you would be disgusted by her.
Lumineuse conducted this affair herself, knowing that
nothing could deprive you of the princess if you
destroyed her enchantment by either marrying or skinning her. You chose the former alternative, and you
know what followed. By night she resumed her natural
form and lamented spending all her days in your royal
mother's pocket, for Marmotte had been permitted by
Lumineuse to torment the princess until you had fulfilled your destiny, which was to skin her. Marmotte
was enraged at finding that you had married her before
the King of Whiting, her nephew.

Since the princess was no longer a whale, there was
no fish to skin, but Marmotte, who kept creating new
obstacles, was to make you pound her and had forbidden the princess to tell you anything about it at the
cost of your life. Moreover, Marmotte promised her
she would later enjoy the greatest happiness. "How
will he ever make up his mind to pound me?" she

asked while waiting for you. "Ah, my dear Citronette, if it were only my life that Marmotte threatened, I'd give it cheerfully to protect my husband from the tortures they've prepared for him. But they're also after his life—that life which is so dear to me. Ah, Marmotte! Babarous Marmotte! How can you find pleasure in making me so miserable when I've never given you any reason to harm me?" She knew the period prescribed for your separation from her, but she did not dare tell you. You know the last time that you saw her that you found her in tears, and you asked her why. She pretended to accuse you of inconstancy because of your attention to little Camion. You appeased her supposed jealousy, and the fatal hour for Marmotte to fetch her arrived. You were transported to the palace of your father while the princess and I were changed into crayfish and placed into a little cane basket, which the fairy put under her arm. After getting into a chariot drawn by two adders, we arrived at the palace of the King of Whiting. This palace had belonged to the princess's father, but the city had been changed into a lake and formed the reservoir that we inhabited. By the way, all the men-fish that you've seen had once been the wicked subjects of that good king.

I must tell you, my lord, that the unfortunate monarch and his wife were in despair the moment the princess sank to the bottom of the well. The fairies who had formerly come to their aid appeared and consoled them for their loss, but the unhappy couple knew that Camion was to be exiled to their kingdom and chose to be with her rather than far away in spite of what they had to fear from the cruelty and ferociousness of the King of Whiting. The fairies did not conceal the princess's future fate from them, and her father asked to be cook of the kitchen and keeper of the King of Whiting's mortar. The fairy immediately tapped her wand, and he became the pike-headed man you saw in that position. So you need no longer be surprised at his having wept bitterly whenever you brought the cray-fish to pound. Since he knew that his daughter had to undergo this torture, he always thought she might be among them. The wretched monarch did not have a moment's rest because his daughter had no means of making herself known to him. What's more, the queen had requested to be changed into a crayfish in order to be with the princess.

As soon as we arrived at the palace, the fairy presented us to him and ordered him to have crayfish soup made for his dinner every day. We were then thrown into the reservoir. My first concern was to search for the queen in order to soothe the grief of the princess a little. But either by decree of fate or stupidity on my part, I found it impossible to discover her. We spent our days in this mournful search, and our most pleasant moments were those in which we recalled our past. Finally you arrived and they presented us to you, but the fairy had forbidden us to make ourselves known until you interrogated us, and we didn't dare to break this rule because we were severely punished for the most trivial offenses.

The princess told me she thought she was going to die of fright when she observed you talking with the cruel Marmotte. We saw you impatiently searching among our companions, and it was obvious you had little chance of reaching us by the direction you took. We knew we had to be pounded, but we also learned that we would be restored to our former condition immediately after and that the wicked Marmotte would have no further power over us. On the same day you were to begin inflicting this torture on us, we were all gathered in the reservoir weeping over our destiny when Lumineuse appeared. "Don't weep, my children," that remarkable fairy said. "I've come to inform you that you'll escape the punishment with which they've threatened you, provided you go cheerfully to the mortar and don't answer any questions addressed to you. I can say no more at present— I'm in a hurry, but do as I've told you and you won't regret it. The young princess whose fate appears to be the cruelest is not to lose hope—she'll soon find relief."

We all thanked the fairy and appeared before you fully determined to keep our secret. You spoke to some, who gave you only vague replies, and after you had chosen ten, we returned to the reservoir, where the assurance of our imminent rescue invigorated us with a natural gaiety.

Lumineuse's last words relieved the beautiful Camion's heart, and that made her charming in her mother's eyes and mine, and we three were inseparable. Eventually your choice fell on me and the queen, and we had no time to say adieu to the princess. An unknown power acted on us at the moment and caused us to become so cheerful that we thought we'd die of laughter at the absurd things we said to each other. You carried us to the kitchen, and no sooner did we touch the bottom of the fatal mortar than Lumineuse herself came to our aid and restored me to my natural form and transported me to my usual abode. I also had the consolation of seeing the queen and our companions resume their forms, but I don't know what happened to them. The fairy embraced me and told me to wait for you and reveal everything when you came searching for the princess.

"I've awaited this moment with impatience, as you can well believe, my lord," Citronette said to the prince, who had been listening most eagerly to her. "Yesterday I was just about to sit at the mouth of the well when Lumineuse appeared and said, 'Our children are about to be made happy, my dear Citronette. Zirphil has only to retrieve Marmotte's toothpick case to fulfill his tasks since he's finally skinned the princess.' 'Ah, great queen!' I cried. 'Are you sure of this? Have we really been so fortunate?' 'Yes,' she replied. 'It's quite true. He thought he had only skinned Marmotte, but in reality it was the princess. Marmotte was concealed in the handle of the knife that he used, and the instant he had finished his task, she caused the princess to vanish and appeared in her place in order to intimidate him again!' "

"What!" cried the prince. "I actually harmed my charming bride? Was I so cruel? Did I torture her? Ah, heavens! She'll never pardon me. I don't deserve her pardon!" The unhappy Zirphil spoke so impetuously

and upset himself so much that poor Citronette was
sorry she had told him this news.

"What's that?" she said, seeing that he was quite
overcome. "You didn't know it?"

"No, I didn't know that," he said. "What made me
take the shell off that unfortunate and charming crayfish was the sight of Lumineuse in my ring speaking to
a veiled person. She even laughed with her, and I imagined it was my princess. I thought that she had passed
through the mortar like the rest. Ah, I'll never forgive
myself for this mistake!"

"But, my lord," Citronette said, "the charm
depended on your skinning or pounding her, and you
hadn't done either. The person to whom Lumineuse
spoke was the princess's mother. They were waiting
for the end of your adventure in order to seize your
bride and protect her for you. It was quite necessary for
it to happen that way."

"Nevertheless," the prince said, "if I had known it,
I'd rather have pierced my own heart with that horrid
knife!"

"But consider," Citronette said, "that in piercing
your heart, you'd have left the princess eternally in the
power of your frightful rival. It is far better to have
shelled her than to have died and left her in misery."

This argument obviously placated the prince, and he
consented to some nourishment to maintain his
strength. They had just finished when the roof of the
salon opened and Lumineuse appeared, seated on a carbuncle drawn by a hundred butterflies. She descended
from the carbuncle, assisted by the prince, who
drenched the hem of her garment with a flood of tears.
The fairy raised him, saying, "Prince Zirphil, today
you're to reap the fruit of your heroic endeavors. Console yourself, for you shall finally enjoy happiness.
I've vanquished Marmotte's fury by my pleas, and
your courage has disarmed her. Come with me to
receive your princess from her hands and mine."

"Ah, madam," the prince cried, throwing himself at
her feet, "am I dreaming? Can it be that happiness is at
last mine?"

"You can rest assured," the fairy said. "Come to

your kingdom and console the queen, your mother, for your absence and the death of the king, your father. Your subjects are waiting to crown you."

In the midst of his joy the prince felt a bitter pang on hearing about his father's death, but the fairy distracted him from his distress by seating himself beside her. Citronette she permitted to seat herself at their feet. Then the butterflies spread their radiant wings and set out for King Zirphil's empire.

On the way the fairy told him to open his ring, and he found the toothpick case he had to return to Marmotte. The king thanked the generous fairy a thousand times over, and they arrived at the capital of his dominions, where they were awaited with the utmost impatience. Zirphil's mother advanced to greet the fairy as she got out of her chariot, and all the people, who knew about Zirphil's return, shouted and acclaimed him. Such a reception relieved him somewhat of his grief, and he tenderly embraced his mother. Then they all went up to a magnificent apartment that the queen had prepared for the fairy.

No sooner did they enter than Marmotte arrived in a chariot lined with Spanish leather and drawn by eight winged rats. She brought with her the beautiful Camion as well as her father and mother. Lumineuse and the queen hastened to embrace Marmotte while Zirphil respectfully kissed her paw, which she laughingly extended to him. Thereupon he returned the toothpick case to her, and she permitted him to claim his bride and present her to the queen, who embraced her with a thousand expressions of joy.

The large, illustrious group of people began speaking all at once, and joy reigned supreme. Camion and her charming husband were the only ones unable to say a word, for they had too much on their minds. There was, however, an eloquence in their silence that affected everyone present. The good Citronette wept with happiness while kissing the hands of the divine princess.

At last Lumineuse took them both by the hand and advanced with them toward Zirphil's mother. "Behold, madam," she said. "Two young lovers who only await your consent to become happy. Do complete their happiness. My sister Marmotte, the king and queen here present, and I myself, all request that you do so."

The queen tenderly embraced the happy couple. "Yes, my children," she replied courteously, "live happily together, and permit me to participate in that happiness as I relinquish my crown to you."

Zirphil and the princess threw themselves at her feet, and she raised them and embraced them again. They implored her not to abandon them, but to help them by giving them her advice.

Then Marmotte touched the beautiful Camion with her wand: her clothes, already magnificent, became silver brocade embroidered with carat diamonds, and her beautiful locks fell down and rearranged themselves so exquisitely that the kings and queens declared that her appearance was perfectly dazzling. The toothpick case the fairy held was changed into a crown formed entirely from beautiful diamonds so well set that the whole palace became illuminated by it. Marmotte placed it on the head of the princess, and Zirphil in turn appeared in a suit similar to that of Camion's. Lastly, the ring that she had given him produced a crown exactly like hers.

They were married on the spot and proclaimed king and queen of that fine country. The fairies gave the royal wedding breakfast, and nothing was lacking. After spending a week overwhelming them with good things, they departed and conducted the king and queen, Camion's father and mother, back to their kingdom, where they had punished the old inhabitants and repopulated it with new people faithful to their master. As for Citronette, the fairies permitted her to come and spend some time with her beautiful queen, and they allowed Camion to see her whenever she pleased just by wishing for her.

At last the fairies departed, and never has the world seen two people so happy as King Zirphil and Queen Camion. Their greatest happiness they found in each other, and days seemed to them like moments. Having children completed their bliss, and they lived to an extreme old age loving and continually striving to

please each other with the same ardor. When they
died, their kingdom was divided, and after various
changes it has come under the rule of one of their
descendants and become the flourishing empire of the
Great Mogul.

Marie-Catherine d'Aulnoy

Marie-Catherine Le Jumel de Barneville, Comtesse d'Aulnoy (c.1650–1705) was born in Barneville, Normandy, and came from a wealthy aristocratic family. During her youth she had two important formative influences: her aunt told her numerous folk tales, and her mother encouraged her to live as independently as possible. At fifteen she was married to François de la Motte, Baron d'Aulnoy, who was thirty years her senior and a notorious gambler and libertine. She had some children by him, but due to his poor character, she soon became disenchanted with her marriage and had several lovers. In 1669, with the help of her mother, Madame Guadagne (who had remarried after Baron de Barneville's death), and two men, Jacques-Antoine de Courboyer and Charles de la Moizière, who were their respective lovers, Mme. d'Aulnoy tried to implicate her husband in a crime of high treason against the king, which carried a capital punishment. However, the Baron d'Aulnoy managed to extricate himself from the affair and turned the tables on his wife: De Courboyer and de la Moizière were executed; Madame Guadagne escaped and made her way to England; Mme. d'Aulnoy was arrested briefly and then also managed to flee Paris. After taking refuge in a convent, Mme. d'Aulnoy apparently traveled extensively in Holland, England, and Spain, and may have acted along with her adventurous mother as a secret agent for France in those countries. She also had some more children and different lovers. However, it is not clear when she traveled, where she lived at any given time, or who her lovers were. What is known is that in 1685 she received permission to return to Paris and bought a house in the rue Saint-Benoit, which became one of the most interesting literary salons of the period.

By 1690 Mme. d'Aulnoy, an exceedingly bright and beautiful woman, began her public literary career with the publication of the novel *L'Histoire d'Hippolyte, comte de Douglas,* which contained the prose fairy tale, *L'île de la Félicité,* which anticipated the great fairy-tale vogue that commenced five years later. Her novel was a huge success, and that same year she published *Mémoires de la cour d'Espagne,* which appears to have been largely taken from an English book, since there is no evidence that Mme. d'Aulnoy had ever been at the Spanish court. The same holds true for her next book, *Relation du voyage d'Espagne* (1691), which contained the tale *Histoire de Mira,* based on the theme of Melusine. Her last book about journeys to foreign countries was *Mémoires de la cour d'Angleterre* (1695), which may also have been a fictive account and based on Mme. d'Aulnoy's own readings about the English court.

It became customary at Mme. d'Aulnoy's salon to recite fairy tales and on festive occasions to dress up like characters from fairy tales. She herself became one of the most gifted storytellers at her salon, and eventually she began publishing several volumes of fairy tales: *Les Contes des Fées,* vols. I–III (1696–97), *Les Contes des Fées,* vol. IV (1698), and *Contes Nouveaux ou Les Fées à la Mode,* vols. I–IV (1698). More than Charles Perrault, it was Mme. d'Aulnoy who was responsible for the extraordinary vogue of French fairy tales that swept the Parisian literary circles during the next ten years and continued less intensely until the publication of the *Cabinet des Fées* (1786–89).

On the basis of her so-called memoirs and fairy tales, Mme. d'Aulnoy was elected a member of the Académie des Ricovrati in Padova, and she continued to be active in the literary field by publishing other works such as *Sentiments d'une Ame pénitente* (1698) and *Le Comte de Warwick* (1703). In addition, Mme. d'Aulnoy managed to make time for intrigues. In 1699 she supposedly assisted her friend Mme. Ticquet, who assassinated her husband, a member of Parlement, because he had allegedly abused her. Mme. Ticquet was beheaded, and Mme. d'Aulnoy was fortunate to be exculpated from any wrongdoing.

In 1700 her husband died. Since they had been on terrible terms, his last act was to disinherit her. Nevertheless, she continued to maintain her salon and participate in the cultural life in Paris until her death in 1705.

Although Mme. d'Aulnoy was a mediocre stylist and her poetry is maudlin at times, she had such a powerful imagination and remarkable command of folk tale motifs and characters that her fairy tales never ceased to captivate her readers. Moreover, Mme. d'Aulnoy paid close attention to the details of dress, architecture, speech, and manners of her day, and she described these details in her fairy tales so accurately that they always had a ring of authenticity. Of course, her descriptions always tended to be hyperbolic: her heroines were the most beautiful; her heroes were the most charming and handsome; the castles were the most splendid. One refrain continues throughout her tales: "never has anyone seen anything so magnificent as this." This "never" that becomes "forever" in her tales revealed her longing for a world different from the one to which she had been exposed.

Mme. d'Aulnoy did not like constraints. In particular, she did not like the manner in which women were treated and compelled to follow partriarchal codes, and as we know, she did not even stop short of abetting execution or murder of men she considered unworthy or tyrannical. All her tales are filled with violence and violation of some kind or another that must be resolved, and in some cases, like *The Ram,* the resolution is not entirely satisfying. D'Aulnoy's tales are nightmarish because the fairies themselves are not always in agreement with one another, and thus humans must live under laws that they do not always understand and under fairy powers who are arbitrary, not unlike Louis XIV and his ministers. The only saving grace in the tales is love, or *tendresse,* that is, true natural feelings between a man and woman, and these feelings are constantly tested in extreme if not macabre ways. D'Aulnoy's repertoire of tortures and bestial transformations was immense. She stopped at nothing to make her lovers suffer, making their rescue all the sweeter.

Literary critics have often commented that the constant action in d'Aulnoy's tales emanated from the boredom that the aristocracy felt during the ancien régime and that the tales were a form of compensation for the frustration that she and others felt. However, d'Aulnoy was anything but bored, and her tales that originated from her active social life in the salons of that time were a means of confronting the frustrating conditions under which she lived and of projecting possibilities for change. Like her heroine Belle-Belle or the Chevalier Fortune, d'Aulnoy disguised her dreams in her symbolical tales and was not afraid to imagine or try anything if it meant the fulfillment of these dreams.

THE ISLAND OF HAPPINESS

RUSSIA is a frigid country where one rarely sees the beautiful days of a mild climate. Its mountains are almost always covered with snow, and the trees are so loaded with icicles that when the sun casts its rays on them, they appear to be garnished with crystals. There are forests of enormous grandeur where white bears wreak terrible havoc, and the people are continually warring with them. Although they manage to kill the bears, it is not without difficulty and danger. Thus, in Russia hunting bears is considered both the most noble and most ordinary occupation.

Once upon a time the Russians were governed by a young prince named Adolph. Born under a lucky star, he was so handsome, polite, and intelligent that it would have been difficult to convince anyone that a person so accomplished lived in a country so coarse and savage. He had not yet turned twenty when he undertook a great war against the Muscovites and showed dauntless courage and remarkable leadership. When he allowed his army to rest, he himself did not rest. Instead he went on that dangerous quest for bears.

One day when he was carried away once again by his noble passion for hunting, he led a large retinue into a vast forest. All over he roved until he finally got lost. Just as he realized that he was alone, that it was late, and that he no longer knew where he was, a storm took him by surprise. He guided his horse down a wide track and vainly blew his hunting horn in order to alert some of his hunters. All at once the scant daylight that was left was transformed into the most obscure night, punctuated only by lightning. The thunder made a terrible noise as the rain storm increased. The prince at

first took shelter under some trees, but he was soon
compelled to leave that spot. All around the rain fell in
torrents, and the paths were flooded. Deciding to get
free of the forest and to seek some shelter from the
tempest, he struggled with difficulty to reach open
fields, where he found himself even more exposed to
the inclement weather. He looked all around him and
noticed a light in a spot that was very high up. So he
headed in that direction, arduously climbing by foot
and leading his horse to the top of an almost inaccessible mountain. His way was obstructed by a multitude
of boulders and sheer cliffs. For several hours he
pressed on, sometimes on foot, sometimes on horseback, until he found himself nearing a cave. Through
the opening he saw the light that he had already
observed. He hesitated before entering, for he thought
it might be the hideout of some robbers who frequently
ravaged the countryside and who could rob and kill
him. However, since the souls of princes possess a
nobility and pride that sets them apart from other men,
he reproached himself for his fear. Into the cave he
advanced, hand on sword, ready to defend himself in
case someone was bold enough to attack him.

Because of the noise he made when he entered, an
old woman, whose white hair and mass of wrinkles
revealed how ancient she was, emerged from the rear
of the cave. As she approached him, she was visibly
astonished.

"You're the first mortal I've ever seen here," she
said. "Do you know, sir, who dwells here?"

"No, my good woman," Adolph responded. "I have
no idea where I am."

"This is the abode of Eole, god of the winds," she
stated. "This is where he retires with all his children.
I'm their mother, and you've found me alone because
they are all busy, each one doing good or evil in the
world as his wont. But you seem drenched from the
rain that has just fallen. Let me make a fire so you can
dry yourself. I'm afraid, though, that I cannot offer you
much here. The meals that the winds have are very
light, and men need to eat something much more
solid."

The prince thanked her for the kind welcome he had
received and approached the fire, which leapt into
flames almost immediately because the West Wind had
just entered and blown on it. No sooner had he arrived
than the Northeast Wind and many northerly gales
returned to the cave. Eole was not tardy, and Boreas,
the East, Southwest, and North Winds followed. They
were all damp and had puffed cheeks and unkempt
heads of hair. Their manners were not very civil or
polite, and when they ventured to speak to the prince,
they all but froze him with their breath. One recounted
that he had dispersed an entire navy. Another recalled that
he had caused many ships to perish. A third had kindly
saved certain vessels from pirates who had wanted to
seize them. Many of the gales reported how they had
uprooted trees, knocked down houses, and overturned
walls. In short, each one boasted of his exploits. After
listening to all of them, the old woman suddenly
showed signs of great uneasiness.

"Did any of you encounter your brother Zephir
during your adventures?" she asked. "He's already
late, and I confess I'm troubled that he's not going to
return."

While all echoed that they had not seen him, Adolph
noticed a young boy at the entrance of the cave. He was
just as handsome as Cupid: he had wings made of white
feathers mixed with the color of flesh that appeared to
be fine and delicate and in perpetual motion. His blond
hair fell carelessly in a thousand curls to his shoulders.
His head was crowned by roses and jasmine, and he had
a pleasant, jovial air about him.

"Where have you come from, you little rake?" the
old woman cried huskily. "All your brothers are here.
You're the only one who takes his time and who
doesn't care at all about how much I might worry."

"Mother, I had no intention of returning so late," he
said, "for I know that you don't like it. But I was in the
gardens of Princess Felicity. She was taking a walk
there with her nymphs. One made a garland of flowers
for her. Another nymph, who was lying on the grass,
opened her throat a little, and this gave me the freedom
to approach her and give her a kiss. Several were

dancing to songs. The beautiful princess was in an orange orchard, and my breath swept up to her mouth. I dallied around her and played gently with her veil. 'Zephir,' she said, 'I like that! You make everything so pleasant! I'm going to keep walking as long as you tarry. . . .' I must confess that such sweet words uttered by such a charming person captivated me, and I was no longer my own master. I would not have been able to leave her at all if I had not known how this would displease you."

Adolph listened with such great satisfaction that he felt sorry when Zephir fell silent. "Permit me, charming Zephir, to ask you where the country is that the princess reigns," he said.

"It is the Island of Happiness," responded Zephir. "Nobody, sir, can enter it. People have exhausted themselves in trying to find it, but their fate is such that they do not know how to find it. They have traveled all over in vain. Sometimes they even imagine that they have found it because they often arrive at other small ports possessing calm and tranquillity. Many people remain there happily, but these floating islands are quite mediocre compared with the Island of Happiness. People soon lose sight of them, and only desire, which allows mortals to hope for just a shadow of repose, keeps them searching. Every day I see distinguished men perish near there."

The prince continued to ply him with questions, which Zephir answered with great precision and intelligence. It was extremely late, and the good mother ordered all her children to go to their corners of the cave. Zephir offered the prince a bed in a spotless place less cold than the other caverns of this grotto. A small spot of fine grass grew there, covered with flowers, and Adolph threw himself down on it. The rest of the night he spent with Zephir, talking about the Princess Felicity.

"How I'd love to see her," he said. "Is it so absolutely impossible? Couldn't I succeed with your help?"

Zephir told him that such a venture would be very dangerous, but that if he had the courage to abandon himself to Zephir's guidance, he imagined there might be a way: he would put him on his wings and carry him through the vast ethereal regions. "I have a cloak I'll give you," he continued, "and when you put it on with the green side showing, you'll be invisible. No one will be able to perceive you, and this is absolutely vital for your protection, because if the guards of the island, who are terrible monsters, see you, they'll capture you, no matter how brave you may be."

Adolph had such an urgent desire to begin this great adventure that he accepted everything Zephir proposed with all his heart, no matter what danger he faced. No sooner did the sun begin to shine in its chariot of mother-of-pearls than the impatient Adolph woke a still dozing Zephir.

"I've given you hardly any time to rest," the prince said as he embraced him, "but it seems to me, my kind host, that it's already time to depart."

"Let's go, then," Zephir responded. "Far be it from me to complain. Let me thank you instead, for I must confess that I'm in love with a proud and pert rose, and I'd be in a good deal of trouble with her if I weren't there to see her as soon as it turns daylight. She is in one of Princess Felicity's flower beds."

So saying, he gave the prince the cloak that he had promised him. He wanted to carry him on his wings, but he did not find this way comfortable.

"Sir, I'm going to lift you," he said, "just as I lifted Psyche on Cupid's orders when I carried her to the beautiful palace that he had built for her."

So he took him in his arms, and after placing himself at the edge of a cliff, he rocked for some time in a steady motion until he spread his wings, took off, and began soaring through the air.

Although the prince was courageous, he could not help being afraid when he found himself aloft in the arms of a young adolescent. To reassure himself, he recalled that Zephir was a god and that Cupid himself, who seemed the smallest and weakest of all the gods, was the strongest and most awesome. Thus, abandoning himself to his destiny, he collected his wits and gazed attentively at all the places they flew over. But how was it possible to count the places! There were so many cities, kingdoms, seas, rivers, fields, deserts, woods, unknown territories, and diverse peoples! All these sights transported him into such a state of wonderment that he was unable to speak. Zephir told him about the names and customs of all those inhabitants of the earth. He flew gently, and they even took a rest on top of the formidable Caucasian Mountains, on Mount Athos, and on many others that they found along their way.

"Even though the beautiful rose whom I adore," Zephir said, "will sting me with her thorns, I can't cross such vastness without giving you the pleasure of admiring these wonders for the first time."

Adolph expressed his gratitude for Zephir's kindness and at the same time his concern that Princess Felicity would be unable to understand his language and he unable to speak hers.

"Don't fret over that," the god said. "The princess's knowledge is universal, and I'm convinced that you'll speak the same language soon enough."

He flew until that desired island was in sight, and the prince was so struck by all its beauties that he readily believed that it was indeed enchanted. The air was thoroughly perfumed with dew from the excellent waters of Nafre and Cordoue. The rain carried the scent of oranges. The water gushed up to the clouds. The forests were filled with rare trees, and the ground was covered with extraordinary flowers. Streams as clear as crystal flowed all over with a sweet murmur. The birds sang concerts that were superior to the music of the great masters. Exotic fruit grew there naturally, and throughout the island one could find tables covered with all the delicacies that one could desire. But the palace surpassed even all the rest: the walls were made of diamonds, and the ceilings and floors were made of precious gems that formed compartments. Gold glittered everywhere. The furniture was made by the hands of the most gallant fairies. Everything seemed so natural that one could not help but admire the magnificence and assortment all the more. After Zephir set the prince down in a pleasant green lawn, he said, "Sir,

I've kept my word, and now it's up to you to do the rest."

They embraced each other, and Adolph gave him thanks befitting such a favor. Since the god was eager to see his mistress, he left him in those delightful gardens. Venturing down several alleys, Adolph saw grottos made expressly for pleasure. In one he noticed a white marble statue of Cupid so well made that it must have been the work of some divine sculptor. Instead of flames, a jet of water spurted from its torch, and the god was supported by grotto-work and seemed to be reading verses engraved on lapis lazuli. These proclaimed: "Love is the greatest of all blessings. Love alone is able to fulfill our desires. All other sweet things of life become dull if they are not mixed with love's attractive charms."

Adolph entered a honeysuckle arbor, where the sun could not penetrate the charming shade. Here he lay on a carpet of grass surrounding a fountain, and he yielded to the sweetness of slumber, for his heavy eyelids and exhausted limbs begged for a few hours of rest.

It was close to noon when he awoke. He was disappointed to have lost so much time, and to make up for it, he rushed toward the palace. As soon as he got near enough to it, he began to admire its beautiful features at a more leisurely pace than when he had been further away. It seemed that all the arts had competed with equal success to contribute to the magnificence and perfection of the building. Because the prince continued to wear the cloak on the green side, he could view everything without being seen. For a long time he searched for a way to enter the palace, but either the vestibule was closed or the doors of the palace were on the other side of the palace, for he saw no way to enter until he noticed a pretty young nymph opening a window made entirely of crystal. At the very same moment a dwarfish gardener ran to the spot, and the nymph let down a large gold filigree basket that had many ribbons and bows attached. Then she ordered the gardener to gather flowers for the princess, and the gardener promptly did as she was told. Consequently, Adolph threw himself on the flowers in the basket before the nymph had pulled it up to the window. (It should be noted that the green cloak that made him invisible also made him as light as the wind.)

As soon as he was inside, he entered a large salon, where he saw wonders that are difficult to recount. The nymphs were there in large numbers. The oldest among them seemed no more than eighteen, and a great many seemed to be younger. Some were blondes, others brunettes, and all had remarkable white, fresh complexions with beautiful features and regular teeth. In short, the nymphs could pass for the most perfect people imaginable. Adolph could have stayed in the salon all day admiring them if his curiosity had not been aroused by numerous voices marvelously harmonizing with some exceedingly well-played instruments. He advanced toward the chamber from which this pleasant harmony came, and as he entered, he heard the most touching words sung in a manner equally tender.

When first the prince had entered the salon, he had thought that nothing could equal the charms he saw there. However, he was wrong, for the musicians surpassed their beauty by far. Due to some miracle, he understood everything they said even though he did not know the language they used in this palace. He was standing behind one of the prettiest nymphs when her veil slipped to the ground. Without realizing that he would undoubtedly frighten her, he picked up the veil and gave it to her. Since the nymph did not see a soul, she uttered a great cry, and perhaps for the first time someone had become afraid in that beautiful place. All her companions gathered around her, asking her urgently what the matter was.

"You're going to think that I've been seeing things," she said, "but I assure you that my veil that just fell to the ground was returned to my hand by some invisible force."

Everyone burst into laughter, and several nymphs pranced toward the princess's chamber to amuse her with this story. Adolph followed. Thanks to the green cloak, he crossed anonymously through the rooms, galleries, and chambers until he finally reached that of the princess. She sat on a throne made of a single carbuncle more radiant than the sun, but the eyes of Princess Felicity far outshone the carbuncle. Her beauty was so perfect that she seemed a daughter of the heavens. Moreover, she cast a youthful aura of majestic confidence that aroused love and respect. She was dressed more in a gallant than a magnificent fashion: her blond hair was decorated with flowers and a scarf, and her robe was made of gauze mixed with gold. Around her frolicked many small cupids playing a thousand different games. Some took her hands and kissed them; others climbed her throne with the help of their companions and placed a crown on her head. The pleasures were also playing about her. In brief, everywhere the prince turned his eyes, he was struck by the most charming things imaginable, and he stood there like a man entranced. He could hardly stand the princess's explosive beauty, and he could not think of anything but this person whom he already adored. Because he was so agitated and excited, his green cloak fell to the ground, and he became visible.

The princess had never seen a human being, and so she was extremely surprised. In turn, when Adolph saw that he had exposed himself, he threw himself respectfully at her feet.

"Great princess," he said. "I've crossed the universe to admire your divine beauty. I want to offer you my heart and devotion. I hope you will not refuse me."

The princess, who was normally vivacious, remained silent and confused. Until then she had never seen anyone as remarkable as this creature, whom she believed to be unique in the world. This thought convinced her that he was the Phoenix, that bird so rare and vaunted, and feeling she was right in her mistake, she said, "Handsome Phoenix—for I can't believe that you are anyone else but Phoenix since you are so perfect and don't resemble anything that is on my island— I'm extremely grateful to have the pleasure of seeing you. It's a great shame that you are the only kind of your species. If there were many more birds like you, they would fill beautiful bird cages."

Adolph smiled at her gracious naiveté. He did not want the object of his already great passion to remain mistaken for long, for it might lead to misconceptions. Therefore, he took care to tell her everything about himself, and never has a pupil learned her lessons so quickly. In fact, she was ready to give them after just learning them.

Her natural intuition went further than what the prince could tell her. She loved him more than she loved herself, and he loved her more than he loved himself. The two lovers felt everything that love has to offer in sweetness, everything that the mind has to offer in vivacity, and everything that the heart has to offer in delights. Nothing disturbed their repose; everything contributed to their pleasures. They were never sick. They were never troubled by the slightest inconvenience.

Their youthfulness was not changed by the passing of the years, for in this delightful asylum everyone drank long draughts from the Fountain of Youth. Neither the anguishes of love, nor jealous suspicions, not even the petty quarrels that sometimes disturb the happy tranquillity of lovers until they make sweet amends—nothing of this kind happened to them. They were intoxicated with pleasure, and up to that time there had never been a mortal who had enjoyed such good luck as constant as that of the prince. But the condition of mortality bears with it sad consequences. Their good fortune could not last forever.

One day when Adolph was with the princess, it occurred to him to ask her how long he had been enjoying the pleasure of being with her. "The moments pass so quickly where you are," he continued, "that I haven't paid any attention to time since my arrival."

"I'll tell you," she said, "after you reveal to me how long you think you've been here."

He pondered this and said, "If I consult my heart and the gratification I've experienced, I'd believe that I've only spent a week here. But, my dear princess, according to certain things that I can recall to mind, it's been approximately three months."

"Adolph," she said more seriously, "it's been three hundred years."

Ah, if she had only known what those words would cost her, she would have never uttered them.

"Three hundred years!" cried the prince. "What's going on in the world? Who's governing it right now? What are the people doing there? When I return, who will recognize me, and whom will I be able to recognize? My dominions have undoubtedly fallen into somebody else's hands rather than those close to me. I cannot dare hope that there's anything left for me. I'm going to be a prince stripped of his robe. People will regard me like a ghost. I'll no longer know the manners and customs that I'll need to live."

Becoming impatient, the princess interrupted him. "What do you regret, Adolph? Isn't this price worth all the love and kindness I've shown you? I received you in my palace where you are the master. I've preserved your life for three centuries. You haven't aged at all and apparently, until now, you haven't been bored. You wouldn't have had any of this if it weren't for me."

"I'm not ungrateful, beautiful princess," he replied, somewhat confused. "I know all that I owe you. But ultimately, if I were dead at this moment, I would have perhaps performed such great deeds that my name would be eternally engraved in stone. As it is, I see with shame that there has been nothing virtuous about my actions, and my name is not famous. The brave Reginald may have ended in the arms of his Armida, but it was honor that tore him away from her."

"You barbarian!" the princess screamed as a flood of tears streamed from her eyes. "It will be honor that tears you away from me. You want to leave me, and you minimize the pain that it will cause me."

Upon saying this, she collapsed in a dead faint. The prince was greatly moved. He dearly loved her, but he reapproached himself for having spent so much time with a mistress without having done anything that would place his name among the ranks of heroes. He tried in vain to restrain himself and conceal his misgivings. However, he fell into an apathy that soon rendered him unrecognizable.

Now the prince, who had mistaken centuries for

months, mistook months for centuries. The princess saw this and suffered greatly because of it. Not wanting him to remain out of a sense of obligation, she declared, "You are master of your destiny and can depart whenever you wish. All the same, I fear something terrible will happen to you."

Her last words caused him less pain than her first, which were not very pleasing themselves. Although he grew tender and melancholy when he thought about separating, his sense of his destiny was stronger, and at last he said farewell to the woman whom he had adored, and whom he still loved with a great deal of tenderness. He assured her that as soon as he had achieved a measure of glory and made himself more worthy of her magnanimity, he would return and acknowledge her as his sole sovereign and the only treasure of his life. But the princess was too intelligent to be misled, and she had sad forebodings that told her she was going to lose the person she cherished forever.

Despite the fact that she was terribly upset, she did not express her pain. She gave the indifferent Adolph magnificent weapons and the most magnificent horse in the world. "Bichar (that was the name of the horse) will conduct you," she said, "and he will take you wherever you must go to do battle and triumph. But don't place your foot on the ground no matter what happens in your country, for the fairy spirit that the gods have given me enable me to prophesy that if you neglect my advice, Bichar will not be able to extricate you from your trouble."

Promising her that he would obey her wishes, the prince kissed her beautiful hands a thousand times, and he was so eager to leave that delightful place that he even forgot to take his green cloak with him.

Once they reached the border of the island, the vigorous horse threw himself into the river with his master on top of him. After swimming across it, he galloped over hill and dale. He passed through fields and forests with such great speed that it seemed he had wings. But one evening, in a narrow, rutted path, filled with rocks and pebbles and bordered by thorn bushes, they encountered a wagon blocking the path. Loaded with different kinds of old wings, it had turned over on an old man who had been driving the wagon. His head was gray, his voice trembled, and the prince felt pity for the old man's distress since he was bearing the weight of the wagon. Bichar wanted to jump over the wagon blocking the way, and was about ready to soar over it when the good man cried, "Sir, have some compassion for my predicament. If you don't deign to help me, I'll soon be dead."

Adolph could not resist helping the old man. He put his feet on the ground, approached the man, and gave him his hand. But alas! He was tremendously surprised to see the man get up quickly and seize him before he could get ready to defend himself.

"Finally, the Prince of Russia!" the old man said in a terrible, menacing voice, "I've found you. I'm called Father Time, and I've been looking for you for three centuries. I've used all the wings this wagon is carrying to go around the universe in order to find you. But no matter where you may have hidden yourself, nothing that lives can escape me."

Thereupon, he clapped his hand on Adolph's mouth with such force that he prevented the prince from drawing breath until he was smothered. At this sad moment Zephir, who had witnessed everything, passed by, greatly disturbed by the misfortune of his dear friend. When the old barbarian left Adolph, Zephir approached and tried to bring him back to life with his sweet breath. His efforts were in vain, though. He took him in his arms just as he had done the first time, and weeping bitter tears, he brought him back to the gardens of Princess Felicity. He set him down in a grotto on a rock that was flat across the top. Then he covered him and surrounded him with flowers. After taking off his weapons, he formed a trophy with them and engraved an epitaph on a column of jasper that he placed near the unfortunate prince.

The sorrowful princess had been going every day to this grotto since the departure of her lover, adding a flood of tears to the flow of the stream. But then, what unexpected joy to find him again at the very moment when she believed him to be so far away! She imagined that he had just arrived and that, exhausted from the trip, he had fallen asleep. She contemplated whether she should wake him, and finally giving way to her tender feelings, she opened her loving arms to embrace him. As she approached, however, she began to realize her extreme misfortune, and she uttered such bitter cries that they could have moved the most insensitive heart.

She ordered the doors of her palace to be closed forever, and ever since that fatal day nobody has seen her. Her suffering is the reason why she rarely shows herself, and one never finds this princess without her being preceded by some anguish accompanied by sorrow or followed by disturbances. This is the company that is usually with her most of the time. Human beings can certainly bear witness to this, and ever since that deplorable adventure, everyone keeps saying that there is no avoiding Father Time. Nor is there perfect happiness.

THE BLUE BIRD

ONCE upon a time there was a king who was extremely rich. For all his property and money, though, he was inconsolable when his wife suddenly fell ill and died. He shut himself up for a week in a small room and beat his head against the walls in his distress. Since his servants were afraid that he would kill himself, they put some mattresses between the tapestries and the walls so that he would not harm himself no matter how much he knocked himself about. Moreover, his subjects all agreed that they had better speak to him to alleviate his grief as best they could. Some prepared grave and serious speeches; others, charming and even lively addresses. But none made the least impression on him, for he barely heard a word they said.

At last a lady covered by black crape, veils, mantles, and other long mourning garments came before him. She wept so much and sobbed so loudly that he was quite astonished. She told him she would not attempt, as others had done, to mitigate his sorrow. Rather, she came to augment it, since nothing could be more just than to lament the loss of a good wife. "As for myself, I have lost the best of husbands and have made up my mind to weep as long as I have eyes in my head." Thereupon, she redoubled her groans, and the king, following her example, began to howl as well.

He paid more attention to this visitor than all the others and talked to her about the excellent qualities of his dear departed wife. In turn, she recapitulated all those of her beloved dead husband. They talked so much about their sorrow that they were eventually at a loss for words. When the cunning widow saw the subject was nearly exhausted, she raised her veil a little so that the grieving king could get a peek. Indeed, this poor mourner knew how to roll her large blue eyes and flutter long black lashes in a most effective manner. Her complexion was still blooming, and the king examined her with a great deal of attention. Gradually he spoke less and less about his wife, until he stopped discussing her altogether. The widow declared, however, that she would never stop mourning for her husband. In response, the king implored her not to make her sorrow eternal, and soon, to everyone's astonishment, he declared that he would marry her. His mourning garments were exchanged for those with green and rose. Apparently, one needs only to determine a person's weakness in order to gain his trust and do just what one wishes with him.

The king had had only a daughter by his first wife. Considered an eighth wonder of the world, she was named Florine because she was so sweet, young, and beautiful. Seldom was this artless maid seen in splendid attire; she preferred light morning dresses of taffeta fastened with a few jewels and quantities of the finest flowers, which produced an admirable effect when twined with her beautiful hair. She was only fifteen when the king was remarried.

The new queen sent for her own daughter, who had been brought up by her godmother, the fairy Soussio, but she was not particularly more graceful or beautiful because of this upbringing. Because Soussio loved her dearly, she had worked hard to make something out of her goddaughter, but her efforts were in vain. The girl's name was Truitonne, and her face was covered with reddish spots like those on the back of a trout. Her black hair was so greasy and dirty that no one would venture to touch it, and oil oozed out of her yellow skin. Her mother doted on her and talked about nothing but her charming Truitonne.

Since Florine possessed so many advantages over her daughter, however, the queen was stirred to use every possible means to belittle the unfortunate princess in the eyes of her father. Not a day passed that the queen and Truitonne did not play some mischievous trick on Florine. The princess, who was as mild as

she was sensible, merely endeavored to keep herself
beyond the reach of their malice.

One day the king remarked to the queen that Florine
and Truitonne were of an age to be married, and that
they should bestow the hand of one of them on the first
prince who visited their court.

"I want my daughter married first," said the queen.
"She's older than yours, and since she's a thousand
times more charming, there should be no hesitation
about the matter."

The king, who disliked arguments, replied that he
was quite willing to do it this way and she was to
arrange everything as she desired.

A short time afterward, it was learned that King
Charmant was to arrive soon. No prince was more
celebrated for gallantry and magnificence than he. In
mind and appearance he was just as charming as his
name implied. When the queen heard this news, she
employed all the embroiderers, all the tailors, and all
the artisans to make dresses for Truitonne. On the other
hand, she not only requested that the king give nothing
new to Florine, she also bribed the princess's ladies-in-
waiting to steal all her clothes, headdresses, and jewels
on the very day King Charmant arrived so that when
she went to dress she could not find even a ribbon.
Florine knew full well who had done her this turn, and
she sent her servants to purchase materials for a new
dress. However, all the tradesmen responded that the
queen had forbidden them to furnish her with a single
thing. Therefore, she was left only with the gown she
had on her back, and this was very soiled. So ashamed
was she of her appearance that when King Charmant
arrived, she hid herself in a corner of the hall.

The queen received the royal visitor with great pomp
and presented her daughter in a blaze of such magnificence that she looked even more ugly than usual. When
King Charmant averted his eyes, the queen tried to
convince herself that he was so stunned by her that he
had to keep turning away to control his emotions.
Thus, she continually pushed Truitonne before him,
but he responded by inquiring, "Isn't there another
princess, named Florine?"

"Yes," said Truitonne, pointing with her finger, "there she is, hiding herself because she's not dressed properly."

Upon being discovered, Florine blushed. So exceedingly beautiful did she look in her confusion that King Charmant was dazzled. He rose immediately and bowed profoundly to the princess. "Madam," he said, "your incomparable beauty makes the artificial aid of ornaments quite unnecessary."

"Sir," she replied, "I confess I'm not accustomed to wearing such a disgraceful dress as this, and I would have preferred to have escaped your notice."

"It would be impossible for such a marvelous princess like yourself to go anywhere and not have all eyes focused on her," he exclaimed.

"Ah," said the queen, greatly irritated, "it's nice listening to you pay these compliments. But believe me, sir, Florine is already enough of a flirt. She doesn't need such excessive flattery."

King Charmant quickly perceived the queen's motives for speaking this way, but since he was not accustomed to suppressing his inclinations, he continued to manifest his admiration for Florine. Indeed, he conversed with her for three whole hours.

The queen was in despair, and Truitonne inconsolable, because the princess had received such preference. Complaining bitterly to the king, they compelled him to consent to locking up Florine in a tower during King Charmant's stay so that they could not see each other.

No sooner did she return to her room than four masked men seized and carried her to a room at the top of the tower, where they left her greatly distressed, for she saw clearly that she was being treated this way to prevent her from pleasing King Charmant. He had already gained her affections, and she would willingly have accepted him for her husband.

Since he was not aware of Florine's violent abduction, he looked forward with the greatest impatience to the hour when he would meet her again. He talked about her to the gentlemen the king had placed in his company to do him honor, but they had been ordered

by the queen to say the worst possible things about
Florine they could imagine:

"She is coquettish, inconstant, and ill-tempered."

"She torments her friends and her servants."

"It is impossible to imagine anyone more slovenly."

"She is so niggardly that she prefers to dress like a
poor shepherdess than spend the money allowed her by
her father to purchase rich garments befitting her
rank."

As each detail was mentioned, Charmant smarted,
scarcely able to restrain his anger. "No," he said to
himself, "it's impossible that Heaven would permit so
worthless a soul to inhabit this masterpiece of nature. I
admit she was badly dressed when I first saw her, but
the shame she expressed proves that she was not accustomed to dressing so. How can she be ill-tempered and
coquettish with such an enchanting air of mildness and
modesty? It makes no sense! I can much more easily
imagine that it's the queen who's slandering her. She's
not her stepmother for nothing, and the Princess Truitonne, her own daughter, is such an ugly beast that it
wouldn't be unusual for her to envy the most perfect of
beings."

While he was pondering all of this in his mind, the
courtiers suspected from his manner that he was displeased by their abuse of Florine. One courtier more
astute than the rest changed his tune and began
extolling the princess's virtues in order to discover the
prince's true sentiments. Upon hearing this praise,
Charmant woke as from a deep sleep. He participated
eagerly in the conversation, and his features lit up with
joy. Oh love, how hard you are to hide! You are visible
everywhere—on a lover's lips, in his eyes, in the tone
of his voice. When we truly love, both silence and
speech, happiness and misery, equally express the passion we feel.

Impatient to learn if King Charmant was in love, the
queen sent for the courtiers who had won the king's
trust and spent the rest of the night interrogating them.
Everything they reported served only to confirm the
opinion she had already formed—the king was in love
with Florine.

But how can I describe the melancholy state of that poor princess? She lay stretched on the floor in the keep of that terrible tower. "I wouldn't have to be pitied so much," she said, "if I had been locked up here before I had seen that charming monarch. My recollection of him only serves to increase my distress. I'm positive that the queen treated me this cruelly only to prevent my seeing him again. Alas, the little beauty that Heaven has bestowed on me has cost me a great deal of tranquillity." She then began to weep so bitterly that her worst enemies would have pitied her if they had witnessed her torment. And so the night passed.

The queen was anxious to win over King Charmant by showing him all the attention she could. She sent him the most costly and magnificent garments made in the newest fashion of that country, and also the Order of the Knights of Cupid, which she had compelled the king to institute the day they themselves had married in honor of their wedding. This badge was a golden heart enameled and colored like fire. It was surrounded by several arrows and pierced with one that bore the words, "One alone wounds me." For Charmant, however, the queen had a heart cut from a ruby as large as an ostrich's egg; each arrow was made of a single diamond the length of a finger, and the chain of the badge was composed of pearls, the smallest which weighed a whole pound. In short, nothing like it had ever been seen in the world. Charmant was so astonished when he saw it that it was some time before he could speak. At the same time they gave him a beautifully illustrated book with pages of the finest vellum and a binding encrusted with gold and jewels. In it were written the statutes of the Order of the Knights of Cupid in a gallant, refined style. They told him that the princess he had seen requested that he be her knight and had sent him this present. Upon hearing this he imagined that they had come from his beloved. "My goodness," he cried, "does the beautiful Princess Florine think of me in this splendid and flattering way?"

"Sire," they replied, "you've confused the names. We come from the charming Truitonne."

"Truitonne! Is she the one who wants me to be her

champion?" the king asked coldly. "I regret that I
cannot accept this honor. A sovereign is not wholly his
own master and cannot accept just any engagement that
pleases him. I know the duties of a knight and would
like to be able to fulfill them all. But I'd prefer not
receiving the honor she has offered me rather than
proving myself unworthy of it."

So saying, he put the heart, chain, and book back
into the basket and sent them all back to the queen,
who, along with her daughter, almost choked with rage
at the contemptuous manner in which the illustrious
foreigner had declined such a signal honor.

King Charmant visited the king and queen as often
as he was permitted in the hope of meeting Florine in
the royal apartments. His eyes searched everywhere for
her. The moment he heard anyone enter the room, he
turned sharply toward the door and seemed always
restless and unhappy when it was not she. The malicious queen easily guessed what was on his mind, but
she appeared to take no notice of it. She talked to him
only about pleasure parties, and he replied with the
most incongruous answers. At last he asked her
plainly, "Where is the Princess Florine?"

"Sir," the queen replied haughtily, "her father has
forbidden her to leave her apartment until my daughter
is married."

"And what motive," inquired King Charmant, "can
there be for making that beautiful princess a prisoner?"

"I don't know," the queen said, "and even if I did, I
don't feel obligated to inform you."

Enraged, Charmant cast an angry glance at Truitonne. He thought to himself, "This little monster is
the cause of my being deprived of the pleasure of
seeing Florine." So he abruptly left the queen's presence, which gave him too much pain.

On returning to his room, he told a young prince, a
cherished companion of his, to do his utmost to win the
confidence of one of the princess's attendants so that
he could speak to Florine for even one moment. This
prince easily found some ladies of the palace whom he
could trust, and one of them guaranteed him that
Florine would be at a small lower window that very

evening. This window overlooked the garden, and she could converse with Charmant from it, provided he was extremely careful and made sure that no one knew. "The king and queen are so severe," she added, "that they'll put me to death if they discover I've sided with Charmant's feelings."

Delighted that he had succeeded in his mission, the prince promised her anything she desired. Then he returned to his royal master and told him the appointed time of meeting. Meanwhile the confidante, who had deceived him, went and told the queen what had happened and waited for further instructions. The queen immediately decided to place her daughter at the little window and gave Truitonne special instructions. Despite the fact that she was naturally stupid, Truitonne was to carry them out without a mistake.

The night was so dark that King Charmant could not have possibly noticed the trickery, even if he had been suspicious. When he drew near the window, he was overflowing with joy and expressed a wealth of tender thoughts to the supposed Florine to convince her of his affection. Taking advantage of the situation, Truitonne told him that she felt like the most unfortunate person in the world in having such a cruel stepmother, and that she would continue to suffer until the queen's daughter was married. Charmant assured her that if she would accept him for her husband, he would be delighted to share his heart and crown with her. Thereupon, he drew his ring from his finger and, placing it on one of Truitonne's, begged her to receive it as a token of eternal fidelity and added, "You need only fix the hour for our flight."

Truitonne made the best possible answers she could to his ardent appeals. He noticed they were not very sensible, and they normally would have made him uneasy, but he thought they arose from the terror she felt at possibly being surprised by the queen. He left her only on condition that she would meet him again the next night at the same hour, which she promised faithfully to do.

Upon hearing of the good success of this meeting, the queen felt sure of everything. When the day was fixed for the elopement, King Charmant prepared to carry off his beloved in a flying chariot drawn by winged frogs, a present to him by a friend who was an enchanter. The night was pitch black, and Truitonne snuck out mysteriously through a little door. The king, who was waiting for her, received her in his arms with a hundred vows of everlasting affection. But since he was not eager to be flying about in his chariot for a long time before marrying his beloved princess, he asked her to tell him where she wanted their wedding to be held. She answered that she had a godmother named Soussio who was a celebrated fairy, and she felt they should go at once to Soussio's castle. Although the king did not know the way, he only had to mention to his great frogs where he wished to go. They were perfectly acquainted with the whole map of the world, and in no time they brought Charmant and Truitonne to Soussio's abode.

The castle was so brilliantly illuminated that Charmant would have discovered his mistake the moment he entered if the princess had not carefully covered herself with her veil. She asked for her godmother and contrived to see her alone. Telling her how she had ensnared Charmant, she entreated her to pacify him.

"Ah, my child," the fairy said, "the task won't be an easy one, for he is too fond of Florine. I feel certain he'll give us a great deal of trouble."

Meanwhile the king was awaiting them in a salon that had walls made of diamonds so pure and transparent that he saw Soussio and Truitonne conversing together through them. He thought he must be dreaming. "What?" he said. "Have I been betrayed? Have some demons brought this enemy of our peace to this place? Has she come to disturb our wedding? Where's my dear Florine? Perhaps her father has pursued her!"

A thousand thoughts ran through his mind, all of them disconcerting. But matters looked even worse when he entered the salon and Soussio addressed him in an authoritative tone, "King Charmant, here is the Princess Truitonne, whom you have pledged to marry.

She is my goddaughter, and it's my desire that you marry her immediately."

"Me?" he exclaimed. "You want me to marry that little monster? You must think me a docile babe to propose such a thing. I've made no promise to her whatsoever, and if she's told you otherwise, then she has—"

"Hold your tongue," interrupted Soussio. "Don't you dare forget to show me the proper respect."

"I agree to respect you as much as a fairy can be respected," the king replied, "provided that you restore my princess to me."

"Aren't I your princess, faithless one?" Truitonne said, showing him his ring. "To whom did you give this ring as a pledge of your troth? With whom did you converse at the little window if not with me?"

"How's this possible?" he cried. "Have I been deceived? No! No, I'll not be your dupe! Come, my frogs, come! I want to leave here immediately!"

"Oho, it's not in your power to leave without my consent," exclaimed Soussio. At her touch his feet were fastened to the floor as if they had been nailed to it.

"You may stone me to death, you may flay me alive," cried the king. "I'll marry no one but Florine. My mind is made up. So you can do with me as you please."

Soussio tried sweet talk, threats, promises, prayers. Truitonne wept, shrieked, groaned, stomped, and became sullen again. The king merely surveyed them both with an air of the greatest indignation, not giving the slightest response to anything they said.

Twenty days and twenty nights passed without their ceasing to talk and without eating, sleeping, or sitting down. Finally Soussio became exhausted and lost her patience. "Well, since you so obstinately refuse to listen to reason," she said to the king, "choose right now whether you'll marry my goddaughter, or do penance for seven years as a punishment for breaking your word."

All of a sudden the king, who up to this time had been perfectly silent, exclaimed, "Do what you want with me, just so that I'm freed from this wretch."

"You're a wretch yourself!" Truitonne said angrily.

"A petty king like you, with your marsh-bred postures. You come to my country, break your word to me, and insult me. Had you a groat's worth of honor in you, you'd behave differently!"

"How touching," said the king in an ironical tone. "I must be making a mistake not to take such a lovely person for my wife."

"No, no, she won't be your wife!" screamed Soussio in a rage. "You may now fly out of that window if you like, for you're to be a blue bird for the next seven years!"

At that very moment the king underwent a complete transformation: his arms grew feathers and formed wings; his legs and feet became black and scrawny and furnished with crooked talons; his body shrank. He was entirely covered with long, fine, thin feathers of celestial blue; his eyes became round and as bright as two stars; his nose was but an ivory beak; a white crest rose on his head in the form of a crown. He was able to sing and talk in a remarkable fashion, but all he uttered was a cry of anguish at seeing himself transformed into this condition. Then he flew from Soussio's fatal palace as fast as his wings could carry him.

Overwhelmed with grief, he flitted from branch to branch, selecting only those trees consecrated to love or sorrow. Sometimes he landed on myrtles, other times on cypresses, and sang the most lamentable tunes, deploring his sad fate and that of Florine. "Where have her enemies hidden her?" he asked. "What has become of that beautiful victim? Has the queen's barbarity permitted her to remain alive? Where should I search? Am I condemned to spend seven years without her? Perhaps during that period they'll compel her to marry, and I'll never regain the hope that sustains me." This whirl of thoughts tormented the blue bird to such a degree that he would have welcomed death.

Meanwhile the fairy Soussio sent Truitonne back to the queen, who was anxiously waiting to learn all about the nuptials. When she heard from her daughter's lips all that had transpired, she became terribly enraged, and poor Florine was to feel her backlash. "She shall repent more than once for having captivated Charmant," the queen said.

To the tower she went with Truitonne, whom she had dressed in her richest clothes with a crown of diamonds on her head and a royal mantle whose train was carried by three daughters of the richest barons in the realm. On her thumb was King Charmant's ring, which Florine had noticed the day she had conversed with him. Florine was greatly surprised to see Truitonne in such splendid apparel.

"My daughter's come to bring you a wedding present," she said. "King Charmant was so madly in love with her that he's married her. Oh, you've never seen such a happy couple." Thereupon, they showed the princess heaps of gold and silver tissues, jewels, lace and ribbons, all contained in large baskets worked in gold filigree. While presenting these objects, Truitonne made sure that Florine noticed King Charmant's sparkling ring, and the latter became convinced of her misfortune. With an air of desperation she told them to remove the base gifts from her sight. "I wish to wear nothing but black, and indeed, I shall soon be dead." Upon saying this, she fainted.

The cruel queen was delighted to have succeeded so well. She did not permit anyone to assist her, but left her alone in the most wretched state imaginable. Then she maliciously reported to the king that his daughter was so carried away by her emotions that she had lost control of her wits, and great care should be taken to prevent her leaving the tower. The king told her to manage the matter as she thought best, and that he would be satisfied as always.

When the princess recovered from her swoon and began to consider how they had behaved toward her, how her wicked stepmother had mistreated her, and how her hope of becoming King Charmant's wife had been destroyed, her anguish became so keen that she wept the entire night. In this wretched condition she went to an open window, where she uttered the most tender and touching lamentations. When day began to break, she shut the window, but continued to weep. The following night she again opened the window, sobbing and sighing and shedding a torrent of tears. Morning dawned, and she hid herself in the recesses of her chamber.

In the meantime King Charmant—or, to speak more correctly, the beautiful blue bird—kept flying around the palace, for he believed his dear princess was confined somewhere in it. If her lamentations were distressing, his were no less so. He approached the windows as near as he could in order to look into the rooms, but the fear of being noticed and recognized by Truitonne prevented his examining the rooms as closely as he wished. "It would cost me my life," he said to himself. "If these wicked princesses were to discover where I am, they'd take their revenge on me. I must keep my distance, or else I'll be exposed to extreme danger." For these reasons he took the greatest precautions and rarely sang except at night.

Now, there happened to be a towering cypress right in front of the window at which Florine usually sat. The blue bird came to perch on it, and no sooner had he done so than he heard someone lamenting. "How much longer shall I suffer?" she said. "Won't death kindly come to my aid? Those who fear death see him too soon. Yet I long for his coming, and he cruelly avoids me. Oh, barbarous queen! What have I done to you that you keep me in this horrible captivity? Don't you have ways enough to torment me? You need only make me witness the happiness of your unworthy daughter enjoying the company of King Charmant!"

The blue bird heard every syllable of this lament in astonishment. He could hardly wait for daylight to arrive in order to catch a glimpse of the distressed lady, but just before morning dawned, she closed her window and retired. The bird, whose curiosity was awakened, did not fail to return the following night, and in the moonlight he saw a girl begin to sigh at the tower window.

"Oh, fortune," she exclaimed, "you who flattered me with the prospect of reigning, you who had kept my father's love alive, what have I done to deserve being plunged so suddenly into such bitter grief? Is it at such a tender young age as mine that one must begin to experience your inconstancy? Return, you cruel thing! Return, if you can. The only favor I ask of you is to end my unhappy fate."

The blue bird listened attentively, and the more he did, the more convinced he became that it was his charming princess who was doing the lamenting.

"Adorable Florine," he cried, "wonder of our days, why do you desire to terminate your life so hastily? Your misfortunes can still be remedied."

"Ah! Who's that speaking in such a consoling way?" she asked.

"An unfortunate king," replied the bird, "who loves you and will never love any other than you."

"A king who loves me!" replied Florine. "Is this a trap set for me by my enemy? Yet what would she gain by it? If she seeks to discover my sentiments, I'm ready to frankly own up to them."

"No, my princess," replied the bird. "The lover who's speaking to you is incapable of betraying you"—and as he uttered these words he few to the window.

At first Florine was alarmed at the appearance of such an extraordinary bird, who spoke with as much sense as a man and yet had the small, sweet voice of a nightingale. The beauty of his plumage, however, and the words he uttered soon reassured her.

"May I be permitted once more to behold you, my princess?" he exclaimed. "Can I taste such perfect happiness and not die with joy? But, alas, how this happiness is troubled by your captivity, and the condition that the wicked Soussio has reduced me to for seven years."

"And who are you, charming bird?" the princess inquired, caressing him.

"You've pronounced my name," said the king, "and you pretend you do not know me?"

"What? The greatest monarch in the world, King Charmant?" cried the princess. "Can the little bird I hold in my hand be you?"

"Alas, beautiful Florine, it is but too true," the bird replied. "And if anything can console me, it's the feeling that I chose this pain instead of renouncing my love for you."

"For me?" said Florine. "Ah, don't attempt to deceive me. I know that you've married Truitonne. I recognized your ring on her hand. I saw her glistening with the diamonds you had given her. She came to insult me in my sad prison, wearing the rich crown and royal mantle she had received from your hands, while I was bound in chains and fetters."

"You've seen Truitonne dressed that way?" interrupted the king. "Did she and her mother dare tell you those jewels came from me? Oh, Heaven! Is it possible that I hear such awful lies, and that I cannot gain immediate revenge on the liars? I want you to know that they tried to deceive me: by basely using your name, they succeeded in getting me to elope with the ugly Truitonne. But the instant I discovered my error, I tried to flee from her, and eventually I chose to become a blue bird for seven years rather than betray the pledge of fidelity I made to you."

Florine was so pleased by her charming lover's explanation that she forgot the misery of her prison. She told him many things to console him in his sad circumstances, and assured him that she would have done as much for him. Day had dawned and the majority of the officers of the royal household risen before the blue bird and the princess had finished conversing. It cost them a thousand pangs to part, but they agreed they would meet every night in the same manner.

Their delight at having found each other was so great that it cannot be described. Both offered thanks to love and fortune, but Florine's happiness was tempered by her anxiety about the blue bird. "Who will protect him from the hunters?" she asked. "Or from the sharp talons of some eagle or hungry vulture? They'll eat him with relish not knowing that he's a great king. Oh, Heaven! What would become of me if some of his delicate feathers were blown to my window and announced to me the dreaded disaster?" This thought prevented the poor princess from closing her eyes, for when one loves, thoughts appear like facts, and what one would at another time think impossible seems certain to occur. So she spent the day in tears until the hour arrived for her to return to the window.

Hiding in a hollow tree, the charming bird occupied himself all day by thinking of his beautiful princess. "How happy I am to have found her," he said. "How fascinating she is! How deeply I appreciate the kindness she's extended to me." The tender lover counted every second he was condemned to spend in the shape that prevented his marrying her, and never was the termination of a sentence more ardently desired. Since he was eager to be as gallant to Florine as possible, he flew to the capital city of his own kingdom. Landing at his palace, he entered his cabinet through a broken pane of glass in one of the windows, took a pair of diamond earrings more perfect than any other in the world, and brought them that evening to Florine's cell, where he requested that she wear them.

"I'll consent," she said, "if you visit me by daylight, but since I only see you at night, I won't put them on."

The bird promised he would find a way to come to the tower whenever she wished. In response, she put on the earrings, and the night passed in tender discourse just like the night before.

The next day the blue bird returned to his palace, entered his cabinet by the broken window, and carried away the richest bracelets ever seen. Each was made of a single emerald cut in facets with a hole through the center to enable the wearer to pass her hands and arms through them. "Do you think," the princess said to him, "that my affection for you can be measured by presents? Ah, how you misjudge me."

"No, madam," he replied, "I don't believe that the trifles I offer you are required to keep your love, but mine will not permit me to neglect the least opportunity of showing you my respect, and when I am absent, these little trinkets will bring me to mind."

Florine said a thousand kind things to him on this subject, and he replied with as many no less tender. The following night the enamoured bird brought his beautiful lady a watch. It was encased in a single pearl, and the workmanship was superior to its luster.

"It's useless to present me with a watch," said the

princess sweetly. "When you are absent, the hours seem endless, and when you are with me they pass so like a dream that I cannot time them with any precision."

"Alas, my princess," exclaimed the blue bird, "I agree with you and I am certain that I feel the pain of absence and the pleasure of returning even more deeply than you do."

"After what you have suffered to remain true to me," replied the princess, "I truly believe that your affection and respect cannot be carried further."

As soon as morning appeared, the bird flew back to his hollow tree, where he lived on wild fruits. Sometimes he sang the finest tunes, to the great delight of all who passed that way. Since they could not see anything, they believed it must be the voice of a spirit. This belief became so widespread that eventually nobody dared enter the wood. A thousand fabulous adventures were told about those who had done so, and the general alarm insured the blue bird's safety. Not a day passed without his making Florine some present, either a pearl necklace, or the most brilliant and uniquely wrought rings, diamond loops, bodkins, and bouquets of jewels in imitation of natural flowers, entertaining books, and interesting medals, until she possessed a stack of marvelous valuables. She wore her jewels only by night to please the king, and in the daytime, since she had no other place to put them in, she hid them carefully in the straw of her mattress.

Two years passed this way without Florine once complaining about her captivity. Indeed, how could she? She had the pleasure of conversing all night with the man she loved. Never were so many pretty speeches made. Though the bird spent the whole day in a hollow tree and never saw anyone, they had a thousand new things to tell each other. Their love and wit alone furnished them with an inexhaustible abundance of subject matter for their conversation.

In the meantime the malicious queen vainly endeavored to marry off Truitonne. She sent ambassadors with proposals to every prince she had ever heard of, but these envoys were sent packing almost as soon as they arrived. "If your mission concerned Princess Florine, you would be joyously received," was the answer. "But as for Truitonne, let her remain a virgin, for nobody will object."

These tidings infuriated both mother and daughter, and they vented their anger against the innocent princess. "What? This arrogant creature continues to thwart us despite her captivity?" they cried. "We shall never be able to forgive the injuries she has caused us! She must have some secret correspondence with foreign countries and thus must be guilty of high treason at the very least. Let's act on this suspicion and use every possible means to convict her."

So late did they finish their talk about this matter that it was past midnight when they decided to climb the tower to interrogate Florine. At the window with the blue bird, she was arrayed in all her jewels. Her beautiful hair was dressed with a nicety unusual for tormented souls. Her room and bed were strewn with flowers, and some Spanish pastilles that she was burning emitted an exquisite perfume. Listening at the door, the queen thought she heard a melody sung in a duet (Florine's voice was nearly divine), and these are the tender words she heard:

> "Oh, how wretched is our lot,
> Nor can we forget our torment,
>   Loving thus—while forced to part.
> But even though our woes are deep,
> And our cruel foes force us to weep,
>   Nothing will destroy our hearts."

A few deep sighs finished this little concert.

"Ah, my Truitonne, we've been betrayed," exclaimed the queen. All at once she opened the door and rushed into the room. Imagine the alarm of Florine at this sight! She promptly pushed open the window to give the royal bird an opportunity to fly off unperceived. She was much more anxious about protecting his life than her own, but he felt unable to fly away. His sharp eyes had discovered the danger—the queen and Truitonne—to which the princess was exposed. As they approached like Furies bent on devouring her, how troubled he was not to be able to defend her!

"Your intrigues against the state are detected," cried the queen. "Do not imagine your rank can save you from the punishment you deserve."

"Intrigues with whom, madam?" inquired the princess. "Haven't you been my jailer these two years? Have I seen any other people than those you have sent me?" While she spoke, the queen and her daughter examined her with great surprise. Her remarkable beauty and her extraordinary attire dazzled them.

"And where, madam, have you obtained these jewels that outshine the sun?" the queen asked. "Are we to believe there are mines in this tower?"

"I found them," answered Florine. "That's all I know about it."

The queen gazed at Florine with a penetrating look, trying to ascertain what was happening in the core of her heart. "We are not your dupes," she cried. "You think you can deceive us, but, Princess, we are aware of all you do from morning till night. These jewels have been given to you with the sole object of inducing you to sell your father's kingdom."

"I'm in a good position to deliver, aren't I?" replied Florine with a disdainful smile. "An unfortunate princess who has languished in captivity so long can be of great service, certainly, in a conspiracy of such a nature."

"And for whom, then," added the queen, "are you so coquettishly dressed up? Your room is so full of perfume, and your attire so magnificent that it is as if you were at court."

"I have plenty of time on my hands," said the princess. "It's not unusual I should strive to wile away a few moments by taking care of the way I look. I spend so many hours in weeping over my misfortunes that my innocent occupation surely cannot be a subject of reproach."

"Indeed, indeed!" said the queen. "Let us just see if this innocent miss is not in league with our enemies." She began to hunt everywhere and, emptying the mattress, she found such an immense quantity of dia-

monds, pearls, rubies, emeralds, and topazes that
she could not imagine where they all had come from.
All the while she was intending to hide incriminating
documents in some place so that their discovery would
inculpate the princess. When she thought nobody was
looking, she began thrusting them into the chimney,
but by good luck the blue bird was perched there. He
had eyes as sharp as a lynx and saw everything.

"Beware, Florine!" he cried. "Your enemy is trying
to betray you."

This voice was so unexpected that it frightened the
queen, and she became afraid to conceal the papers.

"Madam," said the princess, "you see that the spirits
of the air are my friends."

"I believe," exclaimed the queen in a fit of rage,
"that you are in league with demons. In spite of them,
though, your father will have justice done."

"Would to heaven," cried Florine, "I only had to fear
the fury of my father. But yours, madam, is much more
terrible."

The queen left her, greatly disturbed by all she had
seen and heard. She consulted her friends as to what
should be done to the princess. They remarked that if
Florine was being protected by some fairy or
enchanter, any further persecution would only irritate
her powerful friend. "It would be better first to discover the mystery." The queen approved this idea. She
sent a young girl to sleep in Florine's apartment under
the pretext that she was there to wait on her. The girl
pretended to be naive, but Florine did not fall for such
an obvious ruse. The princess regarded her as a spy,
and she could only feel her torment more violently.
"What now? Won't I ever be able to converse again
with my dear bird?" she asked. "He has helped me
endure my misfortunes, and I have soothed his troubles. Our affection was everything to us! What will
become of him? What will become of me?" While
thinking all these things, she shed rivers of tears. She
no longer dared go to the little window, though she
heard the bird fluttering around it. She was dying to
open it, but she feared exposing the life of her dear
lover.

A whole month passed without her appearing at the window. The blue bird was in despair. Complaint after complaint did he utter. How could he live without seeing his princess? He had never felt the pangs of solitude and the misery of his transformation so sharply. He sought in vain a remedy for both. Nothing brought him consolation.

After watching day and night for a whole month, the spy was eventually overwhelmed by drowsiness, and at last she sunk into a sound slumber. When Florine saw this, she opened her little window and said:

> "Bird as blue as cloudless sky,
> Come to my window, quickly fly!"

Those were her exact words without the slightest alteration. The bird heard them so distinctly that he was at the window in an instant. What delight once more to behold each other! How much they had to say to each other! They renewed their vows of love and fidelity a thousand times over. Seeing the princess unable to restrain her tears, her lover was tormented and did his utmost to console her. At last the hour of parting arrived without the spy awakening, and they said good-bye to each other in the most touching manner.

The next night the spy fell asleep again. The princess lost no time in going to the window and calling as before:

> "Bird as blue as cloudless sky,
> Come to my window, quickly fly!"

The bird immediately arrived, and the night passed without discovery like the preceding one. The lovers were delighted. They hoped that the spy would find so much pleasure in sleeping that she would do so every night, and, in fact, the third did pass as happily.

On the one following, though, the sleeper was disturbed by a noise. Listening without appearing to be awake, and peeping as best she could, she saw the most beautiful bird in the world by the light of the moon. He

talked to the princess, caressed her with his claw, and
pecked her gently with his bill. She overheard part of
their conversation and was extremely surprised, for the
bird spoke like a lover, and the beautiful Florine
answered him most tenderly. When day broke and they
said their farewells, they parted with extreme sorrow,
as though they had a presentiment of their coming misfortune. Bathed in tears, the princess threw herself on
her bed, and the king returned to his hollow tree.

The spy ran to the queen and told her all she had
seen and heard. The queen in turn sent for Truitonne
and her confidantes. They talked the matter over for a
long time and concluded that the blue bird was King
Charmant. "What an affront!" cried the queen. "What
an affront, my Truitonne! This insolent princess, whom
I thought was so wretched, was quietly enjoying the
most charming conversations with that ungrateful
prince. Oh, I'll take such a bloody revenge that it will
be the talk of the whole world!"

Truitonne begged her not to lose a moment, and
since she considered herself more interested in the
matter than the queen, she was bursting with joy at the
thought of all that would be done to destroy the happiness of the lover and his mistress. The queen sent the
spy back to the tower, ordering her not to show any
suspicion or curiosity, but to appear more sleepy than
ever. She went to bed early and snored as loudly as she
could. The poor, deceived princess opened the little
window and called:

> "Bird as blue as cloudless sky,
> Come to my window, quickly fly!"

but she called in vain the whole night long. He did not
come, for the wicked queen had ordered swords,
knives, razors, and daggers to be attached to the
cypress tree so that when he darted toward the window
these murderous weapons cut off his feet. In addition,
some others lacerated his wings and stabbed his chest.
Only with great difficulty, leaving behind him a long
trail of blood, did he reach his own tree. Why weren't
you there, lovely princess, to comfort that royal bird?

And yet it would have been the death of her to have
seen him in such a dismal condition.

Since he was convinced that it was Florine who had
been guilty of this cruel treachery, he did not care a fig
about his life. "Oh, barbarous princess," he exclaimed
mournfully, "is this the way you repay the most pure
and tender passion that ever was or will ever be? If you
had wanted me to die, why didn't you perform the deed
yourself? Death would have been sweet from your
hand! I looked for you with so much love and trust. I
suffered for you and suffered without complaining.
And now you have sacrificed me to the cruelest of
women, our common enemy! You've made your peace
with her at the price of my life. It is you, Florine—you
who has stabbed me! You have borrowed Truitonne's
hand and guided it to my bosom!" These furious
thoughts so overwhelmed him that he looked forward
to his death.

However, his friend the enchanter, who had seen the
flying frogs return without the king in the chariot,
became so concerned about him that he went around
the world eight times in search of him. On his ninth
journey he passed through the forest in which the poor
king was lying. As was his custom, he blew a long
blast on his horn and then cried five times in a loud
voice, "King Charmant! King Charmant! Where are
you?"

The king recognized his best friend's voice and
cried, "Come over to this tree, and behold the wretched
king you cherish drowning in his own blood."

Quite surprised, the enchanter looked all around
without seeing anyone. "I'm a blue bird," the king
exclaimed in a feeble, plaintive voice.

After hearing this, the enchanter had no trouble
locating him in his nest. Another person might have
been dumbfounded, but he was well versed in every
aspect of necromancy. He needed but a few words to
stop the blood from flowing, and along with some
herbs he found in the wood, he murmured a short spell
and cured the king so well that it seemed he had never
been wounded. Then he asked the king to tell him how
he had become transformed into a bird, and who had

wounded him so cruelly. The king satisfied his curiosity and informed him that it must have been Florine who had revealed the amorous mystery of the secret visits he paid her. To make her peace with the queen, she had consented to have the cypress tree filled with the daggers and razors that had almost hacked him to pieces. He denounced the treachery of the princess a thousand times and said he would have been happier if he had died without knowing the wickedness of her heart. The magician inveighed against her and against all her sex, and he advised the king to forget her. "What a misfortune it would be," he said, "if you were to continue loving that ungrateful lady. After what she's done to you, you have everything to fear."

The blue bird, however, could not share this view, for he still loved Florine too dearly, and the enchanter, who knew his real sentiments despite the care the king took to conceal them, said to him in a friendly manner:

"Crushed by Fortune's cruel blow,
Vainly Reason's voice is heard;
We but listen to our woe,
Neglecting wise and soothing words.
Leave old Time his work to do.
All things have their sunny side.
But until he brings it within view,
Naught but darkness will be spied."

The royal bird admitted the truth of these remarks and asked his friend to take him home and put him in a cage, where he would be safe from a cat's paw or murderous weapon.

"But," said the enchanter, "do you really want to remain in such a deplorable condition for five years? It is ill-suited to your duties and your dignity. Remember, you have enemies who claim that you're dead. They want to seize your kingdom. I fear very much that you'll lose it before you regain your proper form."

"Can't I enter my palace and govern as I used to do?" asked the king.

"Oh," exclaimed his friend, "the situation has changed. Those who would obey a man will not bow to a parrot. Those who feared you when you were a king surrounded by grandeur and pomp would be the first to pluck out all your feathers now that you're a little bird."

"Alas, for human weakness," cried the king. "Although a glittering exterior is nothing compared to virtue, it still wields a power over the minds of men that is difficult to combat. Well, then, let us be philosophers, and despise that which we cannot obtain. Our lot will be none the worse for it."

"I don't give up so easily," said the magician. "I still hope to hit upon some means of restoring you to your proper form."

Florine, sad Florine, was in despair at no longer seeing the king. She spent her days and nights at the window and constantly repeated:

> "Bird as blue as cloudless sky,
> Come to my window, quickly fly!"

The presence of her watchful attendant did not stop her, for her despair was so great that she did not care about the consequences. "What has happened to you, King Charmant?" she cried. "Have our mutual enemies made you feel the cruel effects of their rage? Have you fallen victim to their fury? Alas, alas! Have you perished? Shall I never see you again? Shall I never weary of my woes? Have you abandoned me to my hard fate?"

What tears, what sobs followed these tender complaints. How did the absence of such a dear and charming lover lengthen the dreary hours of her captivity. The princess was dejected, ill, thin, and changed. So convinced that something fatal had happened to the king, she could scarcely sustain herself.

The queen and Truitonne had triumphed. Their revenge gave them more pleasure than the offence that had annoyed them. And just what was this offence after all? King Charmant had refused to marry a little monster he had a thousand reasons to hate. In the meantime, Florine's father, who had reached a considerable age, fell ill and died. Now the fortunes of the wicked

queen and her daughter assumed a new aspect. They
were looked upon as favorites who had abused their
influence. The people rose up and ran to the palace,
demanding Princess Florine and claiming they would
recognize her alone as their sovereign. The queen was
affronted by this and tried to handle the affair in a
haughty manner. She appeared on a balcony and threatened the insurgents. But the revolt became widespread,
and the people broke into the apartments, pillaged
them, and stoned her to death. Truitonne fled for protection to her godmother, the fairy Soussio, or she
would have shared the fate of her mother. The nobles
of the kingdom met immediately and climbed the
tower, where the princess was lying gravely ill. She
knew neither of her father's death nor of her enemy's
punishment. When she heard the noise of people
approaching, she was convinced they were coming to
put her to death. She was not in the least alarmed, for
life had become hateful since she had lost the blue bird.
So when her subjects flung themselves at her feet and
informed her of the happy change in her fortunes, she
was quite indifferent. Still, they carried her to the
palace and crowned her. Then her frail body was given
great care, and her desire to search for the blue bird
combined to restore her health. Soon she was able to
appoint a council to govern the kingdom during her
absence. Providing herself with jewels to the value of a
thousand million francs, she set out on her journey one
night quite alone, without anyone knowing where she
was going.

The enchanter who managed the affairs of King
Charmant, not having sufficient power to undo what
Soussio had done, decided to seek her out and propose
some arrangement whereby she would restore the king
to his natural form. He called for his frogs and flew to
the fairy, who was at that moment conversing with
Truitonne. Enchanters and fairies are on an equal
footing. These two had known each other for five or six
hundred years, and during that time they had quarreled
and made up again at least a thousand times.

She received him very politely. "What does my
compeer want?" she said (this is the way they all

address one another). "Is there anything I can do for you?"

"Yes, compeer," answered the magician, "you can. It concerns one of my best friends, a king whom you have made very unhappy."

"Aha! I understand you, compeer," cried Soussio. "I'm very sorry, but there's no hope for him unless he consents to marry my goddaughter. There she is in all her beauty, as you may see. Let him think it over."

The enchanter was almost struck dumb when he caught sight of Truitonne, so hideous did she appear to him. Nevertheless, he could not leave without coming to some sort of agreement with Soussio. "The king has run a thousand risks since he has begun dwelling in a cage." Once, the nail on which the cage had been hanging had broken, and the cage had fallen to the ground with a severe shock to his feathered majesty. Minet, the cat, who happened to be in the room when this accident occurred, gave the poor king a scratch on the eye that nearly blinded him. On another occasion they neglected to give him any fresh water, and he barely escaped having the pip. A little rogue of a monkey got loose, caught hold of some of his feathers through the bars of the cage, and toyed with him as if he were a jay or a blackbird. But worst of all, he was on the verge of losing his kingdom. His heirs were trumping up new stories every day to prove he was dead.

Finally the enchanter came to an understanding with his compeer Soussio: she would bring Truitonne to King Charmant's palace, where she would reside for some months. During that time the king would be allowed to make up his mind to marry her. Soussio would permit him to resume his original form with the proviso that he would become a bird again if he eventually refused to marry her goddaughter.

The fairy presented Truitonne with magnificent dresses made of gold and silver, seated her on a pillion behind herself on a dragon, and proceeded directly to Charmant's kingdom, where they found him with his faithful friend the enchanter. With three taps of Soussio's wand King Charmant was again the handsome, charming, intelligent, and magnificent sovereign he had been before. However, his reprieve was dearly bought. The mere thought of marrying Truitonne made him shudder. The enchanter reasoned with him as well as he could, but made little impression on him. The king was less occupied with the government of his dominions than with devising means to prolong the period Soussio had allowed before he must marry Truitonne.

In the meantime Queen Florine had disguised herself as a peasant. Her hair was disheveled and hanging about her ears to conceal her features, and she wore a straw hat on her head and a sack upon her shoulder. Onward she proceeded, by turns walking and riding. She went by sea and land as fast as she could. However, not being certain of the route, she feared that every turn she took might lead her away from her charming monarch instead of toward him.

One day she stopped to rest beside a fountain whose silvery water flowed over little pebbles. Taking the opportunity of washing her feet, she sat on the grassy bank, tied up her fair locks with a ribbon, and put her feet into the little stream. She looked like Diana bathing on her return from the chase. A little old woman, bent over and leaning on a stout stick, happened to be passing that way and stopped. "What are you doing there so all alone, my pretty girl?"

"My good mother," the queen answered, "I have plenty of company, for I'm beset by sorrows, anxieties, and misfortunes." And upon uttering these words, her eyes filled with tears.

"What? So young and you're crying?" asked the good woman. "Ah, my child, don't give in to sorrow. Tell me truly what's wrong, and hopefully I may be able to comfort you."

The queen willingly told her about all her misfortunes, about the conduct of the fairy Soussio, and how she was presently searching for the blue bird.

The little old woman suddenly drew herself up as straight as possible, changing her whole appearance. She was lovely, young, and superbly attired. She smiled graciously at the queen as she said, "Incomparable Florine, the king you seek is no longer a bird. My sister Soussio has restored him to his former shape. He's in his kingdom. Don't torture yourself, for you will reach it and obtain your goal. Here are four eggs. Break one of them whenever you need help the most, and you'll find something in each that will be useful." In that instant she disappeared.

Florine felt much consoled by what she had heard. Putting the eggs into her sack, she resumed her journey toward Charmant's kingdom. After walking eight days and nights without stopping, she arrived at the foot of an enormously high mountain that was made entirely of ivory and so steep that one could not keep one's footing on it. She made a thousand vain attempts, but slipped back every time, until she became exhausted. In despair at encountering such an insurmountable obstacle, she lay down at the bottom of the mountain and decided to die right there.

Then she remembered the eggs the fairy had given her and took one out of her sack. "Let's see if the lady was merely making fun of me when she promised that the eggs would help me in my need." Breaking the egg, she found some small golden clamps, which she fastened on her hands and feet. With their help she climbed the ivory mountain without the least trouble, for the points of the clamps penetrated the ivory and prevented her from slipping. When she reached the top, she found herself in just as much trouble with regard to the descent. The entire valley was a sheet of mirrored glass in which upward of sixty thousand women were admiring themselves, for this looking glass was two whole miles in width and six in height. Everyone appeared in it exactly as she wished to be. The carroty-haired women seemed to have locks of gold; a coarse brunette appeared to be a glossy raven black. The old looked young—the young never looked older. In sum, no fault could be seen in this wonderful mirror, and consequently the fair sex from all parts of the world resorted to using it. It was enough to make you die laughing to see the airs and graces that most of these coquettes gave themselves. Nor were men less eager to consult this magical mirror, which pleased them just as well. To some it seemed to give fine, curly hair, to others taller stature or better shape, a more martial mien or a nobler deportment. The ladies they laughed and laughed at them just as much in return.

The mountain was called by a thousand different names as a result. No one had ever been able to get to the top of it. Therefore, when Florine appeared on the summit, the ladies uttered shrieks of despair. "Where is that mad creature going?" they cried. "No doubt she must know how to walk on glass, or the first step she takes, she'll break our mirror to pieces!"

Thereupon a terrific hubbub arose. The queen did not know what to do, for she saw the imminent danger of descending by that road. So she broke another egg, and two pigeons popped out, attached to a tiny chariot that grew sufficiently large for her to sit in comfortably. The pigeons then gently descended with the queen and landed at the bottom without the least accident.

"My little friends," she said to them, "if you'll carry me to the spot where King Charmant holds his court, you won't find me ungrateful."

The civil, obedient pigeons kept going night and day until they reached the gates of the city. Florine got out and gave each of them a sweet kiss worth more than a royal diadem.

Oh, how her heart beat as she entered the city! Staining her face so that she would not be recognized, she asked a group of people she passed where she might see the king. Some of them began to laugh at her. "See the king?" they said. "Ho, what do you want with him, my young slut? Go, go and clean yourself! You are not worthy enough to look at such a monarch."

The queen made no reply, but quietly moved on and asked the next group she met where the best place would be to see the king.

"He'll soon be going to the temple with Princess Truitonne, for he has finally consented to marry her" was the answer.

"Heavens, what tidings! Truitonne, the worthless Truitonne, on the verge of marrying the king?" Stricken, Florine felt like dying, and collapsed dumbfounded on a heap of rubble under a gateway, her face covered by her disheveled hair and her large straw hat. "How unfortunate I am!" she cried. "I've come here only to add to the triumph of my rival and witness her contentment. It was for her, then, that the blue bird deserted me! It was for this little monster that he was guilty of the most cruel inconstancy. While I grieved over him and trembled for his life, the traitor had already turned away and thought no more of me than if he had never seen me. Indeed, he left me to lament his absence without a sigh."

Miserable souls rarely have much appetite, so when the poor queen sought out a lodging for the night, she went to bed without any supper. Rising with the sun, she hurried to the temple. After repeated rebuffs from soldiers and attendants, she succeeded in obtaining admission. There she saw the king's throne and that of Truitonne, whom the people already looked upon as their queen. How painful it was for such a sensitive lover as Florine! She approached the throne of her rival and paused, leaning against a marble pillar. The king arrived first, looking more handsome and fascinating than ever. Truitonne followed him, richly attired and ugly enough to frighten everybody. She frowned as soon as she noticed Florine. "Who do you think you are to dare approach our august person and our golden throne in this way?"

"I'm called Mie Souillon," replied Florine. "I've come from a distant country to sell you some rare objects." Thereupon, she took out of her sack the emerald bracelets that King Charmant had given to her.

"Aha," said Truitonne, "these are pretty glass ornaments. Will you take five coins for them?"

"Show them to a connoisseur, madam," said the queen, "and then we'll make our deal."

Truitonne, who loved the king as much as such a creature could, was delighted in having a reason to speak to him. Approaching his throne, she showed him the bracelets and requested his opinion with regard to their value. As soon as he saw them, he immediately recalled those he had given to Florine. Sighing, he turned pale and could not speak for some time. At last, fearing that people might notice how upset his conflicting emotions were making him, he made an effort to compose himself and answered, "I believe these bracelets are worth almost as much as my kingdom. I had thought there was only one pair like this in the world, but these are certainly just like the pair I knew."

Truitonne returned to her throne, and once she was seated, she looked less noble than an oyster in its shell. Then she asked Florine what was the lowest price she would ask for the bracelets.

"You would find it difficult to pay, madam," she answered. "I had better propose another kind of bargain to you. If you'll obtain permission for me to sleep one night in the cabinet of echoes, I'll give you the emeralds."

"Gladly, Mie Souillon," said Truitonne, laughing like an idiot and showing teeth longer than the tusks of a wild boar.

The king did not ask where the bracelets came from, not because he did not care about the person who possessed them—in any case, her appearance was not such as to inspire much curiosity—but because he was so overwhelmingly repulsed by Truitonne. Now, it is important to know that when Charmant had been a blue bird, he had told Florine that beneath his apartments was a small room called the cabinet of echoes, so ingeniously constructed that the slightest whispers uttered there could be heard by the king while reposing in his bedroom. And since Florine's intention was to reproach him for his inconstancy, she could not have imagined a better method. After she was conducted to the cabinet that evening on Truitonne's orders, she immediately began her complaints and lamentations.

"The catastrophe that I never dreamed would occur has come about, cruel blue bird," she cried. "You've forgotten me! You love my unworthy rival. The bracelets I received from your disloyal hand could not make you remember me, so entirely have you banished me from your recollection." Here her sobs choked off her speech, and when she was able to speak again, she resumed her lamentations and continued them until daybreak.

The king's servants, who had heard her moan and

sigh all night long, asked Truitonne why Florine had
made such a disturbance. The queen answered that
when she slept soundly, she was in the habit of
dreaming and often talked aloud in her sleep. As for
the king, a fatal aberration had prevented him from
hearing her. Ever since he had fallen so deeply in love
with Florine, he could not sleep soundly. So whenever
he went to bed, he took a dose of opium in order to
gain some rest.

Florine spent part of the next day in a strange, anxious mood. "If he heard me," she thought, "he's certainly showing his cruel indifference. If he didn't hear
me, how shall I get him to do so?" Although she
did not possess any more of those rare objects, she did
have plenty of beautiful jewels. However, she needed
something that would particularly catch Truitonne's
fancy. So Florine resorted to using her eggs. She broke
one, and out sprang a coach of polished steel inlaid
with gold. It was drawn by six green mice and driven
by a rose-colored rat, and the postilion, also of the rat
species, was a grayish-violet color. In the coach sat
four puppets who were more sprightly than any ever
seen at the fairs of St. Germain or St. Lauren. They
could do all sorts of wonderful things, particularly two
little gypsies, who could dance a saraband or a jig and
hold their own with the famous Leance.

Florine was enraptured at the sight of this new
masterpiece of necromancy. Remaining perfectly mum
until evening, the time Truitonne usually took a walk,
she took up a place on one of the paths and set the mice
galloping with the coach, rats, and puppets. This nov-
elty so astonished Truitonne that she called out two or
three times, "Mie Souillon, Mie Souillon! Will you
take five coins for your coach and set of mice?"

"Ask the men of letters and learned scholars of this
kingdom," said Florine, "what such a wonder is worth,
and I'll abide by the estimation of the best judge."

Truitonne, who did everything arbitrarily, replied,
"Without offending me any longer by your filthy presence, tell me the price."

"All I ask," said Florine, "is to sleep again in the
cabinet of echoes."

"Go, poor idiot," answered Truitonne, "you shall have your wish." Turning to her ladies-in-waiting, she said, "What a stupid creature to reap no greater advantage from such rare objects."

Night came. Florine uttered all the most touching reproaches she could think of, but again it was in vain, for the king never forgot to take his opium. His servants said to one another "That country wench must surely be mad. What is she muttering about all night?"

"Whatever the case may be," some remarked, "there is both reason and feeling in what she says."

She waited impatiently for morning to ascertain what effect her words had produced. "What?" she cried. "Has this barbarous man become deaf to my voice? Will he no longer listen to his dear Florine? Oh, how weak I am to love him still! How well do I deserve the scorn with which he treats me!" But all her reproaches were for naught, for she had no power over her feelings for him.

There was only one more egg left in her sack that could help her. She broke it, and out came a pie composed of six birds, which were larded, dressed, and quite ready for eating. Yet they sang admirably, told fortunes, and knew more about medicine than Sculapius himself. Florine was enchanted at the sight of such a wonderful thing and carried her talking-pie into Truitonne's antechamber. While waiting for her to come, one of the king's servants came up to Florine and said, "My friend, Mie Souillon, are you aware that if the king did not take opium to make him sleep, you would be disturbing him immensely, for you chatter all night long in the most extraordinary manner."

Now Florine was no longer surprised that the king had not heard her. She took a handful of jewels out of her sack and said, "I'm not afraid of interrupting the king's sleep. So if you'll prevent him from taking opium tonight, assuming I'll be sleeping in the cabinet of echoes, all these pearls and diamonds shall be yours."

The servant agreed to do it and gave her his word. A few minutes afterward Truitonne arrived. She noticed

Florine with her pie, which she pretended to be eating. "What are you doing there, Mie Souillon?"

"Madam," replied Florine, "I am eating astrologers, musicians, and physicians."

At that moment all the birds began to sing more melodiously than sirens and then to cry, "Give us a piece of silver, and we'll tell you your fortune." A duck that was particularly prominent called out in a voice louder than any of the others, "Quack! quack! quack! quack! I'm a physician; I cure all disorders and every sort of madness, except that of love."

Truitonne was most surprised by so many wonders. Indeed, she had never seen so many in her entire life. Thinking it an excellent pie, she coveted it. "Come, come, Mie Souillon, what shall I give you for it?"

"The usual price," answered Florine, "permission to sleep in the cabinet of echoes—nothing more."

"Why," said Truitonne generously (for she was in a good mood due to her acquisition of such a pie), "you shall have a gold coin as part of the bargain."

Florine was now happier than she had been for some time because she hoped the king would hear her. So she took her leave of Truitonne with many thanks. As soon as night came, she requested to be led to the cabinet, ardently hoping that the servant would keep his word, and that instead of giving the king his opium, he would substitute something that would keep his majesty awake. When she thought everybody else was asleep, she began her usual lamentations. "How many dangers did I confront searching for you," she said, "while you fled from me and sought to marry Truitonne? What did I do to you, you cruel person, to make you forget your vows? Remember your transformation, my favors, and our tender conversations." She repeated nearly all of them, her memory sufficiently proving that nothing was dearer to her than such recollections.

The king was not asleep and heard Florine so distinctly that he could not imagine where they came from. But his heart, pierced by tenderness, brought back the image of his incomparable princess so vividly that he felt his separation from her just as keenly as he had at the moment the knives had wounded him in the cypress tree. He began to speak aloud on his part, as the queen had done on hers. "Ah, princess," he said, "too cruel to a lover who adored you. Is it possible that you would have sacrificed me to our mutual enemies?"

Florine heard what he said and replied that if he would grant Mie Souillon an audience, he would learn about all the mysteries he had been unable to grasp until now. At these words the impatient king called one of his servants and asked him if he could find a Mie Souillon and bring her to him. The servant answered that nothing could be easier: she was sleeping in the cabinet of echoes.

The king did not know what to think. How could so great a queen as Florine be disguised as a scullion? And yet, how could Mie Souillon have the queen's voice and know such particular secrets unless she were not Florine herself? In his uncertainty he arose and dressed himself in the greatest haste. He descended by a back staircase to the door of the cabinet of echoes. Florine had taken the key out of the lock, but the king had a master key that unlocked every door in the palace.

A lamp at some distance cast a faint light on the scene. Lying on a couch, she was dressed in a light robe of white taffeta, which she wore beneath her coarse disguise, and her beautiful hair bathed her shoulders. The king entered in a rush, his love getting the better of his anger. The moment he saw for certain it was she, he flung himself at her feet, bathed her hands with his tears, and felt he would die of joy, grief, and a thousand different emotions that swirled inside of him.

The queen was no less moved. Her heart seemed to stop beating; she could scarcely breathe. She looked earnestly at the king without saying a word, and when she found the strength to speak to him, she had no power to reproach him, for the joy of beholding him again made her forget all of her groundless complaints. At length they explained to each other what had happened and justified what they had done. Their tender feelings were revived more strongly than ever, and the only obstacle that remained was the fairy Soussio.

But at this moment the enchanter who was so fond of the king arrived with a famous fairy, who was none other than the one who had given the four eggs to Florine. After initial compliments were exchanged, the enchanter and the fairy declared that their power had united in favor of the king and queen and that Soussio could do nothing against them. Consequently their marriage could take place without delay.

We may readily imagine the delight of these two young lovers. As soon as it was daytime, the news spread throughout the palace, and everybody was enchanted at the sight of Florine. When the tidings reached Truitonne, she ran to the king's apartments. To her surprise she found her beautiful rival there, and the moment she attempted to open her mouth to abuse her, the enchanter and the fairy appeared and changed her into a sow. Since *Truie* in French means sow, she still retained part of her name, plus her natural disposition to grumble. She ran out of the room grunting and then into the kitchen courtyard, where long peals of laughter greeted her and completed her despair.

Now that King Charmant and Queen Florine had been rescued from such a hideous person, they thought of their wedding and how elegant and magnificent it would be. Indeed, it is easy to judge how great their happiness was after so many prolonged misfortunes.

> When Truitonne tried to force that charming king
> To tie a knot which death alone could sunder,
> Regardless of the consequences it would bring,
> She certainly committed a great blunder.
> Of course, it's possible she did not know, a marriage
> Unblessed by mutual love is wretched slavery.
> But Charmant's bold, uncompromising carriage,
> Showed as much prudence, I maintain, as bravery.
> Better to be a bird of any hue—
> A raven, crow, an owl—I do protest,
> Than stick for life to a partner like glue
> Who scorns you, or whom you detest.
> Too many matches of this sort I've seen,

And wish that now there were some king magician
To stop these ill-matched souls at once and lean
On them with force to keep his prohibition.
He must be vigilant and forbid the banns,
Whenever true affection might be slighted.
And Hymen must be prevented from joining hands,
Whenever hearts have not first been united.

THE RAM

IN those happy times when fairies still existed, there reigned a king who had three daughters. Young and beautiful, all three possessed considerable qualities, but the youngest was the most charming and the favorite by far. Indeed, they called her Merveilleuse. Her father gave her more gowns and ribbons in a month than he gave the others in a year, and she was so good-natured that she shared everything with them so that there might be no misunderstandings.

Now, the king had some evil neighbors who grew tired of keeping peace with him. Therefore, they formed a powerful alliance and compelled him to arm his country in self-defence. Once he had raised a large army, he assumed command and rode off to battle. The three princesses remained with their tutors in a castle, and every day they received good news about the king's exploits. One time he took a city, another he won a battle. Finally he succeeded in routing his enemies and driving them out of his dominions. Then he returned to the castle as fast as he could to see his little Merveilleuse, whom he adored so much.

The three princesses had ordered three satin gowns to be made for themselves—one green, one blue, one white. Jewels were selected to match their dresses—the green enriched with emeralds, the blue with turquoises, and the white with diamonds. Thus attired, they went to meet the king, singing the following verses, which they had written to celebrate his victories:

"With conquest crowned on many a glorious plain,
What joy to greet our king and sire again!

Welcome him back, victorious, to these halls,
With new delights and countless festivals.
Let shouts of joy and songs of triumph prove
His people's loyalty, his daughters' love!"

When the king saw his lovely daughters in such splendid attire, he embraced them all tenderly, but caressed Merveilleuse more than the others. A magnificent banquet was set up, and the king and his three daughters sat down to eat. Since it was his habit to draw inferences from everything, he said to the eldest, "Tell me, please, why have you put on a green gown?"

"Sire," she answered, "having heard of your achievements, I imagined that green would express the joy and hope with which your return inspired me."

"That is very prettily said," the king exclaimed. "And you, my child," he continued, "why are you wearing a blue gown?"

"My liege," the princess said, "I want to indicate that we should constantly implore the gods to protect you. Moreover, your sight is to me like that of Heaven and all the Heavenly Host."

"You speak like an oracle," the king said. "And you, Merveilleuse, why have you dressed yourself in white?"

"Because, sire," she answered, "it becomes me better than any other color."

"What?" the king cried, very much offended. "Was that your only motive, you little coquette?"

"My motive was to please you," said the princess. "It seems to me that I ought to have no other."

The king, who loved her dearly, was so perfectly satisfied with this explanation that he declared himself quite pleased by the little turn she had given to her meaning and the art with which she had at first concealed the compliment.

"Now, then," he said, "I've had an excellent supper, but I won't yet go to bed. Tell me what you all dreamed of the night before my return."

The eldest said she had dreamed that he had brought her a gown with gold and jewels that glistened brighter

than the sun. The second said she had dreamed he had
brought her a golden distaff to spin herself some shifts.
The youngest said she had dreamed that he had married
off her second sister and on the wedding day he had
offered her a golden vase and said, "Merveilleuse,
come here. Come here so you can wash."

Infuriated by this dream, the king knit his brow and
made such an exceedingly wry face that everybody saw
he was enraged. He retired to his room and flung himself onto his bed, but he could not forget his daughter's
dream. "This insolent creature," he said, "she wants to
turn me into her servant. I wouldn't be at all surprised
if she put on that white satin dress without thinking of me at all. She doesn't take me seriously. But
I'll frustrate her wicked designs while there's still
time." He rose in a fury, and though it was still dark
outside, he sent for the captain of his guards and
said, "You heard Merveilleuse's dream. It forecasts
strange things against me. I command you to seize her
immediately, take her into the forest, and kill her.
Afterward, you're to bring me her heart and tongue so
I'll be sure you haven't deceived me. If you fail, I'll
have you put to death in the most cruel manner
imaginable."

The captain of the guards was astounded by this barbarous order. He did not dare argue with the king, however, for fear of increasing his rage and causing him to
give the horrifying order to another. He assured him he
would take the princess and kill her and bring him back
her heart and tongue.

The captain strode directly to the princess's apartment, where he had some difficulty in obtaining permission to enter, for it was still quite early. He
informed Merveilleuse that the king desired to see her.
She arose immediately, and a tiny Moorish girl named
Patypata carried her train. A young ape and a little dog
who always accompanied her also ran after her. The
ape was called Grabugeon and the little dog, Tintin.
The captain of the guards made Merveilleuse descend
into the garden, where he told her the king was taking
in the fresh morning air. She entered it, and the captain pretended to look for the king. When he did not

find him, he said, "No doubt his majesty has walked
farther on into the wood." He opened a small gate
and led the princess into the forest. It was just getting light, and the princess saw that her escort had
tears in his eyes and was so dejected that he could
not speak.

"What's the matter?" she inquired kindly. "You
seem very much distressed."

"Ah, madam," he exclaimed, "how could I be otherwise, for I've been given the most dreadful order
that has ever been given! The king has commanded me
to kill you in this forest and to take your heart and
tongue to him. If I fail to do so, he will put me to
death."

Turning pale with terror, the poor princess began to
weep softly, like a lamb about to be sacrificed. Then
she turned her beautiful eyes to the captain of the
guards and looked at him without anger. "Do you
really have the heart to kill me?" she asked. "I've never
done you any harm, and I've always spoken well of
you to the king. If I really deserved my father's hate,
I'd suffer the consequences without a murmur. But
alas, I've always shown him so much respect and
affection that he has no just reason to complain."

"Fear not, beautiful princess," said the captain, "I'm
incapable of such a barbarous deed. I'd rather have him
carry out his threat and kill me. But if I were to kill
myself, you would be no better off. We must find some
way that will enable me to return to the king and convince him you're dead."

"What way is there?" asked Merveilleuse. "He's
ordered you to bring him my heart and tongue, and if
you don't, he won't believe you."

Patypata had witnessed everything, though neither
the captain nor the princess was aware of her presence
because they were so overcome by sadness. Advancing
courageously, she threw herself at Merveilleuse's feet.
"Madam," she said, "I want to offer you my life. You
must kill me. I'd be most happy to die for such a good
mistress."

"Oh, I could never permit it, my dear Patypata!" the
princess said, kissing her. "After such an affectionate

proof of your friendship, your life is as dear to me as my own."

Then Grabugeon stepped forward and said, "You have good reason, Princess, to love such a faithful slave as Patypata. She can be of much more use to you than I. Now it's my turn to offer you my heart and tongue with joy, for I wish to immortalize myself in the annals of the empire of monkeys."

"Ah, my darling Grabugeon," Merveilleuse replied, "I can't bear the idea of taking your life."

"I'd find it intolerable," exclaimed Tintin, "good little dog as I am, if anyone but myself were to sacrifice his life for my mistress. Either I die or nobody dies."

Upon saying this, a great dispute arose between Patypata, Grabugeon, and Tintin, and they exchanged a great many harsh words. At last Grabugeon, who was quicker than the others, scampered up to the top of a tree and flung herself down headfirst, killing herself on the spot. As much as the princess grieved over her loss, she agreed to let the captain of the guards cut out her tongue since the poor thing was dead. To their dismay, however, it was so small (for the creature was not much bigger than one's fist) that they felt certain the king would not be deceived by it.

"Alas, my dear little ape," cried the princess, "there you lie, and your sacrifice hasn't saved my life!"

"That honor has been reserved for me," interrupted the Moor, and as she spoke, she snatched the knife that had been used on Grabugeon and plunged it into her bosom. The captain of the guards would have taken her tongue, but it was so black that he knew he would not be able to deceive the king with it.

"Look at my misfortune!" the princess said tearfully. "I lost all those I love, and yet my fate remains unchanged."

"Had you accepted my offer," Tintin said, "you would have only had to mourn my loss, and I would have had the satisfaction of being the only one mourned."

Merveilleuse kissed her little dog and wept such bitter tears over him that she became quite exhausted.

She turned hastily away, and when she ventured to look around again, her escort was gone, and she found herself alone with the dead bodies of her Moor, her ape, and her little dog. She could not leave the spot until she had buried them in a hole that she found by chance at the foot of a tree. Afterward she scratched these words into the tree:

> Three faithful friends lie buried in this grave.
> They saved my life with deeds most brave.

Then she began to think about her own safety. It was certainly dangerous for her to remain in that forest, especially since it was so close to her father's castle. The first person who saw her would recognize her. Then again, she might be attacked and devoured like a chicken by the lions and wolves that infested it. So she set off walking as fast as she could.

The forest was so enormous, however, and the sun so strong that she was soon nearly ready to collapse from heat, fear, and exhaustion. She looked around in every direction, but was unable to see an end to the woods. Every movement frightened her. She continually imagined that the king was in hot pursuit, seeking to kill her. Indeed, she uttered so many cries of woe that it is impossible to repeat them all here.

As she walked on, not following any particular path, the thickets tore her beautiful dress and scratched her ivory skin. At last she heard some sheep bleating. "It is probably some shepherds with their flocks," she said. "Perhaps they'll be able to direct me to a village where I can disguise myself in peasant garb. Alas, kings and queens are not always the happiest people in the world! Who in all this kingdom would have ever believed that I'd become a fugitive, that my father would want to take my life without reason, and that I'd have to disguise myself to save my neck?"

Even as she made these remarks, she was approaching the spot where she had heard the bleating. Upon reaching an open glade encircled by trees, she was astonished to see a large ram with gilded horns and fleece whiter than snow. He had a garland of flowers around his neck, his legs were entwined with ropes of enormous pearls, and chains of diamonds hung all about him. As he lay on a couch of orange blossoms, a pavilion of gold cloth suspended in the air sheltered him from the rays of the shun. There were a hundred brightly decked sheep all around him, and instead of browsing on grass, some were having coffee, sherbet, ices, and lemonade; others, strawberries and cream, and preserves. Some were playing at *basset,* others at *lansquenet.* Several wore collars of gold ornamented with numerous fine emblems, earrings, ribbons, and flowers. Merveilleuse was so astounded that she remained stock still. Her eyes were roving in search of the shepherd in charge of this extraordinary flock when the beautiful ram ran over to her in a sprightly manner. "Approach, divine princess," he said. "You have nothing to fear from such gentle and peaceful animals of our kind."

"What a miracle! A talking ram!" the princess exclaimed.

"What's that, madam?" the ram replied. "Your ape and your little dog spoke very prettily. Why weren't you surprised by that?"

"A fairy endowed them with the gift of speech, which made everything less miraculous," Merveilleuse stated.

"Perhaps we had a similar experience," the ram answered, smiling sheepishly. "But what caused you to come our way, my princess?"

"A thousand misfortunes, my lord ram," she said to him. "I'm the most unhappy person in the world. I'm seeking a place of refuge from my father's fury."

"Come, madam," the ram replied, "come with me. I can offer you one that will be known only by you, and you will be completely in charge of everything there."

"I can't follow you," Merveilleuse said. "I'm about to die from exhaustion."

The ram with golden horns called for his chariot, and immediately six goats were led forward, harnessed to a pumpkin of such tremendous size that two persons could sit in it with the greatest ease. The hollowed-out pumpkin was dry inside and fitted with splendid down cushions and lined all over with velvet. Getting into the pumpkin, the princess was astounded by such a unique equipage. The master ram seated himself in the pumpkin beside her, and the goats took them at full gallop to a cave. The entrance was blocked by a large stone, but the golden-horned ram touched the stone with his foot and it fell away at once. He told the princess, "Enter without fear."

She imagined that the cave would be a horrible place, and if she had not been so afraid of being captured, nothing would have induced her to go into it, but her fear was so great that she would have thrown herself into even a well to avoid capture. So she followed the ram without hesitation. He walked in front of her to show her the way down, which ran so very deep that she thought she was going at least to the other end of the earth. At moments she feared he was conducting her to the region of the dead.

Suddenly she came upon a vast meadow bursting with a thousand different flowers, whose sweet aroma surpassed that of any she had ever smelled. A broad river of orange-flower water flowed around it; fountains of Spanish wine, rossolis, hippocras, and a thousand other liqueurs formed charming cascades and rivulets. The meadow was home to entire avenues of unusual trees, and partridges greased and dressed better than those eaten at the restaurant La Guerbois hung from the branches. In other avenues the branches were festooned with quails, young rabbits, turkeys, chickens, pheasants, and ortolans. In certain parts, where from afar the atmosphere appeared hazy, it rained bisques d'écrevisse and other soups, foies gras, ragouts of sweetbreads, white puddings, sausages, tarts, patties, jam, and marmalade. There were also louis d'ors, crowns, pearls, and diamonds. Showers so rare—and so useful—would no doubt have attracted excellent company if the great ram had been more inclined to mix in general society, but all the chronicles in which he is mentioned concur in assuring us that he was as reserved as a Roman senator.

Merveilleuse had arrived in this beautiful region
during the finest time of the year. Thus, she was fortunate to see that there was also a palace, surrounded by
long rows of orange trees, jasmines, honeysuckles, and
tiny musk roses, whose interlaced branches formed
cabinets, halls, and chambers, all hung with gold and
silver gauze and furnished with large mirrors, chandeliers, and remarkable paintings. The master ram told
the princess to consider herself the sovereign of this
realm. "I have been suffering from grief for many
years, and it is now up to you to make me forget all my
misfortunes."

"Your behavior is so generous, charming ram," she
said, "and everything I see appears so extraordinary
that I don't know what to make of it."

No sooner had she uttered these words than a group
of the most remarkable and beautiful nymphs appeared
before her. They gave her fruit in baskets of amber,
but when she stepped toward them, they shrank
back slightly. When she extended her hands to
touch them, she felt nothing—they were only phan-
toms. "What does this mean?" she exclaimed. "Who
are these things around me?" She began to weep,
and King Ram (for so they called him), who had left
her momentarily, returned and found her in tears,
causing him such despair that he felt he would die at
her feet.

"What's the matter, lovely princess?" he inquired.
"Has anyone here been disrespectful to you?"

"No," she answered, "I can't complain. It's only that
I'm not accustomed to living among the dead and with
sheep that talk. Everything here frightens me, and
though I'm greatly obliged to you for bringing me here,
I'd be even more obliged if you'd bring me back into
the world."

"Don't be alarmed," the ram replied. "Please deign
to listen to me calmly, and you shall hear my sad story:

I was born to inherit a throne. A long line of kings,
my ancestors, had ensured that the kingdom I'd
be taking over was the finest in the universe. My subjects loved me. Feared and envied by my neighbors, I

was thus justly respected. It was said that no king had ever been more worthy of such homage, and my physical appearance was not without its attractions as well.

I was extremely fond of hunting, and once, when I was zealously pursuing a stag, I became separated from my attendants. Suddenly seeing the stag plunge into a pond, I spurred my horse in after him. This was as unwise as it was bold. But instead of the coldness of water, I felt an extraordinary heat. The pond dried up, and through an opening gushing with terrible flames I fell to the bottom of a precipice, where nothing was to be seen but fire.

I thought I was lost when I suddenly heard a voice saying, "No less fire could warm your heart, ungrateful one!"

"Hah! Who is it that complains of my coldness?" I said.

"An unfortunate who adores you without hope," the voice replied.

Just then the flames were extinguished and I perceived a fairy whose age and ugliness had horrified me ever since I had known her in my early childhood. She was leaning on a young slave of incomparable beauty, and the golden chains she wore sufficiently indicated who she was. "What miracle is this, Ragotte?" I asked her (since that was the fairy's name). "Have you really ordered this?"

"Who else should have ordered it?" the fairy replied. "Has it taken you this long to learn the way I feel? Must I undergo the shame of explaining myself? Have my eyes, once so certain of their power, lost all their influence? Just look how low I'm stooping! I'm the one who's confessing my weakness to you, who, great king though you may be, are less than an ant compared to a fairy like me."

"I am whatever you please," I said impatiently, "but what is it you demand of me? Is it my crown, my cities, my treasures?"

"Ah, wretch," she replied disdainfully, "if I so desire it, my scullions would be more powerful than you. No, I demand your heart! My eyes have asked you for it

thousands and thousands of times. You haven't understood them, or rather, you don't want to understand
them. If you had been desperately in love with
someone else," she continued, "I wouldn't have interrupted the progress of your ardor, but I had too great an
interest in you not to discover the indifference that
reigned in your heart. Well, then, love me!" she added,
rolling her eyes and pursing her mouth to make it look
more pleasant. "I'll be your little Ragotte, and I'll add
twenty kingdoms to what you possess already, a hundred towers filled with gold, five hundred filled with
silver—in a word, all you can wish for."

"Madame Ragotte," I said to her, "I would never
think of declaring myself to a person of your merit at
the bottom of a pit in which I expect to be roasted. I
implore you, by all the charms that you possess, to set
me free, and then we'll consider together what we can
do to satisfy you."

"Ha, traitor!" she exclaimed, "if you loved me, you
wouldn't seek the road back to your kingdom. You'd
be happy in a grotto, in a foxhole, in the woods or the
desert. Don't think that I'm such an ingenue. You hope
to escape, but I warn you that you'll remain here. Your
first task will be to tend my sheep. They are intelligent
animals and speak just as well as you do."

Upon saying this, she took me to the plain where we
now stand and showed me her flock. I paid scant attention to them, for I was struck by the marvelous beauty
of the slave beside her. My eyes betrayed me. The
cruel Ragotte noticed my admiration and attacked her.
She plunged a bodkin into one of her eyes with such
violence that the adorable girl fell dead on the spot. At
this horrible sight I threw myself on Ragotte, and with
my sword in hand, I would have made her into a sacri-
ficial victim for the spirits of the underworld if she
hadn't used her power to freeze me as I stood. All my
efforts were in vain. I fell to the ground and sought
some way to kill myself and end my agony. But the
fairy said to me with an ironical smile, "I want you to
become acquainted with my power. You're a lion right
now, but soon you'll become a sheep."

As she pronounced this sentence, she touched me

with her wand, and I found myself transformed as you now behold me. I haven't lost the faculty of speech, nor the sense of torment caused by my condition. "You are to be a sheep for five years," she said, "and absolute master of this beautiful realm. Meanwhile I'll move far from here so I won't have to see your handsome face. But I'll brood over the hate I owe you."

Then she disappeared and, in truth, if anything could have relieved my misfortune, it would have been her absence. The talking sheep you see here acknowledged me as their king, and they informed me that they were unfortunate mortals who had in various ways offended the vindictive fairy. They had been changed into a flock, and some had to serve longer penances than others. In fact, every now and then they become what they were before and leave the flock. As for the shadows you've seen, they are Ragotte's rivals and enemies whom she has deprived of life for a century or so and who will return to the world later on. The young slave I mentioned is among them. I've seen her several times with great pleasure, although she didn't speak to me. When first I approached her, I was disturbed to discover it was nothing but her shadow. However, I noticed that one of my sheep was giving this phantom a lot of attention and learned that he was her lover. Ragotte had separated them out of jealousy, and this is the reason why I've avoided the shadow of the slave since then. During the past three years I've longed only for my freedom.

"In the hope of regaining it, I frequently wander into the forest," he continued. "It was there that I saw you, beautiful princess. Sometimes you were in a chariot that you drove yourself with more skill than Apollo does his own. Sometimes you followed the chase on a steed that seemed would obey no other rider, or you were in a race with the ladies of your court, flying lightly over the plain, and you won the prize like another Atalanta. Ah, Princess, if I had dared to speak to you during this time in which my heart paid you secret homage, what wouldn't I have said? But how would you have received the declaration of an unhappy sheep like me?"

Merveilleuse was so stirred by all she had heard that she scarcely knew how to answer him. She said something civil, however, which gave him some hope, and also told him that she was less alarmed by the ghosts now that she knew their owners would revive again. "Alas," she continued, "if my poor Patypata, my dear Grabugeon, and the pretty Tintin, who died to save me, could have met with a similar fate, I wouldn't be so melancholy here."

Despite the disgrace of the royal ram, he still possessed some remarkable prerogatives. "Go," he said to his grand equerry (a splendid-looking sheep), "go fetch the Moor, the ape, and the little dog. Their shadows will amuse our princess."

A moment later they appeared, and although they did not approach near enough for Merveilleuse to touch them, their presence was a great consolation to her.

The royal ram possessed all the intelligence and refinement required for pleasant conversation, and he adored Merveilleuse so much that she began to have some regard for him and soon after came to love him. A pretty sheep, so gentle and affectionate, is not a displeasing companion, particularly when one knows that he is a king and that his transformation will eventually end. Thus the princess spent her days peacefully, awaiting a happier future. The gallant ram devoted himself entirely to her. He gave fetes, concerts, and hunts in which his flock aided him and even the shadows played their part.

One day when his couriers arrived—for he regularly sent out couriers for news and always obtained the best—he learned that the eldest sister of Princess Merveilleuse was about to marry a great prince, and the most magnificent preparations were being made for the wedding.

"Ah," the young princess said, "how fortunate I am to be deprived of witnessing so many fine things! Here I am underground, among ghosts and sheep, while my sister is about to be made a queen. Everybody will pay their respects to her, and I'm the only one who won't be able to share in her joy."

"What reason do you have to complain, madam?" asked the king of the sheep. "Have I refused you permission to attend the wedding? Depart as soon as you please. Only give me your word that you'll return. If you don't agree to that, I'll perish at your feet, for my love for you is too passionate and I'd never be able to live if I lost you."

Touched, Merveilleuse promised the ram that nothing in the world could prevent her return. So he provided her with an equipage befitting her birth. She was superbly attired, and nothing was omitted to embellish her beauty. She got into a chariot of mother-of-pearl drawn by six Isabella-colored hypogriffins that had just arrived from the other end of the earth. She was accompanied by a great number of exceedingly handsome, richly attired officers. These the royal ram had ordered to come from a distant land to form the princess's train.

She arrived at her father's court at the moment the marriage was being celebrated. As soon as she appeared, she dazzled everyone by her glittering beauty and the jewels that adorned her. She heard nothing but acclamation and praise. The king gazed at her with such zeal and pleasure that she was afraid he would recognize her, but he was so convinced that his daughter was dead that he did not have the least inkling who she was.

Nevertheless, she was so afraid that she might be detained that she did not stay to the end of the ceremony. She departed abruptly, leaving a small coral box garnished with emeralds, on which was written in diamonds: "JEWELS FOR THE BRIDE." They opened it immediately, and what extraordinary things they found! The king, who was burning to know who she was, was despondent about her departure. He gave strict orders that if she ever returned, they were to shut the gates and detain her.

Brief though the absence of Merveilleuse had been, it had seemed like ages to the ram. Waiting for her by the side of a fountain in the thickest part of the forest, he had immense treasures displayed there with the intention of giving them to her in gratitude for her return. As soon as he saw her, he ran toward her, romping and frisking like a real sheep. He lay down at her feet, kissed her hands, and told her all about his anxiety and impatience. His love for her so inspired him that he managed to speak with an eloquence that completely captivated the princess.

A short time afterward, the king was to marry off his second daughter, and Merveilleuse heard about it. Once again she asked the ram for permission to attend a fete in which she took the closest interest. Of course, he felt a pang he could not suppress when he heard her request, for a secret presentiment warned him of a catastrophe. But since we cannot always avoid evil, and since his consideration for the princess overruled any other feeling, he did not have the heart to refuse her. "You desire to leave me, madam," he said, "and I must blame my sad fate for this unfortunate situation more than you. In consenting to your wish, I'll never make you a greater sacrifice."

She assured him that she would return as quickly as she had the first time. "I would be deeply grieved if anything were to keep me from you. I beg you, don't worry about me."

She went in the same pomp as before and arrived just as they were beginning the marriage ceremony. Although everyone was following the nuptials, her presence caused exclamations of joy and admiration that drew the eyes of all the princes to her. They could not stop gazing at her: her beauty, they felt, was so extraordinary that they could easily have been convinced that she was more than mortal.

The king was charmed to see her once more, and he never took his eyes off her, except to order all the doors to be closed to prevent her departure. When the ceremony was nearly concluded, the princess rose hastily in order to disappear in the throng, but was shocked and distressed to find that all the gates locked against her.

The king approached with a respectful, submissive air that reassured her. He begged her not to deprive

them so soon of the pleasure of admiring her and
requested that she remain and grace the banquet he was
about to give the princes and princesses who had honored him with their presence on this occasion. He led
her into a magnificent salon, in which the entire court
was assembled, and offered her a golden basin and a
vase filled with water so that she might wash her beautiful hands. No longer could she restrain her feelings.
She flung herself at his feet, embraced his knees, and
exclaimed, "Look, my dream has come true! You've
offered me water to wash with on my sister's wedding
day without anything evil happening to you."

The king had no difficulty recognizing her, for he
had been struck by her strong resemblance to Merveilleuse more than once. "Ah, my dear daughter!" he
cried, embracing her with tears in his eyes. "Can you
ever forgive my cruelty? I wanted to take your life
because I thought your dream predicted I would lose
my crown. Indeed, it did just that, for now that your
two sisters are married, each has a crown of her own.
Therefore, mine shall be yours." Upon saying this, he
rose and placed his crown on the princess's head,
crying, "Long live Queen Merveilleuse!"

The entire court took up the shout. The two sisters
threw their arms around her neck and kissed her a thousand times. Merveilleuse was so happy she could not
express her joy. She cried and laughed at the same
time. She embraced one, talked to another, thanked the
king, and in the midst of all this, she recalled the captain of the guard, to whom she was so much indebted.
When she asked eagerly to see him, though, they
informed her he was dead, and she felt a pang of
sorrow.

After they sat down to dinner, the king asked her to
relate all that had happened to her ever since the day he
had given his fatal orders. She immediately began
telling the story with the most remarkable grace, and
everybody listened to her attentively.

While she was engrossed in telling her story to the
king and her sisters, though, the enamored ram
watched for the princess as the hour set for her return
passed. Indeed, his anxiety became so extreme that he

could not control it. "She'll never come back!" he
cried. "My miserable sheep's face disgusts her. Oh,
unfortunate lover that I am, what will become of me if
I have lost Merveilleuse? Ragotte! Cruel fairy! How
you have avenged yourself for my indifference to
you!" He indulged in such lamentations for hours, and
then, as night approached without any signs of the
princess, he ran to the city. When he reached the king's
palace, he asked to see Merveilleuse, but since everybody was now aware of her adventures and did not
want her to return to the ram's realm, they harshly
refused to let him see her. He uttered cries and lamentations capable of moving anyone except the Swiss
guard who stood sentry at the palace gates. At length
broken-hearted, he flung himself to the ground and
breathed his last sigh.

The king and Merveilleuse were completely unaware
of the sad tragedy that had taken place. The king sug-
gested to his daughter that she ride in a triumphal
coach and show herself to everyone in the city by the
lights of thousands and thousands of torches illumi-
nating the windows and all the great squares. But what
a horrible spectacle she encountered as she left the
palace gates—her dear ram stretched out breathless on
the pavement! Jumping out of the coach and running to
him, she wept and sobbed, for she knew that her delay
in returning had caused the royal ram's death. In her
despair she felt she would die herself.

Now we know that people of the highest rank are
subject, like all others, to the blows of fortune, and that
they frequently experience the greatest misery at the
very moment they believe themselves to have attained
their heart's goal.

> The choicest blessings sent by Heaven
> Often tend to cause our ruin.
> The charms, the talents, that we're given,
> May often end on a sad tune.
> The royal ram would have surely seen
> Happier days without the charms that led
> The cruel Ragotte to love, then hurl her mean
> But fatal vengeance on his head.

In truth he should have had a better fate,
For spurning a sordid Hymen's chains;
Honest his love—unmasked his hate—
How different from our modern swains!
Even his death may well surprise
The lovers of the present day:
Only a silly sheep now dies,
Because his ewe has gone astray.

FINETTE CENDRON

ONCE upon a time there was a king and a queen who managed the affairs of their realm very badly. As a consequence, they were driven out of their kingdom and had to sell their crowns to support themselves. After that they had to part with their wardrobes, their linen, lace, and all their furniture, piece by piece. Soon the brokers tired of purchasing their goods, for every day something else was sent for sale. When they had disposed of nearly everything, the king said to the queen, "We're exiled from our own country and no longer have any possessions. We must do something to earn a living for ourselves and our poor children. Give some thought as to what we can do. Up to now the only trade I've known is the very pleasant one of a king's."

The queen, who was endowed with a wealth of good sense, asked for a week to think the matter over. At the end of that time she announced, "Sire, there's no need for us to be unhappy. You need only to make nets with which you can catch both fowl and fish. As the lines wear out, I'll spin new ones. With regard to our three daughters, they're downright idle girls who still think themselves as fine ladies and would like to continue living in that style without sullying their hands. We must take them so far away that they'll never be able to find their way back again, since we cannot possibly support them as well as they would like."

The king began to weep when he found he had to separate himself from his children, for he was a kind father. The queen was mistress, however, and he agreed to whatever she proposed. "Get up early tomorrow morning," he said to her, "and take your three daughters wherever you think fit."

While they were thus plotting together, the Princess Finette, who was the youngest daughter, listened at the keyhole, and when she discovered her father and mother's plans, she set off as fast as she could in the direction of a large grotto a considerable distance away, which was the abode of her godmother, the fairy Merluche.

Finette took two pounds of fresh butter, some eggs, milk, and flour to make a nice cake for her godmother and ensure she would be given a warm reception. She began her journey in good spirits, but the farther she went, the more weary she became. The soles of her shoes were worn completely through, and her pretty little feet became so sore that they were a sad sight to see. Indeed, she became so exhausted that she sat on the grass and cried. Just then a beautiful Spanish horse came by, already saddled and bridled. He had more than enough diamonds on his saddle cloth to purchase three cities. When he saw the princess, he stopped and began to graze quietly beside her. Bending his knees, he appeared to pay homage to her. Thereupon, she took him by the bridle and said, "Gentle hobby, would you kindly carry me to my fairy godmother's? You'd do me great service, for I'm so weary that I am ready to expire. If you help me on this occasion, I'll give you good oats and hay and a litter of fresh straw to lie upon."

The horse bent himself almost to the ground, and when young Finette jumped upon him, he galloped off with her as lightly as a bird until he came to a halt at the entrance of the grotto, as if he had known where to go to. In fact, he knew well enough, for Merluche herself had foreseen her goddaughter's visit and had sent the fine horse for her.

As soon as Finette entered the grotto, she made three respectful curtsies to her godmother. Then she took the hem of her gown, kissed it, and said to her, "Good day, godmother, how are you doing? I've brought you some butter, milk, flour, and eggs to make you a cake according to the custom of our country."

"You're welcome, Finette," the fairy said. "Come hither so I may embrace you." She kissed her twice and

this delighted Finette a great deal, for Madame Merluche was not one of those fairies one finds by the
dozen. "Come, goddaughter," she said, "you'll be my
lady's maid. Take down my hair and comb it." The
princess took her hair down and adroitly combed it. "I
know full well why you've come. You overheard the
king and queen discussing how they might lose you,
and you want to avoid such a calamity," Merluche said.
"Here, you have only to take this skein of unbreakable
thread. Fasten one end to the door of your house and
keep the other in your hand. When the queen abandons
you, you'll easily find your way back by following the
thread."

The princess thanked her godmother, who gave her a
bag filled with fine dresses made of gold and silver.
She embraced her, placed her again on the pretty horse,
and in two or three minutes he had carried Finette to
the door of her parents' cottage.

"My friend," Finette said to the horse, "you're very
handsome and clever, and your speed is as great as the
sun's. I thank you for your service. You may now
return whence you came."

She entered the house quietly and hid her bag under
her pillow. Then she went to bed appearing to know
nothing that had taken place. At daybreak, the king
woke his wife. "Come, come, madam," he said. "Get
ready for your journey."

She got up immediately, took some sturdy shoes, a
short petticoat, a white jacket, and a stick. Then she
summoned her eldest daughter, who was named Fleur
d'Amour; her second, who was named Belle-de-Nuit;
and her third, named Fine-Oreille, whom they famil-
iarly called Finette. "I've been thinking all last night
that we ought to go and see my sister," the queen said.
"She'll entertain us in splendid fashion. We can feast
and laugh as much as we like there."

Fleur d'Amour, who despaired of living in such a
desert, said to her mother, "Let us go, madam, wherever you please. Just as long as I can stroll somewhere,
anywhere." The two others agreed and took their leave
of the king. They set off all four together and walked
so very far that Fine-Oreille was terrified her thread

would not be long enough, for they walked nearly a thousand miles. She always kept behind the others, drawing the thread skillfully through the thickets.

When the queen thought her daughters would be unable to find their way back, she entered a dense forest and told them, "Sleep, my little lambs. I'll be like the shepherdess who watches over her flock for fear the wolf will devour them." Once they had lain down on the grass and fallen asleep, the queen left them there, believing she would never see them again.

Finette had shut her eyes but not gone to sleep. "If I were an evil-natured girl," she said to herself, "I'd go straight home and leave my sisters to die here." (The fact is, they beat her and scratched her until they drew her blood.) Yet despite their malice she did not abandon them. She roused her sisters and told them the whole story. They began to cry and begged her to take them with her, promising that they would give her beautiful dolls, a child's set of silver plates, and all their other toys and candy. "I'm quite sure you'll do nothing of the kind," Finette said. "Nevertheless, I'll behave as a good sister should." So saying, she rose and followed her thread with the two princesses, and thus they reached home almost as soon as the queen.

While they were at the door, they heard the king say, "It troubles my heart to see you come back alone."

"Pshaw," said the queen. "Our daughters were much too great a burden for us."

"If you had brought back my Finette," the king said, "I might have felt consoled about the loss of the others, for they loved nothing and nobody."

At that moment they knocked at the door—rap, rap. "Who's there?" asked the king.

"Your three daughters," they replied. "Fleur d'Amour, Belle-de-Nuit, and Fine-Oreille."

The queen began to tremble. "Don't open the door!" she exclaimed. "It must be their ghosts, for they could not have possibly found their way back alive."

The king, who was as great a coward as his wife, called out, "You're lying! You're not my daughters!"

But shrewd Fine-Oreille said, "Papa, I'll stoop down so that you can look at me through the hole made for

the cat to come through. If I'm not Finette, I agree to
be whipped."

The king did as he was told, and as soon as he recognized her, he flung open the door. Pretending to be
delighted to see them again, the queen said that she had
forgotten something and come home to fetch it, but that
she would surely have returned to them. They pretended to believe her and went upstairs to a snug
hayloft in which they always slept.

"Now, sisters," Finette said, "you promised me the
doll. Give it to me."

"Don't hold your breath, you little scamp," they
said. "You're the reason why they care so little for us."

Thereupon, they grabbed their distaffs and beat her
terribly. After they had abused her as much as they
desired, they let her go to bed. However, since she was
covered with wounds and bruises, she could not sleep.
Because of this, she heard the queen say to the king,
"I'll take them much farther in another direction, until
I'm positive they'll never return."

When Finette heard this plan, she rose silently to see
her godmother again. She went into the chicken yard,
where she wrung the necks of two hens, a cock, and
two little rabbits that the queen was fattening on cabbages for the next festive occasion. She put them all
into a basket and set off, but she had not gone a mile,
groping her way and quaking with fear, when the
Spanish horse approached at a gallop, snorting and
neighing. Thinking that some soldiers were about to
seize her, she cried, "Alas, it's all over for me." When
she saw the beautiful horse all alone, though, she
jumped upon his back, delighted to travel so comfortably, especially since she arrived almost immediately
at her godmother's.

After the usual greetings she presented her with the
hens, cock, and rabbits, and asked for her sage advice,
since the queen had sworn she would lead them to the
end of the world. Merluche told her goddaughter not to
trouble herself and gave her a sackful of ashes. "Carry
this sack in front of you and shake it as you go along.
You'll walk on the ashes, and when you wish to return, you'll only have to follow your footsteps," she said.

"Don't bring your sisters back with you, though, for they're too malicious. If you do bring them back, I'll never see you again."

Finette bid farewell to her and was given thirty or forty millions of diamonds in a little box, which she put in her pocket to take with her. The horse was ready and waiting and carried her home as before.

At daybreak the queen called the princesses and said, "The king isn't well, and I dreamed last night that I must go and gather some flowers and herbs that'll help him recuperate. There's a particular country where they grow to perfection, so let us be off right away."

Fleur d'Amour and Belle-de-Nuit, who never imagined that their mother intended to lost them again, were quite grieved at hearing that they had to make another long trip. Yet they had to go, and they went farther than any journey had ever been made. Finette, who never said a word, kept behind them and shook her sack of ashes with such wonderful skill that neither wind nor rain spoiled them.

The queen was perfectly convinced that they would not find their way back again, and one evening, when she observed her three daughters fast asleep, she used the opportunity to leave them and returned home. As soon as it was light and Finette found her mother gone, she woke her sisters. "We're alone," she said. "The queen has left us."

Fleur d'Amour and Belle-de-Nuit began to weep. They tore their hair and beat their own faces with their fists. "Alas, what will become of us?" they exclaimed.

Finette was the best-hearted girl in the world, and therefore she took pity on her sisters once again. "See how vulnerable I'm leaving. myself," she told them. "When my godmother furnished me with the means to return, she forbade me to show you the way and told me that if I disobeyed her, she'd never see me again."

Fleur d'Amour and Belle-de-Nuit threw themselves on Finette's neck, kissing her so affectionately that it required nothing more to bring all three back together to the king and the queen. Their majesties were greatly surprised at the return of the princesses, and they conversed long into the night. Meanwhile, their youngest daughter, who was not called Fine-Oreille for nothing, heard them concoct a new plan that involved the queen taking them on another journey the next morning. Again Fine-Oreille ran to wake her sisters.

"Alas," she said to them, "we're lost! The queen is determined to lead us into some wilderness and leave us there. I offended my godmother for your sakes, so I don't dare go to her for advice as I did before."

Faced with such a terrible prospect, they asked each other, "What shall we do, sister? What shall we do?"

At last Belle-de-Nuit said to the two others, "Why should we worry ourselves? Old Merluche doesn't possess all the wit in the world. There are other folks who possess just as much. We need only take plenty of peas and drop them all along the road as we go. Then we'll be sure to trace our way back."

Fleur d'Amour thought this was a remarkable idea, and they loaded all their pockets with peas. But instead of peas, Fine-Oreille packed her bag filled with fine clothes and the little box of diamonds, sensing that they might be gone a long time.

As soon as the queen called them, they were ready to go. "I dreamed last night," she said, "that in a country, which is unnecessary to name, there are three handsome princes who are waiting to marry you. I'm going to take you there to see if my dream was true."

The queen went first and her daughters followed her, confidently dropping their peas, for they were sure of finding their way home. This time the queen went farther than she had ever gone before, and during one dark night she left the princesses. She reached home very weary, but delighted for having gotten rid of the great burden of her three daughters.

After sleeping until eleven, the three princesses awoke, and Finette was the first to discover the queen's absence. Although she was perfectly prepared for it, she could not help crying, especially because she trusted the power of her fairy godmother much more than the cleverness of her sisters. Frightened, she went to them and said, "The queen's gone. We must follow her as soon as possible."

"Hold your tongue, you little hussy," replied Fleur d'Amour. "We can find our way well enough when we choose. There's no need in making such a fuss."

Finette did not dare to answer. However, when they did try to retrace their steps, there were no signs or paths to be found. Since immense flocks of pigeons inhabited that country, they had eaten up all the peas. The princesses began to scream with grief and terror. After spending two days without eating, Fleur d'Amour said to Belle-de-Nuit, "Sister, don't you have anything to eat?"

"Nothing."

She put the same question to Finette.

"Nor do I," she answered, "but I've just found an acorn."

"Ah! Give it to me," one sister said.

"Give it to me." said the other.

Each insisted on having it.

"An acorn will not go far among the three of us," Finette said, "Let us plant it, and maybe a tree will spring from that which will be useful to us."

Although there was scant chance of a tree growing in a country where none were to be seen, they agreed. The only things they could find to eat were cabbages and lettuces, and this was what the princesses lived on. If their constitutions had been delicate, they would have starved a hundred times. They slept almost always in the open air, and every morning and evening they took turns watering the acorn and saying, "Grow, grow, beautiful acorn!"

Indeed, it began to grow so fast that they could watch it grow. When it had reached a certain height, Fleur d'Amour tried to climb it, but it was not strong enough to bear her. Feeling it bend under her weight, she came back down again. Belle-de-Nuit was no more successful. Since Finette was lighter, she managed to climb up and remain there a long time.

Her sisters called to her, "Can you see anything, sister?"

She answered, "No, I can't see a thing."

"Ah, then, the oak is not tall enough," said Fleur d'Amour.

So they continued to water it and say, "Grow, grow, beautiful acorn!" Finette kept climbing it twice a day, and one morning, when she was upon the tree, Belle-de-Nuit said to Fleur d'Amour, "I've found a bag that our sister has hidden from us. What can be in it?"

Fleur d'Amour replied, "She told me it contained some old lace she had brought along to mend."

"I believe it's full of candy," Belle-de-Nuit said. Since she had a sweet tooth, she decided to look. When she opened the bag, she did find a good deal of old lace belonging to the king and queen, but hidden beneath it were the fine clothes and the box of diamonds the fairy had given to Finette.

"Well, now! Was there ever such a sly little scamp?" exclaimed Belle-de-Nuit. "We'll take out all the things and put some stones in their place."

This they did hastily, and when Finette rejoined them, she did not notice what they had done, for she never dreamed of decking herself out in a desert. She thought only about the oak, which quickly became the finest that the world has ever seen. One day when she had climbed it and her sisters as usual had asked if she could see anything, she exclaimed, "I can see a large mansion so very beautiful that I can't find the words to describe it. The walls are composed of emeralds and rubies, the roof of diamonds. It's covered all over with golden bells and weathercocks that whirl about as the wind blows."

"You're lying," they said. "It can't be as beautiful as you say."

"Believe me," Finette replied, "I'm not a liar. Come and see for yourselves. My eyes are quite dazzled by it."

Fleur d'Amour climbed up the tree. When she saw the château, she could talk about nothing else. Greatly curious, Belle-de-Nuit climbed in her turn and was just as enchanted as her sisters at the sight.

"We must certainly go to this palace," they said. "Perhaps we'll find those handsome princes who'll be happy to marry us."

They spent all evening long discussing the subject before they lay down to sleep on the grass. But when

Finette seemed to be fast asleep, Fleur d'Amour said to Belle-de-Nuit, "I'll tell you what we should do, sister. Let's get up and dress ourselves in the fine clothes Finette has brought."

"That's a splendid idea," Belle-de-Nuit responded.

Rising, they curled their hair, powdered it, put patches on their cheeks, and dressed themselves in the beautiful gold and silver gowns arrayed with diamonds. What a magnificent sight they made!

The next morning, unaware of her wicked sisters' theft, Finette took her bag with the intention of dressing herself, and was greatly distressed to find nothing in it but flint stones. At that moment she turned and saw her sisters shining like suns. She wept and complained about their treachery, but they only laughed and joked about it.

"I can't believe," Finette said, "that you have the effrontery to take me to the château without dressing and making me as beautiful as you are."

"We have barely enough for ourselves," Fleur d'Amour replied, "and you'll get nothing but blows if you pester us."

"But the clothes you have on are mine. My godmother gave them to me. They don't belong to you."

"If you say one more word about it," they responded, "we'll knock you on the head and bury you without anyone being the wiser!"

Poor Finette did not dare provoke them, but followed them slowly, walking a short distance behind them, as if she were merely their servant.

The nearer they approached the mansion, the more wonderful it appeared. "Oh," Fleur d'Amour and Belle-de-Nuit said, "what fun we'll have! What splendid dinners we'll have! We'll dine at the king's table. But Finette will have to wash the dishes in the kitchen, for she looks like a scullion. If anybody asks who she is, we must take care not to call her 'sister.' We must say she's the little cowherd from the village."

Of course, the lovely, sensible Finette was distressed at being treated so badly.

When they reached the castle gate, they knocked at it, and it was opened immediately by a terrifying old hag. She had just one eye, located in the middle of her forehead, but it was bigger than five or six ordinary ones. Her nose was flat, her complexion swarthy, and her mouth so horrible that it was frightening to behold. She was fifteen feet high and had a waist thirty feet wide. "Unfortunate wretches," she said to them, "What's brought you here? Don't you know that this is the ogre's castle, and that all three of you would scarcely make do for his breakfast? But I'm more good-natured than my husband. Come in. I won't eat you all at once. You'll have the consolation of living two or three days longer."

Upon hearing the words of the ogress, they began to flee, but one of her strides was equal to fifty of theirs. Thus she pursued and caught them, one by the hair and the others by the nape of the neck. Then she tucked them under her arm, took them into the castle, and threw all three into the cellar, which was filled with toads and adders and strewn with the bones of those the ogres had eaten. Desiring to eat Finette right away, the ogress went to fetch some vinegar, oil, and salt to make her into a salad. At that moment, however, she heard the ogre approaching and thought, "The princesses are so white and delicate that I want to eat them all myself." So she popped them quickly under a large tub, from which they could only look through a hole.

The ogre was six times as tall as his wife. When he spoke, the building shook, and when he coughed, they resembled peals of thunder. He had just one huge, filthy eye, and his hair stood all on end. Using a log of wood for a cane, he entered with a covered basket in his hand, from which he pulled fifteen children he had stolen on the road and swallowed them like fifteen freshly laid eggs. When the princesses saw him, they trembled under the tub. They were afraid to cry, lest they be heard, but they whispered to each other, "He'll eat us alive. How can we possibly save ourselves?"

The ogre said to his wife, "You know, I smell fresh meat. Give it to me."

"That's a good one," the ogress said. "You always think you smell fresh meat. It's your sheep that have just passed by."

"You can't fool me. I smell fresh meat for certain, and I'll search everywhere for it."

"Search," she said. "You won't find anything."

"If I do find something, and you've hidden it from me, I'll cut your head off and make a ball out of it."

She was frightened by this threat and said, "Don't be angry, my dear ogre. I'll tell you the truth. Three young girls came here today, and I hid them away. It would be a pity to eat them, though, for they know how to do everything. I'm old and need some rest. You can see that our fine house is very dirty, our bread is badly made, and your soup rarely pleases you. Moreover, I myself no longer appear so beautiful in your eyes ever since I began working so hard. These girls will be my servants. I beg you not to eat them just now. If you should desire one of them some other day, they'll always be within your reach."

The ogre was loath to promise that he would not eat them immediately. "Let me do as I please," he said. "I'll only eat two of them."

"No, you won't eat them."

"Well, then, I'll only eat the smallest."

"No, you won't touch a single one of them."

After a great deal of bickering, he at last promised he would not eat them, but she thought to herself, "When he goes hunting, I'll eat them and tell him they managed to escape."

The orge emerged from the cellar and told his wife to bring the girls to him. The poor princesses were nearly paralyzed with fright, and the ogress had to coax them to come forward. When they were brought before the ogre, he asked them what they could do. They answered, "We can sweep, sew, and spin exceedingly well."

"We can make ragouts so delicious that people are tempted to eat even the plates."

"As for bread, cakes, and patties, people have been known to order them from a thousand miles around."

Since the orgre was fond of good cooking, he said, "Aha! Set these good housewives to work immediately. I say," he asked, testing them, "after you light the fire, how do you know when the oven is hot enough?"

"I throw some butter into it, my lord," Finette replied, "and then I taste it with my tongue."

"Very well," he said, "light the over fire, then."

The oven was as big as a stable because the ogre and ogress ate more bread than two armies could eat. The princess built a terrific fire, until the oven was as hot as a furnace. In the meantime the ogre became impatient waiting for his new bread. So he ate a hundred lambs and a hundred suckling pigs, while Fleur d'Amour and Belle-de-Nuit made the dough. "Well," the mammoth ogre asked, "is the oven hot?"

"You shall see, my lord," said Finette. She threw in a thousand pounds of butter and then said, "It should be tasted with the tongue, but I'm too short to reach it."

"I'm tall enough," the ogre said as he stooped. He thrust his body so far into the oven though, that he could not keep his balance, and all the flesh was burned off his bones. When the ogress approached the oven, she was astounded to find her husband a mountain of cinders!

Fleur d'Amour and Belle-de-Nuit, who saw how distressed she was, consoled her as well as they were able, but they feared her grief would subside all too soon, and once her appetite returned, she would make a salad out of them, as she had been about to do before. "Don't be discouraged, madam," they said to her, "you'll find some king or some marquis who'll be delighted to marry you."

She smiled slightly, showing teeth that were longer than most people's fingers. When they saw her in such a good mood, Finette said, "If you would only take off these horrible bearskins that you wrap yourself in and follow the fashion, we'll dress your hair to perfection. Then you'll resemble a star."

"Come," the ogress said, "let's see what you can do. But rest assured that if I find any ladies more lovely than me, I'll make mincemeat out of you."

Thereupon, the three princesses took off her cap and began combing and curling her hair. While they entertained her with their chatter, Finette took a hatchet and struck her from behind with such a blow that her head was sliced clean off her shoulders.

Never was there such rejoicing! Climbing to the roof of the mansion, the three princesses amused themselves by ringing the golden bells. Then they ran through all the apartments, which were made of pearls and diamonds and filled with costly furniture. They nearly fainted with pleasure. They laughed, they sang, they had all they wanted: corn, marmalade, fruit, and dolls in abundance. Going to sleep in beds of brocade and velvet, Fleur d'Amour and Belle-de-Nuit said to each other, "Look at us, we're richer than our father was when he still had his kingdom."

"On the other hand, though, we want to be married, and nobody will dare to come here. People assume this mansion remains a cutthroat den because they don't know that the ogre and the ogress are dead. We must go to the nearest city and show ourselves in our fine dresses. Then we're bound to find some honest bankers who'll be quite glad to marry princesses."

As soon as they were dressed, they told Finette they were going to take a stroll. "But you must stay home and cook and wash and clean the house. We'd better find everything as it should be on our return. If not, you'll be beaten within an inch of your life!"

Poor Finette, whose heart was full of grief, remained alone in the house, sweeping, cleaning, washing, and crying without cease. "How unfortunate," she lamented "that I disobeyed my godmother! All sorts of awful things have happened to me. My sisters have stolen my precious dresses and adorned themselves with my ornaments. If it weren't for me, the ogre and his wife would be alive and well at this moment. What have I gained from killing them?"

Saying this, she broke into sobs until she almost choked. Shortly afterward her sisters returned loaded with Portugal oranges, preserves, and sugar. "Ah," they announced, "what a splendid ball we attended! How crowded it was! The king's son was among the dancers, and we received a thousand compliments. Come take off our shoes and clean them. It's one of your tasks."

Finette obeyed them, and if by accident she let drop a single word of complaint, they jumped on her and beat her savagely. The next day and the next they went out and returned with accounts of new wonders.

One evening Finette was sitting in the chimney corner on a heap of cinders, idly examining the cracks in the chimney, when she discovered a little key lodged in one of them. It was so old and so dirty that she had the greatest trouble cleaning it, but after she had done so, she found it was made of gold. Assuming that a golden key ought to open some beautiful little casket, she ran all over the mansion, trying it in all the locks. Eventually she found it fit the lock of a casket that was a masterpiece of art. When she opened it, she found it filled with clothes, diamonds, lace, linen, and ribbons worth immense sums. She said not a word to her sisters about her good fortune, but waited impatiently for their departure the next day. As soon as they were out of sight, she adorned herself until she looked more beautiful then the sun and the moon combined.

In this altered condition she went to the ball where her sisters were dancing, and though she was not wearing a mask, she had changed so much for the better that they did not recognize her. As soon as she appeared, a murmur arose throughout the gathering. Some were filled with admiration, others with jealousy. Asked to dance, she soon showed that she surpassed all the other ladies in grace as well as beauty. The mistress of the mansion came to her, and after making a respectful curtsy, she asked her name so that she would always have the pleasure of remembering such a marvelous person. Finette replied civilly that her name was Cendron. Now, there was not a lover who did not leave his mistress for Cendron, not a poet who did not write verses about Cendron. Never did such a shabby name cause so much commotion in so short a time. Every echo repeated the praises of Cendron. People did not have eyes enough to gaze at her, nor tongues enough to extol her.

Fleur d'Amour and Belle-de-Nuit, who had previously created a sensation wherever they appeared, were ready to burst with spite as they observed the reception accorded to this newcomer. But Finette extricated herself from all such rivalry with the best grace in the world. Her manners seemed to be those of one born to command. Fleur d'Amour and Belle-de-Nuit, who never saw their sister except with her face covered with chimney soot and looking as dirty as a dog, had completely forgotten how beautiful she was. Consequently, they did not have the slightest inkling who she was. Like all the rest, they paid their respects to Cendron.

As soon as she saw the ball was nearly over, she hurried home, undressed herself quickly, and put on her old rags. When her sisters arrived, they said to her, "Ah, Finette, we've just seen a perfectly charming young princess! She's not a baboon like you. She's as white as snow with a richer complexion than the roses. Her teeth are pearls and her lips are coral. She was wearing a gown so decked with gold and diamonds it must have weighed more than a thousand pounds. How beautiful, how charming she was!"

Finette murmured, "So was I, so was I."

"What are you muttering there?" her sisters asked.

She repeated even more softly, "So was I, so was I."

This little game was played for some time. Hardly a day passed that Finette did not appear in a new dress, for the casket was a fairy one. The more she took out, the more it was filled, and every item was so fashionable that all the ladies dressed themselves in imitation of Finette.

One evening when Finette had danced more than usual and had delayed her departure to a later hour, she was so anxious to get home before her sisters that she walked too hurriedly and lost one of her slippers, made of red velvet and embroidered with pearls. She tried to find it on the road, but the night was so dark, that she searched in vain. Thus she entered the house with one foot shod and one foot not.

The next day, Prince Chéri, the king's eldest son, went out hunting and found Finette's slipper. He picked it up and examined it, admiring its diminutive size and elegance. After turning it over and over, he kissed it and carried it home with him.

From that day on, he refused to eat, and his looks

underwent a great change: he became as yellow as a
quince, thin, melancholy, and depressed. The king and
queen, who were devoted to him, had the choicest
game and best confiture brought in from everywhere,
but they meant nothing to him. He gazed blankly at
everything and did not respond when his mother spoke
to him. They summoned the best physicians from all
around even as far as Paris and Montpellier. After
observing him continually for three days and three
nights, they concluded that he was in love and that he
would die if they did not find the sole remedy for him.

The queen, who doted on her son, burst into tears
because she did not know the object of his love and
could not help him marry her. She had the most beautiful ladies she could find brought into his chamber, but
he did not deign to glance at them. At last she said,
"My dear son, you're going to be the cause of our
death, for you're in love and you're hiding it from us.
Tell us whom you love and we'll give her to you, even
if she's just a simple shepherdess."

Taking courage from the queen's promise, the prince
drew the slipper from under his pillow. Showing it to
her, he said, "Look, madam, this is the cause of my
malady. I found this petite, delicate slipper when I
went out hunting, and I refuse to marry anyone but the
woman who can wear it."

"Very well, my son," said the queen, "there's no
need to trouble yourself. We'll organize a search for
her."

She rushed to the king with this news. He was very
surprised and immediately ordered a proclamation to
be made with drum and trumpet: all single women
were to come and try on the slipper, and she whose
foot fit the slipper would marry the prince.

Upon hearing this, every woman washed her feet
with the sorts of waters, pastes, and pomades. Some
ladies actually had them peeled, while others starved
themselves in order to make their feet smaller and prettier. They converged in hordes to try on the slipper, but
no one could fit into it, and the more they came and
failed, they more the prince's suffering increased.

One day Fleur d'Amour and Belle-de-Nuit dressed

themselves so superbly that they looked astonishingly beautiful.

"Where are you bound?" asked Finette.

"We're going to the capital city where the king and queen reside," they replied. "We're going to try on the slipper the king's son has found. If it fits one of us, the prince will marry her, and then one of us will become queen."

"And why can't I go?" Finette responded.

"Really! You're awfully stupid!" they said. "Go and water our cabbages. That's all you're fit for."

Without a second's thought Finette decided she should put on her finest clothes and take her chance with the rest, for she had a vague suspicion that she would be successful. She was troubled because she did not know her way, for the ball she had attended had not been held in the capital, but she dressed herself magnificently nevertheless. Her gown was made of blue satin and covered with diamond stars. She had a corona of them in her hair and a full moon on her back, and all these jewels glistened so brightly that no one could look at her without blinking. Upon opening the door to go out, she was quite surprised to find the pretty Spanish horse that had carried her to her godmother's. He was covered all over with golden bells and ribbons, and his saddle clothe and bridle were beyond compare. She patted him and said, "You're a most welcome sight, my little hobby. I'm much obliged to my godmother, Merluche." When he knelt down and she bounded atop him like a nymph, she was thirty times more beautiful than fair Helen of Troy.

The Spanish horse galloped off sprightly, his bells ringing ting, ting, ting. When Fleur d'Amour and Belle-de-Nuit heard these sounds, they turned around and saw her coming. They were completely taken by surprise, for they now recognized her both as Finette and Cendron. "Sister!" Fleur d'Amour cried to Belle-de-Nuit, "Look, that's Finette Cendron!"

As the other echoed the cry, Finette passed so close to them that her horse splashed them all over and left their fine dresses dripping with mud. Finette laughed at them and called, "Your highnesses, Cendrillon despises you as you deserve."

Then she passed them like a shot and disappeared. Belle-de-Nuit and Fleur d'Amour looked at each other. "Are we dreaming?" they asked. "Who could have supplied Finette with clothes and a horse? It's a miracle! She's got luck on her side. Her foot will fit the slipper, and we'll have made a long journey in vain."

While they were bemoaning their situation, Finette arrived at the palace. The moment she appeared, everybody thought she was a queen. Guards presented arms, drums rolled, and trumpets sounded a flourish. All the gates were flung open, and those people who had seen her at the ball preceded her and cried, "Make room! Make room for the beautiful Cendron, the wonder of the world!"

Such was the state that she entered the room of the dying prince. Casting his eyes on her, he was enraptured by the sight of her and prayed fervently that her foot would be small enough to fit into the slipper. Instantly she slipped it on and produced its fellow, which she had brought with her for this purpose. Immediately the cry could be heard: "Long live the Princess Chérie! Long live the princess who will be our queen!"

The prince rose from his couch and advanced to kiss her hand, and she was struck by how handsome and intelligent he was. While he paid her a thousand courteous attentions, the king and queen were informed of the event. Consequently, they came in all haste. The queen took Finette in her arms, called her daughter, her darling, her little queen! She gave her several magnificent presents, and the generous king added many more. They ordered the guns be fired, and violins, bagpipes, and every sort of musical instrument began to play. No one talked of anything but dancing and rejoicing. The king, queen, and prince begged Cendron to consent to let the marriage take place immediately.

"No," she said, "I must first tell you my story," which she did in a few words. When they found that she was born a princess, they again were so filled with joy that they thought they would burst. And when she

told them the names of her father and mother, they recognized them as sovereigns of dominions they had conquered. When they informed Finette of this fact, she
immediately vowed that she would not consent to
marry the prince until they had restored the estates of
her father. Of course, they promised to do so, for they
had upward of a hundred kingdoms, and one more or
less was not worth haggling over.

In the meantime Belle-de-Nuit and Fleur d'Amour
had arrived at the palace, and the first news that
greeted them was the Cendron had put on the slipper.
They did not know what to do or say. They decided to
return again without seeing her, but when Finette heard
they had arrived, she insisted that they come in. Instead
of berating and punishing them as they deserved, she
advanced to embrace them tenderly and then presented
them to the queen, "Madam, these are my sisters. They
are very charming, and I ask you to love them."

So confused were they by Finette's kindness that
they were rendered speechless. She promised them
they could return to their own kingdom, which the king
was restoring to their family. At these words they
threw themselves on their knees before her and wept
for joy.

The wedding was the most splendid that has ever
been seen. Finette wrote to her godmother and put the
letter along with valuable presents on the back of the
pretty Spanish horse. The letter requested that she visit
the king and queen, tell them of their good fortune, and
inform them they could now return to their kingdom,
an errand the fairy Merluche performed most graciously. Thus did Finette's father and mother regain
their estates and her sisters later became queens just
like her.

> If it's revenge on the ungrateful you want to see,
> Then follow Finette's wise policy.
> Do favors of the undeserving until they weep.
> Each benefit inflicts a wound most deep,
> Cutting the haughty bosom to the core.
> Finette's proud, selfish sisters suffered more,
> When by her generous kindness overpower'd,

Than if the ogres had made them into a mess,
For she overcame them with her kindness.
For her example, then, this lesson learn,
And give good for evil in your turn
No matter what wrong may awake your wrath,
There is no greater vengeance than this kind path.

THE YELLOW DWARF

ONCE upon a time there was a queen who had only one daughter, but that one was worth a thousand. Since the queen was a widow, nothing in the world was as dear to her as the young princess, and she was so afraid of losing her affection that she never corrected any of her faults. Is it any wonder that this marvelous being began to view her beauty as more divine than mortal? She appeared nearly always dressed as Pallas or Diana, followed by the principal ladies of the court attired as nymphs. And since she knew she was destined to wear a crown, she became so vain of her inherent charms that she snubbed everyone around her. If all this weren't enough, the queen capped her daughter's vanity by naming her Toutebelle.

When the princess reached the age of fifteen, the queen had her portrait painted by the best artists and sent it to several kings with whom she was on friendly terms. As soon as they saw this portrait, everyone without exception yielded to the inevitable power of her charms. Some fell ill, others lost their wits, and those fortunate enough to maintain their health and senses rushed to her court. No sooner did they lay eyes on the fair original than the poor princes became her devoted slaves.

Never in the world was a court more gallant and polite. Twenty kings vied with one another in endeavoring to please the princess. After spending three or four hundred million francs on a single entertainment, they felt more than repaid by her curt response: "It was pretty." The queen was delighted by all the worship that her daughter was receiving. Not a day passed that the princess did not find seven or eight thousand sonnets and as many odes, madrigals, and songs, sent to her by all the poets in the universe. Toutebelle was the sole theme of all the prose and verse written by the authors of the time. All the bonfires were made with these compositions, which burned and sparkled better than any other sort of fuel.

No one ventured to claim the honor of proposing to become her husband, though everybody wanted to. Yet how could anyone touch a heart like hers? A man might have hanged himself five or six times a day to please her, and she would have thought it but a trifle. Her lovers complained bitterly about her cruelty, and her mother, now that she wanted her to marry, saw no means of inducing her to decide in favor of one of them. "Won't you soften that intolerable pride of yours and stop criticizing all the kings who visit our court?" she asked. "I want to give you one for a husband. Don't you want to please me?"

"But I'm so happy," Toutebelle replied. "Please permit me, madam, to enjoy my serene indifference. If I were to change, you might be very sorry."

"Yes," said the queen, "I'd be angry if you were to love anyone beneath you. But look at those who want you, and you will see that none are more worthy than the suitors you have."

This was quite true, but the princess had such a high opinion of her own perfection that she considered herself worth someone even better. After some time had passed, her obstinate determination to remain single upset her mother so much that she now regretted her extreme indulgence, even though it was too late. Not knowing what to do, she journeyed all alone to consult a famous fairy called the fairy of the desert. Gaining access to her, however, was no easy task, for she was guarded by a pride of lions. The queen's plight would have been hopeless if she had not known that she had to feed these beasts a cake made of millet seed, sugar candy, and crocodiles' eggs. She made one of these cakes herself and put it into a hand basket.

Since she was not accustomed to walking so far, she lay down at the foot of a tree to take a short rest.

Gradually she fell asleep, and on reawakening she found her basket empty. The cake was gone, and to complete the calamity, she heard the tremendous roars of the great lions coming ever nearer, for they had detected her scent.

"Alas, what will become of me?" she exclaimed piteously. "They're going to devour me!" Weeping, not having strength to flee, she clung to the tree under which she had slept. Just then she heard, "Psst! Psst! Ahem! Ahem!" She looked all around her and, raising her eyes, saw a little man up in the tree, He was no more than a foot tall, and he was eating oranges. "I know you quite well, Queen," he said, "and I know you're afraid the lions will devour you. To be sure, you have good reason to be afraid, for they've devoured many before you, and to make matters worse, you have no cake."

"I must prepare myself to die!" the queen said, sighing. "Alas, I'd die much happier if my dear daughter were but married!"

"What? You have a daughter?" the yellow dwarf exclaimed. (He was given this name because of the color of his skin and because he dwelled in an orange tree.) "Truly, I'm delighted to hear it, for I've sought a wife by land and sea. Look, if you promise her to me, I'll save you from lions, tigers, or bears."

Looking at him, the queen was scarcely less frightened by his horrible little figure than by the lions. She pondered for some time without replying.

"What, you hesitate, madam?" he cried. "You can't be very fond of life."

At that very moment the queen perceived the lions on the top of a hill charging toward her. Each had two heads, eight feet, four rows of teeth, and their skin was as hard as rock and as red as morocco. At this sight the poor queen trembled more than a dove that spots a falcon, and she cried out with all her might, "My lord dwarf! Toutebelle is yours."

"Oh," he said disdainfully. "Toutebelle is too much of a belle. I don't want anything to do with her. You may keep her."

"Ah, my lord," the troubled queen continued, "don't

reject her. She's the most charming princess in the world."

"Very well," he said, "I'll accept her out of charity, but remember the gift you've given me!"

Suddenly the trunk of the orange tree opened and the queen rushed headlong into it just as it closed, thwarting the lions of their prey. The queen was so upset that she did not see that a door had been constructed inside the tree as well. Eventually she noticed it and, opening it, saw a field of nettles and thistles surrounded by a muddy ditch. Not far from the door stood a low-roofed cottage thatched with straw, and from it emerged the yellow dwarf, grinning mirthfully. Wearing wooden shoes and a jacket of coarse yellow cloth, he had large ears and no hair and looked just like a little villain. "I'd be delighted, my lady mother-in-law," he said, "to show you the little château in which your Toutebelle will reside with me. She may keep an ass in this field of nettles and thistles to ride about on. This rustic roof will shelter her from inclement weather. She'll drink this water and eat some of the frogs that live off it freely. And she'll have me day and night beside her—handsome, gay, and gallant, as you see me—for I'd be very angry if her shadow were to follow her better than I could."

The unfortunate queen was suddenly struck by the wretched life the dwarf planned for her daughter, and since she could not stand such a terrible prospect, she fainted dead away without uttering a word in reply. In this state was she transported to the palace and placed neatly in her own bed with the finest nightcap and most beautiful ribbons that she had ever worn. When the queen awoke and recalled what had happened to her, she could not believe it was true, for when she found herself in her palace with her ladies and her daughter by her side, there was little to show that she had been in the desert, that she had encountered such great dangers, and that the dwarf had saved her from them by making such a hard condition as the gift of Toutebelle. Nevertheless, the rare lace of the cap and the beauty of the ribbon astonished her just as much as the dream she assumed she must have had.

Due to her extreme anxiety, she fell into a melancholy so extraordinary that she could scarcely speak, eat, or sleep. The princess, who loved her mother with all her heart, was very concerned about her. She asked her frequently to tell her what the matter was, but the queen kept giving excuses. Sometimes she answered that she was not feeling well, other times that one of the neighboring states threatened to declare war against her.

Toutebelle saw clearly enough that these were plausible reasons, but also that there was something else at the bottom of the matter that the queen carefully concealed from her. Unable to suppress her disquiet, she decided to seek out the famous fairy of the desert, whose wisdom was widely celebrated in the region. She also desired her advice about marrying or remaining single, for everybody kept urging her to choose a husband. With her own hands she carefully kneaded the cake that had the power to appease the fury of the lions. That evening she pretended to go to bed early, but instead went out by a back staircase, her face covered by a large white veil that came down to her feet. All alone she took the road toward the clever fairy's grotto.

When she arrived at the fatal orange tree of which I have already spoken, however, she found it so laden with fruit and blossoms that she was overcome by an irresistible desire to pick some. Setting her basket on the ground, she plucked some oranges and ate them. When she turned to look for her basket and the cake again, they had disappeared. Already quite distressed, she was jolted when suddenly, right beside her, appeared the frightful dwarf whom I described before.

"What's troubling you, fair maid? Why are you weeping?" he asked.

"Alas, who wouldn't weep?" she replied. "I've lost my basket and my cake, which I need to insure my safe arrival at the abode of the desert fairy."

"Ah, and what do you want with her, fair maid?" the

little monkey asked again. "I'm her kinsman, her
friend, and just as clever as she is."

"My mother has lately been so despondent that I
tremble for her life," the princess replied. "I think that
I may be the cause of it all. You see, she wants me to
marry, and I must confess that I haven't met anyone yet
whom I deem worthy of me. This is why I want to consult the fairy."

"Don't trouble yourself, Princess," the dwarf said.
"I'm better suited to enlighten you about such subjects
than she. Your mother regrets that she has promised
your hand in marriage—"

"The queen's promised me to someone?" the
princess cried, interrupting him. "Oh, you must be mistaken. She would have told me, for I'm far too interested in this affair for her to arrange my engagement
without seeking my consent beforehand."

"Beautiful princess," said the dwarf, suddenly
flinging himself at her feet, "I hope that her choice will
not displease you when I tell you that it is I who is destined to enjoy such happiness."

"My mother wants you for her son-in-law?" Toutebelle exclaimed, retreating a few steps. "You must be
insane!"

"I don't really care about this honor," the dwarf said
angrily. "Here come the lions! In three bites they'll
avenge me for your unjust disdain."

All at once the poor princess heard the loud roars of
the approaching monsters. "What will become of me?"
she cried. "Is this how my young days are to end?"

The wicked dwarf looked at her and laughed con-
temptuously. "At least you'll have the glory of dying a
maiden," he said, "and not disgracing yourself by
having a person of your dazzling worth united with a
miserable dwarf like me."

"For mercy's sake, don't be angry," the princess begged, clasping her beautiful hands. "I'd rather
marry all the dwarfs in the universe than perish so
frightfully."

"Regard me well, Princess, before you give me your
word," he replied, "for I don't want to take advantage
of you."

"I've looked at you more than enough," she said. "The lions terrify me more than your looks. Save me! Save me or I'll die of fright!"

Scarcely had she uttered these words than she fainted. When she at last recovered from her swoon, she found herself, without knowing how she got there, in her own bed lined with the finest linen in the world, the most beautiful ribbons on her dress, and a ring made of a single red hair, which fitted her finger so tightly that the skin would have come off sooner than the ring.

When the princess saw all these things and remembered what had taken place that night, she fell into a melancholy that shocked and upset the entire court. More alarmed than anyone, her mother asked her hundreds of times what the matter was, but the princess persisted in concealing this incident from her. At length the great estates of the kingdom became impatient to see the princess married, and they assembled in council. Afterward they obtained an audience with the queen, whom they petitioned with the request that she choose a husband for her daughter as soon as possible. She answered that she desired nothing better, but that her daughter demonstrated so much repugnance to marriage that she advised them to talk to the princess herself about the subject, whereupon they left immediately.

Toutebelle had lost a good deal of her haughtiness since her encounter with the yellow dwarf. She saw no other way of escaping her dilemma than by marrying a great king with whom the little monkey would not dare to dispute such a glorious prize. To the members of the council she gave a more favorable answer than they had expected: "Although I would consider myself content to remain single all my life, I agree to marry the king of the gold mines." This was a powerful, handsome prince who had loved her passionately for several years and who until that moment had never dared to hope that she would in the least return his affection.

You can well imagine how ecstatic he was when he received such glorious news, and you can also imagine

the rage of all his rivals when they learned about the
extinction of the fond hopes they had nourished. But
Toutebelle could not marry twenty kings. She had
already had a great deal of difficulty in choosing one,
for her vanity was as great as ever, and she was still
fully convinced that nobody in the world was suitable
enough for her.

Everything necessary for the finest celebration that
the universe has ever seen was prepared. The king of
the gold mines sent home for such prodigious sums
that the sea was swamped with the ships that returned
with them. Agents were dispatched to all the most
refined and gallant courts, particularly that of France,
to purchase the rarest materials for the wardrobe of the
princess. Of course, she had less need than anybody for
ornamentation to highlight her beauty, which was so
perfect that it was impossible to embellish. As the
blissful day approached, the king of the gold mines
never left the side of his charming princess.

The evident importance of becoming acquainted
with the character of her future husband induced the
princess to observe him carefully. As a result she discovered in him so much merit, so much sense, such
deep and delicate feeling—in short, such a fine mind in
such a perfect body—that she began to return his affection to some degree. They spent happy moments wandering in the most beautiful gardens in the world,
where they found themselves at liberty to express their
mutual sentiments, a pleasure often heightened by the
charms of music. The king, always gallant and
amorous, sang verses of his own composition to the
princess. The following is one she especially liked:

> "The groves for you have donned a richer green.
> The fields reveal the brightest flowers seen.
> Your footsteps fall, fresh blossoms spring;
> Without your bowers, the sweet birds sing.
> All nature smiles, around, below, above,
> All hail the daughter of the god of love!"

Everyone in the palace was filled with joy but the
king's rivals. Enraged by his success, they left the

court and returned to their own dominions, too over-whelmed by grief to be able to bear the pain of wit-nessing Toutebelle's marriage. In fact, they took their leave of her in such a touching manner that she could not help pitying them.

"Ah, madam," the king of the gold mines asked her on that occasion, "why are you being so unfair to me today? These lovers were more than repaid for their sufferings by one glance from your eyes, and yet you've blessed them with your pity."

"I'd be angry," Toutebelle said, "if you were indif-ferent to the compassion I've shown those princes who have lost me forever. It's proof of your sensitivity, and I'm indebted to you for it. But, my lord, their position is so different than yours. You have good reason to be satisfied with my conduct toward you, and they have little cause to congratulate themselves. So don't let your jealousy get the better of you."

Disarmed by how kindly the princess received a reproach that might have annoyed her, the king of the gold mines threw himself at her feet, kissed her hand, and asked her pardon a thousand times.

At last the day they had awaited so fervently arrived. Everything was ready for the marriage: trumpets and musical instruments announced the commencement of this grand fete all over the city; the streets were car-peted and strewn with flowers; the people flocked in crowds in the great square in front of the palace. In a state of rapture, the queen had scarcely gone to bed before she got up again long before daybreak to give the necessary orders and to select the jewels the princess was to wear. She was diamonds down to her very shoes, which were also fashioned of them. Bought at an enormous price, her gown of silver brocade was striped with a dozen rays of the sun, and their radiance was matched only by the beauty of the princess. A magnificent crown adorned her head. Her hair fell to her feet in wavy curls. Her majestic form glittered brilliantly among the crowd of ladies who accompa-nied her.

The king of the gold mines was no less magnificent in his appearance, and his happiness was apparent in

his every look and gesture. No one approached him
who did not return loaded with his generous gifts, for
he had ordered a thousand barrels to be filled with gold
and large sacks of pearl-embroidered velvet to be
crammed with coins. Placed around the banquet hall,
each held a hundred thousand and were given indis-
criminately to all who held out their hands. The result
was that this pleasant ceremony drew many people
who had scant regard for the other entertainment
events during the wedding festivities.

The queen and princess advanced to meet the king
and proceeded with him to the altar. As they passed
through the long nave, they saw two large turkey cocks
drawing a very clumsily made box. Behind them came
a tall old crone, whose great age and decrepitude were
as striking as her ugliness. She walked with a crutch
and wore a black taffeta ruff, a red velvet hood, and a
farthingale all in tatters. She took three turns around
the gallery with her turkey cocks before she said anything. Then, stopping in the center and brandishing her
crutch in a threatening manner, she cried, "Ho, ho,
queen! Ho, ho, princess! Do you think you can break
your promise to my friend the yellow dwarf with
impunity? I'm the fairy of the desert! Don't you realize
that if it weren't for him and his orange tree that my
great lions would have devoured you? We don't put up
with such insults in fairyland. Ponder quickly the consequences of what you're about to do, for I swear by
my cap that you shall marry the dwarf, or I'll burn my
crutch."

"Ah, Princess!" the queen exclaimed, bursting into
tears. "What do I hear? What was the promise you
made?"

"Ah, Mother!" Toutebelle cried sorrowfully. "What
was the promise you yourself made?"

The king of the gold mines was enraged by this
interruption and by the wicked old woman's opposition
to his marriage. He advanced toward her, sword in
hand, and placing the point to her throat, he cried,
"Leave this palace forever, or you'll pay for your mali-
ciousness with your life."

No sooner had he said these words than the lid of the

box popped open with a terrific noise and shot to the ceiling. Out came the yellow dwarf, mounted on a large Spanish cat. In a wink he had assumed a position between the fairy of the desert and the king of the gold mines.

"Not so quick, young man," he said. "Don't think you can assault this illustrious fairy. You're going to have to deal with me alone! I'm your foe, nay, I'm your rival. The faithless princess who means to wed you promised to be mine, and I promised to be hers. Look and see if she doesn't have a ring of my hair on her finger. Try to remove it and you'll learn how inferior your power is to mine."

"Miserable monster," the king replied, "you have the audacity to declare yourself the lover of this divine princess? You're nothing but a monkey, whose hideous figure is painful to behold. I would have long since eliminated you if you had really been worthy of dying by my hand."

Stung to the quick, the yellow dwarf stuck his spurs into the sides of his cat, who began squalling horribly. As the cat flew here and there, it terrified everyone except the brave king, who pressed the dwarf so closely that he drew a large cutlass from his side and challenged the king to a single combat.

The dwarf descended into the palace courtyard amid an extraordinary uproar, and the enraged king followed him with rapid strides. No sooner had they confronted each other, as the entire court watched from the balconies, than the sun suddenly became as red as blood, and it grew so dark that they could scarcely see each other. Such thunder and lightning exploded that the world seemed to be coming to its end. The two turkey cocks appeared at the yellow dwarf's side: they were twin giants larger than mountains, spewing so many flames from their mouths and eyes that each one looked like a fiery furnace. Still, none of those horrors frightened the dauntless young king. Through his intrepid glare and swirling sword he reassured all who were interested in his welfare and brought embarrassment to the yellow dwarf.

Alas, the king's mettle failed him when he saw the

fairy of the desert—her head covered with long serpents like Tisiphone, mounted upon a winged griffin
and armed with a lance—rush at his dear princess and
strike her with such a fierce blow that she fell into the
queen's arms bathed in her own blood. That tender
mother was more deeply wounded by the blow than
even her daughter, and she uttered shrieks and groans
that are impossible to describe. As soon as he saw this,
the king's reason abandoned him, and he ceased
fighting. Immediately he dashed to rescue the princess
or to die with her, but the yellow dwarf anticipated his
movements. Leaping with his Spanish cat onto the balcony, he snatched the princess from the arms of the
queen and the ladies who surrounded her. Then he
jumped onto the roof of the palace and disappeared
with his prize.

Paralyzed with astonishment, the king witnessed
this extraordinary incident in utter despair. Not only
did he have no power to prevent it, but to complete
his disgrace, he felt his eyesight fail him as an irresistible power carried him off through a vast expanse
of some vacuum. What misfortunes! Love, cruel Love!
Is this how you treat those who acknowledge you as
their lord?

The wicked fairy of the desert had no sooner laid
eyes on the king of the gold mines than her barbarous
heart was touched by his charms. Marking him as her
prey, she carried him off to the depths of a frightful
cave, where she bound him with chains anchored to a
rock in the hope that the fear of impending death would
make him forget Toutebelle and do whatever she
desired. As soon as they had arrived, she restored his
sight. Through the power of fairy art, she acquired the
graces and charms denied her by nature, and appeared
before him as a lovely nymph who just happened to
show up at that spot by chance.

"What do I see?" she cried. "Can it be you, charming
prince? What's happened to you? What misfortune has
brought you to languish in this miserable abode?"

Deceived by her appearance, the king replied, "Alas,
fair nymph, I don't know why the infernal fairy has
brought me here. Although she prevented me from

seeing when she carried me and hasn't shown herself since, I do know from her voice that it was the fairy of the desert."

"Ah, my lord," the false nymph exclaimed, "if you are in the power of that woman, you won't escape without marrying her. She has snared more than one hero, and of all beings in the world, she is the most obstinate when she sets her mind on something."

While she thus pretended to take a great interest in the king's distress, he caught sight of the nymph's feet, which resembled those of a griffin. The fairy of the desert could always be recognized by her feet, which remained unaltered no matter how she changed herself. Pretending not to notice, the king continued conversing as though he fully trusted her. "I don't feel any aversion toward the fairy of the desert," he said, "but I can't stand her protecting the yellow dwarf and keeping me in chains like a criminal. What have I done to offend her? I loved a charming princess, but if the fairy restores my liberty to me, I feel that gratitude will induce me to love no one but her."

"Are you sincere about this?" the nymph asked, faltering.

"There's no need to doubt me," the king replied. "I'm not experienced in the art of deception, and I must confess that my vanity would be more flattered by the attention shown by a fairy than by a mere princess. But even if I desperately loved her, I'd show her nothing but hatred until I had regained my liberty."

Deceived by these words, the fairy of the desert decided to transport the king to a spot as beautiful as the cave he now inhabited was horrible. Compelling him to get into her chariot, to which she now harnessed swans instead of the bats that usually drew it, she flew with the king of the gold mines from one pole to the other. What a shock the king received, though, enroute! While coursing through the boundless ethereal regions, he caught a glimpse of his dear princess in a castle made entirely of steel. Its walls reflected the rays of the sun and became burning glass sheets that scorched to death all who approached them. The princess was reclining in a bower beside a streamlet, and one of her hands was beneath her head, while the other appeared to be wiping away tears. As she lifted her eyes to Heaven, imploring its aid, she saw the king pass by with the fairy of the desert. Just as she had used her skillful power to appear beautiful in the eyes of the young monarch, so she also seemed to be the most marvelous creature in the world to the princess.

"What now?" she exclaimed. "Aren't I sufficiently wretched in this inaccessible castle where the dreadful yellow dwarf has transported me? Must the demon of jealousy torture me to complete my misery? Must I learn through this extraordinary incident that the king of the gold mines is unfaithful to me? Now that I'm out of sight, he obviously believes that he's absolved from all his vows. But who is this formidable rival whose fatal beauty surpasses mine?"

While the princess mused, the enamored king was in mortal agony at being whisked away from the dear object of his affections. If he had not been so fully cognizant of the fairy's power, he would have risked escape either by killing her or by using some other means that his love or courage might have proposed. But what could be done against so powerful a being? "Be patient," he told himself. "You must wait for the right opportunity to free yourself of her clutches."

Having seen Toutebelle as well, the fairy sought to discover in the king's eyes what effect the sight of his darling had induced in his heart. "No one but myself," the king said, interpreting her glances, "can tell you what you want to know. This unexpected meeting with an unhappy princess with whom I had an attachment has aroused some feelings in me. But you are so far superior to her in my mind that I'd rather die than be unfaithful to you."

"Ah, Prince!" the fairy said. "Dare I hope that I've inspired you with sentiments so favorable?"

"Time will convince you, madam," he replied. "But if you want to convince me that I'm in your good graces, you'll not refuse me when I ask you to protect Toutebelle."

"Reflect on what you ask of me," said the fairy, frowning and looking askance at him. "Do you want me to use my skills against the yellow dwarf, my best friend, in order to release a proud princess from his power—a princess whom I must still regard as my rival?"

The king sighed without replying. What answer could he make to such an calculating fiend?

They arrived at a vast prairie sprinkled with a thousand different flowers. A deep river surrounded it, and streams from many fountains flowed gently beneath tufted trees offering refreshing shade. In the distance could be seen a superb palace whose walls were made of transparent emeralds. As soon as the swans drawing the fairy's chariot had descended beneath a portico roofed with rubies and paved with diamonds, thousands of lovely nymphs appeared from every quarter and advanced to receive them with loud shouts of joy and the following song:

"When victory is what Love seeks to gain,
Defiance is idle—we struggle in vain.
Resistance gives force to the weapons he wields.
The greater the hero, the sooner he yields."

The fairy of the desert was delighted at hearing this allusion to her conquest. Leading the king into the most superb apartment known in the memory of fairies, she left him alone for a few minutes so that he would not think that he was utterly her prisoner. For his part, he felt certain that she was not far off and that no matter where she was keeping herself, she had an eye on all his actions. Therefore, he advanced to a large looking glass and addressed it by saying, "Loyal counselor, let me see what I can do to make myself more pleasant to the charming fairy of the desert, for I'm terribly eager to please her." Thereupon, he combed and powdered his hair, put a patch on his cheek, and upon noticing a suit of clothes on a table more magnificent than his own, he changed into them as quickly as possible. When the fairy reentered, she was so ecstatic that she could not control her joy.

"I appreciate the pains you've taken to please me," she said. "You've found the secret of pleasing me without searching for it. You must judge, sir, whether it will be difficult to continue to do so."

The king, who had his reasons for saying sweet things to the old fairy, kept flattering her, and by degrees he obtained permission to take a daily walk by the seaside. She had used her art to make that coast so dangerous and terrifying that not a captain was courageous enough to navigate in the vicinity. Thus she had nothing to fear by granting this favor to her captive. It was, however, some comfort to him to be able to indulge in solitary musings uninterrupted by the presence of his wicked jailer.

After having strolled for some time on the sands, he stooped and inscribed the following lines in them with a cane that he carried at his side:

At last I am at liberty to weep:
My tears in torrents now unchecked may pour,
And ease my laboring bosom's anguish that's so deep.
Alas! I shan't behold my love anymore.
Oh you, that make this rock-girted shore
To mortals inaccessible! Dread sea,
Whose mountain billows as the wild roar,
Now high as Heaven, now low as Hell, can flee.
Your state, compared to mine, is calm tranquillity.

Toutebelle! Oh cruel destiny! Forever,
Forever lost! The idol of my heart!
You gods, when dooming me for her to sever,
Why didn't you ask my life as well to part?
Spirit of Ocean, whoever you are.
If it be true that even beneath the wave
Love has the power to reach you with his dart,
Rise from your pearly grotto, your coral cave,
And from despair a fond and faithful lover save.

As he finished, he heard a voice that irresistibly attracted his attention. Noticing the tide rising in an extraordinary manner, he quickly turned around and saw a female of extraordinary beauty. Her torso was adorned only by her waist-long hair, and the breeze brushed it gently so that her hair floated on the water. She held a looking glass in one hand and a comb in the other, and her lower extremities took the form of a long fish's tail furnished with fins. Needless to say, the king was astounded by such an extraordinary sight.

As soon as she was near enough to speak, she said, "I know of your sad predicament with your lost princess as well as the bizarre attachment that the fairy of the desert has for you. If you're willing, I'll take you away from this fatal spot. Otherwise you may languish another thirty years."

The king knew not how to reply to this proposal. Though he needed no inducement to escape from captivity, he feared the fairy of the desert had taken this form to deceive him. As he hesitated, the siren, who could read his thoughts, said, "Don't think I'm laying a trap for you. I'm too honest to want to serve your enemies. The conduct of the fairy of the desert and the yellow dwarf has incensed me. I see your unhappy princess daily, and her beauty and merit have aroused my compassion. So, let me repeat, if you'll trust me, I'll rescue you."

"I trust you completely," the king said, "and I'll do whatever you command. But since you've seen my princess, please tell me some news of her."

"We'd lose too much time by talking here," said the siren. "Come, I'll take you to the steel castle and leave a figure here on the shore that will resemble you so closely that it will deceive the fairy."

She immediately cut some sea rushes and made a large bundle of them. Blowing on them three times, she said, "Sea rushes, my friends, I order you to lie motionless on the sand until the fairy of the desert comes to take you away." The rushes became covered with skin and so resembled the king of the gold mines that he was astonished by the transformation. The figure wore clothes exactly like his, and its countenance was pale and wasted, as if he had drowned. The friendly siren then made the king sit on her large fish's tail, and in this manner, agreeable to both, they plied the sea together.

"Now," the siren said, "I'll gladly tell you what transpired after the fairy of the desert had wounded Toutebelle and the wicked dwarf carried her off on the back of his horrible Spanish cat. The princess lost so much blood and was so terrified by all that had occurred that her strength failed her, and she was unconscious the entire journey. Despite her condition, the yellow dwarf did not stop to help her in the least until he had safely arrived in his terrible steel palace, where he was welcomed by the most beautiful nymphs in the world, whom he had already transported there. They vied with one another in their eagerness to serve the princess. She was put into a bed with sheets made of gold and covered with pearls as large as walnuts."

"Ha!" exclaimed the king of the gold mines, interrupting the siren. "So he's married her. I feel faint! I'm going to die!"

"No," she said, "compose yourself, my lord. Toutebelle's vigor has protected her from the violence of that hideous dwarf."

"Proceed then," the king said.

"What more can I tell you?" the siren continued. "She was in the grove when you flew over it. She saw you with the fairy of the desert, who was so well disguised that she appeared to be more beautiful than the princess herself. You cannot imagine how desperate she is. She believes you love the fairy."

"Good heavens!" the king cried. "She believed that I love the fairy? What a mistake she's made! What must I do to put these matters right?"

"Consult your own heart," the siren replied with a gracious smile. "When we are deeply in love, we need no advice about such things."

Even as she spoke, they arrived at the steel castle. The side facing the sea was the only border that the yellow dwarf had not fortified with those formidable walls that burned everyone who approached them. "I know for certain," that siren said, "that Toutebelle sits beside the same fountain that you saw when you passed over the castle gardens. But you'll have some foes to

contend with before you can approach her. Here is a
sword: armed with it you may dare to brave the
greatest dangers. But beware that you never let it drop.
Adieu, I'm going to rest beneath the rock you see over
yonder. If you need my help to convey you and your
dear princess any farther, I won't fail you, for her
mother is my best friend and it was for her sake that I
went to find you."

So saying, she gave the king a sword fashioned from
a single diamond, which glistened more brightly than
the rays of the sun. The king understood its incalcu-
lable value, and since he could find no words to
express his gratitude, he begged her to make amends
for his deficiency by imagining all that an honest heart
could feel under such great obligations.

We must now say a word about the fairy of the
desert. When she found that her charming lover had not
returned, she went in search of him. Down to the
seashore she walked with a hundred maidens in her
train, all bearing magnificent presents for the king.
Some carried large baskets filled with diamonds, other
golden vases marvelously wrought; many were carrying ambergris, coral, and pearls; others had bales of
amazingly rich materials on their heads while still
others bore fruit, flowers, and even birds. Thus you can
imagine the feelings of the fairy who followed this
bounteous troop when she saw the sea rushes that
exactly resembled the king of the gold mines. The sight
of him dead caused her such pain that she uttered a
dreadful shriek that pierced the skies, shook the hills,
and echoed even in the infernal regions. The Furies,
Megara, Alecto, and Tisiphone, could not have assumed a more terrible aspect than did the fairy of
the desert at that moment. Throwing herself on the
apparent corpse of the king, she wept, she howled, she
tore apart fifty of the most beautiful maidens accompanying her, immolating them to the manes of her dearly
departed. After this she invoked eleven of her sister
fairies to appear and help her construct a stately mausoleum in which she might deposit the remains of the
young hero. Like the desert fairy every one of the
eleven was deceived by the appearance of the sea

rushes. This circumstance is rather surprising, for fairies generally know everything, but the clever siren proved in this case that she knew more than they.

Even as they were collecting porphyry, jasper, agate, marble, statues, emblems, gold, and bronze to immortalize the king they believed dead, he was thanking the charming siren and implored her to continue protecting him. She kindly promised she would vanish from sight. Nothing was left but for him to advance on the steel castle.

Guided by his love, he strode forth to inspect every part of the castle and discover his adorable princess. But he encountered trouble all too quickly. Four terrible sphinxes surrounded him, and when they lashed out with their sharp talons, they would have quickly torn him to pieces if the diamond sword had not proved as useful as the siren had predicted. No sooner had he flashed it before the eyes of these monsters than they fell powerless at his feet, and he dealt each of them its death blow. When he advanced again, he encountered six dragons covered with scales harder to pierce than iron. Alarmed though he was, his courage remained unshaken, and he made such good use of his redoubtable sword that he cut each one in half with one blow. He was hoping he had surmounted the greatest obstacles when a most embarrassing one presented itself. Twenty-four beautiful, graceful nymphs advanced toward him with long garlands of flowers, which they stretched across his path to impede his progress.

"Where do you wish to go, sire?" they asked. "We've been entrusted to protect these regions. If we permit you to pass, we shall all experience a wealth of misfortunes. For mercy's sake, don't continue. Do you want to stain your victorious hand with the blood of twenty-four innocent maidens who have never done anything to displease you?"

Irresolute, the king stood transfixed before them. He who professed such respect for the fair sex and eagerly championed them to the death on every occasion was presently to destroy a group of the fairest! But while he was hesitating, he heard a voice say: "Strike! Strike! or your princess is lost forever!"

Swayed by these words, he did not utter a word in reply to the nymphs, but instead he rushed upon them, broke through their garlands, attacked them without mercy, and scattered them about.

This proved his last obstacle before he found himself entering the grove in which he had previously seen Toutebelle, who was seated beside the fountain, pale and suffering. Trembling as he approached her, he would have thrown himself at her feet, but she fled from him as hastily and indignantly as if he had been the yellow dwarf. "Don't condemn me without hearing me out," he said. "I'm neither unfaithful nor guilty of any intentional wrong toward you. I'm an unhappy lover who was compelled despite himself to offend you."

"Ah, cruel prince," she exclaimed, "I saw you sail through the air with a lady of extraordinary beauty. Was it despite yourself you made that voyage?"

"Yes, Princess," he replied, "it was. The wicked fairy of the desert was not satisfied with chaining me to a rock. So she dragged me in her chariot to one of the ends of the world, where I would still be languishing in captivity if it were not for the unexpected assistance of a beneficent siren who brought me here. I've come, my princess, to release you from the power of the villain who holds you prisoner. Don't reject the aid of the most faithful of lovers!"

He flung himself at her feet and caught the hem of her gown to detain her, but in so doing, he unfortunately let the formidable sword drop to the ground. The yellow dwarf, who lay hidden beneath the leaves of a lettuce, no sooner saw it fall from the king's grasp than he sprang forward and seized it, for he was aware of its power.

The princess uttered a terrified shriek at the sight of the dwarf, but her anguish only exasperated the little monster. With two cabalistic words he conjured up two giants, who bound the king with chains and fetters.

"Now," the dwarf said, "I'm master of my rival's fate, but I'll spare his life and give him liberty to leave this place, provided you consent to marry me immediately."

"Oh, I'd rather die a thousand deaths!" the enamored king exclaimed.

"You die? Alas, my lord," said the princess, "what could be more terrible for me than such a calamity?"

"Your becoming the victim of this monster. Can any horror exceed that?"

"Let's die together, then."

"No, Princess," the king answered. "Grant me the consolation of dying for you."

"Before I allow that," the princess said, turning to the dwarf, "I will consent to your wishes."

"In front of my eyes?" the king exclaimed. "In front of my eyes you intend to make him your husband? Cruel princess, life will be hateful to me!"

"No," the yellow dwarf said, "you will see no such thing. A beloved rival is too dangerous to be endured."

With these words, despite the tears and shrieks of Toutebelle, he stabbed the king in the heart and laid him dead at his feet. Unable to bear life without her lover, the princess fell on his body, and her spirit quickly fled to join his. Thus this illustrious but unfortunate pair perished without the siren being able to help, for the power of the spell had been centered in the diamond sword.

The wicked dwarf preferred having the princess dead than seeing her in the arms of another, and once the fairy of the desert was informed of what had occurred, she destroyed the mausoleum she had erected and developed as much hatred for the king as she had formerly felt love.

The friendly siren was overwhelmed with grief by such a great misfortune, but she could obtain no other favor from Fate than the permission to change the two lovers into palm trees. Their two bodies, which had been so perfect during life, became two graceful trees, and since they still cherished a faithful love for each other, they joined their branches in fond embraces and immortalized their ardor by that tender union.

Those who in danger on the stormy main
Vow hecatombs to all the gods they know,
When safe on shore they find themselves again,
Not even near their altars do they care to go.
In peril anyone will swear anything for his sake,
But let the tragic tale of poor Toutebelle
Warn you no promise in your fear to make
You would not gladly keep when all is well.

THE GREEN SERPENT

ONCE upon a time there was a great queen who, having given birth to twin daughters, invited twelve fairies who lived nearby to come and bestow gifts upon them, as was the custom in those days. Indeed, it was a very useful custom, for the power of the fairies generally compensated for the deficiencies of nature. Sometimes, however, they also spoiled what nature had done its best to make perfect, as we shall soon see.

When the fairies had all gathered in the banquet hall, they were about to sit at the table and enjoy a magnificent meal. Suddenly the fairy Magotine entered. She was the sister of Carabossa and no less malicious. Shuddering when she saw her, the queen feared some disaster since she had not invited her to the celebration. However, she carefully concealed her anxiety, personally went looking for an armchair for the fairy, and found one covered with green velvet and embroidered with sapphires. Since Magotine was the eldest of the fairies, all the rest made way for her to pass and whispered to one another, "Let us quickly endow the infant princesses, sister, so that we may get the start on Magotine."

When the armchair was set up for her, she rudely declined it, saying that she was big enough to eat standing. She was mistaken in this, though, because the table was rather high and she was not tall enough to see over it. This annoyance increased her foul mood even more.

"Madam," the queen said, "I beg you to take your seat at the table."

"If you had wished me to do so," the fairy replied, "you would have sent an invitation to me as you did to the others, but you only want beauties with fine figures and fine dresses like my sisters here. As for me, I'm too ugly and old. Yet despite it all, I have just as much power as they. In fact, without boasting about it, I may even have more."

All the fairies urged her strongly to sit at the table, and at length she consented. A golden basket was placed before them, containing twelve bouquets composed of jewels. The fairies who had arrived first each took a bouquet, leaving none for Magotine. As she began to mutter between her teeth, the queen ran to her room and brought her a casket of perfumed Spanish morocco covered with rubies and filled with diamonds, and asked her to accept it. But Magotine shook her head and said, "Keep your jewels, madam. I have more than enough to spare. I came only to see if you had thought of me, and it's clear you've neglected me shamefully."

Thereupon she struck the table with her wand, and all the delicacies heaped on it were turned into fricasseed serpents. This sight horrified the fairies so much that they flung down their napkins and fled the table. While they talked with one another about the nasty trick Magotine had played on them, that cruel fairy approached the cradle in which the princesses, the loveliest children in the world, were lying wrapped in golden swaddling. "I endow you with perfect ugliness," she quickly said to one of them, and she was about to utter a malediction on the other when the fairies, greatly disturbed, ran and stopped her. Then the mischievous Magotine broke one of the window panes, dashed through it like a flash of lightning, and vanished from sight.

All the good gifts that the benevolent fairies proceeded to bestow on the princess did not alleviate the misery of the queen, who found herself the mother of the ugliest being in the universe. Taking the infant in her arms, she had the misfortune of watching it grow more hideous by the moment. She struggled in vain to suppress her tears in the presence of their fairy ladyships, whose compassion is impossible to imagine. "What shall we do, sisters?" they said to one another.

"How can we ever console the queen?" They held a grand council about the matter, and at the end they told the queen not to give into her grief since a time would come when her daughter would be very happy.

"But," the queen interrupted, "will she become beautiful again?"

"We can't give you any further information," the fairies replied. "Be satisfied, madam, with the assurance that your daughters will be happy."

She thanked them very much and did not forget to give them many presents. Although the fairies were very rich, they always liked people to give them something. Throughout the world this custom has been passed down from that day to our own, and time has not altered it in the least.

The queen named her elder daughter Laidronette and the younger Bellotte. These names suited them perfectly, for Laidronette, despite her boundless intelligence, became too frightful to behold, whereas her sister's beauty increased hourly until she looked thoroughly charming.

After Laidronette had turned twelve, she went to the king and queen, and threw herself at their feet. "Please, I implore you, allow me to shut myself up in a lonely castle so that I will no longer torment you with my ugliness." Despite her hideous appearance, they could not help being fond of her, and not without some pain did they consent to let her depart. However, since Bellotte remained with them, they had ample consolation.

Laidronette begged the queen not to send anyone except her nurse and a few officers to wait on her. "You needn't worry, madam, about my being abducted. I can assure you that, looking as I do, I shall avoid even the light of day."

After the king and queen had granted her wishes, she was conducted to the castle she had chosen. It had been built many centuries before, and the sea crashed beneath its windows and served it as a moat. In the vicinity was a large forest in which one could stroll, and in several fields leading to the forest, the princess played various instruments and sang divinely.

Two years she spent in this pleasant solitude, even writing several volumes recording her thoughts, but the desire to see her father and mother again induced her to take a coach and revisit the court. She arrived just as they were to celebrate the marriage of Bellotte. Everyone had been rejoicing, but the moment they saw Laidronette, their joy turned to distress. She was neither embraced nor hugged by any of her relatives. Indeed, the only thing they said to her was that she had grown a good deal uglier, and they advised her not to appear at the ball. "However, if you wish to see it, we shall find some hole for you to peep through."

She replied that she had come there neither to dance nor to hear the music, that she had been in the desolate castle so long that she had felt a longing to pay her respects to the king and queen. Painfully aware that they could not endure the sight of her, she told them that she would therefore return to her wilderness, where the trees, flowers, and springs she wandered among did not reproach her for her ugliness. When the king and queen saw how hurt she was, they told her reluctantly that she could stay with them two or three days. Good-natured as always, though, she replied, "It would be harder for me to leave you if I were to spend so much time in your good company." Since they were all too eager for her to depart, they did not press her to stay, but coldly remarked that she was quite right.

For coming to her wedding the Princess Bellotte gave her a gift of an old ribbon that she had worn all winter in a bow on her muff, and Bellotte's fiancé gave her some zinzolin taffeta to make a petticoat. If she had expressed what she thought, she would have surely thrown the ribbon and rag of zinzolin in her generous donors' faces, but she had such good sense, prudence, and judgment that she revealed none of her bitterness. With her faithful nurse she left the court to return to her castle, her heart so filled with grief that she did not say a word during the entire journey.

One day as she was walking on one of the gloomiest paths in the forest, she saw a large green serpent at the foot of a tree. As it reared its head, it said to her,

"Laidronette, you aren't the only unhappy creature. Look at my horrible form. And yet at birth I was even handsomer than you."

Terrified, the princess heard not one half of this. She fled from the spot, and for many days thereafter did not dare to leave the castle, so afraid was she of another such encounter.

Eventually she tired of sitting alone in her room, however, and one evening she went for a walk along the beach. She was strolling slowly, pondering her sad fate, when she noticed a small gilt barque painted with a thousand different emblems gliding toward her. With a sail made of gold brocade, a mast of cedar, and oars of eagle wood, it appeared to be drifting at random. When it landed on the shore, the curious princess stepped on board to inspect all of its beautiful decorations. She found its deck laid with crimson velvet and gold trimmings, and all the nails were diamonds.

Suddenly the barque drifted out to sea again, and the princess, alarmed at her impending danger, grabbed the oars and endeavored in vain to row back to the beach. The wind rose and the waves became high. She lost sight of land and, seeing nothing around her but sea and sky, resigned herself to her fate, fully convinced not only that it was unlikely to be a happy one, but also that this was another one of the fairy Magotine's mean tricks. "If I must die, why do I have such a secret dread of death?" she asked. "Alas, have I ever enjoyed any of life's pleasures so much that I should now feel regret at dying? My ugliness disgusts even my family. My sister is a great queen, and I'm consigned to exile in the depths of a wilderness where the only companion I've found is a talking serpent. Wouldn't it be better for me to perish than to drag out such a miserable existence?" Having thus reflected, she dried her tears and courageously peered out to discover whence death would come, inviting its speedy approach. Just then she saw a serpent riding the billows toward the vessel, and as it approached her, it said: "If you're willing to be helped by a poor green serpent like me, I have the power to save your life."

"Death is less frightful to me than you are," the

princess exclaimed, "and if you want to do me a kind favor, never let me set eyes on you again."

The green serpent gave a long hiss (the manner in which serpents sigh), and without saying a word it immediately dove under the waves.

"What a horrible monster!" the princess said to herself. "He has green wings, a body of a thousand colors, ivory claws, fiery eyes, and a bristling mane of long hair on his head. Oh, I'd much rather die than owe my life to him! But what motive does he have in following me? How did he obtain the power of speech that enables him to talk like a rational creature?"

As she was entertaining these thoughts, a voice answered her: "You had better learn, Laidronette, that the green serpent is not to be despised. I don't mean to be harsh, but I assure you that he's less hideous in the eyes of his species than you are in the eyes of yours. However, I do not desire to anger you but to lighten your sorrows, provided you consent."

The princess was dumbfounded by this voice, and the words it uttered seemed so unjust to her that she could not suppress her tears. Suddenly, though, a thought occurred to her. "What am I doing? I don't want to cry about my death just because I'm reproached for my ugliness!" she exclaimed. "Alas, shouldn't I perish as though I were the grandest beauty in the world? My demise would be more of a consolation to me."

Completely at the mercy of the winds, the vessel drifted on until it struck a rock and immediately shattered into pieces. The poor princess realized that mere philosophizing would not save her in such a catastrophe, and grabbed onto some pieces of the wreck, so she thought, for she felt herself buoyed in the water and fortunately reached the shore, coming to rest at the foot of a towering boulder. Alas, she was horrified to discover that her arms were wrapped tightly around the neck of the green serpent! When he realized how appalled she was, he retreated from her and said, "You'd fear me less if you knew me better, but it is my hard fate to terrify all those who see me."

With that he plunged into the surf, and Laidronette

was left alone by the enormous rock. No matter where she glanced, she could see nothing that might alleviate her despair. Night was approaching. She was without food and knew not where to go. "I thought I was destined to perish in the ocean," she said sadly, "but now I'm sure that I'm to end my days here. Some sea monster will come and devour me, or I'll die of hunger." Rising, she climbed to the top of the crag and sat down. As long as it was light, she gazed at the ocean, and when it became dark, she took off her taffeta petticoat, covered her head with it, and waited anxiously for whatever was to happen next. Eventually she was overcome by sleep, and she seemed to hear the music of some instruments. She was convinced that she was dreaming, but a moment later she heard someone sing the following verse, which seemed to have been composed expressly for her:

> "Let Cupid make you now his own.
> Here he rules with gentle tone.
> Love with pleasure will be sown.
> On this isle no grief is known."

The attention she paid to these words caused her to wake up. "What good or bad luck shall I have now?" she exclaimed. "Might happiness still be in store for someone so wretched?" She opened her eyes timidly, fearing that she would be surrounded by monsters, but she was astonished to find that in place of the rugged, looming rock was a room with walls and ceiling made entirely of gold. She was lying in a magnificent bed that matched perfectly the rest of this palace, which was the most splendid in the universe. She began asking herself a hundred questions about all of this, unable to believe she was wide awake. Finally she got and ran to open a glass door that led onto a spacious balcony, from which she could see all the beautiful things that nature, with some help from art, had managed to create on earth: gardens filled with flowers, fountains, statues, and the rarest trees; distant woods, palaces with walls ornamented with jewels, and roofs composed of pearls so wonderfully constructed that each was an architectural masterpiece. A calm, smiling sea strewn with thousands of vessels, whose sails, pendants, and streamers fluttered in the breeze, completed the charming view.

"Gods! You just gods!" the princess exclaimed. "What am I seeing? Where am I? What an astounding change! What has become of the terrible rock that seemed to threaten the skies with its lofty pinnacles? Am I the same person who was shipwrecked last night and saved by a serpent?" Bewildered, she continued talking to herself, first pacing, then stopping. Finally she heard a noise in her room. Reentering it, she saw a hundred pagods advancing toward her. They were dressed and made up in a hundred different ways. The tallest were a foot high, and the shortest no more than four inches—some were beautiful, graceful, pleasant, others hideous, dreadfully ugly. Their bodies were made of diamonds, emeralds, rubies, pearls, crystal, amber, coral, porcelain, gold, silver, brass, bronze, iron, wood, and clay. Some were without arms, others without feet, others had mouths extending to their ears, eyes askew, noses broken. In short, nowhere in the world could a greater variety of people be found than among these pagods.

Those pagods who presented themselves to the princess were the deputies of the kingdom. After a speech containing some very judicious ideas, they informed her that they had traveled about the world for some time past, but in order to obtain their sovereign's permission to do so, they had to take an oath not to speak during their absence. Indeed, some were so scrupulous that they would not even shake their heads or move their hands or feet, but the majority of them could not help it. This was how they had traveled about the universe, and when they returned, they amused the king by telling him everything that had occurred, even the most secret transactions and adventures in all the courts they had visited. "This is a pleasure, madam," one of the deputies added, "which we shall have the honor of occasionally affording you, for we have been commanded to do all we can to entertain you. Instead

of bringing you presents, we now come to amuse you
with our songs and dances."

They began immediately to sing the following verses
while simultaneously dancing to the music of tam-
bourines and castanets:

> "Sweet are pleasures after pains,
> Lovers, do not break your chains;
> Trials though you may endure,
> Happiness they will insure.
> Sweet are pleasures after pains,
> Joy from sorrow luster gains."

When they stopped dancing and singing, their
spokesman said to the princess, "Here, madam, are a
hundred pagodines, who have the honor of being
selected to wait on you. Any wish you may have in the
world will be fulfilled, provided you consent to remain
among us."

The pagodines appeared in their turn. They carried
baskets cut to their own size and filled with a hundred
different articles so pretty, so useful, so well made, and
so costly that Laidronette never tired of admiring
and praising them, uttering exclamations of wonder
and delight at all the marvels they showed her. The
most prominent pagodine, a tiny figure made of diamonds, advised her to enter the grotto of the baths,
since the heat of the day was increasing. The princess
proceeded in the direction indicated between two ranks
of bodyguards, whose appearance was enough to make
one die with laughter.

She found two baths of crystal in the grotto ornamented with gold and filled with scented water so delicious and uncommon that she marveled at it. Shading
the baths was a pavilion of green and gold brocade.
When the princess inquired why there were two, they
answered that one was for her, and the other for the
king of the pagods.

"But where is he, then?" the princess asked.

"Madam," they replied, "he is presently with the
army waging war against his enemies. You'll see him
as soon as he returns."

The princess then inquired if he were married. They answered no. "Why, he is so charming that no one has yet been found who would be worthy of him." She indulged her curiosity no further, but disrobed and entered the bath. All the pagods and pagodines began to sing and play on various instruments. Some had *theorbos* made out of nut shells; others, bass viols, made out of almond shells, for it was, of course, necessary that the instruments fit the size of the performers. But all the parts were arranged in such perfect accord that nothing could surpass the delight their concert gave her.

When the princess emerged from her bath, they gave her a magnificent dressing gown. A pair of pagods playing a flute and oboe marched before her, and a train of pagodines singing songs in her praise trailed behind. In this state she entered a room where her toilet was laid out. Immediately the pagodines in waiting, and those of the bedchamber, bustled about, dressed her hair, put on her robes, and praised her. There was no longer talk of her ugliness, of zinzolin petticoats, or greasy ribbons.

The princess was truly taken aback. "To whom am I indebted for such extraordinary happiness?" she asked herself. "I was on the brink of destruction. I was waiting for death to come and had lost hope, and yet I suddenly find myself in the most magnificent place in the world, where I've been welcomed with the greatest joy!"

Since the princess was endowed with a great deal of good sense and breeding, she conducted herself so well that all the wee creatures who approached her were enchanted by her behavior. Every morning when she arose, she was given new dresses, new lace, new jewels. Though it was a great pity she was so ugly, she who could not abide her looks began to think they were more appealing because of the great pains they took in dressing her. She rarely spent an hour without some pagods coming to visit and recounting to her the most curious and private events of the world: peace treaties, offensive and defensive alliances, lovers' quarrels and betrayals, unfaithful mistresses, distractions,

reconciliations, disappointed heirs, matches broken
off, old widows remarrying foolishly, treasures discovered, bankruptcies declared, fortunes made in a minute,
favorites disgraced, office seekers, jealous husbands,
coquettish wives, naughty children, ruined cities. In
short, they told the princess everything under the sun to
entertain her. She occasionally saw some pagods who
were so corpulent and had such puffed-out cheeks that
they were wonderful to behold. When she asked them
why they were so fat, they answered, "Since we're not
permitted to laugh or speak during our travels and are
constantly witnessing all sorts of absurdities and the
most intolerable follies, our inclination to laugh is so
great that we swell up when we suppress it and cause
what may properly be called risible dropsy. Then we
cure ourselves as soon as we get home." The princess
admired the good sense of the pagodine people, for we
too might burst with laughter if we laughed at all the
silly things we see every day.

Scarcely an evening passed without a performance
of one of the best plays by Corneille or Molière. Balls
were held frequently, and the smallest pagods danced
on a tightrope in order to be better seen. What's more,
the banquets in honor of the princess might have
served for feasts on the most solemn occasions. They
also brought her books of every description—serious,
amusing, historical. In short, the days passed like minutes, although, to tell the truth, all these sprightly
pagods seemed insufferably little to the princess. For
instance, whenever she went out walking, she had to
put some thirty or so into her pockets in order for them
to keep up. It was the most amusing thing in the world
to hear the chattering of their little voices, shriller than
those of puppets in a show at the fair.

One night when the princess was unable to fall
asleep, she said to herself, "What's to become of me?
Am I to remain here forever? My days are more
pleasant than I could have dared to hope, yet my heart
tells me something's missing. I don't know what it is,
but I'm beginning to feel that this unvarying routine of
amusements is rather insipid."

"Ah, Princess," a voice said, as if answering her

thoughts, "isn't it your own fault? If you'd consent to love, you'd soon discover that you can abide with a lover for an eternity without wishing to leave. I speak not only of a palace, but even the most desolate spot."

"What pagodine addresses me?" the princess inquired. "What pernicious advice are you giving me? Why are you trying to disturb my peace of mind?"

"It is no pagodine who forewarns you of what will sooner or later come to pass," the voice replied. "It's the unhappy ruler of this realm, who adores you, madam, and who can't tell you this without trembling."

"A king who adores me?" the princess replied. "Does this king have eyes or is he blind? Doesn't he know that I'm the ugliest person in the world?"

"I've seen you, madam," the invisible being answered, "and have found you're not what you represent yourself to be. Whether it's for your person, merit, or misfortunes, I repeat: I adore you. But my feeling of respect and timidity oblige me to conceal myself."

"I'm indebted to you for that," the princess responded. "Alas, what would befall me if I were to love anyone?"

"You'd make a man who can't live without you into the happiest of beings," the voice said. "But he won't venture to appear before you without your permission."

"No, no," the princess said. "I wish to avoid seeing anything that might arouse my interest too strongly."

The voice fell silent, and the princess continued to ponder this incident for the rest of the night. No matter how strongly she vowed not to say the least word to anyone about it, she could not resist asking the pagods if their king had returned. They answered in the negative. Since this reply did not correspond in the least with what she had heard, she was quite disturbed. She continued making inquiries: was their king young and handsome? They told her he was young, handsome, and very charming. She asked if they frequently received news about him.

They replied, "Every day."

"But," she added, "does he know that I reside in his palace?"

"Yes, madam," her attendants answered, "he knows

everything that occurs here concerning you. He takes great interest in it, and every hour a courier is sent off to him with an account about you."

Lapsing into silence, she became far more thoughtful than she had ever been before.

Whenever she was alone, the voice spoke to her. Sometimes she was alarmed by it, but at others she was pleased, for nothing could be more polite than its manner of address. "Although I've decided never to love," the princess said, "and have every reason to protect my heart against an attachment that could only be fatal to it, I nevertheless confess to you that I yearn to see a king who has such strange tastes. If it's true that you love me, you're perhaps the only being in the world guilty of such weakness for a person so ugly."

"Think whatever you please, adorable princess," the voice replied. "I find that you have sufficient qualities to merit my affection. Nor do I conceal myself because I have strange tastes. Indeed, I have such sad reasons that if you knew them, you wouldn't be able to refrain from pitying me."

The princess urged him to explain himself, but the voice stopped speaking, and she heard only long, heavy sighs.

All these conversations made her very uneasy. Although her lover was unknown and invisible to her, he paid her a thousand attentions. Moreover, the beautiful place she inhabited led her to desire companions more suitable than the pagods. That had been the reason why she had begun feeling bored, and only the voice of her invisible admirer had the power to please her.

One very dark night she awoke to find somebody seated beside her. She thought it was the pagodine of pearls, who had more wit than the others and sometimes came to keep her company. The princess extended her arm to her, but the person seized her hand and pressed it to a pair of lips. Shedding a few tears on it, the unseen person was evidently too moved to speak. She was convinced it was the invisible monarch.

"What do you want of me?" she sighed. "How can I love you without knowing or seeing you?"

"Ah, madam," he replied, "why do you make conditions that thwart my desire to please you? I simply cannot reveal myself. The same wicked Magotine who's treated you so badly has condemned to me suffer for seven years. Five have already elapsed. There are two remaining, and you could relieve the bitterness of my punishment by allowing me to become your husband. You may think that I'm a rash fool, that I'm asking an absolute impossibility. But if you knew, madam, the depth of my feelings and the extent of my misfortunes, you wouldn't refuse this favor I ask of you."

As I have already mentioned, Laidronette had begun feeling bored, and she found that the invisible king certainly had all the intelligence she could wish for. So she was swayed by love, which she disguised to herself as pity, and replied that she needed a few days to consider his proposal.

The celebrations and concerts recommenced with increased splendor, and not a song was heard but those about marriage. Presents ere continually brought to her that surpassed all that had ever been seen. The enamored voice assiduously wooed her as soon as it turned dark, and the princess retired at an earlier hour in order to have more time to listen to it. Finally she consented to marry the invisible king and promised him that she would not attempt to look upon him until the full term of his penance had expired. "It's extremely important," the king said, "both for you and me. Should you be imprudent and succumb to your curiosity, I'll have to begin serving my sentence all over again, and you'll have to share in my suffering. But if you can resist the evil advice that you will soon receive, you'll have the satisfaction of finding in me all that your heart desires. At the same time you'll regain the marvelous beauty that the malicious Magotine took from you."

Delighted by this new prospect, the princess vowed a thousand times that she would never indulge her curiosity without his permission. So the wedding took place without any pomp and fanfare, but the modesty of the ceremony affected their hearts not a whit.

Since all the pagods were eager to entertain their

new queen, one of them brought her the history of
Psyche, written in a charming style by one of the most
popular authors of the day. She found many passages
in it that paralleled her own adventures, and they
aroused in her a strong desire to see her father, mother,
sister, and brother-in-law. Nothing the king could say
to her sufficed to quell this whim.

"The book you're reading reveals the terrible ordeals
Psyche experienced. For mercy's sake, try to learn
from her experiences and avoid them."

After she promised to be more than cautious, a ship
manned by pagods and loaded with presents was sent
with letters from Queen Laidronette to her mother,
imploring her to come and pay a visit to her daughter in
her own realm. (The pagods assigned this mission were
permitted, on this one occasion, to speak in a foreign
land.)

And in fact, the princess's disappearance had
affected her relatives. They believed she had perished,
and consequently her letters filled them with gladness.
The queen, who was dying to see Lairdonette again,
did not lose a moment in departing with her other
daughter and son-in-law. The pagods, the only ones
who knew the way to their kingdom, safely conducted
the entire royal family, and when Laidronette saw
them, she thought she would die from joy. Over and
over she read the story of Psyche to be completely on
her guard regarding any questions that they might put
to her and to make sure she would have the right
answers. But the pains she took were all in vain—she
made a hundred mistakes. Sometimes the king was
with the army; sometimes he was ill and in no mood to
see anyone; sometimes he was on a pilgrimage and at
others hunting or fishing. In the end it seemed that the
barbarous Magotine had unsettled her wits and doomed
her to say nothing but nonsense.

Discussing the matter together, her mother and sister
concluded that she was deceiving them and perhaps
herself as well. With misguided zeal they told her what
they thought and in the process skillfully plagued
her mind with a thousand doubts and fears. After refusing for a long time to acknowledge the justice of

their suspicions, she confessed at last that she had never seen her husband, but his conversation was so charming that just listening to him was enough to make her happy. "What's more," she told them, "he has only two more years to spend in this state of penance, and at the end of that time, I shall not only be able to see him, but I myself shall become as beautiful as the orb of day."

"Oh, unfortunate creature!" the queen exclaimed. "What a devious trap they've set for you! How could you have been so naive to listen to such tales? Your husband is a monster, and that's all there is to it, for all the pagods he rules are downright monkeys."

"I believe differently," Laidronette replied. "I think he's the god of love himself."

"What a delusion!" Queen Bellotte cried. "They told Psyche that she had married a monster, and she discovered that it was Cupid. You're positive that Cupid is your husband, and yet it's certain he's a monster. At the very least, put your mind to rest. Clear up the matter. It's easy enough to do."

This was what the queen had to say, and her husband was even more emphatic. The poor princess was so confused and disturbed that, after having sent her family home loaded with presents that sufficiently repaid the zinzolin taffeta and muff ribbon, she decided to catch a glimpse of her husband, come what may. Oh, fatal curiosity, which never improves in us despite a thousand dreadful examples, how dearly you are about to make this unfortunate princess pay! Thinking it a great pity not to imitate her predecessor, Psyche, she shone a lamp on their bed and gazed upon the invisible king so dear to her heart. When she saw, however, the horrid green serpent with his long, bristling mane instead of a tender Cupid young, white, and fair, she let out the most frightful shrieks. He awoke in a fit of rage and despair.

"Cruel woman," he cried, "is this the reward for all the love I've given you?"

The princess did not hear a word. She had fainted from fright. Within seconds the serpent was faraway. Upon hearing the uproar caused by this tragic scene, some pagods ran to their post, carried the princess to her couch, and did all they could to revive her. No one can possibly fathom Laidronette's depths of despair upon regaining consciousness. How she reproached herself for the misfortune she had brought upon her husband! She loved him tenderly, but she abhorred his form and would have given half her life if she could have taken back what she had done.

These sad reflections were interrupted by several pagods who entered her room with fear written on their faces. They came to warn her that several ships of puppets with Magotine at their head had entered the harbor without encountering any resistance. Puppets and pagods had been enemies for ages and had competed with each other in a thousand ways, for the puppets had always enjoyed the privilege of talking wherever they went—a privilege denied the pagods. Magotine was the queen of the puppets, and her hatred for the poor green serpent and the unfortunate Laidronette had prompted her to assemble her forces in order to torment them just when their suffering was most acute.

This goal she easily accomplished because the queen was in such despair that although the pagods urged her to give the necessary orders, she refused, insisting that she knew nothing of the art of war. Nevertheless, she ordered them to convene all those pagods who had been in besieged cities or on the councils of the greatest commanders and told them to take the proper steps. Then she shut herself up in her room and regarded everything happening around her with utter indifference.

Magotine's general was that celebrated puppet Punch, and he knew his business well. He had a large body of wasps, mayflies, and butterflies in reserve, and they performed wonders against some lightly-armed frogs and lizards. The latter had been in the pay of the pagods for many years and were, if truth be told, much more frightening in name than in action.

Magotine amused herself for some time by watching the combat. The pagods and pagodines outdid themselves in their efforts, but the fairy dissolved all their superb edifices with a stroke of her wand. The charming gardens, woods, meadows, fountains, were soon in ruins, and Queen Laidronette could not escape the sad fate of becoming the slave of the most malignant fairy that ever was or will be. Four or five hundred puppets forced her to go before Magotine.

"Madam," Punch said to the fairy, "here is the queen of the pagods, whom I have taken the liberty of bringing to you."

"I've known her a long time," Magotine said. "She was the cause of my being insulted on the day she was born, and I'll never forget it."

"Alas, madam," the queen said, "I believe you were sufficiently avenged. The gift of ugliness that you bestowed on me to such a supreme degree would have satisfied anyone less vindictive than you."

"Look how she argues," the fairy said. "Here is a learned doctor of a new sort. Your first job will be teaching philosophy to my ants. I want you to get ready to give them a lesson every day."

"How can I do it, madam?" the distressed queen replied. "I know nothing about philosophy, and even if I were well versed in it, your ants are probably not capable of understanding it."

"Well now, listen to this logician," exclaimed Magotine. "Very well, Queen. You won't teach them philosophy, but despite yourself you'll set an example of patience for the entire world that will be difficult to imitate."

Immediately thereafter, Lairdonette was given a pair of iron shoes so small that she could fit only half her foot into each one. Compelled nevertheless to put them on, the poor queen could only weep in agony.

"Here's a spindle of spider webs," Magotine said, "I expect you to spin it as fine as your hair, and you have but two hours to do it."

"I've never spun, madam," the queen said. "But I'll try to obey you even though what you desire strikes me to be impossible."

She was immediately led deep into a dark grotto, and after they gave her some brown bread and a pitcher of water, they closed the entrance with a large rock. In trying to spin the filthy spider webs, she dropped her spindle a hundred times because it was too heavy. Even though she patiently picked it up each time and began her work over again, it was always in vain. "Now I know exactly how bad my predicament is. I'm wholly at the mercy of the implacable Magotine, who's not just satisfied with having deprived me of all my beauty, but wants some pretext for killing me." She began to weep as she recalled the happiness she had enjoyed in the kingdom of Pagodia. Then she threw down her spindle and exclaimed, "Let Magotine come when she will! I can't do the impossible."

"Ah, Queen," a voice answered her. "Your indiscreet curiosity has caused you these tears, but it's difficult to watch those we love suffer. I have a friend whom I've never mentioned to you before. She's called the Fairy Protectrice, and I trust she'll be of great service to you."

All at once she heard three taps, and without seeing anyone, she found her web spun and wound into a skein. At the end of the two hours Magotine, who wanted to taunt her, had the rock rolled from the grotto mouth and entered it, followed by a large escort of puppets.

"Come, come, let us see the work of this idle hussy who doesn't know how to sew or spin."

"Madam," the queen said, "it's quite true I didn't know how, but I was obliged to learn."

When Magotine saw the extraordinary result, she took the skein of spider web and said: "Truly, you're too skillful. It would be a great pity not to keep you employed. Here, Queen, make me some nets with this thread strong enough to catch salmon."

"For mercy's sake!" the queen replied. "You see that it's barely strong enough to hold flies."

"You're a great casuist, my pretty friend," Magotine said, "but it won't help you a bit." She left the grotto, had the stone replaced at the entrance, and assured Laidronette that if the nets were not finished in two hours, she was a lost creature.

"Oh, Fairy Protectrice!" the queen exclaimed, "if it's true that my sorrows can move you to pity, please don't deny me your assistance."

No sooner had she spoken than, to Laidronette's astonishment, the nets were made. With all her heart she thanked the friendly fairy who had granted her this favor, and it gave her pleasure to think that it must have been her husband who had provided her with such a friend. "Alas, green serpent," she said, "you're much too generous to continue loving me after the harm I've done you."

No reply was forthcoming, for at that moment, Magotine entered. She was nonplussed to find the nets finished. Indeed, they were so well made that the work could not have been done by common hands. "What?" she cried. "Do you have the audacity to maintain that it was you who wove these nets?"

"I have no friend in your court madam," the queen said. "And even if I did, I'm so carefully guarded that it would be difficult for anyone to speak to me without your permission."

"Since you're so clever and skillful, you'll be of great use to me in my kingdom."

She immediately ordered her fleet to make ready the sails and all the puppets to prepare themselves to board. The queen she had heavily chained down, fearing that in some fit of despair she might fling herself overboard.

One night when the unhappy princess was deploring her sad fate, she perceived by the light of the stars that the green serpent was silently approaching the ship.

"I'm always afraid of alarming you," he said, "and despite the reasons I have for not sparing you, you're extremely dear to me."

"Can you pardon my indiscreet curiosity?" she replied. "Would you be offended if I said:

"Is it you? Is it you? Are you again near?
My own royal serpent, so faithful and dear!
May I hope to see my fond husband again?
Oh, how I've suffered since we were parted then!"

The serpent replied as follows:

"To hearts that love truly, to part causes pain,
With hope even to whisper of meeting again.

In Pluto's dark regions what torture above
Our absence forever from those whom we love?"

Magotine was not one of those fairies who fall asleep,
for the desire to do mischief kept her continually awake.
Thus, she did not fail to overhear the conversation
between the serpent king and his wife. Flying like a Fury
to interrupt it, she said, "Aha, you amuse yourselves
with rhymes, do you? And you complain about your fate
in bombastic tones? Truly, I'm delighted to hear. Proserpine, who is my best friend, has promised to pay me if I
lend her a poet. Not that there is a dearth of poets below,
but she simply wants more. Green serpent, I command
you to go finish your penance in the dark manor of the
underworld. Give my regards to the gentle Proserpine!"

Uttering long hisses, the unfortunate serpent departed, leaving the queen in the depths of sorrow.
"What crime have we committed against you, Magotine?" she exclaimed heatedly. "No sooner was I born
than your infernal curse robbed me of my beauty and
made me horrible. How can you accuse me of any
crime when I wasn't even capable of using my mind at
that time? I'm convinced that the unhappy king whom
you've just sent to the infernal regions is as innocent as
I was. But finish your work. Let me die this instant. It's
the only favor I ask of you."

"You'd be too happy if I granted your request."
Magotine said. "You must first draw water for me from
the bottomless spring."

As soon as the ships had reached the kingdom of
puppets, the cruel Magotine took a millstone and tied it
around the queen's neck, ordering her to climb to the
top of a mountain that soared high above the clouds.
Upon arriving there, she was to gather enough four-leaf
clovers to fill a basket, descend into the depths of the
next valley to draw the water of discretion in a pitcher
with a hole in the bottom, and bring her enough to fill
her large glass. The queen responded that it was impossible to obey her: the millstone was more than ten
times her weight and the pitcher with a hole in it could
never hold the water she wished to drink. "Nay, I
cannot be induced to attempt anything so impossible."

"If you don't," Magotine said, "rest assured that your green serpent will suffer for it."

This threat so frightened the queen that she tried to walk despite her handicap. But, alas, the effort would have been for naught if the Fairy Protectrice, whom she invoked, had not come to her aid.

"Now you can see the just punishment for your fatal curiosity," the fairy said. "Blame no one but yourself for the condition to which Magotine has reduced you."

After saying this, she transported the queen to the top of the mountain. Terrible monsters that guarded the spot made supernatural efforts to defend it, but one tap of the Fairy Protectrice's wand made them gentler than lambs. Then she proceeded to fill the basket for her with four-leaf clovers.

Protectrice did not wait for the grateful queen to thank her, for to complete the mission, everything depended on her. She gave the queen a chariot drawn by two white canaries who spoke and whistled in a marvelous way. She told her to descend the mountain and fling her iron shoes at two giants armed with clubs who guarded the fountain. Once they were knocked unconscious, she had only to give her pitcher to the canaries, who would easily find the means to fill it with the water of discretion. "As soon as you have the water, wash your face with it, and you will become the most beautiful person in the world." She also advised her not to remain at the fountain, or to climb back up the hill, but to stop at a pleasant small grove she would find on her way. She could remain there for three years, since Magotine would merely suppose that she was either still trying to fill her pitcher with water or had fallen victim to one of the dangers during her journey.

Embracing the knees of the Fairy Protectrice, the queen thanked her a hundred times for the special favors she had granted her. "But, madam," the queen added, "neither the success I may achieve nor the beauty you promise me will give me the least pleasure until my serpent is transformed."

"That won't occur until you've spent three years in the mountain grove," the fairy said, "and until you've

returned to Magotine with the four-leaf clovers and the
water in the leaky pitcher."

The queen promised the Fairy Protectrice that she
would scrupulously follow her instructions. "But,
madam," she added, "must I spend three years without
hearing any news of the serpent king?"

"You deserve never to hear any more about him for
as long as you live," the fairy responded. "Indeed, can
anything be more terrible than having made him begin
his penance all over again?"

The queen made no reply, but her silence and the
tears flowing down her cheeks amply showed how
much she was suffering. She got into her little chariot,
and the canaries did as commanded. They conducted
her to the bottom of the valley, where the giants
guarded the fountain of discretion. She quickly took
off her iron shoes and threw than at their heads. The
moment the shoes hit them, they fell down lifelessly
like colossal statues. The canaries took the leaky
pitcher and mended it with such marvelous skill that
there was no sign of its having ever been broken.

The name given to the water made her eager to drink
some. "It will make me more prudent than I've been,"
she said. "Alas, if I had possessed those qualities, I'd
still be in the kingdom of Pagodia." After she had drunk
a long draught of the water, she washed her face with
some of it and became so very beautiful that she might
have been mistaken for a goddess rather an a mortal.

The Fairy Protectrice immediately appeared and
said, "You've just done something that pleases me very
much. You knew that this water could embellish your
mind as well as your person. I wanted to see to which
of the two you would prefer the most, and it was your
mind. I praise you for it, and this act will shorten the
term of your punishment by four years."

"Please don't reduce my sufferings," the queen
replied. "I deserve them all. But comfort the green serpent, who doesn't deserve to suffer at all."

"I'll do everything in my power," the fairy said,
embracing her. "But since you're so beautiful now, I
want you to drop the name of Laidronette, which no
longer suits you. You must be called Queen Discrète."

As she vanished, the queen found she had left a pair of dainty shoes that were so pretty and finely embroidered that she thought it almost a pity to wear them. Soon thereafter she got back into her little chariot with her pitcherful of water, and the canaries flew directly to the grove of the mountain.

Never was a spot as pleasant as this. Myrtle and orange trees intertwined their branches to form long arbors and bowers that the sun could not penetrate. A thousand brooks running from gently flowing springs brought a refreshing coolness to this beautiful abode. But most curious of all were the animals there, which gave the canaries the warmest welcome in the world.

"We thought you had deserted us," they said.

"The term of our penance is not over yet," the canaries replied. "But here is the queen whom the Fairy Protectrice has ordered us to bring you. Try to do all you can to amuse her."

She was immediately surrounded by all sorts of animals, who paid her their best compliments. "You shall be our queen," they said to her. "You shall have all our attention and respect."

"Where am I?" she exclaimed. "What supernatural power has enabled you to speak to me?"

One of the canaries whispered in her ear, "You should know, madam, that several fairies were distressed to see various persons fall into bad habits on their travels. At first they imagined that they needed merely to advise them to correct themselves, but their warnings were paid no heed. Eventually the fairies became quite upset and imposed punishments on them. Those who talked too much were changed into parrots, magpies, and hens. Lovers and their mistresses were transformed into pigeons, canaries, and lapdogs. Those who ridiculed their friends became monkeys. Gourmands were made into pigs and hotheads into lions. In short, the number of persons they punished was so great that this grove has become filled with them. Thus, you'll find people with all sorts of qualities and dispositions here."

"From what you've just told me, my dear canary,"

the queen said, "I've reason to believe that you're here only because you loved too well."

"It's quite true, madam," the canary replied. "I'm the son of a Spanish grandee. Love in our country has such absolute power over our hearts that one cannot resist it without being charged with the crime of rebellion. An English ambassador arrived at the court. He had a daughter who was extremely beautiful, but insufferably haughty and sardonic. In spite of all this, I was attracted to her. My love, though, was greeted with so much disdain that I lost all patience. One day when she had exasperated me, a venerable old woman approached and reproached me for my weakness. Yet everything she said only made me more obstinate. When she perceived this, she became angry. 'I condemn you,' she said, 'to be a canary for three years, and your mistress to be a wasp.' Instantly I felt an indescribable change come over me. Despite my affliction I could not restrain myself from flying into the ambassador's garden to determine the fate of his daughter. No sooner had I arrived than I saw her approach in the form of a large wasp buzzing four times louder than all the others. I hovered around her with the devotion of a lover that nothing can destroy, but she tried several times to sting me. 'If you want to kill me, beautiful wasp,' I said, 'it's unnecessary to use your sting. You only have to command me to die, and I'll obey you.' The wasp did not reply, but landed on some flowers that had to endure her bad temper.

"Overwhelmed by her contempt and the condition to which I was reduced, I flew away without caring where my wings would take me. I eventually arrived at one of the most beautiful cities in the universe, which they call Paris. Wearily, I flung myself on a tuft of large trees enclosed within some garden walls, and before I knew who had caught me, I found myself behind the door of a cage painted green and ornamented with gold. The apartment and its furniture were so magnificent that I was astounded. Soon a young lady arrived. She caressed me and spoke to me so sweetly that I was charmed by her. I did not live there long before learning whom her sweetheart was. I witnessed this braggart's visits to her, and he was always in a rage because nothing could satisfy him. He was always accusing her unjustly, and one time he beat her until he left her for dead in the arms of her women. I was quite upset at seeing her suffer this unworthy treatment, and what distressed me even more was that the blows he dealt the lovely lady served only to increase her affection.

"Night and day I wished that the fairies who had transformed me into a canary would come and set to rights such ill-suited lovers. My wish was eventually fulfilled. The fairies suddenly appeared in the apartment just as the furious gentleman was beginning to make his usual commotion. They reprimanded him severely and condemned him to become a wolf. The patient lady who had allowed him to beat her, they turned into a sheep and sent her to the grove of the mountain. As for myself, I easily found a way to escape. Since I wanted to see the various courts of Europe, I flew to Italy and fell into the hands of a man who had frequent business in the city. Since he was very jealous of his wife and did not want her to see anyone during his absence, he took care to lock her up from morning until night, and I was given the honor of amusing this lovely captive. However, she had other things to do than to attend to me. A certain neighbor who had loved her for a long time came to the top of the chimney in the evening and slid down it into the room, looking blacker than a devil. The keys that the jealous husband kept with him served only to keep his mind at ease. I constantly feared that some terrible catastrophe would happen when one day the fairies entered through the keyhole and surprised the two lovers. 'Go and do penance!' the fairies said, touching them with their wands. 'Let the chimney sweeper become a squirrel and the lady an ape, for she is a cunning one. And your husband, who is so fond of keeping the keys of this house, shall become a mastiff for ten years.'

"It would take me too long to tell you all the various adventures I had," the canary said. "Occasionally I was obliged to visit the grove of the mountain, and I rarely

returned there without finding new animals, for the
fairies were always traveling and were continually
upset by the countless faults of the people they encountered. But during your residence here you'll have
plenty of time to entertain yourself by listening to the
accounts of all the inhabitants' adventures."

Several of them immediately offered to relate their
stories whenever she desired. She thanked them
politely, but since she felt more inclined to meditate
than to talk, she looked for a spot where she could be
alone. As soon as she found one, a little palace arose
on it, and the most sumptuous banquet in the world was
prepared for her. It consisted only of fruits, but they
were of the rarest kind. They were brought to her by
birds, and during her stay in the grove there was
nothing she lacked.

Occasionally she was pleased by the most unique
entertainments: lions danced with lambs; bears whispered tender things to doves; serpents relaxed with lin-
nets; a butterfly courted a panther. In short, no amour
was categorized according to species, for it did not
matter that one was a tiger or another a sheep, but
simply that they were people whom the fairies had
chosen to punish for their faults.

They all loved Queen Discrète to the point of adora-
tion, and everyone asked her to arbitrate their disputes.
Her power was absolute in this tiny republic, and if she
had not continually reproached herself for causing the
green serpent's misfortunes, she might have accepted
her own misfortune with some degree of patience.
However, when she thought of the condition to which
he was reduced, she could not forgive herself for her
indiscreet curiosity.

Finally the time came for her to leave the grove of
the mountain, and she notified her escorts, the faithful
canaries, who wished her a happy return. She left
secretly during the night to avoid the farewells and
lamentations, which would have cost her some tears,
for she was touched by the friendship and respect that
all these rational animals had shown her.

She did not forget the pitcher of discretion, the
basket of four-leaf clovers, or the iron shoes. Just when

Magotine believed her to be dead, she suddenly appeared before her, the millstone around her neck, the iron shoes on her feet, and pitcher in her hand. Upon seeing her, the fairy uttered a loud cry. "Where have you come from?"

"Madam," the queen said, "I've spent three years drawing water into the broken pitcher, and I finally found the way to make it hold water."

Magotine burst into laughter, thinking of the exhaustion the poor queen must have experienced. But when she examined her more closely, she exclaimed, "What's this I see? Lairdonette has become quite lovely! How did you get so beautiful?"

The queen informed her that she had washed herself with the water of discretion and that this miracle had been the result. At this news Magotine dashed the pitcher to the ground. "Oh, you powers that defy me," she exclaimed, "I'll be revenged. Get your iron shoes ready," she said to the queen. "You must go to the underworld for me and demand the essence of long life from Proserpine. I'm always afraid of falling ill and perhaps dying. Once I have that antidote in my possession, I won't have any more cause for alarm. Take care, therefore, that you don't uncork the bottle or taste the liquor she gives you, or you'll reduce my portion."

The poor queen had never been so taken aback as she was by this order. "Which way is it to the underworld?" she asked. "Can those who go there return? Alas, madam, won't you ever tire of persecuting me? Under what unfortunate star was I was born? My sister is so much happier than I. Ah, the stars above are certainly unfair."

As she began to weep, Magotine exulted at her tears. She laughed loudly and cried, "Go! Go! Don't put off your departure a moment, for your journey promises to benefit me a great deal." Magotine gave her some old nuts and black bread in a bag, and with this handsome provision the poor queen started on her journey. She was determined, however, to dash her brains out against the first rock she saw to put an end to her sorrows.

She wandered at random for some time, turning this

way and that, thinking it most extraordinary to be sent
like this to the underworld. When she became tired, she
lay down at the foot of a tree and began to think of the
poor serpent, forgetting all about her journey. Just then
appeared the Fairy Protectrice, who said to her, "Don't
you know, beautiful queen, that if you want to rescue
your husband from the dark domain where he is being
kept under Magotine's orders, you must seek the home
of Proserpine?"

"I'd go much farther, if it were possible, madam,"
she replied, "but I don't know how to descend into that
dark abode."

"Wait," said the Fairy Protectrice. "Here's a green
branch. Strike the earth with it and repeat these lines
clearly." The queen embraced the knees of her generous friend and then said after her:

"You who can wrest from mighty Jove the thunder!
    Love, listen to my prayer!
    Come, save me from despair,
And calm the pangs that rend my heart asunder!
As I enter the realm of Tartarus, be my guide.
Even in those dreary regions you hold sway.
It was for Proserpine, your subject, that Pluto sighed;
So open the path to their throne and point the way.
A faithful husband from my arms they tear!
My fate is harder than my heart can bear;
    More than mortal is its pain;
    Yet for death it sighs in vain!"

No sooner had she finished this prayer than a young
child more beautiful than anything we shall ever see
appeared in the midst of a gold and azure cloud. He flew
down to her feet with a crown of flowers encircling his
brow. The queen knew by his bow and arrows that it was
Love. He addressed her in the following way:

"I have heard your tender sighs,
And for you have left the skies.
Love will chase your tears away,
And try his best in every way.
Shortly shall your eyes be blest

With his sight you love the best.
Then the penance will be done,
And your foe will be overcome."

The queen was dazzled by the splendor that surrounded Love and delighted by his promises. Therefore, she exclaimed:

"Earth, my voice obey!"
Cupid's power is like my own.
Open for him and point the way
To Pluto's dark and gloomy throne!"

The earth obeyed and opened her bosom. The queen
went through a dark passage, in which she needed a
guide as radiant as her protector, and finally reached
the underworld. She dreaded meeting her husband
there in the form of a serpent, but Love, who sometimes employs himself by doing good deeds for
the unfortunate, had foreseen all that was to be foreseen: he had already arranged that the green serpent
become what he was before his punishment. Powerful
as Magotine was, there was nothing she could do
against Love.

The first object the queen's eyes encountered was
her charming husband. She had never seen him in such
a handsome form, and he had never seen her as beautiful as she had become. Nevertheless, a presentiment,
and perhaps Love, who made up the third in the party,
caused each of them to guess who the other was. With
extreme tenderness the queen said to him:

"I come to share your prison and your pain.
Though doomed no more the light of heaven to see,
Here let but love unite our hearts again,
No terrors these sad shades will have for me!"

Carried away by his passion, the king replied to
his wife in a way that demonstrated his ardor and pleasure. But Love, who is not fond of losing time, urged
them to approach Proserpine. The queen offered Magotine's regards and asked her for the essence of long

life. Proserpine immediately gave the queen a phial
very badly corked in order to induce her to open it.
Love, who is no novice, warned the queen against
indulging a curiosity that would again be fatal to her.
Quickly the king and queen left those dreary regions
and returned to the light of day with Love accompanying them. He led them back to Magotine and hid
himself in their hearts so that she would not see him.
His presence, however, inspired the fairy with such
humane sentiments that she received these illustrious
unfortunates graciously, although she knew not why.
With a supernatural effort of generosity she restored
the kingdom of Pagodia to them, and they returned
there immediately and spent the rest of their days in as
much happiness as they had previously endured trouble
and sorrow.

> Too oft is curiosity
>   The cause of fatal woe.
> A secret that may harmful be,
>   Why should we seek to know?
>
> It is a weakness of womankind,
>   For witness the first created,
> From whom Pandora was designed,
>   And Psyche imitated.
>
> Each one, despite a warning, on the same
>   Forbidden quest intent,
> Did bring about her misery and become
>   Its fatal instrument.
>
> Psyche's example failed to save
>   Poor Laidronette from erring.
> Like warning she was led to brave.
>   Like punishment incurring.
>
> Alas, for human common sense,
>   No tale, no caution, schools!
> The proverb says, Experience
>   Can make men wise, and change dumb fools.

But when we're told, yet fail to listen
  To the lessons of the past,
I fear the proverb lies quite often,
  Despite the shadows forward cast.

THE WHITE CAT

ONCE upon a time there was a king who had three brave, handsome sons, and he was afraid lest they become eager to reign during his lifetime. He had even heard rumors that they were seeking to win over adherents to help them take over the kingdom. The king knew he was growing old, but his mind was still alert, and he had no desire to yield a position he still filled worthily. Therefore, he thought that the best way to keep them from growing restive was to tantalize them with promises that he would always avoid fulfilling.

One day he called them into his room, and speaking to them kindly, he remarked, "You'll agree with me, my dear sons, that my great age prevents me from managing the affairs of state as assiduously as before. I fear my subjects may suffer from this circumstance, and I want to transfer my crown to one of you. To deserve such a gift, however, it is only just that you in turn try to please me. Now, since I contemplate retiring to the country, I believe that a pretty, faithful, and intelligent little dog would make an excellent companion. So, instead of showing preference to my eldest, I declare that whichever one of you brings me the handsomest little dog will immediately become my heir."

The princes were exceedingly surprised by the king's inclination for a little dog, but the two younger realized they could profit from this proposition and gladly accepted the task, while the eldest was too timid or too respectful to stand up for his rights. So they took leave of the king, who distributed money and jewels among them and added, "Return without fail next year on the same day and hour, and bring me your little dogs."

Before setting out, they withdrew to a castle a mile

from the city and gathered their most intimate friends for several splendid banquets. There the three brothers pledged eternal friendship to one another. They would act without jealousy or regrets in this particular affair, they declared, and the successful candidate would be willing to share his fortune with the others. At last they departed, agreeing to meet at the same castle on their return before proceeding together to the king. So that they might not be known, they refused to take any assistants and even changed their names.

Each took a different road. The two elder met with many adventures, but let me recount only those of the youngest. He was well mannered and possessed a gay, cheerful temperament, even though his courage was most intrepid. He had a noble figure, a striking face, regular features, and fine teeth. He was very talented in all those skills that a prince was expected to perform: he could paint, he sang with a pleasant voice, and played the lute and *theorbo* with a sensitivity that charmed everyone. In short, he was a highly accomplished young fellow.

Scarcely a day passed that he did not purchase dogs. They were big and little: greyhounds, mastiffs, bloodhounds, pointers, spaniels, water dogs, lapdogs. The instant he found one handsomer than the next, he let the previous one go, since he could not have possibly led around thirty or forty thousand dogs by himself, and he remained firm in his determination not to have gentlemen, servants, or pages in his company.

Continuing on without any fixed destination, he was surprised one night by a thunderous rainstorm in a forest, and he lost the path he was following. So he took the first he could find, and after having walked a long way, he saw a glimmer of light that indicated there was some habitation nearby in which he might find shelter until morning. Guided by the light, he came to the gate of the most magnificent castle you could ever imagine. This gate was made of gold and covered with carbuncles, and their pure, vivid light illuminated everything in the vicinity. It was this light that the prince had perceived at a distance. The walls were transparent porcelain of various colors, and the histories of all the fairies from the beginning of time were painted there. The famous adventures of Donkey-Skin, Finette, the Orange Tree, Gracieuse, Sleeping Beauty, the Green Serpent, and a hundred others, were not omitted. He was delighted to see Prince Sprite among them, for he was his uncle, according to the legends of Brittany. The rainstorm prevented him from lingering before this mural because he was being drenched to the skin. Besides, he could hardly see anything beyond the rays cast by the gate's carbuncles. Thereupon he returned to the golden gate, where he saw a kid's foot dangling from a chain of diamonds. He admired all the magnificence and apparent security in which the owners of the castle seemed to live. "Indeed," he said to himself, "what's to prevent thieves from cutting off this chain and pulling the carbuncles off the gate? They could make themselves rich for the rest of their lives."

Pulling the kid's foot, he immediately heard a bell ring, which by its sound seemed to be made of gold or silver. A moment later the gate was opened without his seeing anything but a dozen hands, each holding torches, suspended in midair. He was so astonished that he hesitated to move forward. However, he felt other hands that gently pushed him forward. Therefore, he advanced with some distrust, and to be on the safe side, he kept his hand on the hilt of his sword. On entering a vestibule entirely decorated with porphyry and lapis lazuli, he heard two enchanting voices raised in song:

> "Be not startled by the hands you see.
> Have no fear in this delightful place.
> There's nothing here except a lovely face,
> Nothing at all but love to flee."

Unable to believe that he was being invited so graciously for the purpose of eventually being harmed, he let himself be pushed toward a large coral gate that opened before his eyes. Into a salon of mother-of-pearl he entered and then passed through several apartments variously ornamented with such an abundance of paint-

ings and jewels that he was captivated by the sight of
them. Thousands and thousands of lights, from the
vaulted roof of the salon down to the floor, illuminated
parts of the other apartments, which were also filled
with chandeliers, girandoles, and stages lined with wax
candles. Such magnificence was so resplendent that he
had difficulty imagining how all this had been made
possible.

After passing through sixty rooms, he was stopped
by the hands that had been guiding him and watched
as a large easy chair moved by itself toward the fire-
place. At the same instant a fire was lighted, and the
hands, which appeared to him handsome, white, small,
plump, and well shaped, began to undress him, for he
was soaked, as I have already told you, and they were
afraid he would catch cold. Although they did not
reveal themselves, they gave him a splendid shirt
suitable for a wedding day and a morning gown made
of rich golden material embroidered with emerald
ciphers. The bodiless hands carried over a dressing
table that had everything he needed. Nothing could be
more magnificent. They combed him with a lightness
and pleasing skill. Finally, they dressed him again, not
in his own clothes, but with others much richer. He
observed all that took place with silent wonder and a
certain alarm that he could not altogether conquer.

After they had powdered, curled, perfumed, attired,
and adorned him to look handsomer than Adonis, the
hands led him into a hall that was superbly gilt and furnished. All around were paintings of the stories about
all the most famous cats: Rodilardus hung by the heels
in the Council of Rats, Puss in Boots, Marquis of
Carabas, The Writing Cat, The Cat That Became a
Woman, Witches in the Shape of Cats, and their Sabbath and all its ceremonies. In a word, these paintings
were highly unusual.

A table was set with two places, each with a golden
cadenas. The buffet astonished him, for it held innumerable cups of rock crystal studded with a thousand rare stones. The prince was trying to figure out
why there were two place settings when he saw several
cats take their places in a small orchestra that had been

designed expressly for them. One held a music book with the most extraordinary notes, another held a roll of paper to beat time with, and the rest had miniature guitars.

Suddenly each cat began to mew in a different tone and strummed the strings of their guitars with their claws, producing the strangest music that he had ever heard. The prince would have thought he was in the lower regions if he had not found the palace so marvelously beautiful; this fact alone prevented him from making such an error. He was, however, obliged to stop up his ears, and he laughed heartily at the sight of the various postures and grimaces of these novel musicians.

As he pondered the odd things that had already happened to him in the château, he saw a figure scarcely a foot tall enter the hall. This puppet was draped with a long black crape veil, and the two cats preceding it, wearing cloaks and swords, were also dressed in deep mourning. A large retinue of cats followed, some carrying rat traps filled with rats and others mice in cages. The prince could not get over his astonishment. He did not know what to think. The little black figure approached, and as it lifted its veil, he perceived the most beautiful white cat that ever has been or ever will be seen. In a very youthful, melancholy air she began mewing so softly and sweetly that it went straight to his heart. "Prince," she said, "you are welcome. My mewing majesty regards you with pleasure."

"Madam cat," the prince said, "it's very generous of you to receive me with so much ceremony, but you don't appear to me to be any ordinary little animal. Your gift of speech and the superb castle you inhabit are sufficient evidence to the contrary."

"Prince," the white cat replied, "please forgo paying me these compliments. I'm plain in my speech and my manners, though I have a generous heart. Come, let them serve supper. And put an end to the concert, for the prince doesn't understand what they are singing."

"Are they actually singing words, madam?" he inquired.

"Yes, indeed," she answered. "We have poets here

of considerable talent, and if you remain among us for long, you'll become convinced of this fact."

"You need only say so, and I'll believe it," the prince responded politely. "All the same, madam, I regard you as a most unusual cat."

The supper was placed on the table by the hands of invisible bodies. First, there were two soups, one of pigeons and the other of very plump mice. The sight of the latter prevented the prince from touching the former, believing that the same cook had concocted both, but the cat, who guessed from his face what was going on in his mind, assured him that their meals had been cooked separately and that he could eat it with the perfect assurance that it contained neither rats nor mice. The prince did not wait to be told twice, for he felt that the pretty cat had no wish to deceive him.

At that moment he noticed to his surprise that she had a miniature set in a bracelet on her paw. He begged her to show it to him, supposing it to be that of some Master Minagrobis. He was astonished to find the portrait of an extraordinarily handsome young man who resembled himself so nearly that he could not have asked for a better likeness. Sighing, the white cat became even more melancholy, lapsing into a profound silence. The prince saw clearly that there was some unusual story connected with the portrait, but did not venture to ask any questions for fear of displeasing her. Instead, he entertained her by telling all the news he had and in the process found her well acquainted with the various concerns of princes and other events occurring in the world.

After supper the white cat invited her guest to enter a salon, in which was constructed a theater where twelve cats and twelve monkeys danced a ballet. One party was dressed as Moors, the other as Chinese. You can easily imagine the leaps and capers they performed, and every now and then they gave each other a scratch or two. So did the evening end, and the white cat bade "Good night" to her guest.

The hands who had been his conductors so far took hold of him again and led him into an apartment quite different from any he had seen, for it was not so much magnificent as it was elegant. All the decorations were made of butterflies' wings whose various colors formed a thousand different flowers. There were also the feathers of exceedingly rare birds that perhaps have never been seen anywhere else. The furnishings of the bed were made of and tied with a thousand bows of ribbon. Large mirrors hung from the ceiling to floor in frames of chased gold representing a thousand tiny cupids.

The prince went to bed without saying a word, for there were no means of talking with the hands that waited upon him. He slept but little and was wakened early by a muffled noise. The hands immediately lifted him out of bed and dressed him in hunting attire. Looking into the castle courtyard, he saw more than five hundred cats, some of whom led greyhounds in the slips, while others blew horns. It was a grand holiday. The white cat was going to hunt and wanted the prince to accompany her. The officious hands gave him a wooden horse, and though he made some objection to mounting it, saying that he could never become a knight-errant like Don Quixote, his resistance was useless. It had a bridle and saddle embroidered with gold and diamonds, and in fact it went at full gallop and kept pace wonderfully. The white cat rode a monkey, the handsomest and proudest ever seen. She had thrown off her long veil in favor of a dragoon's cap, which made her look so bold that she frightened all the mice in the vicinity. Never was there a more charming hunting party. The cats outran the rabbits and hares, and as fast as they caught them, the white cat had a *curée* made in her presence, and a thousand skillful feats were performed to the great delight of the whole company. The birds, in turn, were by no means safe, for the kittens climbed the trees, and a great monkey carried the white cat up even to the nests of the eagles so that their eaglets were at her mercy.

Once the hunt was over, the white cat took a horn, and though it was about the length of one's finger, it emitted a call so clear and loud that it was easily heard ten miles away. As soon as she had sounded two or three flourishes, she was surrounded by all the cats in the country. Some rode chariots through the air, and others came in boats by water. Never before had so many cats been gathered, nearly all dressed in different fashions. Attended by this splendid entourage, the white cat returned to the castle, requesting the prince to accompany her. He was perfectly willing to do so, even though all this caterwauling smacked of a witch's festival.

As soon as they reached home, she put on her long black veil and dined with the prince, who was hungry and did justice to the good cheer. They brought him some liqueurs, which he sipped with great satisfaction, and they soon made him forget all about the little dog he was to find for the king. He no longer thought of anything but mewing with the white cat, that is to say, remaining her kind and faithful companion. He spent his days by amusing himself in pleasant ways, followed by ballets, carousals, and a thousand other events that provided him with a good deal of entertainment. Even the beautiful cat herself frequently composed verses and sonnets so full of passionate tenderness that made him suspect she had a susceptible heart, for no one could speak as she did without being in love. Unfortunately, her secretary, who was an old cat, wrote in such a vile scrawl that it is impossible to read them today, even though her works have been preserved.

The prince had forgotten all about the land of his birth. The hands of which I have spoken continued to wait upon him, and he regretted sometimes that he was not a cat so he could spend his whole life long in such excellent company. "Alas," he said to the white cat, "how wretched I'll be when I must leave you! I love you so dearly! Either become a woman or make me a cat."

Amused by his wish, she gave him some mysterious answers that he did not understand in the least.

A year flies by quickly when one has neither care nor pain, when one is merry and in good health. The white cat knew when the prince was supposed to return, and since he had forgotten it, she reminded him. "Don't you know," she asked, "that you have only three days left to look for the little dog that your father desires? Your brothers have already found several that are very beautiful."

The prince's memory of his task returned to him, and he was astonished by his negligence. "What secret spell could have made me forget the most important thing in the world to me?" he exclaimed. "My honor and fortune are staked on this. Where shall I find a dog that can win the kingdom for me, or a horse swift enough to complete the journey, in such a short time?"

Seeing him become so anxious and sad, the white cat said to him sweetly, "Prince, do not be distressed. I'm your friend, and you may stay here one more day. Although it's five hundred miles from here to your country, the good wooden horse will carry you there tomorrow in less then twelve hours."

"I thank you, beautiful cat," the prince said, "but I cannot simply return to my father without bringing him a little dog."

"Wait," said the white cat, "here's an acorn that contains one more beautiful than the Dog Star."

"Oh, madam cat," the prince cried, "your majesty is jesting with me."

"Put the acorn to your ear," she replied, "and you'll hear it bark."

He obeyed her, and immediately the little dog went "bow-wow." The prince was extremely delighted, for any dog that could be kept in an acorn was bound to be diminutive indeed.

He was going to open the acorn, so eager was he to see the dog, but the white cat told him that the dog might catch cold on the journey, and it would be better for him to wait until he was in his royal father's presence. He thanked her a thousand times and bade her a most tender farewell. "I assure you," he said, "that the days I have spent with you have flown by so quickly that I deeply regret leaving you behind. Although you're the sovereign here and all the cats that compose your court possess much more wit and gallantry than ours, I'd be honored if you came with me."

The cat replied to this invitation only with a deep sigh: "Prince, depart."

The prince was the first to reach the castle where he had agreed to meet his brothers. Arriving shortly thereafter, they were surprised to see in the courtyard a wooden horse that curveted with more grace than the horses in the riding schools. When the prince came forward to receive them, they embraced several times and recounted their travels to one another, though our prince kept the bulk of his adventures a secret from his brothers. Showing them an ugly turnspit, he remarked, "I think it's so beautiful that I've selected it for the king." Despite the close friendship of the brothers, the two elder felt a secret joy at their young brother's awful taste. Since they were sitting at a table, they nudged each other's feet by way of signifying that they did not have much to fear from him.

The next morning they set out together in the same coach. The king's two elder sons carried a few little dogs in baskets so beautiful and delicate that everyone was afraid to touch them. The youngest son carried the poor turnspit, which was so filthy that nobody could bear the sight of it. As soon as they set foot in the palace, everybody surrounded them and welcomed them back to court. Once they had entered the king's apartment, he was at a loss to make a decision, for the little dogs given to him by his two elder sons were nearly equal in beauty. In fact, the two brothers had already begun to dispute the right of succession when their younger brother reconciled them by taking out of his pocket the acorn that the white cat had given him. He opened it immediately, and everybody saw a tiny dog lying on cotton. He got up and jumped through a ring without touching any part of it. The prince placed it on the floor, and instantly it began dancing a saraband with castanets that was as sprightly as the most celebrated Spanish dancer. It was a thousand different colors, and its hair and ears swept the ground. The king was dumbfounded, for how could he possibly criticize the beauty of Toutou?

Nevertheless, he was by no means inclined to give over his crown, for the smallest fleur-de-lis in its circlet was dearer to him than all the dogs in the universe. Therefore, he told his sons that he was gratified by the trouble they had taken. Indeed, they had succeeded so well in fulfilling his first request that he wanted to test their ability again before he fulfilled his promise. "You have a year to travel over land and sea in quest of a piece of cloth so fine that it will pass through the eye of a needle used to make Venetian point lace."

All three were extremely disappointed to learn that they were obliged to undertake a new voyage of discovery, but the two elder princes, whose dogs were less beautiful than that of the youngest, readily consented. Both went their own ways without declaring their friendship to him as they had done before, for the trick of the turnspit had rather cooled their ardor.

Our prince remounted his wooden horse, and since he did not wish for any assistance other than that obtained from the friendship of the white cat, he set off at a gallop toward the castle where she had so kindly received him. He found all the doors open, and the windows, roofs, towers, and walls were all illuminated by a hundred thousand lamps, which produced a brilliant effect. The hands that had attended him so well advanced to meet him and took the bridle of the excellent wooden horse, which they led to the stable while the prince entered the white cat's apartments.

Wearing her morning cap, she was lying in a little basket on a fine mattress of white satin. She seemed in low spirits until she saw the prince. Then she cut a thousand capers and played as many gambols to show him her delight. "Whatever hope I had that you'd return," she said, "I confess, Prince, that I didn't want to deceive myself by indulging in it. I'm generally so unfortunate in matters that concern me that this is a pleasant surprise."

The grateful prince caressed her a thousand times and told her about the success of his journey, which she knew perhaps better than he did. "Only now the king wants a piece of cloth that can pass through the eye of a needle." In truth, he believed it was impossible to find such a thing, but he did not hesitate to ask her to make the attempt, relying implicitly upon her friendship and assistance. Becoming more serious, the white cat told him it was a matter that demanded considera-

tion. Fortunately, there were some cats in her castle
who spun extremely well. She intended to put a claw to
it herself and speed up the work as much as possible.
"Rest assured that you have no need of searching any
farther for what you will more readily find in my castle
than in any other place in the world."

The hands appeared bearing torches, and the white
cat and prince followed them. They entered a magnificent arbor running along the side of a large river, over
which was to be shot an astonishing display of fireworks. Four cats were simultaneously to be burnt there,
for they had been tried and sentenced in due form for
having eaten the roast meat, cheese, and milk, provided
for the white cat's supper, and even of having conspired against her life with Martafax and L'Hermite,
two famous rats of that country, and regarded as such
by La Fontaine, a very dutiful historian. It was well-
known there had been a great deal of intrigue in the
matter, and that the majority of the witnesses had been
bribed. Despite all this, the prince managed to obtain
their pardon. The fireworks did not harm anyone, and
never had such splendid skyrockets been seen before.

Afterward, a splendid supper was served. This gratified the prince more than the fireworks because he was
famished: the wooden horse had carried him at such a
rapid pace that he had never ridden so hard before in
his life. The following days were spent like those of the
previous year and the ingenious white cat set forth a
thousand diverse entertainments to regale her guest.
Our prince was probably the first mortal who ever
found so much amusement among cats without human
company.

The truth is, the white cat possessed charming, sweet,
and well-rounded qualities. She was wiser than a cat is
allowed to be, and the prince was sometimes astonished
by her knowledge. "No," he said, "it's not natural for
you to possess all these wonderful qualities I've discovered in you. If you love me, charming pussy, explain to
me what miracle has enabled you to think and speak so
perfectly that you might be elected a member of the
most famous Academy of Arts and Sciences?"

"Stop questioning me, Prince," she said. "I'm not

allowed to answer, and you may conjecture as much as you like without the least contradiction from me. Let it suffice that I'll always have a velvet paw for you, that I take a tender interest in all that concerns you."

The second year slipped away like the first—without their being aware of it at all. The prince could scarcely think of anything he desired without the diligent hands instantly providing him with it, whether it be a book, jewel, picture, or antique medal. He had but to say, "I want a certain gem in the cabinet of the Great Mogul or of the King of Persia, or such a statue in Corinth or any part of Greece," and it was instantaneously before him, without his knowing how it came or who brought it. This pastime was not without its charms, for it is sometimes very pleasant to possess the finest treasures in the world.

The White Cat, who constantly attended to the prince's welfare, warned him that the hour of departure was approaching. There was no need to worry, however, about the piece of cloth he needed. She had made a most wonderful one for him, and she added that she intended this time to furnish him with an equipage worthy of his birth. Without waiting for his reply, she told him to look into the great courtyard of the castle. He saw an open calèche made of gold and enameled in scarlet with a thousand gallant emblems that stimulated the mind as much as the eye. It was drawn by twelve horses as white as snow, four-and-four abreast, bearing harnesses of scarlet velvet embroidered with diamonds and plated with gold. The calèche was lined to match, and a hundred coaches followed in its train. Each was led by eight horses and filled with superbly attired noblemen of high bearing. There was as well an escort of a thousand bodyguards, whose uniforms were covered so much with embroidery that you could not see the stuff they were made of. Most striking about this cavalcade was the portrait of the white cat, which could be seen on the emblems on the calèche or the uniforms of the bodyguards or attached by a ribbon to the doublets of those who formed the train, as if it were a new order with which she had decorated them.

"Go," she said to the prince. "Appear at the court of

your father in such a sumptuous state that your magnificence may make an impression on him and prevent
him from refusing again to bestow you with the crown
you deserve. Here's a walnut. Crack it only in his presence, and you'll find in it the piece of cloth you asked
of me."

"Charming white cat," he said, "I must confess
that your kindness has so infused me that, if you consent, I'd prefer spending my life here with you than
enjoying all the grandeur that I have reason to expect
elsewhere."

"Prince," she replied, "I'm convinced that you have a
good heart, a rare quality among princes. Usually they
want to be loved by everyone. Rarely do they want to
love anyone themselves. You're proof that the rule has
its exception. I give you credit for the affection you've
demonstrated for a white cat that, after all, is good for
nothing but catching mice."

The prince kissed her paw and departed. We would
have some difficulty in believing the speed with which
he traveled if we were not already aware of the pace at
which the wooden horse had previously covered the
five-hundred-mile distance from the castle. Impelled
by a like power, these swift steeds traveled for twenty-
four hours straight and stopped only when they reached
the king's palace.

The two elder brothers had already arrived, and when
they did not see the youngest prince, they congratulated
themselves on his negligence. "Here's a piece of good
luck!" one whispered to the other. "He's either dead or
very ill. He won't be our rival in the important business
about to be decided." They immediately displayed their
cloths, which were so fine that they could pass through
the eye of a large needle, though not that of a small
one. Elated by this, the king used it as a pretext to deny
their claims. He ordered the magistrates to bring the
needle that he had selected out of the City Treasury,
where it had been carefully kept during the princes'
absence. there was a good deal of murmuring when he
did this. The friends of the princes, particularly those
of the eldest, whose cloth was made of the finer material, protested, "It's downright chicanery." "The king is

too cunning and deceptive." The king's followers con-
tended that he was merely bound by the conditions he
had proposed. The matter seemed settled when suddenly they heard a fine flourish of trumpets, kettle
drums, and oboes, announcing the arrival of our prince
in all his pomp and accoutrements. The king and his
two other sons were all equally thunderstruck by such
splendor.

After the prince had respectfully greeted his father
and embraced his brothers, he revealed a box dotted
with rubies. In it was the walnut. He cracked it
expecting to find the boasted piece of cloth, but instead
found a hazel nut, which he also cracked. Lo, he was
surprised to find a cherrystone! Everybody looked at
one another, and the king laughed up his sleeve at his
son, who had been naive enough to believe he could
bring a whole piece of cloth in a walnut. Yet, why
shouldn't the prince have believed it when he had
already given the king a dog that had emerged from
an acorn? Therefore, he cracked the cherrystone and
found a kernel. A great murmur arose in the room.
Everyone was convinced that the young prince had
been duped in this adventure, but he did not respond to
the courtiers' raillery. Opening the kernel, he found in
it a grain of wheat and in the grain of wheat a millet
seed. In truth, he began to have doubts himself and
muttered between his teeth, "White cat, white cat,
you've fooled me!" Instantly he felt a cat's claw on his
hand give him such a scratch that blood began to
flow. He knew not whether this scratch was given to
encourage or to dishearten him, but he nevertheless
opened the millet seed, and the entire company was
astonished when he drew out a piece of cloth four hundred yards long, so wonderfully wrought that all the
birds, beasts, and fish were depicted in their natural
colors along with the trees, fruits, and plants of the
earth; rocks, rare gems, and shells of the ocean; the
sun, the moon, the great and lesser heavenly bodies.
There were also portraits of all the kings and lesser
sovereigns reigning in the world at that time, with
those of their wives, mistresses, children, and all their
subjects, not omitting the smallest urchin—everyone in

his particular walk of life accurately represented and dressed in the garb of his country.

When the king saw this piece of cloth, he became as pale as the prince had become red with bewilderment when he had not at first found it. The needle was produced, and the prince passed and repassed the cloth through the eye of it six times. The king and the two elder princes looked on in sullen silence, except at those moments when the beauty and uniqueness of the cloth forced them to acknowledge that nothing in the universe could compare to it.

The king heaved a deep sigh and, turning toward his sons, said, "Nothing gives me as much consolation in my old age as observing the deference paid by you to my wishes. Consequently, I want to put your obedience to a new test. Go and travel for another year, and he who at the end of it brings back the most beautiful maiden shall marry her and be crowned king on his wedding day. It's necessary anyway that my successor should marry, and I pledge my troth that I'll no longer defer bestowing the reward I have promised."

This unjust decision went especially against our prince, for the little dog and piece of cloth were worth more than ten kingdoms. He was so well bred, though, that he would not contest his father's will, and he promptly reentered his calèche. His whole entourage followed him, and he took the road back to his dear white cat. She knew the day, the very moment he would arrive. The entire way was strewn with flowers; thousands of vases exuded perfume everywhere and particularly within the castle. The white cat was seated on a Persian carpet under a pavilion of cloth of gold in a gallery, and from there she saw him approach, received by the hands that had always attended him. All the cats climbed up into the gutters to welcome him with a desperate squalling.

"So, Prince," the white cat said, "you've returned once more without a crown."

"Madam," he replied, "your generosity has placed me in a position to obtain it, but I'm convinced that it would have given the king more pain to part with it than the pleasure I would have gained from acquiring it."

"It matters not at all," she said. "Nothing shall be overlooked if you want to win it, for I'll help you in this affair. Since you're obliged to return with a beautiful maiden to your father's court, I'll find one who'll help you obtain the prize. In the meantime let us be merry. I've ordered a naval combat between my cats and the terrible rats of this country. My cats will perhaps be embarrassed a little, for they're afraid of water. On the other hand, they would have too much of an advantage, and one ought to equalize matters as much as possible."

Admiring the prudence of madam puss, the prince heaped praises on her and accompanied her to a terrace that overlooked the sea.

The ships in which the cats embarked were large pieces of cork, on which they managed to sail conveniently enough, and the rats had bound several eggshells together for their navy. The battle was long and cruel. The rats flung themselves into the water and swam much better than the cats so that they triumphed and were defeated alternately twenty times. However, Minagrobis, admiral of the feline fleet, reduced the rattish race to utmost despair when he devoured the general of their forces, an old rat of great experience, who had been around the world three times in splendid ships where he had been neither captain nor common sailor but simply a lickspittle. The white cat would not permit the utter destruction of all these poor unfortunate creatures. A smart politician, she calculated that if there were no more rats or mice left in the country, her subjects would live in a state of idleness that might work to her disadvantage.

The prince spent this year as he had the two previous ones, hunting, fishing, or playing chess, which the white cat did extremely well. He could not help occasionally questioning her as to the miraculous power that enabled her to speak. He asked her whether she was a fairy, or been transformed into a cat, but since she never said anything but what she chose, she never gave answers that did not wholly suit her.

Consequently, her replies consisted of a number of fragments that signified nothing in particular, and he clearly perceived she was not inclined to share her secret with him.

Nothing flies faster than time spent without trouble or sorrow, and if the cat had not been careful to remember the day when the prince had to return to court, he certainly would have forgotten it. On the eve of his departure she told him that everything depended on him taking home one of the most beautiful princesses in the world. "The hour to destroy that fatal work of the fairies has finally arrived. You must cut off my head and tail and fling them quickly into the fire."

"Me?" the prince exclaimed. "Blanchette, my love! I can't be so barbarous as to kill you! Ah, you undoubtedly mean to test my heart. But rest assured that it is incapable of forgetting the love and gratitude it owes you."

"No, Prince," she replied, "I don't suspect you of ingratitude. Well I know your worth. Neither you nor I control our destiny in this matter. Do as I bid you, and then we'll both begin to be happy. On my word of honor as a noble cat, you'll discover that I'm truly your friend."

The eyes of the young prince welled up with tears at the mere thought of being obliged to cut off the head of his little kitten, so pretty and so charming. He said all the most tender things he could think of in order to induce her to spare him such a trial. However, she persisted in replying that she wanted to die by his hand, and that only this way would he prevent his brothers from obtaining the crown. In a word, she urged him so earnestly that he drew his sword tremblingly, and with a faltering hand he sliced off the head and tail of his dearly beloved cat.

The very next moment he beheld the most charming transformation imaginable. The body of the white cat swelled in size and changed suddenly into that of an indescribably perfect young maiden. Her eyes enthralled everyone's heart, and her sweetness held them captive. Her form was majestic, her demeanor noble

and modest, her spirit, gentle, her manners, engaging.
She was, in sum, the most charming being in the world.

The prince was so struck with amazement at the
pleasant sight of her that he thought he was enchanted.
He could not speak or open his eyes wide enough to
take her in enough. His astonishment became even
greater when he saw an extraordinary number of lords
and ladies enter the room. Each had his or her cat's
skin flung over a shoulder as they advanced and threw
themselves at the feet of their queen. "How great is our
pleasure at seeing you restored to your natural form!"
She received them with signs of affection that clearly
indicated the goodness of her heart, and after spending
a short time in their company, she requested that they
leave her alone with the prince, to whom she told the
following tale:

I don't want you to think, my lord, that I've always
been a cat, or that my birth was an obscure one in the
eyes of men. My father was king of six realms. He
loved my mother tenderly and gave her complete liberty to do whatever she liked. Her great love was traveling, and shortly before I was born, she took a journey
to a certain mountain about which she had heard the
most extraordinary tales. While traveling there, she
was told that she was then passing near an ancient fairy
castle, the most beautiful in the world. At least this
is what people believed according to legend. Since
nobody ventured there, they could not know for certain, but they did know that the fairies had in their
garden the finest, most delicious, and most delicate
fruit that one could ever eat.

My mother immediately had such an overwhelming
desire to taste some that she turned her steps toward
the castle. She arrived at the gate of that superb edifice,
which blazed with gold and azure on all sides, but
when she knocked, nobody appeared to answer. It
seemed as if everyone in the castle were dead. Her
desire grew in proportion to the obstacle. She sent for
ladders so that her attendants might climb over the
garden walls, and they would have succeeded had not
the said walls visibly increased in height, even though

no one was seen to cause this. They lengthened the ladders by tying two or three together, but they broke under the weight of those who mounted them, and the attendants were either crippled or killed.

The queen was in despair. She saw the large trees laden with what looked like delicious fruit, and was determined to eat some or die. Ordering several splendid tents to be pitched before the castle, she remained there six weeks with her entire entourage. She neither slept nor ate, but sighed unceasingly and talked of nothing but the fruit in the inaccessible garden. In the end she fell dangerously ill without anyone being able to find a cure for her illness, for the inexorable fairies had never appeared so much as once since she had set up the tents. All her officers were deeply troubled. Nothing was to be heard but sobs and sighs, and the dying queen kept asking for fruit from her attendants and cared only for that which was denied her.

"One night, awakening from a doze, she opened her eyes and saw an ugly, decrepit old woman seated in an armchair at the head of her bed. Even as she stared, shocked that her women had allowed a stranger to come so near her, the old woman said, "We think your majesty is very obstinate in persisting in your desire to eat our fruit, but since your life is precariously hanging on this, my sisters and I consent to give you as much as you can eat on the spot as well as whatever you can carry away with you. However, you must give us something in exchange."

"Ah, heavens! I can't purchase such fruit at too high a price."

"We wish to have the daughter whom you are about to bring into the world," she said. "As soon as she is born, we'll come and fetch her, and she'll be brought up among us. There are no virtues, charms, or accomplishments with which we shall not endow her. In a word, she'll be our child, and we'll make her happy. But be advised that your majesty will not be allowed to see her anymore until she is married. If this proposal is agreeable to you, I'll cure you instantly and lead you into our orchard. Even though it's night, you'll be able to see well enough to pick whatever fruit you desire. If what I have said does not please you, then good night, Queen, I'm going to bed."

"Hard as the condition may be that you impose upon me," the queen replied, "I'll accept it sooner than die, for I know I cannot live another day, and my infant would therefore perish with me. Cure me, wise fairy," she continued, "and don't postpone for one moment the opportunity of enjoying the privilege you've promised."

The fairy touched her with a golden wand, saying, "Let your majesty be free from all the ills that confine you to this bed!"

It seemed to the queen that someone had instantaneously stripped off a heavy, stiff robe that had oppressed her, though some portions of it still clung to her, apparently in the places most affected by her disorder. Sending for all her ladies, she told them with a smiling countenance that she was quite well and was going to get up. "Soon those gates of the fairy palace, so well bolted and barred, will be opened for me to enter, and I'll be able to eat the fine fruit and take away as much as I like."

All of her ladies thought the queen was seeing things in her delirium because she wanted the fruit so much. Instead of replying, they began to weep, and some went to waken all the physicians to come and see the state their majesty was in.

This delay exasperated the queen, but when she ordered them to bring her clothes to her instantly, they refused. She flew into a passion, turning red with rage. This they attributed to fever, but once the physicians arrived, felt her pulse, and went through the usual ceremonies, they could not deny that she was in perfect health. Her women, who realized the mistake that their zeal had caused them to make, tried to atone for it by asking her majesty's pardon and dressing her as quickly as possible. Peace was restored, and the queen quickly followed the old fairy, who was still waiting for her.

She entered the palace, which required nothing to make it the most beautiful place in the world. Two other fairies, somewhat younger than the one who con-

ducted my mother, received her at the gate and welcomed her graciously. She asked them to lead her
straight into the garden and to those espaliers where
she would find the best fruit.

"Everything is equally good," they said to her, "and
if it weren't for the fact that you desire the pleasure of
picking it yourself, we need only call the fruit we wish
for, and it will come to us here."

"I implore you, ladies," the queen said, "to show me
such an extraordinary sight."

The eldest fairy put her finger into her mouth
and whistled three times. Then she cried, "Apricots,
peaches, nectarines, *brunions,* sherries, plums, pears,
bigaroons, melons, muscatel grapes, apples, oranges,
lemons, gooseberries, strawberries, raspberries, come
at my call!"

"But," the queen said, "all the fruit that you've summoned cannot be found at the same season."

"In our orchard," they replied, "we have all the fruits
of the earth. They're always ripe, always excellent, and
they never spoil."

Meanwhile, the fruit rolled in over the floor pell-mell,
but without being bruised or dirtied. So, the queen,
eager to satisfy her longing, threw herself on them and
took the first that came to hand, devouring rather than
eating it.

After having partly satisfied her appetite, she begged
the fairies to let her proceed to the espaliers so that she
might have the pleasure of choosing the fruit on the
tree and then gathering it. "We freely give you permission," they said, "but remember the promise you've
made us. You won't be allowed to rescind it!"

"I'm convinced," she said, "that you live so well
here, and this palace appears to me so beautiful that if I
did not love my husband dearly, I'd propose remaining
here with you along with my daughter. Therefore, you
need have no fear about my retracting my word."

Completely satisfied, the fairies opened all their gardens and enclosures to her. She remained there three
days and three nights without wishing to go out again
because she found everything so delicious. She gathered the fruit to take home with her, and since it did not

spoil, she had four thousand mules loaded with the
fruit. In addition, the fairies gave her the most exquisite golden baskets in which to carry it and many
other precious items. They promised her that I would
be educated like a princess and that they would make
me a model of perfection and choose a husband for me.
"You will receive notice of the wedding, and we hope
you will attend."

The king was delighted by the queen's return, and
the entire court rejoiced as well. There were nothing
but balls, masquerades, runnings at the ring, and banquets, at which the queen's fruit was served as a delicious treat. The king preferred to eat the fruit over
anything else offered him, but he knew not of the bargain the queen had made with the fairies.

He often asked her where she had traveled to
find such good things. One time she told him that she
had found them on an almost inaccessible mountain.
Another time she said they grew in some valleys. Other
times she named a garden or great forest. Surprised by
so many contradictions, the king questioned those who
had accompanied her, but she had so strictly forbidden
them to tell anyone of her adventure that they dared not
talk about it. Eventually the queen became uneasy
about the promise she had made the fairies, and as the
time for her to give birth approached, she fell into an
alarming state of melancholy. She kept sighing constantly and looked worse and worse every day. After a
great deal of probing, she informed him of everything
that had occurred with her and the fairies, and how she
had promised to give them the daughter she was about
to bring into the world.

"What?" said the king. "We have no other children.
You know how much I want some, and for the sake
of eating two or three apples you gave away our
daughter? You have no feelings for me!" He overwhelmed her with a thousand reproaches, which were
almost the death of my poor mother, but that did not
satisfy him. He had her locked up in a tower and
surrounded it with soldiers to prevent her from having communication with anyone except the officers of
her household. These, too, he changed so they were not

the same as those who had been with her at the fairy castle.

The misunderstanding between the king and the queen threw the whole court into consternation, and everybody changed into clothes more suitable to the general sorrow. The king, for his part, appeared inexorable. He never saw his wife, and as soon as I was born, he had me brought into the palace to be nursed, while she remained a most unhappy prisoner.

The fairies, knowing all that took place, became annoyed. They regarded me as their property and my detention as a theft. Before seeking vengeance appropriate to their anger, they sent a grand embassy to the king to warn him that he had better set the queen free, restore her to his favor, and surrender me to their ambassadors so that I could be nursed and brought up by the fairies. The ambassadors were so little and deformed (for they were hideous dwarfs) that they did not have the power to persuade the king to comply with their request. He refused bluntly, and if they had not taken their departure instantly, something worse might have befallen them. When the fairies heard of my father's conduct, they were highly indignant, and after demolishing his six kingdoms by inflicting every ill they could devise on them, they let loose a terrible dragon that poisoned the air whenever he breathed, wilting all the trees and plants, and devoured man and child.

In the throes of despair, the king consulted all the wise men in his dominions as to what he should do to protect his subjects from the misfortunes that were overwhelming them. They advised him on the one hand to seek out the best physicians and the most excellent remedies throughout the world, and on the other, to offer a free pardon to all criminals under the death penalty who would agree to fight the dragon. The king approved of this advice and acted on it immediately, but without success, for the pestilence continued and the dragon devoured all those who attacked him. Finally the king turned to a fairy who had been his friend from childhood. She was very old and rarely left her bed. Going to see her, he reproached her a thousand times for permitting fate to persecute him without coming to his rescue. "What would you have me do?" she said. "You've irritated my sisters. They're as powerful as I am, and we rarely act against one another. Try to appease them by giving them your daughter. The little princess rightfully belongs to them. You've put the queen in prison. What has that charming woman done for you to treat her so severely? It would be best if you decided to keep your wife's pledge to the fairies. I assure you, you'll be rewarded greatly if you do."

My father loved me dearly, but seeing no other way of saving his kingdoms from the lethal dragon, he told his friend he would take her advice. He was willing to surrender me to the fairies since she had assured him that I'd be cherished and treated as a princess of my rank ought to be. He also agreed to allow the queen to come back to the court. Finally he told the fairy that she should name the person who should carry me to the fairy castle, and it would be done. "You may even remain in its vicinity if you desire, to witness the celebration that will take place there."

The king told her that he would go there with the queen within a week's time and asked her to notify her sister fairies of his intention so that they might make the necessary arrangements.

As soon as he returned to the palace, he sent for the queen and received her with as much affection and regard as he had exhibited rashness and anger when he imprisoned her. She was so changed and melancholy that he would hardly have recognized her if his heart had not assured him she was the same person he had formerly loved so tenderly. With tears in his eyes he implored her to forget the misery he had caused her and assured her she would never again experience anything like that on his account. She replied, "I brought it upon myself by my imprudence in promising our daughter to the fairies. If anything could excuse my actions, it was the condition to which I had been reduced at the time."

The king then informed her that he had decided to place me in the hands of the fairies. The queen, in

her turn, opposed this intention. It seemed as if some
fatality was hanging over this affair, and that I was forever doomed to be a subject of dissension between my
father and mother. After she groaned and wept for a
considerable time without obtaining her goal (for the
king saw too clearly the fatal consequences of hesitating, and our subjects continued to perish as if they
were answerable for the faults of our family), she consented to all he desired, and everything was prepared
for the leave taking.

I was placed in a mother-of-pearl cradle ornamented
with the most elegant things that art could ever conceive. Hanging from every side were garlands and fes-
toons of flowers made of jewels, whose different colors
reflected the rays of the sun with such dazzling splendor that you could scarcely look upon them. The magnificence of my swaddling surpassed that of the cradle,
if that be possible, for all the bands of my clothes were
formed of large pearls. Twenty-four princesses of royal
blood carried me on a delicate litter. Though their
dresses were all different, they were not allowed to
wear any color but white in token of my innocence.
The entire court accompanied me according to rank.

While we were climbing the mountain, we heard
a melodious symphony more and more distinctly. At
length thirty-six fairies appeared, for the trio of before
had invited their friends to accompany them. Each was
seated in a pearl shell larger than that in which Venus
arose from the ocean. Seahorses, which seemed rather
awkward in getting overland, drew these pearl cars,
and though the occupants wore more sumptuous finery
than the greatest queens in the universe, they were at
the same time old and ugly hags.

The dragon who had been their instrument of
vengeance followed them in chains of diamonds. They
carried olive branches to signify to the king that his
submission had found favor with them, and when I was
presented, their caresses were so extraordinary that
they seemed to have no other goal in life except to
make me happy. They took me in their arms, kissed me
a thousand times, endowed me with various gifts, and
then began to dance the fairy brawl. It is a very lively

dance, and it's hard to imagine how well these old ladies jumped and capered. Afterward, the dragon that had devoured so many people crawled forward, and the three fairies to whom my mother had promised me seated themselves upon it. Then they placed my cradle between them and struck the dragon with a wand. It immediately spread its great, scaly wings, which were finer than gauze and glittered with all sorts of extraordinary colors, and in this way did they return to their castle. On seeing me aloft on this terrible dragon, my mother could not help shrieking over and over again. The king consoled her, saying "My friend the old fairy has assured me that no misfortune will befall her. She'll be as well taken care of as if she had remained in our own palace." The queen was calmed by this assurance, though she continued to be distraught at the idea of being separated from me for such a long time. She felt she was to blame for everything, for if she had not insisted on eating the fruit of that garden, I would have been brought up in my father's realm and would never have suffered the misfortunes that I still must relate to you.

Know, then, Prince, that my guardians had built a tower expressly for my abode, and it had a thousand beautiful apartments suitable for each season of the year, magnificent furniture, and amusing books. But it was without doors so that one could only enter it by the windows, which were set very high. Atop this tower was a beautiful garden ornamented with flowers, fountains, and green arbors, where you could remain cool on the hottest of dog days. Here was the place where I was brought up by the fairies, and the care they took of me even exceeded what they had promised the queen. She would have thought every day was my wedding day. I was taught everything befitting my age and rank. I didn't give them much trouble because I learned almost everything with the greatest ease. My docility pleased them, and since I never saw another soul, I might have lived there in perfect tranquillity for the rest of my life.

When the fairies came to see me, they were always mounted on the terrible dragon I have already mentioned. Since they never mentioned the king or queen and called me their daughter, I believed myself to be so. Nobody lived with me in the tower except a parrot and a small dog that they had given me to amuse myself, for the creatures were endowed with reason and conversed remarkably well.

On one side of the tower was a path lined with deep ruts and trees that so choked the road that I had never seen anyone pass by since I had been shut up there. But one day when I was at the window talking with my parrot and my dog, I heard a noise. Looking all around, I noticed a young cavalier who had stopped to listen to our conversation. I had never seen a young man before but in a painting, and I was glad that chance provided me with this opportunity. Not dreaming of the danger that accompanies the pleasure of contemplating such a charming object, I leaned forward to gaze at him, and the more I looked, the more I was delighted. He made a profound bow, stared at me, and seemed frustrated that he could not find a way to converse with me, for my window was very high and he feared being overheard, since he knew well enough that I was in the castle of the fairies.

The night came suddenly upon us, or, to be more precise, it came without our noticing it. He blew his horn two or three times, entertaining me with a few flourishes. Then he took his leave, and I was unable to ascertain which way he had gone because the night was so dark. I remained meditative, no longer feeling the same pleasure in talking to my parrot and dog that I had felt before. They said the prettiest things in the world to me, for fairy creatures are very witty, but my mind was proccupied and I was too naive to conceal it. Perroquet noticed it, and since he was a shrewd bird, he revealed no sign of what was going on in his mind.

As soon as it was light, I got up and ran to my window. Of course, I was most pleasantly surprised to see the young knight at the foot of the tower. He was so magnificently dressed that I imagined that it must be partly on my account, and I wasn't mistaken. He addressed me through a sort of speaking horn, informing me that until then he had been indifferent to

the charms of all the beautiful women he had seen, but
now he was so overwhelmed by my beauty that he
could not imagine how he could live without seeing me
every day. Greatly pleased by this compliment, I was at
the same time very disturbed that I dared not reply, for
I would have been compelled to cry out with all my
might and run the risk of being better heard by the
fairies than by him. I threw him some flowers I had in
my hand that he received as a favorable sign. Kissing
them several times and thanking me, he asked me if I
would approve of his standing under my window every
day at the same hour, and if so, to throw him something
else. A turquoise ring I had on my finger I instantly
pulled off and flung to him. Then I gave him a signal to
depart as quickly as possible because I heard the fairy
Violente mounting her dragon on the other side of the
tower to bring me my breakfast.

The first words she uttered on entering my room
were "I smell the voice of a man here. Search, dragon!"

Oh, how upset I was! My heart was sinking, for I
was afraid the monster would fly out through the opposite window and follow the cavalier. "Indeed, my good
mama," I said (for the old fairy liked me to call her so),
"you're jesting, surely, when you say you smell the
voice of a man. Is it possible to smell a voice? And
if so, what mortal would be rash enough to venture
climbing this tower?"

"What you say is true, daughter," she replied. "I'm
delighted to hear you reason so nicely, and I suppose
the hatred I bear all men sometimes makes me imagine
they're near." Giving me my breakfast and my spindle,
she said, "After you've had your breakfast, don't forget
to spin, for you did nothing yesterday, and my sisters
will be angry with you." In fact, I had been so preoccu-
pied by the stranger that I had found it quite impossible
to spin.

As soon as the fairy was gone, I rebelliously tossed
my spindle aside and ascended to the terrace to look
out as far as I could see. I had an excellent telescope,
and there was nothing to interrupt the view. In every
direction I looked until I discovered my cavalier on the
summit of a mountain. He was resting beneath a rich

pavilion of gold cloth and surrounded by a large entourage. I was convinced that he was the son of some king who reigned in the vicinity. Since I feared that if he returned to the tower, he would be discovered by the terrible dragon, I fetched my parrot and told him to fly to the mountain. "There you will find the person who had spoken to me. Beg him in my name never to come again, for I fear my vigilant guardians will surely do him harm."

Perroquet carried out his task like a clever parrot. The courtiers were all surprised to see him flying at full speed, and watched him perch on their master's shoulder and whisper in his ear. The king (for that's what he proved to be) was both delighted and troubled by this message. My anxiety on his account he found encouraging, but the many obstacles barring him from speaking to me distressed him. Still, he was bent on wooing me and asked Perroquet a hundred questions. Perroquet asked him as many in return, for he was naturally inquisitive. The king gave him a ring to bring to me in return for my turquoise. It was a turquoise as well, but much finer than mine, for it was shaped like a heart and encircled by diamonds. "It's fitting," he told the parrot, "that I treat you as an ambassador. Therefore, let me give you my portrait. Show it to no one but your charming mistress." He tied the miniature under the bird's wing, and the ring he brought me in his beak.

I awaited the return of my little green courier with an impatience I had never known before. He told me that the person to whom I had sent him was a great king. "I was most kindly received by him, and you may rest assured he only lives for your sake. Despite the grave danger in coming to the foot of the tower, he is determined to brave everything rather than renounce the pleasure of seeing you."

Those tidings greatly perplexed me, and I began to weep. Perroquet and my little dog Toutou did their best to console me because they loved me with a great deal of tenderness. Then Perroquet gave me the king's ring and showed me his portrait. I confess I had never been so delighted as by being able to regard the king's image closely, since I had only seen him at a distance.

He appeared to me much more charming than I had supposed. A hundred notions rushed into my mind, some pleasant, some distressing, and my conflict made me appear extraordinarily anxious.

The fairies who came to see me noticed it. They remarked to one another that I undoubtedly tired of my dull life. "It's time we find her a husband of the fairy race." Several were proposed and eventually they settled on little King Migonnet. His kingdom was some five hundred miles away, but that was, of course, a trifle for them.

Overhearing their discussion, Perroquet darted away to give me an account. "Ah," he said, "how I'd pity you, my dear mistress, if you were to become the queen of Migonnet. He's a frightful monkey. I'm sorry to relate this, but to tell you the truth, the king who loves you wouldn't condescend to have him for his footman."

"Have you seen him, Perroquet?"

"Indeed, I have," the bird continued. "I was brought up on the same branch with him."

"What? On a branch?" I exclaimed.

"Yes," he said, "he has talons like an eagle."

I was extremely disturbed by this account. I gazed at the charming portrait of the young king, certain he had given it to Perroquet so I could have the opportunity of beholding him. When I compared it to the description of Migonnet, I felt I had nothing more to hope for in life, and I was determined to die rather than marry this creature.

I did not sleep a wink that night, talking matters over with Perroquet and Toutou. I dozed a little toward daybreak, and since my dog had a good nose, he smelled the king at the foot of the tower and woke Perroquet. "I'll wager," he said, "the king's below."

Perroquet replied, "Hold your tongue, babbler. Just because your eyes and ears are almost always open, you envy others their peace."

"Wager something, then," insisted good Toutou. "I'm sure he's there."

"And I'm sure he's not," replied Perroquet. "Didn't I forbid him to come here in my mistress's name?"

"Oh, you amuse me with your forbiddances," my dog exclaimed. "A man in love consults only his heart." All at once he began roughly tugging Perroquet by the wings, making him quite vexed. The clamor they made woke me, and they told me what had started their quarrel. I ran, or rather flew, to my window, and I saw the king, who extended his arms toward me and said through his horn that he could no longer live without me. "I implore you, find some way to escape from your tower, or find some way I can enter." He called upon all the gods and all the elements to witness that he would marry me immediately and make me one of the mightiest queens in the world.

I ordered Perroquet to tell him that what he desired was quite impossible. Nevertheless, relying on his pledge and the oath he had taken, I was willing to attempt to carry out his wishes. But I implored him not to come every day since he might eventually be observed, and the fairies would show him no mercy.

He withdrew filled with joy at the hope I had given him, and I found myself in a great quandary when I began to consider the promise I had made him. How was I to escape from a tower that had no doors? I had no one to help me but Perroquet and Toutou! I? So young and inexperienced and timid? After considering this, I decided against an attempt that would never succeed, and I sent word to that effect by Perroquet to the king. At first he was going to kill himself before the bird's eyes, but then he charged him to persuade me either to witness his death or to bring him some comfort. "Sire," exclaimed my feathered ambassador, "my mistress is more than willing. She just lacks the means."

When the bird repeated to me all that had transpired, I felt more wretched than ever. The fairy Violente came to see me and noticed my eyes red and swollen. She observed that I had been crying and said, "Unless you tell me the cause, I shall burn you alive."

Her threats were always terrible, and I replied, trembling, that I was tired of spinning and wanted instead to make some nets to snare the young birds that pecked the fruit in my garden. "Cry no longer, my daughter,"

she said. "I'll bring you as much twine as you need."
Indeed, I received it that very evening, but she advised
me to concern myself less about working than about
my personal appearance since King Migonnet was
expected to arrive shortly. I shuddered when I heard
these fateful tidings and gave no reply.

As soon as she had left, I began to make two or
three pieces of net with the object of constructing a
rope ladder, which I succeeded in doing very well,
though I had never seen one. As it happens, the fairy
never furnished me with as much twine as I needed and
continually said to me, "Why, daughter, your work is
like that of Penelope. You never make any progress,
and yet you keep asking for more material."

"Oh, my good mama," I replied, "it's easy for you to
talk. Don't you see I'm very awkward at my work and
burn a good deal of it? Are you afraid I'll cause your
ruin because of the thread?" My naive air amused her,
though she was a very ill-tempered and cruel creature.

I sent Perroquet to tell the king to be under the
window of the tower on a certain evening, and he would
find the ladder and learn the rest when he arrived. I
fastened it as securely as possible since I was determined to make my escape with him. However, when he
saw it, he did not wait for me to descend, but mounted
it eagerly and jumped into my room just as I was preparing everything for my flight.

The sight of him so delighted me that I forgot all
about the danger. He renewed all his vows and implored me not to postpone becoming his wife. We
took Perroquet and Toutou as witnesses of our marriage. Never was a wedding between two persons of
such exalted rank celebrated with less fanfare or commotion, and never were two hearts so perfectly happy
as ours.

Day had not dawned when the king left me. I had
told him of the fairies' dreadful intention to marry me
to little Migonnet, and my description of this creature
horrified him as much as it had me. The hours seemed
long years to me after the king's departure. Running to
the window to follow him with my eyes despite the
darkness, I saw to my astonishment a fiery chariot in

the air being drawn by winged salamanders. It flew so fast that I could scarcely follow it, and it was escorted by several soldiers mounted on ostriches. I didn't have time to distinguish who the ugly creature was speeding through the sky, but I easily surmised that it must be either a fairy or an enchanter.

Shortly afterward, the fairy Violente entered my room. "I bring you good news," she said. "Your lover has just arrived. Be prepared to receive him. Here are some dresses and jewels for you."

"And who has told you," I exclaimed, "that I desire to be married? It's not at all my desire. Send King Migonnet away again. I won't add a pin to my dress. I don't care whether he thinks I'm beautiful or ugly. I'm not going to be his."

"What's this I hear?" the fairy responded. "We have a young rebel here? We've a head without any brains in it! I won't be trifled with, I warn you—"

"What will you do to me?" I cried, reddening at the names she had called me. "Can you make life more miserable for me than it is already? I live in this tower with only a dog and a parrot, and I see only the horrible form of a dreadful dragon several times a day."

"Ha, you ungrateful little wretch," the fairy said, "you haven't deserved in the least all the care and consideration we've shown you. I've often told my sisters we'd reap nothing from all our labors!" She departed to find them, and when she told them about our quarrel, they were just as taken aback as she was.

Perroquet and Toutou scolded me, vowing that if I continued to be so insolent, I'd suffer the terrible consequences. I felt so proud of possessing the heart of a great king that I despised the fairies and the advice of my poor little companions. I didn't dress myself, and I took pleasure in mussing my hair so that Migonnet might think me ugly.

Our meeting took place on the terrace. Arriving in his fiery chariot, he was tinier than the smallest dwarf I'd ever seen. Supporting himself on a pair of diamond crutches, he walked on his eagle's talons and on his knees at the same time because he had no bones in his legs. His royal mantle was only a half yard long, and yet more than a third of it dragged on the ground. His head was as large as a peck measure, and his nose was so big that a dozen birds sat on it, warbling to entertain him. He had such a bushy beard that canaries made their nests in it. His ears rose more than a foot above his head, but they were not so noticeable because of the high-pointed crown that he wore to make him appear taller. The flames of his chariot roasted the fruit, scorched the flowers, and dried up the fountains, and his chief equerry was obliged to lift him. But as soon as he was brought near me, I fled into my room and locked the door and all the windows.

Extremely angry with me, Migonnet returned to the fairies and they begged his pardon a thousand times for my rudeness. To appease him, for they feared him a great deal, they decided to bring him into my room while I slept to tie me hand and foot, place me in his fiery chariot, and take me away with him. After conceiving this plan, they scarcely said a cross word to me about my rude behavior to him. Instead they merely advised me to think about making amends.

Perroquet and Toutou were astonished by such kindness on their part. "Do you know, mistress," my dog said, "I have some sneaking suspicions. My lady fairies are acting strangely, particularly Violente."

I laughed at these fears, while I awaited my dear husband's arrival with great anxiety. He was too impatient to keep me waiting long. I threw him the rope ladder, fully determined to flee with him. He mounted it sprightly and said such tender things that even now I don't dare recall them to mind.

While we were conversing together, as calmly as if we had been in his own palace, the windows of my room suddenly burst open. The fairies entered on their terrible dragon. Migonnet followed them in his fiery chariot flanked by all his guards on their ostriches. Fearlessly drawing his sword, the king thought only of rescuing me from the most dreadful fate that ever awaited a mortal. In brief—I don't know whether I should tell you this, my lord—those barbarous creatures set their dragon on him, and the beast devoured him before my eyes.

Driven to despair by his fate and my own, I flung myself at the jaws of the horrible monster, hoping he would swallow me along with all that I loved in the world. He was quite willing to comply, but the fairies were even crueler than the dragon and would not permit it. "We must save her so that her agony will be prolonged," they cried. "A speedy death is too mild a punishment for this unworthy creature!"

They touched me, and I found myself immediately transformed into a white cat. Then they conducted me to this superb palace, which used to belong to my father. They transformed all the lords and ladies of the kingdom into cats, left only the hands visible of the rest of his court, and reduced me to the deplorable condition in which you found me. Finally, they informed me about my birth and the death of my father and mother, and told me, "You will be released from your catlike form only by a prince who exactly resembles the husband we have just eliminated."

"It is you, my lord, who bear that resemblance," she concluded. "You have the same features, the same air, the same voice. I was struck by it the moment I saw you. I knew about everything that happened, and I'm equally aware of all that will happen. My troubles are about to end."

"And mine, lovely queen," said the prince, flinging himself at her feet. "How long will they last?"

"I already love you more than my life, my lord," the queen said. "You must return to your father, and we'll be able to ascertain there how he feels about me, and if he'll consent to what you desire."

Leaving the castle, the prince gave her his hand as she stepped into a chariot much more magnificent than those she had previously provided for him. The rest of the equipage matched the brilliance of the chariot, and even the hooves of the horses were shod with emeralds and nailed with diamonds. Such a thing has perhaps never been seen except on that occasion. I shall not repeat the pleasant conversation that took place between the queen and the prince on their journey. If her beauty was incomparable, her mind was no less

superb, and the equally perfect young prince exchanged all sorts of charming thoughts with her.

As they neared the castle in which the prince
was to meet his two elder brothers, the queen entered
a little rock of crystal, the points of which were
ornamented with gold and rubies. Completely surrounded by curtains so that no one could see in, it
was carried by some handsome young men superbly
attired. Remaining in the chariot, the prince saw his
brothers walking with two extremely beautiful princesses. As soon as they sighted him, they came forth to
greet him and inquired, "Have you brought a lady with
you?" He replied that he had experienced bad luck on
his journey and had encountered only surpassingly
ugly hags. "The only rare item I've brought back is a
little white cat."

They began to laugh at his naiveté. "A cat?" they
exclaimed. "Are you afraid the mice will eat up your
palace?"

The prince admitted that he had been rather unwise
in selecting such a present for his father.

Thereupon, they continued on their way to the city.
The elder princes rode with their princesses in open car-
riages made of gold and azure, and their horses' heads
were adorned with plumes of feathers and aigrettes.
Nothing was more radiant than this cavalcade. Our
young prince followed them, and behind him came the
crystal rock, which everybody gazed at with wonder.
Meanwhile the courtiers hastened to inform the king
that the three princes were coming.

"Are they bringing beautiful ladies with them?" the
king asked.

"It would be impossible to find any that could surpass them" was the answer, which appeared to displease him.

The two princes eagerly ascended the palace stairs
with their wonderful princesses. The king received
them graciously and could not decide which deserved
the prize. He looked at his youngest son and said,
"Have you returned alone this time?"

"Your majesty will see a little white cat in this
rock," the prince replied. "It meows so sweetly and has

such velvet paws that you'll be delighted with it." The king smiled and went to open the rock himself, but as soon as he approached it, the queen made it fly into pieces by means of a spring, and she suddenly appeared like the sun after it has been hidden in the clouds. Her hair fell in loose ringlets over her shoulders down to her very feet. She was crowned with flowers, and her gown was made of thin white gauze lined with rose-colored taffeta. As she made a most dignified curtsy to the king, he was so overcome by this wondrous appearance that he could not resist exclaiming, "Behold the incomparable beauty who deserves the crown!"

"My liege," she announced, "I come not to deprive you of a throne you fill so worthily, for I was born the heiress to six kingdoms. Permit me to offer one to you and one to each of your elder sons. I ask of you no other recompense than your friendship and this young prince for my husband. Three kingdoms will be quite enough for us."

The king and the entire court joined in shouts of joy and astonishment. The marriage was celebrated immediately, as well as those of the other two princes, and the court subsequently spent several months enjoying entertainment and pleasures of every kind imaginable. Finally each couple departed to reign over their own dominions. The beautiful white cat came to be immortalized in her realm due to her goodness and generosity as well as her rare talent and beauty.

The handsome young prince was fortunate to find
An illustrious princess beneath a cat's skin,
Worthy to be adored and much inclined
To share the throne her affection won for him.

The willing heart is easily subdued
By enchanting eyes set for conquest.
When love's soft flame is fanned by gratitude,
The charm will have more power and be full of zest.

I cannot overlook that mother
Who paid so dearly for her whim.

Like Eve before she did not care about the other,
And was well prepared to sacrifice her kin.

Mothers beware and learn from this greedy queen!
Don't tamper with a daughter's lot
Or gratify the appetite and act so mean.
Condemn her conduct and remember what she got.

BELLE-BELLE OR
THE CHEVALIER FORTUNÉ

ONCE upon a time there was a very good, mild king. He was a powerful monarch, but his neighbor, the Emperor Matapa, was more powerful still. In the last of the great wars they had waged against each other, the emperor had won a tremendous battle. After killing or taking prisoner the greater portion of the king's officers and soldiers, Matapa besieged and conquered the king's capital city, and took possession of all its treasures. The king had just enough time to save himself and the queen, his sister, who had become a widow at a very early age. Though intelligent and beautiful, she was, to tell the truth, also proud, violent, and difficult to approach.

The emperor sent all the king's jewels and furniture to his own palace, and he carried away an extraordinary number of soldiers, women, horses, and anything else that he found useful or pleasant. After he had ravaged the greater part of the kingdom, he returned triumphant to his own, where he was joyously received by the empress and his daughter.

In the meantime, the defeated king was not inclined to accept his misfortune lightly. Rallying the remnants of his troops around him, he gradually formed the nucleus of an army. To increase their numbers as quickly as possible, he issued a proclamation requiring all the noblemen of his kingdom to come and serve him in person, or to send a well-mounted and armed son disposed to support all his ventures.

Now, there was an old nobleman, eighty years of age, who lived on the frontier of the kingdom. He was a wise and prudent man, but fortune had not been kind to him, and he found himself reduced almost to poverty after having been quite wealthy at one time. He would have endured such straits if his three beautiful daughters had not been compelled to share his fate. They were so understanding that they never grumbled at their misfortunes, and if by chance they discussed them at all with their father, they did so more to console him than to add to his disquiet. Without the least desire to seek a better life, they lived with him in their rustic setting.

When the king's proclamation reached the ears of the old man, he called his daughters to him, looked at them sorrowfully, and said, "What can we do? The king has ordered all the noblemen of his kingdom to join him in order to fight against the emperor, and if they refuse, he intends to levy a heavy tax. I'm not in a position to pay the tax, and therefore I'm in a terrible dilemma. This will either be my ruin or my death."

His three daughters were just as distressed as he himself, but they implored him to have courage, for they were convinced that they would find some way out of this predicament. The next morning the eldest daughter went looking for her father, who was walking sadly in an orchard that he tended by himself.

"Sire," she said, "I've come to ask your permission to join the army. I'm tall and strong enough. Let me dress myself in male attire and pass for your son. Even if I don't perform a single heroic deed, I'll at least save you the journey or the tax, and that is a great deal in our situation."

Embracing her affectionately, the count at first objected to such an extraordinary proposition, but she argued so convincingly that he finally had no choice but to consent. All he had to do now was to provide her with the clothes suitable to the person she was to represent. So he furnished her with arms and gave her the best of his four plough horses. Then they bade their tender farewells to each other.

After traveling for several days, she passed through a meadow bordered by a quickset hedge. There she saw a shepherdess who was trying with the greatest difficulty to drag one of her sheep out of a ditch into which it had fallen.

"What's the matter, good shepherdess?" she asked.

"Alas," replied the shepherdess, "I'm trying to save my sheep. It's drowning, and I don't have the strength to drag it out."

"I'm sorry about your plight," she said, riding off without offering her any help.

The shepherdess immediately cried out, "Good-bye, disguised beauty!"

Our lovely damsel was bewildered when she heard that. "How is it possible," she remarked, "that I could be so easily detected? That old shepherdess only saw me for a moment, and yet she knew that I was disguised! What am I to do now? Everyone will know who I am, and if the king finds out, my shame will be great, and so will his anger. He'll think my father's a coward, who shrinks from danger."

After much reflection she decided to return home. The count and his daughters had been talking about her, counting the days she had been gone, when they saw her enter. She told them about the incident with the shepherdess, and the good man responded that he had warned her about this. "If you had listened to me, you would never have set out. Why, it's impossible not to detect a maiden in a man's attire."

Once again, this little family was in a predicament and did not know what to do. Then the second daughter went to the count in her turn and said, "My sister had never been on horseback, so it's not surprising that she was discovered. If you'll allow me to go in her place, I promise that you'll be satisfied with me."

Nothing the old man said in opposing her intention had the slightest effect on her. So he was forced to consent, and she put on different clothes, took some other arms, and another horse. After she had equipped herself, she embraced her father and sisters a thousand times, determined to serve the king bravely. But in passing through the same meadow where her sister had seen the shepherdess and her sheep, she saw her again trying to drag a sheep out of the bottom of the ditch.

"Unfortunate creature that I am!" cried the old woman, "half my flock have perished this way. If someone would help me, I could save this animal, but nobody wants to stop and assist me."

"If you took better care of your sheep, shepherdess, they wouldn't fall into the water," the fair cavalier responded. Without giving her any other consolation, she spurred her horse and rode on.

The old woman bellowed after her, "Good-bye, disguised beauty!"

These words upset our amazon a great deal. "What bad luck! She's recognized me too! Now I've experienced the same fate as my sister. I'm not any luckier than she was, and it would be ridiculous for someone with my effeminate appearance to join the army. Everybody would see right through my disguise!"

She returned at once to her father's house, quite disturbed that she had failed to complete her mission. Though her father received her affectionately and praised her for having had the good sense to return, he fell into a depression. What's worse, he had been put to the expense of purchasing two useless suits of clothes and the other accoutrements. The good old man, however, kept his sorrow to himself, not wishing to add to that of his daughters.

At length the youngest girl came to him and begged him most urgently to grant her the same permission he had granted her sisters. "Perhaps," she said, "it's presumptuous of me to hope I'll succeed where they haven't. Nevertheless, I'd like to try. I'm taller than they are, and as you know, I go hunting every day. This exercise has prepared me in some degree for war, and my great desire to relieve you in your distress has inspired me with extraordinary courage."

The count loved her more than either of her sisters, for she cared for him so tenderly that he regarded her as his chief consolation. She read interesting stories to amuse him, nursed him in his illness, and gave him all the game she killed. Consequently, he argued against her plan much more than he had with her sisters, doing all he could to change her mind. "Do you want to leave me, my dear child?" he asked. "Your absence will be the death of me. If fortune should really smile on you and you should return covered with laurels, I won't

have the pleasure of witnessing them. My old age and
your absence will bring about my demise."

"No, my dear father," said Belle-belle (for this was
her name). "Don't think for a minute that I'll be away
that long. The war will soon be over, and if I find any
other way of fulfilling the king's orders, I won't hesitate to take advantage of them. I assure you, though my
absence will be upsetting to you, it will be even more
distressing to me."

At last he granted her request, and she made a plain
suit of clothes for herself because her sisters' clothes
had cost so much that the poor old count's finances
would not allow more expense. She was also compelled to take a very bad horse since her two sisters had
nearly crippled the other two. All this, however, did
not discourage her. She embraced her father, received
his blessings with respect, and as her tears flowed with
his and those of her sisters, she departed.

In passing through the meadow I have already mentioned, she found the old shepherdess, who was trying
to pull yet another sheep out of the deep ditch.

"What are you doing there, shepherdess?" Belle-
belle stopped and asked.

"I can't do anything more, my lord," the shepherdess
replied. "Ever since daylight I've been trying to save
this sheep in vain. I'm so weary, I can scarcely breathe.
There's hardly a day that passes when some new
misfortune doesn't befall me, and I have nobody to
help me."

"I'm truly sorry for you," Belle-belle said, "and to
prove it, I'll help you."

She instantly dismounted from her horse, which was
so calm that she did not bother tying it to prevent its
running away. Even though she suffered a few
scratches as she jumped over the hedge, she plunged
into the ditch and labored so diligently that she succeeded in dragging out the dear sheep. "Don't cry anymore, my good mother," she said. "Here's your sheep.
Despite the fact that it's been in the water a long time,
it seems quite lively."

"You won't find me ungrateful," the shepherdess
said. "I know you, charming Belle-belle. I know where

you're going and what your intentions are. When your
sisters passed through this meadow, I recognized them
as well and knew their every thought. But they were so
heartless and ungracious toward me that I managed to
prevent their journey. Things will be different in your
case. Let me prove it to you, Belle-belle, for I'm a fairy
and take pleasure in rewarding those who deserve it.
Just watch. You have a miserably poor horse, and now
I'll give you a real one." As she spoke she struck the
ground with her crook, and instantly Belle-belle heard
a neighing behind a bush. Whirling about, she saw the
most dashing horse in the world prancing in the
meadow.

Belle-belle, who was fond of horses, was delighted
to see one so perfect. The fairy called this fine stal-
lion to her and, touching it with her crook, she said,
"Faithful Comrade, I wish you better harnessed than
the emperor Matapa's best horse." Within seconds
Comrade bore a green velvet saddlecloth embroidered
with pearls and rubies, a saddle to match, and a bridle
of pearls with a gold bit and gold studs. In short, not a
horse in the world was as magnificent as this one.
"You've seen only the least remarkable thing about
this horse," the fairy remarked. "Pray, let me enu-
merate his many other qualities. In the first place, he
eats only once a week, and it's not necessary to look
after him, for he knows the present, past, and future.
I've had him a long time, and I've trained him as I'd
train my own horse. Whatever you wish to know, or
whenever you need advice, you need only consult him.
He'll give you such good counsel that most sovereigns
would be blessed to have ministers like him. Consider
him more as your friend than your horse. Lastly, your
attire is not to my liking. Let me give you something
more becoming."

She struck the ground with her crook, and a large
trunk sheathed with Turkey leather appeared. It was
studded with gold nails and bore Belle-belle's initials.
Plucking from the grass a gold key made in England, the fairy opened the trunk, revealing an interior
lined with Spanish leather and profusely embroidered.
Everything within came in dozens; twelve suits, twelve

cravats, twelve swords, twelve feathers, and so forth. The coats were woven with so much embroidery and so many diamonds that Belle-belle could barely lift them. "Choose the suit that pleases you most," the fairy said, "and the others will follow you everywhere. You need only to stamp your foot and say, 'Turkey-leather trunk, come to me brimming with linen and lace,' or 'Turkey-leather trunk, come to me brimming with jewels and coins,' and it will instantly appear before you, whether you are outdoors or in. You must also assume an alias, for Belle-belle will not suit the profession you're about to enter. It occurs to me that you might call yourself the Chevalier Fortuné. Of course, you ought to know who I am. Therefore, let me appear in my natural form." All of a sudden the old woman's skin was shed, and the fairy became so astonishingly beautiful that Belle-belle was dazzled. Her dress was made of blue velvet trimmed with ermine, and her hair was entwined with pearls and adorned by a superb crown.

Transported by her admiration, Belle-belle threw herself at the fairy's feet as a show of her respect and inexpressible gratitude. The fairy raised her and embraced her affectionately. She told her to don a suit of green and gold brocade, and Belle-belle swiftly obeyed. Afterward she mounted her horse and continued her journey so overwhelmed by all the extraordinary things that had just taken place that she could think about nothing else.

Eventually she began to ponder the unexpected good fortune that had helped her attract the kindness of such a powerful fairy, "Because in truth," she said, "she didn't need me to save the sheep. A simple stroke of her wand would have brought an entire flock back from the antipodes if it had wandered off there. I was lucky indeed to have been in a position to oblige her. The trifling service I performed on her behalf is the cause of all she's done for me. She knew my heart and approved of my sentiments. Ah, if my father could see me now, so magnificent and so rich, how delighted he would be! But in any case, I'll have the pleasure of sharing with my family the wealth she has bestowed upon me."

As she finished making these different observa-tions, she arrived in a beautiful, populous city. She attracted a great deal of attention, and the people followed and gathered around her. "Have you ever seen a cavalier more handsome or strapping, or more handsomely dressed?" they cried. "Look how gracefully he manages that superb horse!" They saluted him most respectfully, and he returned their greetings with a kindly, courteous air. As soon as he had stopped at an inn, the governor, who had been out walking and had admired him in passing, sent a gentleman to say that he hoped he would come and make his lodgings in his castle. The Chevalier Fortuné (we will now use this name when discussing Belle-belle) replied that since he had not yet had the honor of making his acquaintance, he would not take that liberty. However, he would come to pay his respects. In addition, Fortuné requested of the governor a man whom he could trust with something of con-sequence that he wanted to send to his father. The governor responded immediately and sent him a very trustworthy messenger.

Asking him to wait since his letters were not ready yet, Fortuné shut himself in his room and stamping his foot, he said, "Turkey-leather trunk, come to me brim-ming with diamonds and coins!" Within seconds it appeared but without its key. Where was he to find it? What a pity to break a golden lock enameled with so many different colors! Then again, he dared not trust a locksmith, for no sooner had he mentioned the cava-lier's treasures than thieves would descend to rob or even kill him.

He looked for the key everywhere, but the more he looked, the more hopeless his search appeared. "How disturbing!" he cried. "I cannot avail myself of the fairy's generosity, nor send my father any of the trea-sures she's given." In the midst of his musing, it occurred to him that his best course of action would be to consult his horse. So he went to the stable and whis-pered, "I beg of you, Comrade, tell me where I can find the key of the Turkey-leather trunk."

"In my ear," the horse replied.

Fortuné peered into the horse's ear and spied a green ribbon. Drawing it out, he found the key he needed. He opened the Turkey-leather trunk, which contained more than a bushel of diamonds and coins. The chevalier filled three caskets, one for his father and two others for his sisters. Then he gave them to the governor's man and told him not to stop night or day until he arrived at the house of the count.

This messenger made a swift journey, and when he told the old man that he had brought him an onerous casket from his son, the cavalier, the count wondered what could be in it. "Belle-belle started with so little money that she had no means to buy a thing or even to pay the journey of the man in charge of this present." But after reading the letter that his dear daughter had written, he thought he would die from joy. What's more, the sight of the jewels and gold confirmed the truth of her story. The most extraordinary thing was that when Belle-belle's two sisters opened their caskets, they found not only bits of glass instead of diamonds but also false coins, for the fairy did not want them to benefit from her kindness. Thinking their sister was laughing at them, they were extremely angry at her, and when the count noticed this, he gave them the greater part of the jewels he had just received. As soon as they touched them, though, they changed like the others. Therefore, they concluded that an unknown power was working against them and begged their father to keep the rest for himself.

The handsome Fortuné did not wait for the messenger to return before he left the city. His business was too urgent; he was bound to obey the king's orders. Paying his visit to the governor's house, he discovered that many people had assembled to see him. His personality and manners revealed such an air of goodness that they could not help but admire and even adore him. He said nothing except what was pleasant to hear, and when so many people crowded around him, he did not know how to account for such an unusual circumstance, especially because he had spent his entire life in the country.

He continued his journey on his excellent horse, which amused him by telling him a thousand stories of the most remarkable events in ancient and recent history. "My dear master," he said, "I'm delighted to have you as my owner. I know you possess a wealth of frankness and honor. Certain people with whom I lived a long time made me weary of life because their circle of friends were so unbearable. Among them was a man who pretended to be my friend. When he spoke in my presence, he placed me above Pegasus and Bucephalus. But as soon as I was out of sight, he called me a jaded and sorry nag. He pretended to admire my faults in order to induce me to commit greater ones. One day, when I tired of his caresses, which properly speaking were treacherous, I gave him such a severe kick that I had the pleasure of knocking out nearly all his teeth. Whenever I've seen him since then, I've told him with the utmost sincerity that it's not right for his mouth to be as handsome as others because he opens it too often to abuse those who do him no harm."

"Ho, ho," the chevalier cried, "you're full of spirit. Aren't you afraid that someday in the heat of passion this man will pass his sword through you?"

"It wouldn't matter, my lord," Comrade replied. "In any case, I'd be aware of his intention before he knew it himself."

As they continued this conversation, they approached a vast forest, and Comrade said to the chevalier, "Master, a woodcutter who lives here may possibly be of great service to us. He is one who has been endowed with gifts."

"What do you mean by that term?" Fortuné interrupted.

"I mean that he's received one or more gifts from fairies," the horse replied. "You must hire him on to accompany us."

Just then they reached the spot where the woodcutter was working, and the young chevalier approached him with a gentle, winning air. He asked him several questions about these woods, if there were many wild beasts there and if he was allowed to hunt them. The woodcutter responded to all of this like an intelligent man. Fortuné then inquired what had happened to the men who had been helping him chop down so many trees. The woodcutter replied that he had felled them all by himself. "It took only a few hours, and I have many others yet to cut to make a load for myself."

"What? Do you mean to say you'll carry off all this wood today?" the chevalier asked.

"Ah, my lord," replied Strongback (for that is what people called him), "my strength is quite out of the ordinary."

"So you make a great deal of money, I suppose?" Fortuné said.

"Very little," the woodcutter replied. "The people hereabouts are poor. Everyone works for himself without asking for his neighbor's help."

"Since you live in such a poor region," the chevalier remarked, "you have only to decide to leave it and travel to another. Come with me and you'll have everything you desire. Whenever you believe it's time to return, I'll give you money for your return journey."

Thinking he would never get a better offer than this, the woodcutter laid his ax aside and followed his new master.

As they passed through the forest, they came upon a man in a glade who was roping his legs so tightly together that it seemed he could do naught but hobble. Stopping, Comrade said to his master, "My lord, here's another gifted man you'll need. You must take him with you."

Fortuné approached this man and with his usual grace asked him, "Why are you tying your legs like that?"

"I'm going hunting," he said.

"What?" the chevalier asked, smiling. "Do you mean to say you can run better when your legs are bound like that?"

"No, my lord," he replied. "I'm aware that I won't be too fast, but that's my goal. There's not a stag, roebuck, or hare I can't outrun when my legs are free. As a

result, I always run right by them, they escape, and I
rarely have the pleasure of catching them!"

"You seem to be an extraordinary fellow," Fortuné
said. "What's your name?"

"They've given me the name of Swift," the hunter
replied, "for I'm well-known in this region."

"If you'd like to see another," the chevalier responded, "I'd be happy to take you with me. You won't
have difficult tasks, and I'll treat you well."

Swift was not particularly well off, and he gladly
accepted the offer.

Continuing his journey, followed by his new servants, Fortuné spied a man binding his eyes on the
border of a marsh the next morning. The horse said to
his master, "My lord, I advise you to hire this man as
well."

Fortuné immediately asked him why he was binding
his eyes.

"I see too clearly," he said. "I can spot game more
than four miles away, and I always kill more than I
wish when I shoot. Therefore, I'm obliged to bind my
eyes, for I wouldn't have any game left once I caught
sight of all the animals around me."

"You're a very talented fellow," replied Fortuné.

"They call me the Sharpshooter," the man said, "and
I wouldn't abandon this occupation for anything in the
world."

"Well, despite what you've just said, I'd like to invite you to travel with me," the chevalier said. "You
won't be prevented from exercising your talent."

The Sharpshooter made some objections, and Fortuné had more difficulty in persuading him than the
others, since sportsmen as a lot are fond of their
freedom. However, he eventually succeeded and left
the marsh with his new servant.

A few days later he passed by a meadow in which
he saw a man lying on his side, and Comrade said,
"Master, this man is most gifted. I can see that you'll
need him very much."

So Fortuné entered the meadow and asked the man
what he was doing.

"I want some herbs," he replied, "and I'm listening

to the grass as it grows to find out which ones I'll need."

"What?" the chevalier remarked. "Are your ears so sharp that you can hear the grass grow and know what's about to sprout?"

"That's why they call me Hear-all," said the man.

"Very well, Hear-all," Fortuné continued, "would you like to join me? I'll give you such high wages that you won't have any regrets."

The man was delighted by such a handsome proposition and joined the others without hesitation.

Continuing his journey, the chevalier saw by the side of a highway a man whose cheeks were so inflated that he looked rather droll. He was facing toward a lofty mountain two miles away where fifty or sixty windmills were standing. The horse said to his master, "Here's another of our gifted ones. Do all you can to make him come with you."

Fortuné, who had the power of fascinating everyone he saw or spoke to, approached this man and asked him what he was doing.

"I'm blowing a little, my lord," he said, "I want to get all those mills turning."

"It appears to me that you're rather far off," the chevalier replied.

"On the contrary," the blower remarked, "I'm afraid I'm too near. If I weren't retaining half of my breath, I'd upset the mills and perhaps the mountains they stand on. I do a great deal of harm this way without intending to, and I can tell you, my lord, that once, when my mistress had treated me badly, I went into the woods to indulge my sorrow, and my sighs tore the trees up by their roots and created a great deal of confusion. So in these parts they now call me Boisterous."

"If they're tired of you," Fortuné said, "and you'd like to come with me, I have some men who'd keep you company. They too possess unusual talents."

"I have a natural curiosity for anything out of the ordinary," Boisterous replied, "and so I accept."

Immensely pleased, Fortuné proceeded on his way. After passing through a densely wooded country, he

came to a large lake that was fed by several springs.
On its shore was a man who was staring at it attentively. "My lord," Comrade said to his master, "this
man will nearly complete your entourage. You'd do
well to induce him to join you."

The chevalier promptly approached him and asked,
"Tell me, what are you doing?"

"My lord," the man replied, "you'll see as soon as
this lake is full. I intend to drink it in one swig, for I'm
still thirsty, although I've already emptied it twice.

Accordingly, he stooped down to drink, and in a few
minutes left hardly enough water for the smallest min-
now to swim in. Just as surprised as his followers, Fortuné asked, "My, are you always so thirsty?"

"No," the man said. "I only drink like this for
a wager or when I've eaten something too salty. I'm
known in these parts as Tippler."

"Come with me, Tippler," said the knight. "I'll give
you wine to tipple, which you'll find much better than
spring water."

This promise pleased the man very much, and he
decided on the spot to join the others.

When the chevalier was within sight of the general
meeting place set for the king's forces, he noticed a
man eating so greedily that although he had more than
sixty thousand loaves of Gonesse bread before him, he
seemed determined to eat every last crumb. Comrade
said to his master, "My lord, this is the final man you
need. Please make him come with you."

The chevalier approached him, smiling. "Do you
really mean to eat all this bread for your breakfast?"

"Yes," he replied. "My only regret is that there's so
little, but the bakers are lazy fellows and refuse to
extend themselves whether you're hungry or not."

"If you require so much every day," Fortuné remarked, "there is hardly a country you wouldn't bring
to the brink of starvation."

"Oh, my lord," replied Gorger (as people called him),
"I'd feel badly if I always had such a huge appetite.
Neither my property nor that of my neighbors would be
enough to satisfy it. To tell the truth, I only feast in this
fashion every now and then."

"My friend Eater," Fortuné said, "join me and I'll show you good cheer. You won't regret choosing me for a master."

Comrade, who had a good deal of sense and fore-thought, then warned the chevalier to forbid his men from boasting about the extraordinary gifts they possessed. So Fortuné lost no time in gathering them around him and said, "Listen to me, Strongback, Swift, Sharpshooter, Hear-all, Boisterous, Tippler, and Gorger. If you want to please me, you'll keep your talents an inviolable secret. In return, I guarantee that I'll try my utmost to keep you satisfied."

Each one of them took an oath to obey Fortuné's orders, and soon after, the chevalier, who stood out more because of his good looks and graceful demeanor than his magnificent attire, entered the ravaged capital city on his excellent horse, followed by the finest attendants in the world. He lost no time in procuring for them horses and uniforms laced with silver and gold. After taking lodgings in the best inn, he awaited the day set for the review. In no time he became the talk of the city, and the king, made aware of his reputation, was eager to meet him.

All the troops assembled on a vast plain, and there the king arrived with his sister and the entire court. Because the queen had not forsworn pomp despite the misfortunes of the kingdom, Fortuné was dazzled by so much splendor. But if the king and his sister attracted his attention, they were just as much struck by his incomparable beauty. Everyone asked who that hand-some, graceful young gentleman was, and the king passed close by him and gave him a signal to approach. Dismounting immediately to make a low bow, Fortuné was unable to help blushing when the king gazed at him so earnestly, and this additional color heightened the radiance of his complexion.

"I'd like to hear from your own lips," the king said, "who you are and what your name is."

"Sire," he replied, "I'm called Fortuné, without hav-ing any reason for bearing this name up to now, for my father, who's a count on the frontier, has been living in

great poverty, although he was born of a rich and noble
family."

"Fortuné, whoever has served as your godmother has
done well to bring you here," the king replied. "I feel a
particular affection for you, for I remember your
father. He once rendered me a great service. Let me
reward him by favoring his son."

"That's quite just of you, brother," said the queen,
who had not spoken yet. "And since I'm older than you
and am more familiar with the service this count rendered the state, I request you to let me take charge of
rewarding this young chevalier."

Enchanted by his reception, Fortuné could not sufficiently thank the king and queen. He did not, however,
venture to extol his feeling of gratitude because he
believed silence more respectful than talking too much.
The little he did say was so correct and to the point that
everyone applauded him. Afterward he remounted his
horse and mixed among the noblemen who accompanied the king, even though the queen called him away
every minute to ask him a thousand questions. Turning toward Floride, her favorite confidante, she asked
softly, "What do you think of this chevalier? Have you
ever seen anyone with a nobler demeanor or more
regular features? I confess to you, I've never laid eyes
on anyone more charming."

Floride agreed with the queen wholeheartedly and
lavished praise on the chevalier, for he seemed just as
charming to her as to her mistress. For his part, Fortuné
could not help regarding the king from time to time. He
was the handsomest prince in the world, and his manners were most engaging. Belle-belle, who had not
renounced her sex with her dress, felt fervently drawn
to him.

After the review, the king told Fortuné, "I fear this
war will be a bloody one, and I've decided to keep you
near me." The queen, who was present, exclaimed that
she had also been thinking the same thing. He ought
not to be exposed to a long campaign, and since the
place of premier *maître d'hôtel* was vacant in her
household, she would give it to him.

"No," the king said. "I intend to make him my squire."

Thereupon, they argued with each other as to who would have the pleasure of promoting Fortuné. Since the queen feared revealing the secret emotions already exciting her heart, she at last yielded to the king's wish.

Hardly a day passed that Fortuné did not call for his Turkey-leather trunk and take out a new garment. He was certainly the most magnificent prince at the court. Sometimes the queen asked him how his father could afford to give him such clothes. Other times she would jest with him, "Tell the truth," she said, "you have a mistress, and she's the one who sends you all these beautiful things."

Though Fortuné blushed, he replied respectfully to the various questions the queen put to him. He also performed his duties remarkably well. He had come to appreciate the king's merits and became more attached to him than he had wanted. "What will be my fate?" he said. "I love a great king without any hope of his loving me. Nor will he ever know what I'm suffering."

In turn, the king overwhelmed him with favors, and he found nothing to his liking unless it was done by the handsome chevalier. Meanwhile the queen, deceived by his dress, seriously contemplated arranging a secret marriage with him, and the inequality of their birth was the only issue that troubled her. She was not the only one who entertained such feelings for Fortuné, however, for the most beautiful women at the court were taken with him. He was swamped with tender letters, assignations, presents, and a thousand gallantries, but he replied to all of them with so much indifference that they were certain he had a mistress in his province. No matter how much he tried to be modest at the great entertainments of the court, he always distinguished himself. He won the prize at all the tournaments. He killed the most game when he went hunting. He danced at all the balls with more grace and skill than any other courtier. In short, it was delightful to watch him and hear him speak.

Anxious to be spared the shame of declaring her

feelings for him, the queen asked Floride to make
him understand that a young and beautiful queen's
many signs of kindness ought not to be a matter of
indifference to him. Floride was taken aback by
this request, for she herself had been unable to avoid
the fate of all those who had seen the chevalier, and
she thought it would be too nice on her part to give
her mistress's interest precedence over her own. So
whenever the queen gave her an opportunity of talking to him, she told him only about the queen's bad
temperament and what injustices her attendants suffered from her instead of speaking about her beauty
and noble qualities. Floride also told him how badly
she abused the power she had usurped in the kingdom. Finally she drew a comparison between their
feelings and said, "I wasn't born a queen, but really I
ought to have been one. I have so much generosity in
my nature that I'm eager to do good for everybody. Ah,
if I were in that high station," she continued, "how
happy I'd make the handsome Fortuné. He'd love me
out of gratitude even if he could not love me from
inclination."

Quite dismayed by this conversation, the young
cavalier did not know what to say. Therefore, he vowed
to avoid any future tête-a-têtes with her.

When Floride returned, the impatient queen constantly inquired, "What impression did you make for
me on Fortuné?"

"He esteems himself so little," she said, "and he's so
bashful that he won't believe anything I tell him about
you. Or he pretends not to believe it because he's
absorbed by some other matter."

"I think so too," said the distressed queen. "But I
can't imagine that he'd curb his ambition to advance
himself."

"And I can't imagine," Floride replied, "that you'd
use your crown to capture his heart. You're so young
and beautiful and possess thousands of charms. Is it
necessary for you to take recourse in the splendor of a
diadem?"

"One may have to take recourse in anything possible," the queen replied, "if it becomes necessary to subdue a rebellious heart."

Floride saw clearly that she could not possibly put an end to her mistress's infatuation. Every day the queen expected some positive result from the confidante's work, but she made such little headway with Fortuné that the queen was eventually compelled to seek some means of speaking to him herself. She knew that he was accustomed to take a walk early every morning in a copse in front of the windows of her apartment. So she arose at daybreak, and as she watched his habitual path, she saw him approaching with a melancholy and distracted air. She called Floride immediately. "You've spoken the truth," she said, "Fortuné is without a doubt in love with some lady at this court or in his province. See how sad he looks."

"I've noticed this sadness in all his conversations," Floride replied. "You'd do well to forget all about him."

"It's too late," the queen exclaimed, sighing deeply. "Since he's already entered that green arbor, let's go there. I want you alone to come with me."

The girl did not dare to stop the queen no matter how much she wanted to, for she feared the queen would induce Fortuné to fall in love with her, and a rival of such exalted rank is always dangerous. As soon as the queen had taken a few steps into the wood, she heard the chevalier singing. His voice was very sweet, and he sang these words in a melody then current:

> "How rare a thing it is for love and peace
> To dwell together in the same heart!
> When my joys begin to surge, my fears increase,
> That they, like a morning dream, will soon depart!
> Dread of the future robs my soul of rest,
> Most unhappy I am when most blessed!"

Fortuné had composed these verses, stirred by his feelings for the king, the favor the king had shown him, and his fear of being found out and forced to leave a court that he preferred above any other in the world.

Stopping to listen, the queen was distraught. "What shall I do?" she whispered softly to Floride. "This ungrateful young man doesn't want to honor or please me. He believes himself content with this conquest of his. He sacrifices me to another."

"He's at that age," Floride replied, "when reason has yet to establish its rights. If I may venture to give some advice to your majesty, forget such a giddy fellow so incapable of appreciating his good fortune."

The queen would have preferred a different answer from her confidante. Casting an angry look at her, she hastened onward and entered the arbor where the knight was. She pretended to be surprised to find him there and to be upset at his seeing her in such disarray, although she had taken great pains to make herself magnificently attractive. As soon as she appeared, he made to withdraw out of respect for her, but she asked him to remain so that he might aid her in walking.

"I was wakened this morning most pleasantly by the singing of the birds. The fine weather and pure air induced me to come outside and listen more closely to their warbling. How happy they are! Alas, all they know is pleasure. Grief does not trouble them!"

"It appears to me, madam," Fortuné replied, "that they're not entirely exempt from pain and sorrow. They're always in danger of a murderous shot or deceitful snares of sportsmen. Moreover, birds of prey make war against these little innocents. When a hard winter freezes the ground and covers it with snow, they die for want of hemp or millet seed, and every year they have difficulty finding a new mistress."

"So you think, then, chevalier," the queen said, smiling, "that this is a difficulty? Some men have a fresh one every month—but you appear surprised by this, as if your heart were not of the same stamp. Can you not change your heart like this?"

"I'm unable to predict how I'd act," the chevalier said, "for I've never been in love. I do believe, however, that if I formed an attachment, it would end only when I breathed my last."

"You've never been in love?" cried the queen,

looking so earnestly at him that the poor chevalier changed color several times. "Fortuné, how can you possibly declare this to a queen who reads in your face and your eyes the passion that occupies your heart? Just now I heard the words you sang to that new melody that's just become so popular."

"It's true, madam," the chevalier replied, "that those lines are my own. My friends ask me every day to write drinking songs for them, although I never drink anything but water. There are others who prefer love songs. So I sing about love and Bacchus without being a lover or a drinker."

As the queen listened to him, she trembled so with emotion that she could scarcely keep standing. All that he told her had rekindled the hope in her bosom that Floride had sought to extinguish. "I'd think you were sincere," she said, "but I'd indeed be surprised if you hadn't found one lady at this court sufficiently lovely to attract your attention."

"Madam," Fortuné replied, "I try so hard to carry out the duties of my office that I have no time for sighing."

"You love nothing, then?" she responded vehemently.

"No, madam," he said, "my heart is not so gallant. I'm a kind of misanthrope who loves his liberty and doesn't want to lose it for anything in the world."

Sitting down, the queen gave him the kindest of looks. "There are some chains so beautiful and glorious," she replied, "that anyone might feel happy to wear them. If fortune has made this your destiny, I'd advise you to renounce your liberty."

As she spoke, her eyes revealed her meaning too clearly for the chevalier to mistake what she meant. He already had strong suspicions and was now convinced they were correct. Fearing the conversation might lead even further, he looked at his watch and held up his hand. "I must beg your majesty to permit me to go to the palace," he said. "It's time for the king to get up, and he asked me to be at his side."

"Go, callous youth," she said, sighing profoundly. "You're doing the right thing by paying court to my brother, but remember, it's not wrong to pay some attention to me."

The queen followed him with her eyes, then let them fall. After reflecting on what had just transpired, she blushed with shame and rage. Her grief was further augmented by the fact that Floride had witnessed everything, and she noticed a smirk of satisfaction on her face that implied: "You would have done better had you taken my advice instead of speaking to Fortuné." She pondered all this for some time. Then she took her tablets and wrote these lines, which she later had set to music by a celebrated court composer:

> "Behold! Behold! The torment I endure!
> My victor knows, but covers the clue.
> My heart shows, but it can't have a cure,
> Still stung by the shaft he's shot so true.

> "He's not concealed his coldness or disdain,
> He hates me, and his hate I should return;
> But ah, my foolish heart tries in vain,
> For it only has love for him to burn!"

Floride played her part cleverly: she consoled her as much as she could and gave her some hope to keep her going. "Fortuné thinks himself so beneath you, madam," she said, "that perhaps he failed to understand what you meant. It seems to me that he's already said a good deal by assuring you that he doesn't love anyone."

It is so natural for us to expect our hopes will be fulfilled that the queen was eventually encouraged to believe she had a chance with Fortuné. She was unaware that the malicious Floride, who knew all too well the chevalier's indifference toward her, wanted to induce him to speak even more forthrightly and offend the queen by his coolness.

As for Fortuné, he was most confused, for he was caught in a cruel dilemma. He would not have hesitated to leave the court if his love for the king had not detained him despite himself. Never did he go near the queen except when she held her court, and then always in the king's entourage. She noticed this change in his conduct instantly and responded by giving him the opportunity of paying her attention several times. He steadfastly refused to do so. But one day as she descended into her gardens, she saw him cross one of the grand avenues and suddenly enter the copse. When she called to him, he was afraid of displeasing her by pretending not to hear and approached her respectfully.

"Do you remember, chevalier," she said, "the conversation we had together some time ago in the green arbor?"

"I'd never forget that honor," he answered.

"No doubt the questions I put to you then were distressing," she said. "Ever since that day you've so avoided me that I haven't been able to quiz you further."

"Since it was happenstance alone that gave me that opportunity," he said, "I thought it would be presumptuous of me to seek another one."

"Why don't you say instead that you've been avoiding my presence, you ungrateful man?" she demanded, blushing. "You know quite well how I feel about you." Fortuné cast down his eyes in an embarrassed and modest manner, and since he hesitated to reply, she continued, "You seem dismayed. Go! Don't try to answer me. Your silence speaks louder than words."

She would have perhaps upbraided him more, but she spotted the king coming their way. She advanced toward him, and upon noticing how melancholy he was, she asked him to tell her the reason.

"You know," the king said, "that about a month ago I received news that an enormous dragon was ravaging the country. I thought my soldiers could kill him and issued the necessary orders for that purpose. But they've tried everything in vain. He devours my subjects, their flocks, and anything he encounters. He poisons all the rivers and springs wherever he quenches his thirst, and ruins the grass and the herbs wherever he lies."

While the king was talking to her, it occurred to the

irritated queen that this would be an opportune way to take her resentment out on the chevalier. "I'm aware of the bad news you received. As you saw, Fortuné was just with me and told me all about it. But, brother, you'll be surprised at what I have to tell you. He's implored me most insistently to ask you for permission to go and fight this terrible dragon. Indeed, he's so skilled in the use of arms that I'm not surprised he's willing to be so daring. Besides, he's told me he has some secret power that he can use to put the most lively dragon to sleep, but that must never be mentioned because it doesn't show much courage on his part."

"No matter how he does it," the king replied, "it will bring him great glory and be of great service to us if he succeeds. But I fear he's overzealous, and it may well cost him his life."

"No, brother," the queen added, "there's no need to fear. You know that he's naturally sincere and thus has no intention in dying so rashly. In short, I've promised to obtain what he wants, and if you refuse him, it will kill him."

"I'll grant your wish," the king said, "but I confess, I do so with a great deal of reluctance. Come, let us call him." He then made a signal for Fortuné to approach and said kindly, "I've just learned from the queen that you want to fight the dragon that is devastating our country. It's such a bold decision that I scarcely believe you've considered the danger involved."

"I've depicted all this to him," the queen said. "But he's so eager to serve you and to distinguish himself that nothing can dissuade him, and I predict he'll succeed."

Fortuné was taken aback by what the king and queen said. Though he quickly grasped the queen's wicked intentions, his natural deference would not permit him to expose them. So he had not responded and simply let her continue. He contented himself by making low bows so that the king thought he was now pleading with him directly to grant him what he desired. "Go, then," the king said, sighing, "go where glory calls you. I know you're skillful in everything you do, especially in the use of weapons. Perhaps this monster won't be able to avoid your blows."

"Sire," the chevalier replied, "no matter what the outcome of this combat, I'll be satisfied. Either I'll rescue you from a terrible scourge, or I'll die for you. But grant me one favor dear to my heart."

"Ask for whatever you wish," said the king.

"May I be bold enough to ask for your portrait?" Fortuné said.

The king was very pleased that he had thought of obtaining his portrait at a time when he should have been occupied with far more weighty matters, and the queen resented once again that he did not make the same request of her. However, he would have had to possess a superabundance of goodness to desire the portrait of such a wicked woman.

Once the king had returned to his palace and the queen to hers, Fortuné mulled over the consequences of the pledge he had made. Going to his horse, he said, "My dear Comrade, I have a good deal of news to tell you."

"I know it already, my lord," he replied.

"What shall we do, then?"

"We must set out posthaste," the horse said. "Go and get the king's order commanding you to fight the dragon, and then we'll do our duty."

These words comforted our young chevalier, and the next morning he awaited the king in a riding dress just as handsome as all the others that he had taken from the Turkey-leather trunk. As soon as the king saw him, he exclaimed, "What? You're ready to go?"

"Your commands cannot be executed too quickly, sire," he replied. "I've come to take my leave of your majesty."

The king could not help feeling pity for Fortuné, seeing that such a young, handsome, and accomplished gentleman was about to expose himself to the greatest danger a man could ever face. He embraced him and gave him a portrait framed by large diamonds. Fortuné accepted it joyfully, for the king's noble qualities had made such an impression on him that he could not imagine anyone in the world more charming.

If Fortuné was upset at leaving him, it was much less from the fear of being devoured by the dragon than from being deprived of the presence of one so dear.

The king added a general order to Fortuné's commission, calling upon all his subjects to aid and assist Fortuné whenever he might be in need. Taking leave of the king, Fortuné went to the queen so that nothing might be taken amiss. She was sitting at her dressing table, surrounded by several of her ladies. She changed color when he appeared, and she began reproaching herself for what she had done. He saluted her respectfully and asked her if she would honor him with her commands since he was on the point of departure. These last words completely disconcerted her, and Floride, who did not know that the queen had plotted against the chevalier, was thunderstruck. She would have liked to have had a private chat with him, but he carefully avoided such an embarrassing situation.

"I pray to the gods," the queen said, "that you may conquer the dragon and return triumphant."

"Madam," the chevalier replied, "your majesty does me too much of an honor. You're sufficiently aware of the danger to which I shall be exposed; however, I'm full of confidence. Perhaps, on this occasion, I'm the only one who has hope."

The queen understood very well what he meant. No doubt she would have replied to this reproach if fewer persons had been present. The chevalier returned to his lodgings and ordered his seven excellent servants to get their horses and follow him. "The time has arrived to prove what you can do." Not one failed to rejoice at having a chance to serve him. In less than an hour everything was ready, and they set out with him, assuring him they would do their utmost to carry out his commands. And, as soon as they had reached the open country and had no fear of being seen, each one gave proof of his talent. Tippler drank the water from the lakes and caught the finest fish for his master's dinner. Swift hunted some stags and caught a hare by its ears, despite the doubles it made. The

Sharpshooter gave no quarter to partridges and pheasants, and when the game was killed by the one, the venison by another, and the fish plucked from the water, Strongback carried everything cheerfully. Even Hear-all made himself useful: he found truffles, morels, mushrooms, salads, and fine herbs by listening to where they grew in the ground. So Fortuné rarely had to pay anything to cover the expenses of his journey. He would have been greatly amused at the sight of so many extraordinary events if he had not been so troubled by all that he had just left. Even as the king's qualities continued to impress him, the queen's malice seemed so great that he could not help hating her.

As he was riding along lost in thought, he was roused from his reverie by the shrieks of a host of poor peasants whom the dragon was devouring. Seeing some who had escaped and running away as fast as they could, he called to them, but they would not stop. So he followed and spoke to them, and he learned that the monster was not far distant. When he asked them how they had managed to escape, they told him that since water was scarce in their region, they had only rain water to drink and had made a pond to conserve it. After making his rounds, the dragon went to drink there and uttered such tremendous roars when he arrived there that he could be heard a mile away. So alarmed did everybody become that they hid themselves and locked their doors and windows.

The chevalier entered an inn, not so much to rest as to seek some sage advice from his handsome horse. After everyone had retired, he went into the stable and asked, "Comrade, how are we to conquer this dragon?"

"My lord," he said, "let me dream about it tonight. Then I'll tell you what I think tomorrow morning."

Accordingly, the next morning when the cavalier came again, the horse said, "Let Hear-all listen to discover if the dragon is close by." Hear-all lay on the ground and heard the rumble of the dragon some seven miles away. When the horse was informed of this, he said to Fortuné, "Tell Tippler to drink up all the water in the pond and have Strongback carry enough wine there to fill it. Then you must scatter dried raisins, pepper, and other herbs around the pond that will make the dragon thirsty. Order all the inhabitants to lock themselves up in their houses. And you, my lord, must stay there and lay in wait with your attendants. The dragon won't fail to drink at the pond, he'll relish the wine, and then you'll see how it will all end."

As soon as Comrade had indicated what was to be done, they all set off on their tasks. The chevalier himself went into a house that overlooked the pond, and no sooner had he done so than the frightful dragon arrived at the pond and took several draughts. Next, he partook of the breakfast they had prepared for him, and then he drank more and then more, until he became intoxicated. Unable to move, he lay on his side, his head hung down, his eyes closed. When Fortuné saw him like this, he knew he did not have a moment to lose. Emerging from the house, sword in hand, he courageously attacked the dragon. Wounded on all sides, the dragon tried to stand up so he could fall on the chevalier, but he lacked the strength because he had lost too much blood. The chevalier was overjoyed that he had reduced him to this sorry state, and called his attendants to bind the monster with cords and chains so that the king would have the pleasure and glory of putting an end to his life. Once they had nothing more to fear from the beast, they dragged him to the city, Fortuné at the head. On approaching the palace, he sent Swift to the king with the news of his great success. Such tidings seemed incredible to everyone until they actually saw the monster tied on a machine constructed for the beheading.

The king descended and embraced Fortuné. "The gods have reserved this victory for you," he said. "I feel more joy at your safe return than at the sight of this horrible dragon reduced to this condition, my dear chevalier."

"Sire," he replied, "it would please me if your majesty would give the monster his death blow. I brought him here expressly to receive it from your hand."

The king drew his sword and terminated the existence of one of his most cruel enemies. Everybody uttered shouts of joy at such unexpected success. Floride, who had been fretting unceasingly, soon heard about the return of her handsome chevalier and ran to tell the queen. She in turn was so astonished and confounded by her love and her hatred that she could not respond to her confidante's news. She had reproached herself hundreds of times for the malicious trick she had played, but she preferred to see him dead than so indifferent to her. She did not know whether she should be pleased or sorry that he had returned to disturb her peace.

Eager to tell his sister of this extraordinary event, the king entered her chamber, leaning on the chevalier's arm. "Here's the dragon slayer," he said. "This faithful subject has performed for me the greatest service that I could have ever demanded. Since you were the one, madam, to whom he first expressed his desire to fight this monster, I hope you appreciate the courage with which he exposed himself to utter peril."

Composing herself, the queen honored Fortuné with a gracious reception and a thousand praises. She thought him handsomer than when he went away, and the way she gazed at him indicated that her heart was not cured of its wound.

She did not, however, want to leave it up to looks alone to explain how she felt. So, as she was hunting with the king, she left off following the hounds, saying she felt suddenly indisposed. Turning to the young chevalier nearby, she said, "Do me the pleasure of remaining with me. I want to get down and rest a little. —Go," she continued, speaking to those who accompanied her, "don't leave my brother!" She dismounted from her horse with Floride and sat by the side of a stream. There she remained for some time in deep silence, trying to think of the best way to start the conversation.

Finally she raised her eyes and fixed them on the

chevalier. "Since good intentions are not always obvious," she said, "I fear you haven't grasped the motives that induced me to urge the king to send you to fight the dragon. I have presentiments that never mislead me, and I felt certain that you'd prove yourself brave. Your rivals have not thought highly of your courage because you didn't join the army. That's why I felt you needed to perform some act of valor to stop their tongues from wagging. Perhaps I ought to have told you what they had been saying about you, but I feared any consequences resulting from your resentment. So I thought it better for you to silence such evilminded people by demonstrating your intrepid conduct in action rather than by exerting influence that would mark you as a favorite, not a soldier. Thus you see, chevalier, that I longed to do something that might contribute to your glory, and you'd be very wrong if you were to judge otherwise."

"The distance is so great between us, madam," he replied, modestly, "that I'm not worthy of the explanation you've been so kind to give me, or the care you took to imperil my life for the sake of my honor. The gods protected me with more beneficence than my enemies had hoped, and I'll always esteem myself lucky to serve the king or you and to risk my life, the loss of which is a matter of more indifference to me than one might imagine."

This respectful reproach from Fortuné nettled the queen, for she wholly comprehended his meaning, but he was still too pleasing for her to feel alienated by such a sharp reply. On the contrary, she pretended to sympathize with his sentiments and asked him, "Tell me again how skillfully you conquered the dragon."

Fortuné had carefully avoided telling anyone how his men had helped him defeat the dragon. He boasted of having faced this redoubtable enemy alone, and that his own skill and courage, even to the point of rashness, had enabled him to triumph. The queen, who scarcely paid attention to what he was saying, interrupted to ask whether he was now convinced of her sincere concern in his affairs. She would have pressed the matter further, but he interrupted her by saying, "Madam, I hear the blast of the horn. The king approaches. Does your majesty want your horse to go and meet him?"

"No," she said spitefully. "It's sufficient for you to do so."

"The king would blame me, madam," he added, "if I were to leave you by yourself in such a dangerous place."

"I can dispense with your attention," she replied imperatively. "Be gone! Your presence annoys me!"

At this command, the chevalier made a dignified bow, mounted his horse, and disappeared from her sight. Concerned by how she would react to this fresh offence, he consulted his fine horse. "Let me know, Comrade," he said, "if this queen, who's too passionate and angry, is going to find another monster for me."

"No, she won't find another one," the handsome horse replied. "But she herself is more of a dragon than the one you've killed, and she'll certainly put your patience and virtue to the test."

"Will she cause me to fall out of favor with the king?" he cried. "That's all I fear."

"I won't reveal the future to you," Comrade said. "Just know that I'm always on the alert." He stopped talking, for the king had appeared at the end of an avenue. Joining him, Fortuné reported that the queen had not felt well and had commanded him to remain at her side.

"It seems to me," the king said, smiling, "you're very much in her good graces, and you speak your mind to her rather than to me. I've not forgotten that you asked her to procure the illustrious opportunity of fighting the dragon."

"I won't dare to contradict you, sire," the chevalier replied, "but I can assure your majesty I make a great distinction between your favors and those of the queen, and if a subject were permitted to make his sovereign a confidant, I'd be most delighted to declare my feelings to you—"

At that point, the king interrupted him abruptly by asking him where he had left the queen, who meanwhile was complaining to Floride of Fortuné's indifference to her. "I'm finding the sight of him more and more hateful," she cried. "Either he leaves the court, or I must withdraw from it. I can no longer tolerate the presence of an ungrateful youth who dares show me so much contempt. Any other mortal would be enraptured to know he pleased a queen who's so powerful in this kingdom! He's the only one in the world who doesn't. Ah, the gods have selected him to disturb my tranquillity!"

Floride was not at all sorry that her mistress was so displeased with Fortuné, and far from endeavoring to oppose her displeasure, she augmented it by recalling a thousand other disturbing signs that the queen had perhaps not wanted to notice. Thus her rage increased, and she began devising some new way to destroy the poor chevalier.

As the king rejoined her and expressed his concern about her health, she said, "I confess I was very ill, but it's difficult to remain so with Fortuné near. He's so cheerful, and his ideas are quite amusing. So I must tell you, he's implored me to obtain another favor from your majesty. He's asked, with the greatest confidence of success, to be allowed to undertake the most rash enterprise in the world."

"What now, sister?" cried the king. "Does he want to fight another dragon?"

"Several all at once," she said, "and he's certain he will triumph. Do you want me to tell you? Very well, he boasts he'll compel the emperor to restore all our treasures, and he doesn't even need an army to achieve this."

"What a pity," the king replied, "that this poor boy has to exaggerate so much."

"His fight with the dragon has made him think of nothing but great adventures," the queen remarked. "But what risk do you run if you permit him thus to serve you?"

"I risk his life, which is dear to me," the king replied. "I'd be extremely sorry to see him throw it away so recklessly."

"No matter what you decide, he's bound to die," she

said. "I assure you that his desire to recover your treasures is so strong that he'll pine away if you refuse him
permission."

The king felt deeply distressed. "I can't imagine," he
said, "how these notions get into his head. I'm extremely disturbed to find him so foolhardy."

"The fact remains," the queen replied, "he's fought
the dragon and conquered him. Perhaps he'll succeed
equally well in this adventure. I'm seldom deceived by
my presentiments, and my heart tells me he'll also
accomplish this mission. Please, brother, don't oppose
his zeal."

"Let him be called," the king said. "In any case, I
must inform him of the risk he runs."

"That's just the way to exasperate him," the queen
replied. "He'll think you won't let him go, and I assure
you he won't be deterred by any consideration for himself, for I've already said all that can be thought about
the subject."

"Very well," the king cried, "let him go. I consent."

Delighted with this permission, the queen sent for
Fortuné. "Chevalier," she said, "thanks be to the king.
He's granted you the permission you desired so
much—to seek out the emperor Matapa and by guile
or by force, recover the treasures he's taken from us.
Prepare to depart as speedily as when you fought the
dragon."

Fortuné was shocked. Was this the extreme to which
the queen's malice and fury had driven her? On the
other hand, he was pleased by the prospect of laying
down his life for a king so dear to him. So without
objecting to this monstrous task, he knelt and kissed
the king's hand. For his part, he was very much moved,
and even the queen felt a degree of shame in witnessing the respect with which he received this order to
charge toward certain death.

"Can it be possible," she said, "that he has some
affection for me? Rather than disavow what I've supposedly done on his behalf, he prefers to suffer without
a complaint. Ah, if this were true, I'd wish a good deal
of harm to myself for having caused him so much!"

The king said little to the chevalier before he

remounted his horse, and the queen entered her chariot again, feigning a return of her indisposition. Fortuné accompanied the king to the end of the forest and then reentered it to converse with his horse. "My faithful Comrade," he said, "it's all up with me. I must die. The queen has plotted a course I'd never have expected."

"My charming master," the horse replied, "don't alarm yourself. Although I wasn't present when all of this occurred, I've known about it for some time. The mission isn't as terrible as you imagine."

"You don't realize that this emperor is the most wrathful man in the world," the chevalier said. "If I suggest to him that he restore all that he has taken from the king, he'll answer by having me strangled and thrown into a river."

"I've heard of his violent ways," Comrade said, "but don't let that prevent you from taking your attendants with you. If you perish there, we'll all perish together. However, I trust we'll have better luck than that."

Somewhat consoled by this, the chevalier returned home, issued the necessary orders, and then received the king's commands along with his credentials. "You'll tell the emperor for me," he said, "that I demand my subjects he holds in bondage, my soldiers who are prisoners, my horses that he rides, and all my goods and treasures."

"What shall I offer him in exchange for all these things?" Fortuné asked.

"Nothing," replied the king, "but my friendship."

The young ambassador's memory was not overburdened by these instructions. He departed without seeing the queen, and though she was offended, he had no reason to treat her with any respect. Besides, what worse could she do to him in a fit of rage that she had not already done in the throes of love? Passions of this kind seemed to him to be the most dreadful thing in the world. Even her wily confidante was exasperated with her mistress for wanting to sacrifice the flower of chivalry.

Taking all he needed for his journey in the Turkey-leather trunk, Fortuné was not satisfied simply with attiring himself magnificently, but wanted his seven attendants to make just as fine an appearance. They all rode on their excellent horses—indeed, Comrade seemed to fly through the air rather than gallop over ground—and soon arrived at Emperor Matapa's capital city. Larger than Paris, Constantinople, and Rome put together, it had so many people that all the cellars, garrets, and lofts were inhabited.

Fortuné was surprised to see such a tremendous city. He demanded an audience with the emperor, but when he announced the purpose of his mission, even though his ample grace made his speech more effective, the emperor could not help smiling. "If you were at the head of five hundred thousand men," he said, "one might listen to you, but they tell me you have but seven."

"I've not undertaken this task, my lord," Fortuné said, "to make you restore what my master wishes by force but by my very humble remonstrances."

"It doesn't matter which way you choose," the emperor responded. "You'll never succeed—unless you can accomplish a task that's just come to my mind; find a man who has such an appetite that he can eat for his breakfast all the hot bread baked for the inhabitants of this great city."

The chevalier was most pleasantly surprised by this proposal, but since he did not answer right away, the emperor burst into a fit of laughter. "It's perfectly natural to respond to a ridiculous request with a ridiculous answer."

"Sire," Fortuné said, "I accept your offer. Tomorrow I'll bring a man who'll eat all the fresh bread and likewise all the stale bread in this city. Just order it to be brought to the great square, and you'll have the pleasure of seeing him devour it down to the very last crumb."

The emperor agreed, swearing he would put him to death if he did not keep his word, and people talked of nothing but the madness of the new ambassador for the rest of the day.

Fortuné returned to the hotel where he had taken up residence and called for Gorger to come to him. "Now's the time for you to prepare yourself to eat

bread," he said. "Everything depends on it." Thereupon
he told him what he had promised the emperor.

"Don't worry, master," Gorger said. "I'll eat until
they weary of feeding me."

Since Fortuné was afraid of any exertion on
Gorger's part, he forbade him to have supper so he
would be better able to eat his breakfast, but this precaution was not really necessary. The next morning,
the emperor, empress, and princess took seats on a balcony so that they would have a better view. Arriving
with his small retinue, Fortuné saw six mountains of
bread higher than the Pyranees rising in the great
square. This sight made him turn pale, but it had the
opposite effect on Gorger. Delighted by the prospect of
eating so much good bread, he asked them not to keep
the smallest morsel from him and declared, "Nothing
will be left even for a mouse." The emperor and the
entire court amused themselves at the expense of Fortuné and his attendants, but Gorger, becoming impatient, demanded the signal to begin.

At a flourish of drums and trumpets, he immediately
threw himself on one of the mountains of bread and
devoured it in less than a quarter hour. All the rest he
gulped down at the same rate. Everyone was astonished and, wondering if their eyes had deceived them,
they had to satisfy themselves by touching where they
had placed the bread. That day everyone, from the
emperor to the cat, was compelled to dine without
bread.

Delighted by his great success, Fortuné approached
the emperor and asked respectfully if he were pleased
by the way he had kept his word with him. The emperor, who was rather irritated at being duped this way,
said, "Monsieur Ambassador, it won't do to satisfy
such hunger without also slaking thirst. Therefore, you,
or one of your men, must drink all the water in the
fountains, aqueducts, and reservoirs in the city, and all
the wine in the cellars."

"Sire," Fortuné said, "you're trying to make it
impossible for me to obey your orders. However, I
don't mind endeavoring to fulfill this task if I can

expect that you'll restore what I've requested for my master."

"I'll do so if you succeed in your undertaking," the emperor stated.

When the chevalier inquired if the emperor would like to be present, he replied that he would certainly attend such an extraordinary event. Thereupon, he got into a magnificent chariot and drove to the fountain of lions, where seven marble lions spouted torrents of water that formed such a mighty river that the inhabitants of the city usually crossed it in gondolas.

Tippler approached the great basin, and without taking a breath, he drained it so dry that the bewildered fish cried out for vengeance. Then Tippler turned to all the other fountains, aqueducts, and reservoirs and did the same. In fact, he could have drunk the sea, he was so thirsty. After seeing such an example, the emperor was convinced Tippler could drink the wine as easily as the water, and he watched his disturbed subjects refuse to give up their wine to him. But Tippler complained that they were being unfair, for he needed the wine to settle his stomach. Not only did he expect all the wine, but also the spirits. Fearing to appear miserly, Matapa consented to Tippler's request.

Once this feat was accomplished, Fortuné reminded the emperor of his promise. At these words the emperor looked very stern and told him he would consider it. Thereupon he convoked his council and expressed his extreme annoyance at what he had promised the young ambassador. Indeed, he had thought the conditions he had set for Fortuné were so impossible to fulfill that he would not have to comply with them. After he had spoken, his daughter, one of the loveliest creatures in the world, remarked, "You're aware, sire, that until now I've beaten all those who have dared to race against me. You must tell the ambassador that if he can reach a certain designated spot before me, you'll stop procrastinating and keep your word."

The emperor thought her advice was excellent and embraced his child. The next morning, he received Fortuné graciously and said, "I have one more condition, which is that you or one of your men must run a race with my daughter. I swear by all the elements that if she's beaten, I'll satisfy your master in every respect."

Since Fortuné did not refuse this challenge, Matapa added that the race would take place in two hours, and immediately informed his daughter that she should get ready. She did so with alacrity, for she had raced since childhood, and soon appeared in an avenue of orange trees three miles long and so beautifully graveled that not a stone the size of a pin's head could be seen in it. She wore a slight rose-colored taffeta dress embroidered down the seams with gold and silver spangles; her beautiful hair was tied by a ribbon in back and fell carelessly on her shoulders; she wore extremely pretty slippers and a belt of jewels that displayed her figure sufficiently to prove that none had ever been as lithe. Even that of the young Atalanta could never have matched hers.

Fortuné arrived, followed by the faithful Swift and his other attendants. The emperor took his seat with his entire court. The ambassador announced that Swift would have the honor of running against the princess. The Turkey-leather trunk had furnished him with a holland suit trimmed with English lace, scarlet silk stockings, feathers to match, and exquisite linen. He looked very handsome in this garb, and the princess accepted him as her competitor. But before they started, she had a liqueur brought to her that she used to strengthen her and give her additional speed. Swift said he ought to have some as well, and that the advantages ought to be equal. "Gladly," she said, "I'm too just to refuse you."

She immediately poured some out for him, but since he was not accustomed to such potent liquid, it went quickly to his head. Turning around two or three times, he collapsed at the foot of an orange tree and fell fast asleep. Meanwhile the signal for starting had already been given three times, and the princess had kindly waited for Swift to wake up. Finally, feeling the grave importance of freeing her father from his predicament she set off with wonderful grace and speed. Since Fortuné was at the other end of the avenue with his men, he was unaware of what was happening until he saw the princess a half mile from the finish line running all alone. "Ye gods!" he cried, speaking to his horse. "We're lost. I see nothing of Swift."

"My lord," Comrade said, "Hear-all must listen. Perhaps he'll be able to tell us what's going on."

Hear-all threw himself onto the ground, and although he was two miles from Swift, he could hear him snoring.

"Truly," he said, "he has no intention of coming. He's sleeping as though he were in bed."

"Ah, what shall we do?" Fortuné cried again.

"Master," Comrade said, "Sharpshooter must shoot an arrow at the tip of his ear to wake him."

The Sharpshooter took his bow and aimed so well that he indeed pierced Swift's ear. Woken by the pain, he opened his eyes to see the princess near the finish, and he heard shouts of joy and mounting applause. At first astonished, he soon regained the ground he had lost in slumber. The very winds seemed to bear him, and nobody could follow him with their eyes. In short, he arrived first with the arrow still in his ear, for he had not had the time to extract it.

So astonished was the emperor by the three events that had occurred since the ambassador had arrived that he believed the gods favored him, and that he better not defer keeping his word. "Approach," he said to Fortuné. "I want you to hear from my own lips that I consent to your taking as much of your master's treasures from here as you or one of your men can carry. Indeed, you couldn't have expected that I'd ever do more than that or that I'd let either his soldiers, his subjects, or his horses go."

Making a profound bow, the ambassador said that he was very much obliged to him. "Pray give your orders to execute your will."

Deeply mortified, Matapa spoke to his treasurer and then rode to a palace just outside the city walls. Fortuné and his attendants immediately asked for permission to enter all those rooms where the king's furniture, rarities, money, and jewels were deposited. The emperor's servants hid nothing from him, but reminded him of the condition that only one man carry them. Strongback made his appearance and carted off all the furniture in the emperor's palace, five hundred statues of gold taller than giants, coaches, chariots, and countless other articles. Everything was taken, and Strongback walked so jauntily, it seemed as though his back bore not a pound.

When the emperor's ministers saw the dismantled palace—sans chairs, chests, saucepans, or even a bed to lie on—they rushed to warn him. You can imagine how astonished he was when he learned that one man carried everything. Exclaiming, "I shall not stand for this," he commanded his guards and musketeers to mount and quickly follow the robbers.

Although Fortuné was more than ten miles away, Hear-all told him that he heard a large body of cavalry galloping toward them, and the Sharpshooter with his excellent vision spotted them at a distance. Having just arrived on the banks of a river with his men, Fortuné said to Tippler, "We don't have any boats. If you could drink some of this water, we might be able to ford the river."

Tippler instantly performed this task. The ambassador was anxious to make the best use of his head start and get away, but his horse counseled, "Don't worry. Let our enemies approach."

They appeared on the opposite bank, and since they knew where the fishermen moored their boats, they speedily embarked in them and rowed with all their might. Then Boisterous inflated his cheeks and began blowing. So tumultuous became the river that the boats were upset, and the emperor's host perished without a single soldier escaping to tell the news.

Fortuné's men rejoiced at this event, and each one's thoughts turned to what reward he might demand as his just deserts. They wanted to make themselves masters of all the treasures they had carried away, and a great dispute arose among them about how to divide everything.

"If I had not won the race," the runner said, "you'd have had nothing."

"And if I hadn't heard you snoring," Hear-all said, "where would we have been then?"

"Who would have wakened you if it weren't for me?" the Sharpshooter responded.

"In truth," Strongback added, "I admire your arguments. But it's clear to me that I should have first choice since I've been carrying it all. Without my help you wouldn't have the opportunity of sharing it."

"You really mean without mine," Tippler responded. "The river that I drank like a glass of lemonade would have defeated you."

"You would have been much more defeated if I hadn't upset the boats," Boisterous said.

"I've been silent up till now," interrupted Gorger, "but I must remark that it was I who started this chain of events. If I had left just a crust of bread, everything would have been lost."

"My friends," Fortuné said commandingly, "you've all done wonders, but we ought to leave it to the king to acknowledge our services. I'd very much regret if we were to be rewarded by some other hand than his. Believe me, let's leave all to his will. He sent us to recover his treasures, not to steal them. Just the thought of it is so shameful that I beg you never to mention it again. I assure you, I shall do everything I can to ensure that you'll have nothing to regret even if the king neglects you."

Deeply moved by their master's remonstrance, the seven gifted men fell at his feet and promised him that his will would be theirs. Onward they went and soon completed their journey. As they approached the city, though, the charming Fortuné was troubled by a thousand different concerns. On the one hand, he was overjoyed at having performed such a great service for the king he loved so tenderly, and the hope of his favorable reception made him eager to return. On the other hand, he feared irritating the queen again and suffering torments anew from her and Floride.

When he finally arrived at the city gates, everyone was overwhelmed by the immense quantity of valuables he had brought back with him, and they followed him with a thousand acclamations. The sounds soon

reached the palace, and the king could not believe the
extraordinary event taking place. He ran to the queen
to tell her about it, and at first she was thunderstruck,
but quickly regained her composure. "You see," she
said, "the gods protect him, and he's fortunately succeeded. I'm not surprised that he's always ready to
undertake what appears impossible to others."

As she uttered these words, she saw Fortuné enter.
He informed their majesties of the success of his journey, adding that the treasures were in the park. Since
there was so much gold, jewels, and furniture, there
was no other place large enough to put them in. You
can easily imagine that the king demonstrated a good
deal of affection for such a faithful, zealous, and
charming subject.

The presence of the chevalier and all the successes
he had achieved reopened the wound in the queen's
heart, which had never been quite healed. She thought
him more charming than ever, and as soon as she was
at liberty to speak to Floride, she began complaining
again. "You've seen what I've done to destroy him,"
she said. "I thought it the only way of forgetting
him. Yet, some sort of irrefutable fate keeps bringing him back to me again. Whatever reasons I had to
despise a man so much my inferior, and who's returned
my affections with the meanest ingratitude, I can't help
but love him still, and I've determined to marry him
privately."

"To marry him?" Floride cried. "I can't believe this!
Have I heard you rightly?"

"Yes," the queen replied. "You've heard my intentions, and you must help me. Bring Fortuné to my
room this evening. I myself shall declare to him how
far I'm willing to go because of my love for him."

In despair at being chosen to assist the queen in her
plans to marry Fortuné, she tried every possible argument to dissuade the queen from seeing him. She maintained that the king would be angry if he discovered
this intrigue, that perhaps he would order the chevalier
to be executed. At the very least he might condemn
him to life in imprisonment, and she would never see
him again. However, all her eloquence was in vain.

Seeing that the queen was beginning to get angry, she decided that there was nothing to be done but obey her.

She found Fortuné in the palace gallery, where he was having the golden statues arranged that he had brought from Matapa, and she told him to come to the queen's room that evening. This order made him tremble, and Floride noticed his distress. "Oh," she said, "how I pity you! What unlucky fate caused the queen to lose her heart to you? Alas. I know one less dangerous than hers, but it's afraid to reveal itself."

The chevalier was not eager for further explanation, for he had endured too much already. Since he cared not a jot for pleasing the queen, he dressed himself so plainly that she could not possibly think him distinguished. Yet even though he dispensed with his diamonds and embroidery, he could not efface the qualities of his person. He was charming and remarkable no matter what he wore. In a word, he was incomparable.

On the contrary, the queen went to great pains to heighten the luster of her appearance by an extraordinary display, and she was quite pleased to see how tongue-tied Fortuné was. "Appearances," she said, "are sometimes so deceptive that I'm delighted to have the chance to defend myself against the charges you no doubt have brought against me in your heart. When I induced the king to send you to the emperor, my object may have seemed to destroy you. Nevertheless, believe me, handsome chevalier, I knew how everything would turn out. I had no other object than to provide immortal glory for you."

"Madam," he said, "you're too far above me to condescend to any explanation. I would never presume to inquire into your motives. The king's commands are sufficient justification for me."

"You're making light of the explanation I want to give you," she remarked. "But the time has come to demonstrate how much I care for you. Approach, Fortuné, approach. Receive my hand as a pledge of my faith."

The poor chevalier was utterly thunderstruck. Twenty times he was on the verge of declaring his sex to the queen, but he did not dare to do so and could only respond to her show of love by an excessive coldness. He tried to explain to her the innumerable reasons why the king would be angry if he were to hear that a subject in his own court had ventured to contract such an important marriage without his sanction. After the queen vainly endeavored to remove the obstacles that alarmed him, she suddenly assumed the voice and countenance of a Fury. Flying into the most violent rage, she threatened him with a thousand punishments, heaped abuse on him, fought and scratched him. Then she turned her rage on herself. She tore her hair, scratched her face and throat until they bled, ripped her veil and lace. Finally she cried out, "Help, guards! Help!" As they rushed into her room, she bellowed at them, "Fling that wretch of a chevalier into a dungeon!"

Running to the king to demand justice for the way that young monster had violated her, she told her brother that Fortuné had had the audacity some time ago to declare his feelings for her. She had hoped that by being severe and sending him away, she could cure him. As the king might have observed, she had used every opportunity to have him removed from the court. However, he was such a villain that nothing could change him. The king could see for himself to what extremes he had gone to possess her. She insisted on his being brought to justice, and that if she were denied such satisfaction, she wanted to know why.

The manner in which she spoke to the king alarmed him, for he knew that she was one of the most violent women in the world. She had a great deal of power and could cause turmoil in the kingdom. Therefore, Fortuné's rash actions demanded an exemplary punishment. Everybody already knew what had happened, and his own feelings should have prompted him to avenge his sister. But, alas, who was to be the target of his vengeance? It was a gentleman who had exposed himself to numerous perils in his service. Indeed, the king was indebted to him for the peace and all his treasures, and he had a particular affection for him. He would have given half his life to have saved his dear favorite. So he explained to the queen how useful he

had been to him, the services he had rendered the
kingdom, his youth, and everything else that might
induce her to pardon him. Yet she would not listen and
demanded his execution.

The king, realizing that he could not avoid having
him tried, appointed the mildest and most tender-
hearted judges in the hope they would weigh the
offence as lightly as possible. His assumption, though,
was mistaken. The judges wanted to establish their
reputation at the expense of this unfortunate prisoner.
Since it was an affair of great notoriety, they were
extremely severe and condemned Fortuné without
deigning to hear his side: he was sentenced to be
stabbed three times in the heart with a dagger because
it was his heart that was guilty.

The king trembled at this sentence as though it had
been passed on himself. He banished all the judges
who had pronounced it, but could not save his beloved
Fortuné. The queen exulted because of the punishment
the chevalier was to suffer, and her eyes thirsted for the
blood of her illustrious victim. The king made various
attempts to intercede, but they served only to exasperate her.

Finally, the day set for the terrible execution arrived.
Off they went to lead the chevalier from his prison.
Because he had been placed in isolation, he was unaware of the crime that he had allegedly committed and
merely imagined that he was to be persecuted once
again because of his indifference to the queen. What
distressed him most was his belief that the king shared
the queen's rage against him.

Meanwhile, Floride was inconsolable at seeing the
predicament in which her lover was placed and made a
most drastic decision: she was prepared to poison the
queen and herself if Fortuné was doomed to die a cruel
death. From the moment she knew the sentence, she
was overcome with despair, and she thought about
nothing but how to execute her plan. The poison she
procured, however, was not as powerful as she desired.
After she had given it to the queen, her majesty seemed
not to feel the slightest effects. Instead she ordered the
charming chevalier to be brought into the palace square

so that the execution could take place in her presence. The executioners brought him from his dungeon according to custom and led him like a tender lamb to the slaughter. The first person who caught his eye was the queen in her chariot, who wanted to be as close as possible in the hope that his blood might splatter her. The king meanwhile had locked himself up in his chamber so that he might freely lament the fate of his beloved favorite.

After they tied Fortuné to the stake, they tore off his robe and vest to pierce his heart. Imagine everyone's astonishment when they uncovered the alabaster bosom of Belle-belle! Immediately the populace realized Fortuné was an innocent girl unjustly accused. So upset and confused was the queen by this sight that the poison began to rampage through her veins. After a series of long convulsions, she recovered only to utter agonized lamentations. The people, who loved Fortuné, had already freed her and ran to announce the wonderful news to the king. He, who had succumbed to the deepest grief, now felt joy take the place of sorrow. Racing into the square, he was delighted to see Fortuné's transformation.

The last sighs of the queen subdued his rapture somewhat, but when he thought about her malice he could not feel sorry for her. He decided to marry Belle-belle in order to repay her for the great debt he owed her, and he declared his intentions to her. You can easily imagine that his wish had been the goal of all that she had ever desired, and it was not the crown she had wanted but the worthy monarch for whom she had long cherished the greatest affection.

The day was set for celebrating the king's marriage, and when Belle-belle assumed her female attire, she appeared a thousand times more charming than in the garb of the chevalier. Consulting her horse with regard to her future adventures, she was assured that she would have nothing but pleasant ones. In gratitude for all the good services he had rendered, she had a stable built of ebony and ivory, and she installed the best satin mattress on which he could take his repose. As for her seven followers, they were rewarded in proportion to their services. Comrade, however, disappeared, and when they came and told Belle-belle, the queen was distressed, for she adored him and ordered her attendants to look for her horse everywhere they could. They did this for three whole days in vain. On the fourth day she was so worried that she got up before sunrise and descended into the garden. Then she crossed the wood and entered a large meadow, calling from time to time, "Comrade, my dear Comrade! Where are you? Have you deserted me? I still need your wise advice. Come back, come back, and give it to me!" While calling out like this, she suddenly noticed a second sun rising in the west. Stopping to gaze at this miracle, she was immensely astonished as she watched it advance toward her by degrees. Within moments she recognized her horse, whose trappings were set with jewels and led a chariot of pearls and topazes drawn by twenty-four sheep. Their wool was of gold thread and purl and extremely radiant. Their traces were made of crimson satin and covered with emeralds, and their horns and ears were ornamented with carbuncles. Belle-belle recognized her fairy protectress in the chariot, and she was accompanied by the count, her father, and her two sisters, who called out to her. They clapped their hands and made affectionate signs to her, intimating that they had come to her wedding. Thinking she would die from joy, she did not know what to do or say to show her delight. She got into the chariot, and this splendid equipage entered the palace, where everything had already been prepared to celebrate the finest wedding ceremony that had ever taken place in the kingdom. Thus the enamored king bound his destiny to that of his mistress, and the story about this charming adventure has circulated for centuries and been passed down to our own.

> The lion roaming Lybia's burning plain,
> Pursued by the hunter, galled by countless darts,
> Is less to be dreaded than that woman vain,
> Whose charms are disdained and foiled in her arts.
>
> Poison and steel are trifles in her eyes,
> As agents of her vengeance and her hate;

The dire effects that from such passions rise
You've now seen in Fortuné's strange fate.

Belle-belle's change saved her innocent soul,
And struck her royal persecutor down.
Heaven protects the innocent and plays its role
By defeating vice and rewarding virtue with a crown.